THE FIRST FORGOTTEN REALMS® NOVEL

The Darkwell emanated death—a black hole in the sunlight. Like a giant sponge, it sucked rays from the sky, holding them for its own evil purposes.

The earthmother tried to marshal her strength, but the beast had grown so strong . . .

She called to her favorite creatures—the Leviathan, the Unicorn, and the Pack.

But as Kazgoroth and its blood-drenched minions surrounded Caer Corwell, and the Ffolk of Moonshae Isles rallied for a courageous last stand, the goddess feared her utmost efforts would be to no avail.

IN AN ALL NEW EDITION

THE
MOONSHAE TRILOGY

BOOK ONE
DARKWALKER ON MOONSHAE

BOOK TWO
BLACK WIZARDS
November 2005

BOOK THREE
DARKWELL
December 2005

FORGOTTEN REALMS

THE MOONSHAE TRILOGY BOOK ONE

DARKWALKER ON MOONSHAE

DOUGLAS NILES

✕✕✕

DARKWALKER ON MOONSHAE
THE MOONSHAE TRILOGY • BOOK ONE

©1987 TSR, Inc.
©2004 Wizards of the Coast, Inc.

Distributed in the United States by Holtzbrinck Publishing. Distributed in Canada by Fenn Ltd.

Distributed to the hobby, toy, and comic trade in the United States and Canada by regional distributors.

Distributed worldwide by Wizards of the Coast, Inc. and regional distributors.

Cover art by J. P. Targete
Text Restored by Dale Donovan and Anne Brown
First Printing: May 1987
This Edition: October 2004
Library of Congress Catalog Card Number: 2004106766

9 8 7 6 5 4 3 2 1

US ISBN: 0-7869-3560-X
UK ISBN: 0-7869-3561-8
620-17608-001-EN

U.S., CANADA,	EUROPEAN HEADQUARTERS
ASIA, PACIFIC, & LATIN AMERICA	Wizards of the Coast, Belgium
Wizards of the Coast, Inc.	T Hofveld 6d
P.O. Box 707	1702 Groot-Bijgaarden
Renton, WA 98057-0707	Belgium
+1-800-324-6496	+322 467 3360

Visit our web site at **www.wizards.com**

✕✕✕

DEDICATION

For Christine,
with all my heart

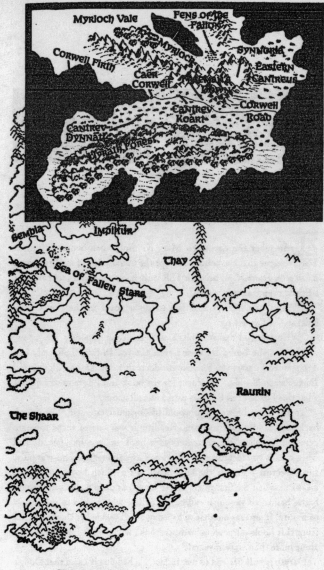

Myrloch Vale

Fens of the Fallon

Corwell Firth

Myrloch

Synnoria

Eastern Cantrevs

Caer Corwell

Freeman's Downs

Corwell Road

Cantrev Koart

Cantrev Dynnatt

Dernall Forest

Sembia

Impiltur

Thay

Sea of Fallen Stars

Raurin

The Shaar

The Great Sea

INTRODUCTION

I remember the day when Mary Kirchoff, then Senior Editor at TSR, told me that she couldn't accept the manuscript of my first novel, *Echoes of the Fourth Magic*, because TSR only had room on its schedule for a FORGOTTEN REALMS® novel.

"Would you like to audition to do a novel in the FORGOTTEN REALMS?" Mary asked.

"What are the FORGOTTEN REALMS?" came my response.

You see, the boxed set wasn't even out yet. In fact, TSR only had one printed FORGOTTEN REALMS product: this one, Doug Niles's novel *Darkwalker on Moonshae*. They sent me the book and I dove in to find out what this FORGOTTEN REALMS world was all about.

To say I was blown away would be an understatement. I still look back very fondly on this novel. Reading it was one of those too-rare experiences, where the characters of a book become like friends and when it ends you feel this special sense of loss and regret. This was pure, fun adventure—exactly the kind of thing for which I play DUNGEONS & DRAGONS® in the first place. These were friends to walk beside, to do battle beside, to vanquish evil beside. These were heroes to salute and to mourn. It amazes me that to this day, I still remember the characters from this book—I never remember books weeks after I read them, let alone more than sixteen years!

Daryth is still a friend to me. In fact, I'd be lying if I said that Doug's book wasn't more than a passing influence on my own first venture into the Realms. In doing my proposal to win the second FORGOTTEN REALMS novel, I had to submit a story outline and a sample chapter. Since the only product I had seen on the Realms was this book, with a map that included only the Moonshae Isles, I thought the Moonshae Isles *were* the FORGOTTEN REALMS. Not a large place, it seemed obvious to me that any book of importance set in this tiny world would have to include some of the major players in Doug's book. I didn't want to use anyone else's characters, but I didn't see a way around it, so in my sample chapter, "Biggrin's Lair," I used one of Doug's characters, Daryth (well, two, if you count Daryth's dog, Canthus the Moorhound), to introduce Wulfgar son of Beornegar, the expected hero of my tale. I figured that Daryth would set up the story, then turn it over to Wulfgar.

Well, soon afterward, I found out the truth of the Realms, the vast scope and size of this enormous continent to the east of the Moonshae Isles. After I won the audition to write *The Crystal Shard*, we reset the tale far, far from Doug's work. The only problem was that I still had Daryth and Canthus in the sample chapter. I replaced them, giving birth to a rogue drow ranger named Drizzt Do'Urden and his loyal panther companion Guenhwyvar.

So thank you, Doug, for inspirational characters and a most memorable book. To this day, after all these years and novels, when people ask me my favorite FORGOTTEN REALMS novel, I point to *Darkwalker on Moonshae*. In fact, after all these years, this book remains one of my very favorite fantasy novels, period, alongside works like *A Canticle for Liebowitz, Master of the Five Magics, Elfstones of Shannara,* and *Lord Foul's Bane.* The FORGOTTEN REALMS could not have gotten off to a better start, and I know that I owe a large part of my own success in that world to the fact that Doug Niles gave the curious audience a wonderful introduction into this gigantic shared world. Simply put, if Doug's book hadn't been so wonderful, I doubt people would have still been around to read my books and all the other FORGOTTEN REALMS novels that followed.

And here we are, sixteen years removed, and Wizards of the Coast has asked me to write an introduction for *Darkwalker on Moonshae.* A very easy assignment, to be sure, and it's a good feeling to be able to lift my mug in toast to Doug Niles and to this wonderful, wonderful book.

Even if the guy is a Packers fan (who rubs it in when they beat my Patriots in the Super Bowl)!

—R.A. Salvatore
May 10, 2004

BOOK
ONE

PRELUDE

The goddess awakened slowly from her cold sleep, awareness returning as the chill blanket of the passing season fell away. Turning with imperial grace, she sought the life-giving force of the renewed sun.

Soon she felt its warmth upon the long and gravelly beaches of her coastlines, and upon the stagnant expanses of her low, flat marshes. Slowly, the sun drove winter's blanket from the rolling moors and tilled fields.

The white mantle remained thick and heavy among the forests and glens of the goddess, and the highlands still showed no sign of acknowledging winter's end This was all as it should be, and the goddess rejoiced in the growing vitality of her body, the earth.

She had grown smaller, of late, but her strength was great. Her lands, though threatened, were in the capable care of her druids, and even the harbingers of the new gods treated her with a certain deference. In the Moonwells—places where her power flowed directly from her spirit to her body—water of high magic lay clear and pristine among thick pines, and in rocky clefts.

Cool seas bathed her lands, cleansing the debris and decay left by the passing of winter. The goddess saw that her children still slept peacefully. They could, she hoped, sleep long years still before she needed to call them.

Through the Moonwells, she saw the clearing skies. No longer did the heavy, iron-gray stormclouds oppress her. The Ffolk were active, preparing for a new season of growth. The druids moved among the trees and mountains of her wild reaches, restoring places where winter had disrupted the Balance. Yet, as she threw off her blanket, she felt a sudden, stabbing pain, penetrating deep within her. Hot and threatening, the injury seemed ready to spread like a cancer through her self.

One of the Moonwells was the source of the pain. Instead of providing a window into the world, full of cool and healthy power, the well burned like a poisoned wound. Very black, it blocked the light and absorbed her power, instead of nourishing it. As she awakened, the goddess felt fear.

And she knew that, once again, the Beast would stalk the land.

The fields around Caer Corwell beckoned brightly, as colored tents, proud banners, and gay costumes all competed for the eye of the fairgoer. The Festival of the Spring Equinox signaled the end of winter, and the beginning of a season of new hope and promise. To such an event, the Ffolk would come from throughout the Kingdom of Corwell, and even beyond, to join the celebration.

The deep harbor at the terminus of Corwell Firth bristled with masts. The deep, sturdy coracles of the Ffolk bobbed next to sleek longships of the northmen, and both were dwarfed by the looming decks of Calishite trading galleons.

Tristan Kendrick, Prince of Corwell, forced his way through the crowd eagerly, barely absorbing the sights and sounds all around him. A troop of Calishite jugglers stood among the crowd, each deftly controlling a ring of glittering scimitars. Tristan, impatient, passed around the jugglers without seeing them. He ignored the hawkers of bright silk, though the oily Calishite trader sold colors never before imagined in Corwell. In his haste, he even passed the booths where the skilled armorsmiths of Caer Calidyrr displayed shining steel swords.

"Hello, Tristan!" called one of the farmers, arranging jugs of milk on a table before him.

"Good morning," added a fisherman from the village.

And so it went as he passed through the crowd, receiving polite and friendly greetings from most of the Ffolk. As usual, Tristan felt a brief flash of annoyance, for no one addressed him by his title. Just once, he would like to hear "Hello, my prince!" or something equally appropriate.

But then he shrugged these thoughts away, just as he shrugged away all serious thought of his rank, and the responsibilities of his name. One day, perhaps, he would give some thought to the duties he would eventually face as king, but today . . . today he had a mission here at the fair!

His step speeded up, and pretty country maids, in fresh gowns of light linen, smiled coyly at him. The prince felt very dashing, reflexively stroking the new coat of hair upon his chin. His first beard had grown in full and curling, slightly darker in color than his wavy brown hair. His new woolen cloak and leather trousers looked clean and shiny against his black leather boots.

He felt alert and alive, full of spring fever.

Passing from the tents and stalls of the goods merchants, Tristan moved between corrals and pens, ignoring the sheep, the cattle, and even the horses. Finally, he reached an expanse of clustered pens, and here he found his objective.

"Greetings, my liege," piped a cheerful voice, and Tristan smiled at the advancing form of Pawldo, the halfling.

"It's good to see you, my friend," the prince said sincerely, clasping the diminutive man's hand. "I'm glad you made it back from your winter voyages safely."

Pawldo beamed at the greeting, but his eyes held a hint of avarice. The halfling was a stout and sturdy little man, perhaps an inch or two over three feet in height. He wore a weathered leather jacket and old, but well-oiled boots. His gray hair hung over his ears and collar, and his smiling face was clean-shaven and free of wrinkles, though Pawldo was over sixty years old.

Halflings lived on all the Isles of the Moonshaes, mostly as neighbors to human settlements. Though they were one of the original races, along with the dwarves and the Llewyrr elves, to inhabit the islands, they had adapted well to the coming of humans. They profited from business dealings with the Ffolk, and benefited from the protection afforded by nearby castles.

"And how are you, old crook?" asked the prince.

"Very well, and better soon, when I've had a chance to part you from your purse!" responded Pawldo. The halfling, shrewdly eyeing the leather pouch hanging from Tristan's belt, quickly concealed a smile of satisfaction.

Tristan could not suppress a surge of affection for his old companion. Pawldo ostensibly lived in Lowhill, the community of Halfling burrows a mere mile from Caer Corwell. The hardy old adventurer, however, spent most of the year traveling about the Moonshae Islands and the rest of the world in pursuit of profit, so the prince saw very little of him. Unlike most Halflings, who were content to enjoy the pastoral comforts of their burrows, pantries, and wine cellars, Pawldo lived a life of excitement and travel.

"I've spent the winter scouring the Sword Coast and the Moonshaes, collecting the finest lot of dogs you've ever seen. And I found the one for you, just to the west of here—on the Isle of Moray. You won't be able to resist him!" Again Pawldo smiled, with a slight twist to the corners of his mouth.

"Let's have a look at him," said Tristan, directing his attention to the small pen behind Pawldo.

This year Pawldo was a dealer in hounds, and as usual, his goods were offered in an assortment of styles, for a variety of purses. Even as his eyes passed quickly over the collection of bored dogs lying in the sun, Tristan saw the one magnificent animal, caught his breath, and whistled.

Trying to sound casual, he said, "Not a bad-looking dog."

"As if you had cause to doubt . . . " Pawldo started to retort, but Tristan was not listening.

The animal was a moorhound—one of the savage hunting dogs bred exclusively on the Moonshae Islands. This was not remarkable—Tristan already owned a dozen of the large dogs. But this moorhound was a large and powerful specimen with a proud bearing quite unusual for its kind.

Among the terriers, racers, and wolfhounds in Pawldo's collection, this great brown moorhound stood out like a princess among scullery maids. His brown coat gleamed, thick and smooth, over broad shoulders and long, slender legs. Even for a moorhound, he was huge. His eyes were riveted on Tristan, just as the prince studied him.

"Where did you find him?" Tristan asked.

"Came across with me from Norland he did. Rode in the bow like he was born to the sea. I've never seen him take any notice of a man—until now that is."

Tristan strode to the dog's side, and knelt on the muddy grass, his eyes level with the dog's. He thought of his hounds. Already they were fierce and loyal hunters—but with a dog such as this to lead them, they would be the finest pack of dogs in the Isles! Tristan slowly took the great head in his hands. The shaggy tail flickered slightly, swaying from side to side.

The prince stared into the moorhound's eyes and whispered, "We shall be the greatest hunters on Gwynneth—no, on *all* the Moonshaes! Even the Firbolgs of the Highlands will tremble in fear at your cry.

"Your name will be Canthus. " The dog regarded the prince keenly, brown eyes shining. His mouth opened slightly as he panted, and Tristan noted teeth the size of his little finger.

A number of onlookers had gathered to observe the prince, and Tristan felt a quick rush of pride as he realized that they looked with equal admiration upon his dog. A pair of savage, yellow-bearded northmen stood behind Pawldo, jabbering in their strange tongue full of *yerg* and *url* sounds. Several fisherfolk, a woodsman, and two young boys also watched. A crimson cloak, among the plain garb of the villagers, marked a young Calishite trader, staring in wonderment.

Tristan tried to conceal his eagerness as he stood and turned back to Pawldo, but his palms were sweating. He must have this dog! Trying to look disinterested, he opened the bidding. "He is indeed a fine animal. I'll give you ten gold for him!"

With a wail of anguish, Pawldo staggered backward. "The sea swelled over the bows," he cried in his high, squeaking voice. "Bold sailors grew pale with fear, and would have retreated, but I pressed on! I knew, I told myself, of a prince who would sacrifice his kingdom for such a dog—a prince who would reward well the steadfastness of an erstwhile friend . . . who would—"

"Hold!" cried Tristan, raising his hand and looking the halfling in the eye while trying to keep from laughing. "You shall have twenty, but no m—"

"Twenty!" The halfling's voice squealed in outrage. He turned to the listeners and threw out his hands, a picture of wounded innocence. The two northmen chuckled at his posturing.

"The sails hung in tatters from the beam! We nearly capsized a dozen times. Waves the size of mountains smashed us . . . and he offers me twenty gold!" Pawldo turned back to the prince, whose smile was growing thin. "Why a dog like this, to one who knew such creatures, would fetch a hundred gold in an instant—in any civilized port in the world!"

The halfling smiled disarmingly. "Still, we are friends, and so I would remain. He is yours . . . for *eighty* gold!" Pawldo bowed with a flourish to the gasps of the growing crowd. Never had a dog been sold for half of that asking price!

"You overestimate the size of my purse," retorted the prince, knowing full well that the price was going to stretch the limits of his allowance. Ruefully, Tristan groped for a bargaining strategy, but his purse felt very vulnerable. Pawldo knew him too well; the prince could not resist such a magnificent dog.

"I can offer you forty, but that is all I—"

"Forty gold," pronounced Pawldo, still playing the crowd. "A respectable sum, for a dog. If we talked of a normal dog, I would say yes in an instant."

"Fifty," declared the prince, starting to get annoyed at the high cost of doing business with Pawldo.

"Sold!"

"Well done! Bravo!"

The praise was accompanied by hearty handclapping and a delighted, feminine laugh.

"Thank you, my dear Lady Robyn," acknowledged Pawldo, with a theatrical bow.

"And you—I'm surprised you got that crooked halfling down from a hundred," Robyn said to Tristan. The young woman's black hair gleamed in the sunlight, and her green eyes sparkled. Unlike most of the young ladies at the festival, she was clad in practical garb—green leggings and a cape the color of bright rust. Yet her beauty outshone that of the most daintily dressed maidens.

The prince returned Robyn's bright smile, pleased to encounter her. The festival would be even more fun if he could enjoy it with her on his arm.

"Are you here to buy a dog?" he asked, ignoring Pawldo's outstretched hand.

"No. I just came down here to see the animals. The castle was too dark and cold for such a lovely day!"

"Did you talk to my father this morning?" Tristan asked, and immediately wished he hadn't when he saw the flash of pain on her face.

"No," she said quietly, turning her head to the side. "The king . . . wanted to be alone."

"I understand," replied Tristan. He looked at the mass of Caer Corwell, towering above the commonsfield on its rocky knoll, and thought briefly of his father. If the king would not even see Robyn—his beloved ward—then he would have nothing to do with anyone.

"Never mind. Let the old coot sit and brood if he wants to!" Tristan ignored the hurt look upon Robyn's face. "Did you see my new prize?"

"He's a fine animal," admitted Robyn somewhat coldly. "But so was his price!"

"Yes, indeed,"chuckled Pawldo. The halfling thrust out his hand again.

Tristan reached for his coin purse. He took minor notice of a crimson flash to the side—the passing of the Calishite in his bright cloak.

And then his hand closed upon air, where the fat pouch had been.

He looked toward the ground, suddenly alarmed, but then turned and stared. The red cloak was nowhere to be seen.

"Thief!" Tristan cursed loudly, and sprinted in the direction he had last seen the flash of crimson. Robyn and Pawldo, momentarily surprised, started after him.

Darting around a tent, and barely avoiding a tall stack of kegs, Tristan saw the flash of red some distance away. He caught a glimpse of dark eyes, and then his quarry disappeared.

The prince dashed through a wine tent, leaping several low benches and scattering several early imbibers. Stumbling from the canvas structure back into the aisle between tents, he looked for the thief.

Again the flash of red, and this time the prince closed the distance.

The Calishite sprang away with renewed speed, pushing roughly through groups of people, and once spilling a stack of pots and pans into the prince's path. The thief ran well, but Tristan's legs carried him quickly over the ground, springing over obstacles or cutting sharply around corners. Often Arlen, the prince's frustrated teacher, had forced his student to run across the moors for hours at a time, developing his endurance and, incidentally, using up boyish energy. That training now paid off as Tristan picked up speed down a straight aisle.

People turned to gape in astonishment at the two runners. Quickly, the chase drew the attention of the festival-goers. Many of the Ffolk, recognizing Tristan and thinking it was some sort of merry game, gave shouts and laughter of encouragement; soon the prince was followed by an enthusiastic throng urging him on.

Finally the prince closed the gap; with a desperate dive, he grabbed the crimson cloak and jerked the thief to the ground. Tristan fell heavily over him, rolling once and then springing to his feet. The thief also recovered, but by the time he stood, the pair were surrounded by a mob of festivalgoers.

Whirling, the swarthy Calishite confronted the prince with a long, curved dagger. Tristan quickly snatched his own hunting blade from its sheath and stopped ten feet from the Calishite. For several seconds, the pair observed and judged each other.

The thief, about Tristan's size and not much older, began to grin in anticipation, though it was mixed with grudging respect for his opponent. The black eyes flashed with humor, and danger, and the thief's stance beckoned.

As Tristan paused, the curved dagger flashed outward and up. The prince instinctively blocked the blow with his own knife, but he was shocked by the swiftness of the hissing blade.

The thief, too, looked surprised at the quickness of the parry. "You use it well," he acknowledged in heavily accented Commonspeech, indicating the heavy knife.

The crowd grew rapidly, but stood well back from the fight. Their mood was tense and quiet now, as they sensed the danger. But no one dared to intervene.

For the first time, Tristan felt a flash of worry. The thief was so cool, even pleasant, yet he must know that he had been caught. Why did he not simply surrender?

Suddenly, catlike, the man sprang. The attack almost caught Tristan off guard, but his keyed instincts sent him darting to the side. He grasped the thief's wrist as his attacker's momentum carried him past. Then, kicking out sharply to the side, the prince knocked the Calishite to the ground.

But suddenly the grip in which Tristan held his foe reversed itself, and the prince felt himself being flung backward. The wind exploded from his lungs as he landed heavily on his back. Like lightning, the thief sprang toward his chest, curved dagger flashing toward the prince's neck.

Ignoring the pain in his chest, Tristan thrust his knife to block the attack, then grasped his attacker's wrist with his free hand. In a dizzying roll, they tumbled across the muddy grass, first one, then the other holding the advantage. Giving a wrenching twist, the thief suddenly broke free and stood. Before he could step clear, however, Tristan swept his leg through a circular kick. His foot landed behind the thief's knee, and the man dropped heavily. Tristan leaped onto him, holding his knife to the stranger's throat.

Slowly, the Calishite relaxed and then, amazingly, began to laugh. Tristan wondered if the man was crazy, then he realized he was nodding toward Tristan's stomach. The prince looked down to see the curved dagger poised a scant hairsbreadth from his gut. As the prince tried to keep from gasping, the thief relaxed his hold, dropping the dagger to the ground.

"I had no wish to hurt you," he announced, in a heavy accent. "I only wanted to see if I could best you." He laughed again with unmistakable good humor.

"Stand aside! Make way!" A squeaking voice parted the crowd, and Pawldo burst through the ring of onlookers. With him came Erian, a great bear of a man and one of Caer Corwell's veteran men-at-arms. Robyn trailed behind.

"Are you all right, my prince?" inquired the halfling.

Tristan was about to answer when he noticed, with some annoyance, that Robyn was not looking at him, nor did she seem in the least bit worried about him. Instead, she stared at the Calishite thief with a curiosity the prince found strangely objectionable. Suddenly she flashed a look at him, and grinned.

"That was a neat trick. Did you ever see a blade move so fast?"

Meanwhile, the thief regarded the prince, the guards, and Robyn with slowly dawning understanding.

"Prince?" he questioned, looking toward Pawldo for confirmation. "So I stole the purse of a prince!" The thief gave a rueful chuckle. "Luck of a she-camel," he declared in disgust, spitting into the grass. "What do we do now?"

"Your luck will only get worse," grunted Erian as he grabbed the Calishite by the scruff of his neck. Lifting the thief easily, the huge man roughly frisked his body.

"Here," grunted the thief, awkwardly reaching into his boot. He tossed the pouch of coins to Tristan. "You'll probably want these back," and he gave that rueful chuckle again. Against his will, Tristan felt himself liking the bravado of the young thief.

"Who are you?" he asked.

"My name is Daryth—of Calimshan."

"Come along, now!" ordered Erian, forcefully pushing the thief forward. "Let's see what the king has to say about this. " Daryth stumbled, and the surly guard cuffed his head.

Robyn tugged at the prince's arm as the guard led the thief away. "If Erian takes him to the king," she whispered, "he'll be executed for certain!" Her eyes were wide with concern.

Tristan looked at the departing thief, and once again felt that strange pang of jealousy. Still, he had his purse back and the incident was over; it was not enough to warrant a death sentence.

"Come on," he grunted. "I don't know what good it'll do, but we might as well go along with them. " He was glad he had said it when Robyn squeezed his hand in gratitude.

X X X X X X X X X X

Black waters swirled and parted, and the form of the Beast rose from the still coolness of the Darkwell. Massive and tight-knit trailing vines crowded close, but the broad, scaly body thrust the interfering plants aside like blades of grass.

Kazgoroth moved slowly, reveling in this new freedom. Yet the Darkwell had served its purpose, for the monster felt power coursing hotly through its body as never before in its long centuries of existence.

The goddess—the Beast's ancient enemy—must be vulnerable. The Beast allowed a trickle of acidic saliva to drool from its widespread jaws, Turning its hot, fiery eyes to the pool, it watched the thick waters of the Darkwell bubble in its wake.

Pulling its feet from the sucking mud, the creature pushed its way into the fens. Tree trunks snapped like brittle twigs as broad shoulders pushed them from its path. A heavy, clawed foot squashed flowers, insects, and rodents with equal lack of note. The sounds of cracking limbs, crushed vegetation, and sticky mud slurping with each mighty footfall shot violently through the wood. Wildlife shrank from the path of the Beast, racing in terror or cowering in abject fear until the monster passed.

As the Beast walked, the Firbolg were called to serve their ancient master—and serve it, they did.

Those misshapen giants—cousins of the Beast itself—ran fearfully at its approach. It took considerable coaxing, and a certain amount of potent enchantment, before the Beast could draw the chief of the Firbolgs to itself.

The ugly giant cringed in fear. His bulbous nose covered with sweat, the Firbolg scratched nervously at a wart, and bobbed his head in mute understanding.

The Firbolg were the first spawn of the Beast, brought by Kazgoroth to the Isles of Moonshae in the dim recesses of the past. Pulling the ancestors of the Firbolg from the sea, the Beast had taken them to Myrlock Vale. Here they lived in isolation, becoming sullen, bored, and lazy.

Emerging eventually from the muck and mire of the fens, the Beast roamed through wilderness for many days. Finally, the monster passed from the wilderness into farmland, and soon came upon a herd of cattle, sheltering in a remote glen.

The fat cows made a fine feast. Blood-spattered jaws gaping, the Beast again moved, this time cautiously. It knew instinctively that it neared the realms of men. The Beast felt no fear, but preferred to avoid detection for as long as possible.

Its mind grew sharper with the fresh blood of its kill and the life-giving oxygen of the spring air flowing through the giant body. The monster realized that its present shape was the wrong one for the Task. What form should the new body take?

Kazgoroth recalled its bovine feast, and was pleased. Slowly, its scaly shoulders shrank, and its lizardlike head shifted into a broad snout. Horns sprouted, and claws and scaly legs became hooves and knobby legs supporting the wide, hairy body. Soon, Kazgoroth concealed itself in the body of a huge bull. The glittering redness of the Beast's eyes seemed to fit the new guise naturally.

And the change was timely, for the monster now felt a disturbance. Humans! Two of them, emerging from woods into the glen. A man and a woman, running to the carcasses of the herd, making strange, keening noises.

Kazgoroth liked this body. This was flesh of power and speed . . . killing flesh. The great head lowered, heavy horns swinging. The charge was swift, the deaths satisfying. The Beast reveled in the human blood, knowing that the slaying of lesser creatures could not compare to this sensual gratification.

The great bull moved majestically from the glen, following a wide track toward the setting sun. The monster knew, without understanding, that it would find many more people in that direction.

As the twilight faded to night, the Beast saw many people quickly shuttering windows, and saw others run in fear at its approach. The crude brain, becoming more adept with each passing second, realized that the body of the bull would attract too much attention from humans in these settled reaches. Something more subtle was necessary.

The monster recalled its human victims. One, the female, had a body that was rounded, and supple, and strangely pleasing. A body that would blend well here. Deep in shadow, the creature again shifted, gradually rising and walking on two smooth, shapely legs. Arms and a face, soft and white, adorned the rounded torso.

This type of body would serve admirably. Instinct guided the monster to make several alterations. Hair, the color of ripe wheat, spilled down its back. Teeth straightened, and the small nose tilted slightly toward the sky. The body became slimmer at the waist and thighs, but other places the Beast kept plump and rounded.

Clothing, the Beast perceived, would be necessary for the disguise to be complete. The night grew darker, and Kazgoroth slipped silently into a small building, where it sensed many humans were asleep. The necessary garments lay within a large trunk. For a moment, Kazgoroth considered with longing the fresh blood coursing through the bodies of the sleeping humans. Caution prevailed and the monster left, allowing these humans to live.

Dawn colored the sky as Kazgoroth again moved west. Now the chill reflection of the sea came into sight, stretching away to the horizon and beyond. But the monster's goal was much closer than the horizon, or even the sea.

Before the waters stood a small castle, and Kazgoroth knew that humans in abundance would lair here. Before the castle spread broad fields, covered with tents and banners and stirring with activity and life. To this field, Kazgoroth moved.

×××××××××××

Enjoying flexing his muscle at his prisoner's expense, Erian firmly propelled the thief toward the castle. Although a capable man-at-arms, the huge fighter had little patience for peacetime, and obviously relished the opportunity for violence. Robyn and Tristan walked behind Erian and his prisoner, who still retained his sense of good cheer. They started up the paved roadway leading to the castle's gatehouse.

Caer Corwell loomed above the festival, and the town and harbor of Corwell, from high upon a rocky knoll. The castle's outer wall—a high, timber palisade—ran along the circumference of the knoll, broken only by the high stone edifice of the gatehouse. The top of the knoll was mainly devoted to the courtyard but the tops of some castle buildings, particularly the three towers of the keep, jutted above the spiked parapet.

The broad parapet of the tallest of the three towers was visible as the

highest point for miles in all directions. Fluttering boldly from this platform streamed the black banner emblazoned with the silver bear—the
Great Bear of the Kendricks.

If the three Ffolk moving up the castle road had been less familiar
with the sight, they might have marveled at the panorama opening
around them as they climbed higher. The commonsfield, sparkling with
the colorful tents and banners of the festival, immediately caught the eye,
its commotion contrasting with the calm, blue waters of Corwell Firth
stretching off to the west. In the center of the commonsfield, the green
and pastoral circle of the Druid's Grove remained pristine, dignified and
natural.

The village of Corwell lay next to the firth on the far side of the
festival grounds. Made up mainly of small wooden cottages and shops,
the little community was nearly empty now, as the villagers were all at
the festival. A low wall, more a symbol of a border than a real bastion of
defense, surrounded the village on three sides. The wooden docks of the
waterfront created the fourth side.

These docks reached into a placid circle of blue, formed by a high
stone breakwater. Within the circle were anchored the dozens of vessels
of the Corwellian fisherffolk, as well as the larger vessels of the visiting
traders.

The little party neared the castle, their steps slowing from the steep-
ness of the climb. The castle road spiraled around the steep knoll,
making a long curve to the gatehouse. To the walkers' left, the side of the
knoll itself dropped rapidly to the commonsfield below. To their right,
the same slope rose steeply to the base of the wooden palisade.

Robyn finally broke the awkward silence among the four. She fell in
step with the thief, caught his eye, and, with a bold smile, spoke.

"I'm Robyn, and this is Tristan."

Daryth looked at the prince quizzically. "Your . . . sister?" he asked,
indicating Robyn.

"No. Robyn was raised as my father's ward," explained Tristan, suddenly eager to clarify the relationship. He remembered, momentarily,
how annoyed he had been at the way Robyn had looked at the thief after
the fight. She was looking at him that way again, something more than
curiosity in her eyes.

"The pleasure is all mine," offered the thief. "I'm afraid circumstances prevent me from——urf! " Erian gave a sharp tug to Daryth's cloak, cutting him off in mid-sentence.

"Not so rough, Erian," Tristan told the guard. "He offers no resistance." Erian almost sneered at the prince, but settled for turning his back in disgust.

"Very perceptive," muttered Daryth, nodding his appreciation. "As a matter of fact, I hope to convince you that this is all a giant misunderstanding. In truth, I like this little town, and intend to stay here——for a while anyway.

"You see," he continued as if in confidence, "I'm really no sailor. I came here on the *Silver Crescent*, working my way.

"I, a master trainer of dogs, forced to such . . . Well, anyway, your little town seemed like a convenient location. I was going to settle down, start an honest business——"

"But temptation got the better of you," concluded the prince.

"Er, I am really very sorry about that. Rather mischievous of me. If I had known then what I do now . . . but I suppose there's no sense crying about it."

The group reached the gatehouse, and the bulk of Caer Corwell towered above them. The great wooden palisade stretched to the right and left until it curved out of sight around the crest of the knoll.

The gatehouse, which stood astride the road at the top of the steep, rocky knoll, consisted of a large stone building with four squat towers at the corners. Since the road allowed the only easy access from the coastal plain to the knoll, it was the most heavily defended approach. As usual, however, the heavy wooden gates stood open, and the sturdy portcullis beyond was raised out of the way.

Daryth stopped for a moment and cast a hurried glance back at the festival grounds and the harbor. For a second, his eyes scanned the scene, as if seeking something.

"Move, you," ordered Erian, giving Daryth a shove through the open archway in the gatehouse. Tristan stepped forward to rebuke the guard, but paused at the pressure of Robyn's hand on his arm.

"What can we do?" she whispered, urgently. "Surely he doesn't deserve to die!"

Her tone brooked no argument, and in any event, Tristan shared her sentiment. "He seems like a decent fellow," he said in a low voice. "But the king will look harshly on any thief who has preyed on festival-goers. What can I do?"

"I don't know," she replied, irritated. "Think of something, for once!" Before he could reply, she dashed forward and caught up with the guard and his prisoner as they entered the sunlit courtyard. Cursing under his breath, Tristan followed.

A dozen moorhounds came racing from the kennel at the far end of the courtyard. Sniffing and wagging, they swarmed around Tristan, investigating Daryth and Robyn as well. They kept their distance from Erian, since the big guard's heavy boots were well known to dogs who ventured too close.

Daryth looked surprised at the savage appearance but friendly dispositions of the large dogs. He talked to them, and stroked their shaggy necks. Soon they all crowded around him, following him as he walked along, prodded by Erian.

Reaching the doors to the great hall, the prince, suddenly inspired, turned to the man-at-arms. "You are dismissed, Erian," he announced. "Tell my father we wish to see him!" Robyn flashed him a look of surprise.

The guard opened his mouth to protest, but Tristan cut him off with a stern gesture. "Very well." The big man shrugged, then turned and moved across the courtyard.

Apparently Daryth, busy scratching the chin of Angus, Tristan's oldest hound, did not notice the exchange. He was absorbed in the veteran hunting dog, which wrinkled his brown face in pleasure, and swung his tail slowly in a circle.

"These are beautiful dogs," declared the awed Calishite. "They are yours, are they not?"

Tristan felt a flush of pride. His hounds were the passion of his life, and he was always pleased to have them complimented.

"Indeed," he said. "Are you familiar with the hounds of the Moonshaes?"

"Any man who enjoys dogs has heard of the moorhound. I have trained many types of dogs in my life. For many years, in Calimshan, I worked with desert racers. I had thought no dog could compare to the racer as a hunter, but these hounds are superior in size and power! Oh, for a chance to train such as these!"

Robyn looked warmly at Daryth, then turned to Tristan, a mute appeal shining from her dark eyes. Again the prince felt that surge of jealousy.

The doors to the great hall swung open, and a maid emerged to escort them in, for Caer Corwell had no heralds. "The King awaits you," she announced with a polite nod.

The trio entered the shadowy hall. They walked between a pair of huge oaken tables toward the great fireplace at the far end of the hall. Before that fireplace, in a heavy wooden chair, sat King Kendrick of Corwell.

The king looked up at their approach, but said nothing. Tristan could not help but feel an irrational flicker of guilt at the sight of the deep lines of sorrow etched into his father's face. He steeled himself for the encounter.

King Bryon Kendrick's hair was black grown heavily streaked with gray. Among the lines on his face, one could see strength and determination, as well as pain and grief. The king's beard, like his hair a mass of black salted with patches of gray and white, flowed down his chest.

As usual, King Kendrick looked bored at the prince's approach. It was no secret to anyone that the prince of Corwell was something of a disappointment to the king. Tristan hoped the king would not harangue him with sarcasm in front of Robyn and the others.

To Tristan's relief, the king turned to smile at Robyn, and his eyes, briefly, flashed a spark of warmth. Then, cold again, they regarded the approaching Calishite.

Next to the king sat Arlen, captain of the king's guard and Tristan's lifelong teacher. The grizzled warhorse looked at Tristan speculatively as he and his companions reached the seated men.

"Hello, Father, Arlen," began Tristan, while Robyn curtseyed quickly.

The prince looked again at Daryth, and the Calishite responded to the glance with a fast smile. And with that smile, Tristan felt the beginning of a deep and true friendship, something stalwart and fine that would last between the two of them for the rest of their lives.

His mind made up, he quickly settled upon a strategy to save the Calishite's life.

"Father," Tristan said again, turning to the king, "I would like us to hire this man as the royal houndmaster."

✕ ✕ ✕ ✕ ✕ ✕ ✕ ✕ ✕

Grunnarch the Red stood boldly upon the rolling deck of his long-ship as the sleek vessel pitched and rocked through looming swells. All around him, like a forest of tall trees, the masts of longships jutted proudly from the Sea of Moonshae. The northmen sailed to war!

Grunnarch, and dozens of the ships of his henchmen—the lesser lords of Norland who owed fealty to him, their king—had taken to sea a tenday earlier than caution dictated. A late winter storm could have caught his fleet unawares, and wreaked fearful havoc.

But the King of Norland was a gambling man, and a fearless one. He had never shirked from risking his own life, and would not tolerate a follower unwilling to do the same. So his men, by the thousand, had followed him to sea.

The gods of war had thundered in Grunnarch's mind throughout the winter, and he had paced his gray fortress like a raging Firbolg. The tension, he knew, had been felt throughout Norland. Thus, even before the weather had broken completely, the northmen had provisioned their longships, bade farewell to their homes, and taken to sea.

The long summer before him beckoned like a seductive woman, and Grunnarch's mind roamed happily over prospects of raiding and stealing, capturing slaves, and fighting glorious battles in the months ahead.

Grunnarch sailed to the Iron Keep, fortress of Thelgaar Ironhand on Oman's Isle. Central among the Moonshae Islands, the keep had a fine deep harbor and, more importantly, the fortress of the northmen's most powerful king, Thelgaar Ironhand. From Iron Keep, the northmen could reach Moray, Gwynneth, or Callidyr—all the lands of the Ffolk. The divided kingdoms of the Ffolk practically begged to be raided. If Thelgaar, with his huge fleet and battle-hardened army, decided to join the campaign, there would be no limit to the summer's potential.

And indeed, two days before landfall, masts were sighted upon the northern horizon. In a matter of hours, Grunnarch recognized the blue whale insignia of Raag Hammerstaad, king of the Norheim Isles. Raag also sailed with many ships. Grunnarch wondered how many other kingdoms might decide to join the warlike throng this summer.

The two fleets merged, and the wind freshened. A hundred ships coursed through the waves, all intent upon Oman harbor. Soon the rocky outline of the island broke the southeast horizon. Grunnarch's vessel in the lead, the fleet filed around the promontory that protected the harbor. Grunnarch grunted in pleasure at the scene in the harbor.

The hundred ships of Thelgaar lined part of the shore of the harbor. In addition to the Iron King's warships were those of many other kingdoms, already arrived and arrayed for war.

This would indeed be a summer of blood and plunder.

XXXXXXXXXX

The goddess shivered, and flinched. She felt her body growing numb—not from fear, but from a distant and wistful sadness. The feeling was remote, and she took no great notice of it. Gradually, though, she began to recognize the numbness for the dire threat it was.

With an effort, she forced herself to stir. Passivity now, she knew instinctively, would be fatal. The call she sent reverberated through the earth, thrumming deep within the mountains and hills, and even rolling along the bottom of the sea.

Hoping that it was not too late, the goddess tried to awaken her children.

A PROPHECY

2

Erian strode rapidly back through the gatehouse and down the road to the festival. He was anxious to return to the fun. *Damn that little gamecock, anyway,* he swore, thinking of the prince. *I save his skin from that slithering spitball of a Calishite, and for what?*

The big guard spat angrily into the dust, and felt a little better. He thought of Geoffrey the aleman, who would undoubtedly have several cool kegs tapped near a comfortable bench. With a dozen silver coins in his pocket, Erian would be able to drink all day and most of the night.

Geoffrey's tent, bigger than most, also rose above the others like a beckoning tower. As Erian had guessed, the fat innkeeper offered uncorked kegs of light and dark ale, as well as thick Callidyrr mead. Splurging, the man-at-arms used one of his silver pieces to purchase a huge tankard of mead.

Turning from the bar, Erian surveyed the other occupants of the tent. Several northmen clustered nearby, drinking quietly. A young bard entertained a group of men and women, farmerffolk, in the far corner.

Then he saw the woman sitting quietly in the darkest corner of the tent. She regarded him with a bold, somewhat amused gaze—a gaze that Erian returned with interest. Her eyes flashed once, very quickly.

He saw that she wore peasant clothes, which seemed much too large for her. Nonetheless, the outlines of her body, he also noticed, stood out clearly against the casually wrinkled cloth, curving deliciously as though to scorn the plain raiment.

Staring, Erian somehow found himself standing before her. Even with her face still masked by shadow, she overwhelmed him. He sat before her, and slowly remembered where, and who, he was.

"My name is Erian," he announced, feeling somehow proud of the fact that he was able to talk at all.

"I am . . . Meridith," responded the woman. She blinked, and he noticed that her eyes were strangely vague, almost empty. Yet they had flashed at him from across the room!

"That is an unusual name. Do you come from Calidyrr, or farther places?" he asked.

She seemed amused, for a moment, as she replied, "I come from, yes, farther places."

"How do you like our festival?" Erian asked, thinking with pleasure of spending a day escorting Meridith about the festival. And of the night that would, perhaps, follow.

"It is quite interesting," responded the woman, as if reading his mind. "But I should like to see more of it."

Erian beamed. "Allow me to be your escort!"

Standing, he offered his arm, playing the part of the gallant. She laughed, and rose also. For just a moment, he saw that flash of fire in her eyes, and his blood raced.

The day passed quickly. Ale and wine stalls were numerous, and Erian found a reason to visit each one and quench his thirst. Meridith drank an occasional glass of wine, but professed a distaste for malt beverage. Nonetheless, she encouraged him not to allow her abstinence to interfere with his thirst.

Later, the coolness of the spring night drove them close together. Meridith's body seemed to harbor a deep chill, and Erian enjoyed the opportunity to wrap her against him in his cloak. She fit nicely at his side, snuggling closer with an eagerness that delighted and excited him.

Once, during the day, they had passed the prince, touring the festival with the king's ward and to Erian's surprise, the Calishite thief who had robbed him that very day. The guard turned to remark about the fact, and Erian saw Meridith watching the prince's party with a look of frightening intensity. Immediately, the guard felt a surge of raw jealousy.

"Who is that?" she asked in a low voice.

"He's the young poppinjay of a prince—carries himself like he owns the whole town," grumbled the guard, in a not altogether accurate description. "He's a disgrace to the Kendrick name! Cares not a whit for the responsibilities of his position—all he's interested in are his blasted hounds and having a good time!"

Erian turned and scowled at Meridith. "What are you looking at him for, anyway? Come on!" He reached for her arm to pull her away, but her voice, strangely urgent, cut him off.

"And the girl? Who is she?"

Now Erian looked back, for Robyn was a sight his eyes had rested upon more than once. Though her shape was hidden beneath her long cape, there were, the guard remembered, gentle curves and soft swells that had turned the lass into a woman over the last two years. The memories inflamed his ardor, and again he reached for Meridith. This time, his arms slipped about her, and she allowed his hand to drop boldly along her back.

"She's the king's ward—an orphan, they say. She's lived in the castle since she was a baby."

"Interesting," mused Meridith, as the guard led her away. Her voice, soft and husky, nearly brought Erian's blood to a boil. As he found another ale tent, the woman's unblinking eyes turned back to Tristan and Robyn, curious, and a little menacing. But when Erian returned with a full mug, Meridith laughed gaily and allowed the big man to take her arm and lead her through the fair.

Eventually they returned to the ale tent where they met, and sat again on the corner bench. Erian felt he must have said something terribly witty, for Meridith was laughing delightedly. And then she paused, regarding him. Again that spark in her eyes, this time a gleaming as of hot coals on a dark night.

She leaned forward and kissed him, and her mouth was hot. The coolness seemed to have left her body, as she leaned against him. She was heat everywhere, and perspiration flowed from his pores.

Erian met her kiss with crushing force, driving his mouth against hers and reaching for her body. She melted backward and he leaned over her. She clasped him, nibbling at his ear and neck. He looked down as she moved again to kiss him, and saw again those fiery eyes. This time, it was as if the door to a furnace had been cast open, and he saw great depths of fire, and heat . . .

And death. She sucked the air and the spirit from his body, replacing it with something foul and perverted. The spirit of the man remained within his body, but it was twisted by the power of the Darkwell into something mightier, but something terribly evil.

×××××××××

"Let's get back to the festival," the prince suggested, after Daryth had been shown his new quarters in the barracks.

The Calishite claimed to have no more possessions than those he carried. He had quickly refused Tristan's suggestion that they visit the galleon in the harbor that had brought him to Corwell. Daryth was pleasant and talkative, but resisted any attempts to question him about his background.

"What's Calimshan like?" asked Robyn.

Daryth shrugged, but then smiled at her disarmingly. "Like any powerful nation, I guess. It's run by the merchants, mostly, under control of the Pasha. I served the Pasha directly—a position of high honor, I suppose." The Calishite's tone showed that he thought very little of the honor.

"How about the festival?" prodded the prince, feeling a little thirsty.

"You two go ahead," said the Calishite. "I'd like to settle in here and relax a bit."

"You're coming with us!" Robyn's tone brooked no argument. "This is the liveliest night Corwell will see until Midsummer, and I'm not going to let you miss it!"

For a moment, it seemed to the prince that a shadow passed across Daryth's face. Tristan hoped he would disagree with the woman and stay behind, but he relented.

"Very well. Let's have some fun."

The golden reflections of sunset still flickered in Corwell Firth as Tristan, Robyn, and Daryth returned to the festival. Many revelers carried torches, and bright lanterns hung from all the stalls, so the meadow was lit against the darkness. Still, just beyond the periphery of the celebration, the cold spring air was black and mysterious.

In the pocket of light, the spring celebration approached frenzy. Bards struck their harps with enthusiasm, the opposing sounds mingling in the air. Hucksters pressed their wares eagerly, the sellers of meads and ales prospered, and much gold and silver changed hands.

Celebrations of the Ffolk were hard-drinking affairs, and the spring festival washed away a winter's worth of boredom. In many places, snoring bodies lay along the aisles or underneath the drinking benches. These were ignored by their fellows who could still walk.

The air of the festival made Tristan bubble with enthusiasm and excitement. Daryth observed the festivities with unabashed wonder.

"Twice better than last year's," observed the prince, watching Robyn laugh happily, "as it should be." Then he paused abruptly and his face went blank as he remembered. "The hound. I'd better stop at Pawldo's and make the arrangements."

"Did I hear my name?" Tristan looked around to see little Pawldo beaming up at him. Clinging to his arm, looking nervously at them, was a young halfling maiden.

"Allow me to introduce Allian," stated Pawldo formally. "My dear, this is Tristan Kendrick, prince of Corwell, the king's ward, Robyn, and—say, aren't you—" Pawldo's eyes widened at the sight of Daryth.

"And this is Daryth of Calimshan," Tristan interjected, bowing to Allian, who blushed deeply.

"Delighted to meet you all," she giggled, her voice even higher pitched than Pawldo's.

Tristan pulled the leather pouch from his pocket. "Here's your coin, Pawldo. Forty gold, right?"

"Tch—with a memory like that, you'll never make a king!" Pawldo grinned. "The figure I recall is fifty!"

"Indeed," muttered Tristan, counting out ten more gold pieces. "I'll pick up the hound in the morning."

"Well, we're off!" announced the halfling, tucking away the coins. "The halflings of Lowhill are having a big dance tonight!" He and the young maid swiftly melted into the crowd.

"I don't know where to begin!" cried Robyn, whirling around and trying to see everything.

A pair of tumblers rolled between the companions, and Robyn, startled, stepped backward. "Look!" she called.

Seizing Tristan's arm, she pulled him along behind the acrobats. But the prince noticed that her other arm was just as warmly clasping Daryth's.

"Perhaps a cool mug of ale . . ." the prince suggested.

In an instant, Robyn had pulled them into a small stall; Tristan found himself buying a round for his companions, as well as the half dozen Ffolk in the place.

"Many thanks, my prince!" acknowledged an old farmer with a broad smile. Tristan reflected that he heard his title only from good friends, or drunks. In a corner of the stall, a lesser bard tried to strum a lively country tune. Several equally lively wenches surrounded the musician, urging him on, dancing and laughing, and kicking high at the growing crowd of onlookers. The festive atmosphere made them ignore the fact that the music was slow and dissonant, for the bard had not thoroughly mastered his harp. The prince thought it was unfortunate that the greater bards all gathered to play at Caer Callidyr, citadel of the High King, for the spring festival.

Tristan watched with interest, but then Robyn was gone again.

"Come on!" she called before disappearing around a huge green and yellow tent of gleaming silk. The canopy seemed to shine brighter in the torchlight than it had in sunlight, perhaps because of the contrast against the inky background.

Following Robyn around the tent, the men found her staring with interest through a hooded doorway, into a darkened tent interior. Acrid smoke puffed from the entrance, and she coughed slightly.

She started to step through the door when Daryth moved forward. "This is a Calishite tent, Robyn, and I know the odor of the ginyak weed. This is not a place for a young lady."

"What makes you think I'd be in trouble there?" she asked, a glare in her eye.

"I did not mean to . . . please!" Daryth stuttered, suddenly nervous. "But trust me, we ought to find our fun elsewhere!"

Robyn looked again at the entrance. Tristan, certain that the head-strong lass would ignore Daryth and charge right in, was more surprised when, without further argument, she spun and turned away.

Brushing past both Daryth and the prince, she walked on. Tristan saw Daryth cast a frightened glance at the tent, and run to catch up with her.

"Here," Robyn called gaily, rushing to the entrance of another silken tent. They crowded inside and spent several minutes watching a snake charmer artfully coerce his serpentine pets from their large, clay jars. In the back of the tent, the snake charmer displayed, chained to a stout post, a great Firbolg. The giant slept, so its ferocity could not be tested.

"Look at that nose!" commented the prince, watching the great organ flex with the Firbolg's heavy snores.

"The poor creature," said Robyn, with an angry look about the tent. "Keeping it chained up like an animal!"

"It's worse than an animal," charged Tristan. "It's a monster!"

"Some monster!" Robyn snorted. "Old and weary, I would say, and better off wherever it came from!" She stalked off.

Once again, the young men found themselves hurrying through the festival grounds, trying to keep Robyn in sight. Shortly, Tristan found himself in a smoky but huge tent, watching oiled dancers undulate to the jarring rhythm of tiny cymbals and wailing pipes. He would have been willing to watch more of the exotic dance, but he found himself annoyed that Robyn so boldly joined the men in watching the sugges-tive movements.

"Let's go," he said gruffly, and Daryth, too, urged Robyn out of the tent.

One after another, they inspected the tents and pavillions of the fair. Several times they lingered in a meadhall, or wine tent, and the flush of many drinks made the evening whirl more madly than ever. In one such tent, Tristan saw the brawny form of Erian, but the big guard had already collapsed in the corner. In another, they ordered a massive limb of mutton, which Daryth tore into as if half starved.

Other tents offered wares for sale, products of the hardworking craftsmen of the Ffolk. Smooth pottery, colorful wool cloaks and capes, and gleaming steel weapons all displayed the skill of Tristan's people, and it was not without pride that he compared the fine weapons to the cheaper, iron implements of the northmen.

Robyn bartered with a crone of a weaver-woman for a new cape, embroidered in a bright, leafy pattern. Throwing it over her slender shoulders, she whirled alluringly for her two companions.

Finally, the trio found themselves standing before the white linen tent of Friar Nolan. The stout cleric rushed from the entrance and fastened on Tristan.

"The shame! The debauchery!" Friar Nolan's bald head glistened with sweat, and his eyes were wide. In emphasis, he bobbed his head excitedly at the dancers and drunks thronging through the festival.

"The gods are forgiving, and will overlook much, but I fear for many souls tonight," the cleric continued in a breathless rush.

Though the clerics of the new gods had been preaching on the Moonshae Islands for a century or more, many of the Ffolk still clung to their traditional worship of the Earthmother. The Ffolk accepted, and even appreciated, the clerics, for their powers were beneficial, and their practices benign. Still, old traditions carried great weight among the Ffolk, and the presence of the druids served as a strong counter to the clerics of the new gods.

The source of the druids' might came from the wild places of the Moonshae Islands—particularly the Moonwells. Mostly solitary, living in secluded groves, the druids gathered at the communities of the Ffolk for occasions such as the festival, or emergencies such as floods, earthquakes, or war.

"And there, as if the rest of this wretchedness is not enough, the final blow is struck." Friar Nolan's pudgy finger, quivering with indignation, pointed across the aisle.

Tristan suppressed a smile as he understood the reason for the cleric's distress. Friar Nolan's tent, dedicated to the greater glory of the new gods, stood directly across the walkway from the central grove of the druids. The large stone arch draped with mistletoe, which provided entrance to the grove, could not have been more of an affront to the easily affronted cleric.

"An unfortunate placement," commiserated the prince, but already he saw that Robyn was getting away again. "Excuse me, but, you understand," he apologized as he raced on.

Robyn passed through the arch and entered the druids' grove, with Daryth and Tristan right behind. The grove was quiet, and very dark. Though central to the festival grounds, the grove seemed a world removed from the madness and noise of the revelry.

Robyn moved slowly, almost reverently, into the grove. She paused briefly under the arch, bowing her head and whispering something softly. Then she stepped forward, seeming to glide across the soft grass toward the heart of the grove.

"What is this place?" Daryth asked, instinctively lowering his voice to a whisper.

"This is the Corwell grove—of the druids," the prince explained. "At the center of the grove is a Moonwell—a magical pool of water. The grove itself is sacred—the trees cannot be cut, and no animal entering here may be harmed."

"Your religion sounds like an important part of your lives," remarked the Calishite.

"Perhaps. Robyn spends a lot of time here. She says it calms her. Sometimes she studies with the druids, I guess."

"Oh?" Daryth raised his eyebrows and peered into the shadows before them. "No wonder she appears to know where she's going, while I can't even see my nose in front of me!"

"Follow me," the prince said. He stepped forward confidently, and tripped over a root. Only Daryth's quick grasp of his cloak prevented him from sprawling headlong.

"Can't you be careful?" Robyn's voice was sharp but hushed, as she returned to the men. "Come with me, carefully."

They advanced slowly until their eyes adjusted and they saw that the scene, in fact, was illuminated. The source of the light, Daryth saw, was a milky pool of water. Surrounding the pool was a ring of tall, broad oak trees. The branches were so thick that they blocked out the light of the full moon.

"Tomorrow, the druids will celebrate the spring equinox here," explained Robyn.

Suddenly, Tristan saw a shadow of movement among the trees around them. Whirling, he saw several hooded shapes emerge into the faint illumination of the Moonwell. The druids were here, he realized, and he wondered why the fact should have surprised him. The figures moved forward with stately grace. Each was concealed, head to toes, in a dark robe.

"Prince of Corwell," spoke the tallest of the robed figures. His voice was rich and deep, but unpracticed, as if he spoke but little. "We have expected you."

"But how . . ." Tristan began, confused.

"I knew it!" Robyn interjected. "It wasn't accident that I felt compelled to enter the grove. And I brought you here!" she said to Tristan, proud of herself.

Daryth had jerked around at the appearance of the figures, his body shaking. "Who are you?" he demanded.

"These are the druids," explained Robyn calmly. "And please, keep your voice down!"

"And you, my child," said another figure. Tristan was startled to see a pleasantly rounded older woman. Unlike the other druids, her hood was thrown back to reveal a plump, lined face, and a warm smile. She looked kindly at Robyn. "My, how time . . ." her voice trailed off, and she cleared her throat.

The other druids remained silent as she looked the trio over. Then she stepped back, nodding slightly to the druid who had spoken first.

"Know this, Prince of the Ffolk," said the tall man in a serious voice, "the images in the well foretell a summer of peril, and an autumn of tragedy. You will earn the right to rule, in this summer, or the tragedy will be upon your shoulders."

"Why? What peril? What are you—"

"The Moonshaes face a dire threat—a menace that thwarts even the power of the goddess. Whether you are the means to end that threat, or will become an agent of its triumph, we cannot yet see."

The woman interrupted the druid, and Tristan noticed that the man quickly deferred to her.

"Oh, such stuff!" she exclaimed. "Yes, of course it will be unpleasant. You might even get killed. But you might not, too! And, my word, it's time someone drew the Sword of Cymrych Hugh again. Just," she concluded, her voice growing tender, "be very careful, please!"

She turned away, and the prince caught the sparkle of moisture in her eyes. Something in the way she looked at Robyn as she moved away caught his interest. And the girl, he saw, watched the departing druidess with an expression of awe.

Then the male druid caught Tristan's attention again.

"Beware, Prince of Corwell, and care well for your companions. The shadow of a mighty evil falls across your path. You must decide whether to drive it back, with light, or be swallowed by its darkness!" The voice rose with power and urgency, until it finally rang throughout the grove like the thrumming of a heavy drum.

"Wait . . . " The prince wanted to question the mysterious figure, but suddenly he saw nothing before him but shifting shadows, rippling fantastically in the white aura from the Moonwell.

xxxxxxxxxx

The Beast, still walking upright in the body of the woman, left the festival throng and moved across the moor, its strength rekindled by its recent feast.

Day or night meant nothing to Kazgoroth. The monster walked always northward as moors gave way to craggy hills. Even the deep snow which still lay among these jagged and stony obstacles proved undaunting. Kazgoroth, with a weight much greater than a woman's, sank through the snow to the ground beneath. Unflinchingly, the female human body plowed a furrow through the deepest drifts.

Finally the monster reached the crest of the low range, and saw the rolling terrain of central Gwynneth spread before it. The crisp spring sunshine glinted off hundreds of rocky peaks, which stretched to the far horizon around a vast, tree-filled bowl. In the center of the bowl, the deep waters of Myrloch also glinted brightly in the sunshine. The flickering ripples of the lake struck pain into the monster's eyes, and it looked away.

Myrloch. Kazgoroth's dim consciousness realized that the lake was still the preserve of the goddess. Central Gwynneth had always been her strongest domain. It was here that the remnants of the Llewyrr fled when they lost their hopeless struggle against the humans for the realms of Moonshae.

The Ffolk believed that the elves called Llewyrr had died out in the Moonshaes; the Beast knew this was not the case. Myrloch Vale hosted populations of dwarves and Firbolgs who preferred to keep their distance from humans. But living also within the secret places of Myrloch Vale were, Kazgoroth knew, communities of Llewyrr. The Beast would avoid these, as their potent magic was one of the few forces upon Gwynneth that gave the monster cause for concern.

The Beast was not yet ready to strike. Shrewd enough to know it needed to acquire more allies, it was on its way to find them. Still in human form, Kazgoroth began the descent into the broad basin. It had no particular business in Myrloch Vale, yet the place stood across its path, and thus the land would bear its passage.

Days of march slowly drained Kazgoroth's strength, and the monster felt a flare of annoyance. The time fast approached when the Beast would need to feast, and so it carried itself with new vigilance, seeking a victim to sate its gnawing hunger.

And soon it found what it sought. Seeing the man alone in the woods, the monster's awakening subconscious suggested a ruse. The female body shrank, twisting eerily into a new shape. Though smaller and more dainty, the body still retained its female roundess and flowing, golden locks.

Flitting lightly through the woods, Kazgoroth moved forward to the kill.   •

×××××××××××

The cool waters pressed heavily against the floor of the sea, far out of range of the sun's warmth. Here, the world knew neither winter nor summer, day nor night. There was only the cool darkness, the eternal darkness that cloaked a region nearly devoid of life.

Yet the goddess's call reached through the pressure of the depths, persistently nudging at the one of her children who slept here. At first, the message was ignored, and the one who was called slept on. Another century or more might pass before the creature stirred.

But the call of the mother was relentless, and finally a bulking form stirred in the deep silt of the sea bottom. Shrugging its giant body free from the clutching muck, the creature rose from the bottom and floated, nearly motionless, in the depths. Time passed, and the form slowly sank toward the bottom again.

But again the goddess prodded gently at her huge child. The great head swung slowly from side to side, and powerful flukes pushed hard against the sea bottom. A mighty tail thrust downward, and the body flexed along its vast length.

Then it began to move, slowly at first, but gaining an awesome momentum. The flukes plowed the water with solid authority, and the broad tail pushed with unstoppable force. Higher, toward the realms of light, and sun, and current, the creature moved.

It gathered speed as it rose, and energy seemed to build in the mighty body. A stream of bubbles flowed from the wide mouth, trickling around layers of huge teeth and seeming to flow downward along the huge body.

The water ahead grew slowly brighter, until the creature saw a pale gray glow spread across the upper reaches of the sea. The grayness became blue, and finally even the sun came into view, a shimmering yellow dot viewed through the filter of the sea.

The body broke the surface of the water with explosive force, sending a shower of brine through the air in all directions. High, and impossibly higher, the creature rose into the air, and still more of its length emerged from the frothing sea. Water spilled from the black skin in thundering waterfalls, until finally the great head slowed, and paused for an instant.

With a crash that rocked the sea for miles around, the body fell back to the surface. Waves exploded outward from the falling body with enough force to capsize a large ship. But the horizon was empty of either land or sail.

There was none to see that the Leviathan had awakened.

THE HUNT

3

Trahern of Oakvale walked silently among the vast trunks of his forest domain. His brown robe blended easily with the knobby trunks, and his sturdy oaken staff provided additional balance as he stepped lightly across fallen tree trunks and other obstacles.

The druid was growing old, but Trahern still felt pride in the state of his forest and the thriving health of his creatures. The caretakership of any of the forests around Myrloch was an honored post among the druids, and Trahern had lived up to the expectations placed upon him. He had avoided conflict with the Llewyrr, though the faeriefolk often traveled and camped in his preserve.

Trahern would be content to live out in peace the remainder of his days tending Oakvale. Every twist in the forest path he now followed, and every piece of lichen and moss that bedecked the numerous tree trunks lying about the woods, was as familiar to Trahern as the interior of his own small cottage. And in this familiarity, he found peace.

But now his peace had been interrupted. The High Druid of Gwynneth, Genna Moonsinger, had summoned the druids of the land to gather in emergency council on the shore of Myrloch. This rare circumstance could only mean that grave danger threatened the land. The old druid found the idea of another crisis particularly annoying now that he was in the autumn of his life. In fact, he had rudely shooed away the owl that had brought him the summons.

A sudden movement at one side caught the druid's eye, and he paused to squint into the brush. His eyes were not what they used to be, but again he saw a shimmer of delicate movement. His heart pounded in excitement as he saw a smoothly curved leg, trailing a filmy gown, disappear behind a tree.

A dryad!

Trahern forgot the council in his eagerness to find the tree sprite. Her lair must be near! Could it be that she was calling him?

Trahern knew that occasionally a dryad would call a druid to come and live with it for a time. These druids never spoke of the experience afterward, but their eyes seemed to return to memories that were most pleasant indeed. Now, perhaps he had been called!

The druid caught sight of the slender form again as it slipped behind another tree. This time, the figure turned back teasingly, and he saw sparkling eyes and heard a tinkle of musical laughter.

Puffing with exertion, Trahern followed the dryad around another tree. In his eagerness, he nearly stumbled but was close behind the sprite as he stepped around the bole of a giant oak.

There, Kazgoroth took him.

XXXXXXXXXX

The feathered decoy wafted high into the air, fluttering like a wounded bird, and Tristan quickly drew and sighted his arrow. Quickly he let the missile fly, cursing as it missed the target by ten feet. The decoy glided on, and underneath it, on the ground, streaked a brown form. Canthus followed the fluttering object for over a hundred yards. As it finally began settling back toward earth, the great dog crouched, and then hurled himself into the air.

The decoy was still eight feet from the ground when the dog's powerful jaws closed over it.

The great moorhound had filled out in the few tendays Tristan had owned him. His square jaw, thick neck encircled by a studded iron collar, and sturdy shoulders made him a very solid dog. His long legs and strength insured that he was very fast.

"Good catch!" applauded Robyn, as Daryth whistled for the dog to return.

"At least one of you might put some meat on the table," grunted Arlen, looking at Tristan in disappointment.

"Forget the damn bow!" cursed Tristan, throwing down the weapon he was having trouble conquering. "I can take care of myself well enough with my sword!"

"Sure ye can," agreed the older man. "But ye'll never be a king of the Ffolk if they can't see that ye wield a bow as well as a blade!"

"I don't want to be king!" retorted the prince. "I'm going to town. " He turned and stalked away from his teacher and Robyn.

"Tristan Kendrick!" Robyn's voice dripped with scorn. "For someone who doesn't want to be king, you sure like to act like one! Where in Gwynneth did you learn to be so rude to your teacher?"

The prince turned, biting back an angry comment, and looked at Robyn and Arlen. Daryth stood off to the side, pretending not to pay attention.

"You're right," he agreed, lowering his gaze and shaking his head. "I'm sorry, old friend. " He held out his hand.

The old warrior took it briefly, then said gruffly, "Get ready. " He prepared another decoy, then turned to the prince. "And pay attention, damn ye! That last shot was pure carelessness—ye forgot about the wind, and it looked like ye took little notice of yer target's motion!"

Again, and again, the decoy fluttered up and the prince shot arrows from the powerful longbow. Each miss made him more annoyed, though several shots grazed the target. The prince noted that Robyn had gone to stand with Daryth, as the Calishite directed the apparently tireless Canthus through his retrieving.

"One more time," Tristan said, almost snarling, as his fingers tightened on the bow.

Arlen swung his arm, the launcher clicked, and again the decoy fluttered into the air. As Canthus raced across the grassy heath, the prince swiftly drew and nocked an arrow. In an instant, the bowstring was taut against Tristan's ear, and he sighted down the shaft as the decoy rose and spun across his path.

Tristan advanced his aim, anticipating the flight of the decoy, and took note of the wind. It had fallen, suddenly, to virtual stillness. Loosing the arrow, the prince watched it streak toward the target.

The shaft struck solidly, sending a spray of feathers fluttering through the air. Even as the decoy changed direction, falling to earth, the great moorhound whirled and leaped, catching the remains of the target in his widespread jaws.

"Well done, lad," grunted Arlen, in what for him was an exuberant expression of pleasure. "There's hope ye'll be an archer yet!"

Tristan smiled wanly, relieved at his success but annoyed by the frustrations it took to get there. Still, the praise pleased him.

"Now stop shooting for a moment and eat!" ordered Robyn, returning with Daryth to the student and teacher. The prince looked at her sharply, but she paid no attention. "Here—I've made you something," she said, offering a covered bowl to the prince.

Tristan, admiring Canthus's strong jaws as Daryth removed the ruined decoy, took the bowl and absently uncovered it. A sound of exasperation caught his attention, and he realized that Robyn had been waiting for him to say something. Too late now, she was already stalking off toward the Calishite. Tristan looked down and saw that she had prepared one of his favorite dishes—a mixture of mushrooms, lettuce, and chives. He started over to thank the lass, but she pointedly turned her back and offered a similar bowl to Daryth. Stung, the prince sat on the ground and chewed his food.

"Hello!" A thin voice trailed up the hill, and Tristan saw the diminutive figure of Pawldo climbing toward them. In a few minutes, the halfling joined them. The stocky little halfling was outfitted for walking but readily dropped to the grass beside them as if he had nowhere very pressing to go.

"I see that he learns quickly," announced Pawldo, nodding toward the great hound that lay, panting, upon the sun-warmed grass.

"Aye. If only his master were half as adept," muttered Arlen to everyone's amusement except Tristan's.

Indeed, Canthus had adapted well to life at Caer Corwell. In less than two tendays, the dog had learned all the hand commands Daryth used to direct him.

He ran faster and leaped higher than any dog the prince, or Daryth, had ever seen. When Canthus first joined the hounds of Tristan's pack, there had been a brief, snarling showdown with Angus. The old dog had blustered and bristled, but sensibly backed down as Canthus had pressed, almost gently, against Angus's skinny neck. Since that moment, Canthus had been the leader.

"When will you take him on a true hunt?" asked the halfling. "I hope you're not going to wait until you learn to shoot—a dog's life is short!"

Again his companions had a laugh at his expense, and Tristan felt his face redden. "Indeed not," he replied. "We've talked of an outing to Llaryth Forest next tenday."

"Splendid!" announced Pawldo. "I'm growing bored of Lowhill—though Allian's company is sweet, I admit. I could use a stint in the forest. To the hunt! When do we leave?"

"We'll have to speak to my father," Tristan replied. "But soon enough, I'm sure."

"Great!" Daryth exclaimed. "I'm eager to see a little more of this island of yours!" Tristan noticed that the Calishite's accent grew less noticeable almost daily.

"I shall come, too," announced Robyn.

The prince looked up in surprise. "But you've always hated hunting . . . " he began.

"And so I do," she replied. "Yet there are some types of fungus that I wish to collect this year, and they can be found nowhere on Gwynneth outside of Llyrath. I shall ignore the senseless slaying that you will no doubt commit . . . unless, of course, you'd rather I went by myself."

"Certainly not!" exclaimed Arlen and Tristan at the same time.

Daryth raised his eyebrows. "What is this Llyrath Forest place? Some kind of deathtrap?"

"No," said Tristan, laughing. "But it is the wildest part of the kingdom. We might meet wild boar or even bear—there are few human residents."

Tristan turned to Robyn. "And I'd like it if you come with us—I was just thinking you wouldn't enjoy it. That's all."

"If you're certain I won't be too much in the way," she declared, frostily.

In fact, Tristan knew Robyn's woodcraft to be superior to his own. Arlen had given him considerable training in the ways of the wild, but Robyn seemed to have an uncanny rapport with it.

"It's settled then!" she cried. "Let's leave tomorrow!"

"How long will it take us to get there?" asked Daryth.

"Just a couple of days, though we'll want to spend some time in the forest. How long should we figure?" the prince asked Arlen.

"Let's plan for ten days. Can we be ready by tomorrow?"

"You'll come with us, of course, Pawldo?" asked the prince. When the halfling nodded happily, Tristan said, "The five of us then!" The group started back toward the castle. "We'll take ten horses—I'll get them from the stables."

"I'll collect sleeping furs and a cookpot," offered Robyn.

Pawldo and Arlen agreed to pack some spare food, in case the hunting was poor, and Daryth would gather the hounds. By the time they reached the castle, the expedition was planned, to depart at dawn.

The group separated at the castle, each going to begin preparations.

Tristan entered the great hall and found his father sitting alone by the embers of a dying fire. He didn't look up as the prince entered. The shutters of the long windows were open, but the room still seemed to harbor a deep, disturbing chill.

"Father, we're going on a hunt—to Llyrath Forest." In silent anger, Tristan cursed the nervousness that always crept into his voice when he talked to his father. "Arlen will accompany us. We'll be gone ten days—perhaps a fortnight."

For a minute, the prince wondered if his father had heard him, for the king displayed no reaction. Finally, the king turned and regarded his son coldly.

"You might as well," King Kendrick declared, his voice heavy with scorn. "It beats wenching and drinking—things I've heard from others that you do so well. You are a disgrace to the crown!"

"What—?" Tristan stopped, cut off by his father's look of disgust. Whatever the prince said now would just inflame his father's anger, he knew.

"Leave me!" growled the king, turning back to the fire.

Suppressing an urge to scream and stomp his feet and once again failing to impress his father, the Prince of Corwell turned and walked, seething, from the hall. As always, he immediately converted his anger into a desire to rush out and have some fun, so he hurried about his preparations for the hunt.

The companions left Caer Corwell before dawn, which spread gray and oppressive from the east. Bundled in woolen cloaks and furs, they led their horses from the castle stable, mounting saddles and supplies on the various steeds. Pawldo, who chose a small, shaggy pony, had to chase his reluctant steed around the courtyard before he could saddle it.

The sunrise brought little warmth, for low clouds hung oppressively over the land. The peaks of the Highlands were buried within the gray blanket, and a penetrating mist hung heavily in the air. The party rode southwest, along the road to Cantrev Dynnatt, for most of the day.

They talked little. Tristan felt a personal gray cloud hanging over his head, following his father's rebuke. In addition, he sensed a remote but forbidding sense of menace in the gray day. For a moment, he recalled the druid's prophecy at the spring festival.

Robyn, too, seemed lost in thought. Every so often, she would start abruptly, and peer into the gray, misty distance as if expecting to see something.

Then she would slump again in the saddle, staring at the gray mane before her.

Arlen rode ahead, naturally assuming the role of the prince's body-guard. He and Tristan accepted this as normal, and the prince barely noticed the old soldier, riding slowly along ahead of them. Only Daryth and Pawldo seemed inclined to talk, and the two quietly rode at the rear of the group, exchanging boasts and stories. The dogs paced along, not interested in running.

At dusk, they arrived at Dynnatt, a small farming community, and found shelter at a cozy inn. In the morning, they would strike southward into the forest, and then turn east. The terrain was rugged, and the tracks were few, so the companions realized that it would probably be several days before they again slept with a roof over their heads.

"Here, have the good table," wheezed the old innkeeper, hobbling toward a large oaken table before a friendly fire. "Haven't had many visi-tors this spring—you'll probably have the place to yourselves tonight."

Tristan had never visited this inn before, and the innkeeper made no sign that he recognized the prince. Clad as he was in plain hunting garb, he felt no desire to call attention to his rank.

They sat down, grateful to escape the damp and cool mist. After several tankards of ale and some tender venison, the prince felt his spirits lifting.

"What business brings you through Dynnatt?" grunted the proprietor, as he cleared away the dirty dishes.

"A hunt!" declared Tristan, raising his mug. "The deer in Llyrath Forest have had their last good night's sleep for the next tenday!"

"The hunting ground is not safe," muttered the old man. "This is not a time to be abroad in Llyrath."

Tristan started to laugh at the old man's warning, but Arlen held up a cautioning hand. "What do ye mean? What have ye seen?"

"Seen? I've seen nothing, but I've heard tales. All winter there's been sheep disappearing in the place. And more than one shepherd has gone in there a-looking for his flock, and never come out again!"

"Surely, old man, you talk like a woman!" objected the prince. "There'll be nothing in the forest to offer a threat to a well-armed band of hunters!"

The old man shrugged, said "So you say, sir," and turned away. Robyn flashed Tristan an angry look, and he felt a moment of guilt. He should not have insulted the innkeeper, he knew. Why did this foolish sense of bravado impel him to make himself look foolish?

Arlen got up, stretched, and walked to his room. Robyn swiftly followed, taking the single room they had hired for her. Pawldo and Daryth, too, slipped away quietly. They all felt the discomfort and general gloominess of the day, renewed and strengthened by the innkeeper's warning.

At least the following day dawned clear, with the promise of more warmth than the previous day had offered. Again the party was off before sunrise, but now they had no road to follow.

"This track should take us to the edge of Llaryth," announced Arlen, as he led the group along a narrow, winding trail. The terrain was rocky and barren, with small lakes and an occasional shepherd's cottage about the only features worthy of notice. Even the cottages disappeared as they moved farther southward. They finally camped in a sheltered niche, surrounded by high rocks that would keep away the knife-edged bite of the wind.

Tristan forged into a thicket of scrub oak, seeking firewood. He gathered several good limbs, and then froze as he heard a rustling behind him. Slowly, he turned, relaxing as Daryth emerged from a thicket, also gathering wood.

"Tristan," asked the houndmaster, "what is it about this place? I don't like the feel of it!"

"I don't know," responded the prince. "I've been here many times, but never felt any danger . . . until now. Bah! It must be our imaginations!"

"Indeed," murmured Daryth, unconvinced.

"Of course, there might be something to that innkeeper's warning," admitted the prince. "But it's more likely he was testing us, or playing some ruse. We've seen nothing out of the ordinary."

"Do you come here a lot?"

"Arlen used to bring Robyn and me camping here when we were children. I guess it's been five or six years since we've been here, though. It's always been a pleasant place—very wild, not many people around. I like that about Llyrath Forest."

"You and Robyn," Daryth asked, a little awkwardly. "Are you . . . ?"

Ignoring a surge of jealousy, Tristan answered thoughtfully. "I don't know. Even though we've known each other all our lives, Robyn excites me like no other girl or woman. But there's something about her that keeps me at arm's length. And—" He had to laugh. "—there's something about *me* that keeps *her* at arm's length."

"She is a lovely woman—more beautiful than anyone I have ever known. I should like to, well . . ." Daryth's desire remained unspoken.

"So would I," laughed Tristan. "So would I."

The next day brought them into the edge of the wood, and here the hunt began. The hounds, pent up by the slow pace of the party's march, were loosed, and soon disappeared among the widely spaced oak trees of the pastoral forest. Urging their horses on, the hunters pursued.

The eager hounds, following the vigorous lead of Canthus, flushed birds from their covers, chased and caught any hapless rabbits that lay in their path, and sniffed the ground in search of larger game. The dogs crisscrossed back and forth across the hunters' path, silently intent on their search.

Only Angus showed signs of slowing. The old dog kept the pace of the pack for several hours, but finally slowed to an amble at the side of the riders.

Over the next few days, as the band worked its way eastward, the archery skill of Arlen and Pawldo put a dozen pheasants and quail into the game bags, but no bigger game.

Finally, the hounds picked up the scent of a deer, and bounded into the brush in pursuit. The prince spurred his horse through a tangled thicket in pursuit, his companions streaming along behind. The hounds eventually brought the animal to bay against a sheer rock wall. Daryth signaled the dogs to halt, and Tristan took careful aim as the slender creature stood, shivering with fear, against the cliff. The prince's arrow flew straight, piercing the creature's neck and swiftly killing it. Suddenly, all those practice sessions were worthwhile.

"Bravo!" clapped Pawldo, trotting up to the prince.

"Nice shot," commented Arlen, and Daryth nodded in agreement.

Robyn turned away as the deer fell—each time the creature kicked, she flinched. Momentarily, Tristan regretted her presence. Why had she insisted on coming, anyway? She took something from the fun . . .

As he stripped and cleaned the kill, his annoyance lifted, and he remembered that Robyn had wished to seek out some fungus or something in the forest. He resolved to give her the opportunity to do so.

They camped that night near a small, clear lake among a grove of lofty pine trees. The ground was cushioned with a thick layer of needles, and firewood was plentiful, so they had a comfortable camp and got a good night's rest. Still, Robyn seemed quiet and depressed that night, and again the following morning.

"Perhaps we should rest here for another day or two," suggested the prince as the party breakfasted on bread and cheese. "Robyn could then have a chance to collect some of her fungi, and we can explore this lake a bit."

"It is indeed a beautiful spot," agreed Arlen, looking around as if for the first time. Low, forested ridges, perfectly reflected in the still morning water, surrounded the lake.

They almost forgot the warnings of the druids and the innkeeper in the pleasant passing of the bright day. Yet, even as they enjoyed watching the girl in her fungus hunt, something in the quiet, almost abandoned forest, something vaguely frightening, impinged on their awareness.

They were all moving in close proximity when Robyn cried, "There!" and leaped to the ground. Racing to a fallen trunk, Robyn pointed glee-fully to a long, shelflike fungus growing from the rotting wood.

Then, yards from her back, the bushes parted, and the grizzled head of a monstrous boar emerged from the undergrowth. Its glittering, blood-red eyes peered angrily about, and it grunted in annoyance.

Tristan's heart froze.

The boar's tusks, nearly a foot long, gleamed wickedly in the shadowy light. Robyn had turned as the bushes rustled behind her, and the color drained from her face as she beheld the angry creature, barely thirty feet away.

And then, with a grunt, the boar charged.

✗ ✗ ✗ ✗ ✗ ✗ ✗ ✗ ✗ ✗

The still, deep waters of Myrloch reflected the silvery rays of a full moon. The sun had just set and the moon risen, when the druids began to gather before the great council ring. The reflected moonlight illumi-nated the gathering, and a watcher could have seen that the mood was somber, perhaps even fearful.

The great stone arches of the council ring sprang, one after the other, from the surrounding shadows as the moon rose higher. In the center of the ring, a pool of bright water reflected the moonlight in all directions, amplifying its brightness.

As the moon climbed, the watchers could see sparkling spots of light, like vivid stars, following it. Common legend held that they were the tears shed by the moon for the sorrows of the present night.

By contrast, the gathering druids stood solemnly among the shadows at the perimeter of the ring, quietly waiting. They did not talk to one another, nor did their attention waver from the Moonwell to acknowl-edge new arrivals. Their number continued to grow, as more and more of the dark-robed figures emerged from the towering pines that ringed Myrloch.

Each wore a robe of brown or dark green, sometimes mottled with a forested pattern. These Ffolk were men and women of both strength and gentleness. Their steps did not disturb the branches and twigs along the ground, nor did their gazes frighten the smallest of woodland creatures. Yet, as a group, they harbored great might indeed.

The druid known as Trahern of Oakvale hobbled into the clearing, looking nervously about. He remained far from any of the other druids, his hands clenched together in the sleeves of his robe. He sneaked glances at the nearest druids and sneered viciously, baring his cracked and bleeding lips. How much he hated them—hated them all!

Licking his lips, he made an effort to keep his body still. It would not do to attract attention to himself. Pulling his deep hood farther down over his face, Trahern waited for the council to begin.

Some of the druids, those who had to travel far, or simply wanted to display their great powers, arrived more theatrically. An owl settled to the ground between two of the great arches. Its shape shimmered and changed into that of a proud, tall man: Quinn Moonwane, master of the forest realm of Llyrath. A hawk dropped suddenly from the sky to land beside Quinn, and quickly changed to human form. Now Isolde of Winterglen stood beside the druid from Llyrath. She whose realm included the woodlands of northern Gwynneth did not greet her peer from the south, but all who watched knew that the time for the council drew near.

Only the Great Druid of Gwynneth still remained absent. The moon climbed higher, its silvery beams casting clear shadows across the great ring. All of the arches now stood out clearly. Each was made from the positioning of three massive stones. Two served as pillars, while the third rested across the tops of the other two. There were twelve of these arches in the outer ring.

In the center of the circle, the Moonwell glistened with a light all its own. Around the Moonwell stood eight pillars of stone, grouped in four pairs. None of the druids approached the center, but in the bright moonlight, perhaps fifty of them were visible gathered around the perimeter of the ring.

Suddenly the waters of the Moonwell parted with a soft *plop*, and a tiny creature emerged from the silvery liquid. With some surprise, the druids watched a small frog cross the ground to the space between one pair of pillars in the center of the ring. In a sudden instant the frog was gone and Genna Moonsinger, Great Druid of Gwynneth, stood before the assembly.

As Genna appeared in her normal guise, so did the moon reach its zenith. Its brilliant light spilled between the two pillars and illuminated the Great Druid for all the rest to see.

Genna Moonsinger looked older, and tired, but she still bore the understanding smile and look of benign patience that had won her this honored post against the competition of more vigorous, but less wise, druids. She slowly turned, giving all present the benefit of that smile, and as she did so the tension that had been building in the ring seemed to lighten, if it did not vanish altogether.

The rays of the full moon highlighted the wrinkles in the Great Druid's aged face but could not overcome the lively sparkle of her eyes. Her body was rounded and stocky, but she carried herself with great dignity. She looked as if the many years of her life had not worn and weakened her, but instead had weathered and strengthened her. The polished oaken staff she held before her gleamed smoothly. Decades of use had worn its surface to a golden sheen.

All eyes in the council rested upon her, but Genna paused lengthily before she spoke. The wind stilled, and the great forest was strangely silent.

"My brothers and sisters," the Great Druid began.

Her voice was soft and musical, yet carried the weight of majesty. The power was well concealed, and her tone seemed wistful.

"The Mother has spoken to me," Genna continued. The druids understood that this meant the Great Druid had had a prophetic dream. "Her next sleep may be her last. Her power wanes grievously, and the instruments of her destruction gather even before the snow has melted from the land."

She turned a slow circle, looking at each of the druids gathered before her. For a moment she paused, wondering if she saw a flash of unnatural light near the rear of the group. Then, her eyes moved on.

Trahern of Oakvale sighed, shivering with tension, and hid his face more deeply within his hood.

Somberly the druids regarded Genna, waiting for her to continue.

"The children of the goddess have been awakened."

This statement drew a few low mutters of astonishment from the gathering, for none but the oldest of the druids recalled a time when the goddess had been forced to call upon her children. The news was heartening, for the children of the goddess—the Leviathan, the Unicorn, and the Pack—were potent allies indeed.

"Yet even this step will not be sufficient to restore the Balance!" Genna's voice took on a note of firmness. "The Firbolgs are abroad, and their activities threaten the Balance on a very direct level.

"The rest of my dream is not clear to me. I can only share these images: somehow, darkness has emerged from light, and now this darkness walks abroad in the land. It is this darkness, whatever its nature, that the Mother fears the most.

"Armies shall gather, and blood will be shed. Very possibly, Myrloch Vale itself will be violated. Should that happen, those of you who are entrusted with the vale's protection are to hinder and slow the passage of the desecrating force, without risking yourselves or your groves. Do not use the animals, if you can possibly avoid it."

Genna paused again, turning a full circle to look at each of her druids. Satisfied, she spoke again. "Remember that the armies, though potent, are not the most dangerous enemy of the Earthmother. Learn all you can about the nature of any strange occurrences in the lands under your care. Whatever the nature of the "darkness from light," we must learn more about it. I fear that it is the most dire threat of all to the Balance.

"Now," Genna continued, her tone mellowing slightly, "what news from the far ends of Gwynneth?"

Quinn Moonwane, master of Llyrath Forest, stepped forward and addressed the gathering. "Your warning fits with tidings of late in Llyrath. That great forest has felt the trod of invading footsteps already. Though I have not discovered the nature of this invasion, I now suspect the Firbolgs."

"And I have seen the armies gathering!" announced Isolde of

Winterglen, stepping to Quinn's side. Her domain covered the vast tract of forest over northern Gwynneth. This forest separated the fortresses of northmen clans that had long ago conquered the northern reaches of Gwynneth.

"The northmen march together, armed heavily, singing songs of war." Isolde's voice did not conceal the scorn with which she regarded the northmen. "They gathered at their ports, a great and warlike throng. Then, several days ago, they boarded their ships and sailed. Their destination I do not know; but the number of their ships was greater than I have yet seen."

"Thank you," acknowledged the Great Druid. The soothing tones of her voice calmed the rising tide of fear that Isolde's words had triggered.

"My brothers, my sisters,"Genna continued, still calming and soothing with her voice. "Our vigilance must be constant. Our enemies are strong, but so are our friends. Oh yes," she added in afterthought, "As in times past when the Balance has been severely strained, a hero will arise from among the Ffolk—a hero who is already a prince."

"This current prince," grunted Quinn, "is young and impetuous—he could make disastrous mistakes."

"Of course he could," agreed Genna cheerfully. "In fact, having met the lad, I'll say that I'm certain he will make mistakes, probably disastrously. But he is greatly steadied by the girl. And indeed, do we have any other choice?"

"Yes, the girl," answered Quinn. "Quite remarkable, indeed. She carries great potential within her, as you had guessed."

Genna smiled discreetly, but made no comment. Her throat tightened, and moisture crept unbidden to her eyes as she thought of the black-haired maiden. Clearing her throat gruffly, she regarded every one of the gathered druids with her bright, sparkling gaze. Her look seemed to spread peace throughout the group.

"May the goddess protect you!"

Genna turned and vanished, though not entirely. Those who watched very closely saw a small, feathered shape dart across the surface of the Moonwell. The swallow flew into the night and quickly disappeared.

The druids turned and moved away from the council ring as silently as they had arrived. Soon, all but one had vanished into the surrounding darkness. That one stood still, staring at the Moonwell, lost in deep thought.

Trahern of Oakvale looked much as he had a few days earlier. Only his eyes were different. They did not glow with vitality, but instead, seemed to glimmer with a hot, angry light. The folds of his brown hood kept his face in shadow, but one who looked within the shadow might think he looked into the embers of a low fire, for such were the eyes of Kazgoroth.

Now, after listening to Genna, and through her the goddess, Trahern understood the pattern that unfolded before him. With his help, the Balance would unravel, leaving Gwynneth in chaos and despair.

Now Trahern the druid, newly the spawn of Kazgoroth, understood the role he would play in the plan.

XXXXXXXXXXX

The rays of the full moon illuminated the sleeping village of Corwell, which was gathered around its protecting castle on the shores of Corwell Firth. A few guards strolled listlessly about the battlements of Caer Corwell or slept at their posts. The village was quiet, as the taverns had closed for the night, and all decent Ffolk were sound asleep.

Erian the guard paced restlessly back and forth in his tiny hut near the castle. Since the night of the spring festival, he had been restless and edgy—often, he grew physically sick. A horse clopped along the street outside, and he turned to the door, an audible snarl curling his lip. He had been unhappy and fearful for the entire month, but never had he felt as restless as now. White moonbeams spilled through the window, and he unconsciously turned his face upward, allowing the cold light of the full moon to wash over him.

Finally, he lay on a straw pallet, but he could not sleep. His body ached, and his mind reeled with confusion. Suddenly, he sat upright, the movement bringing an involuntary groan as his muscles cried out in protest. With a cry, he rolled off the pallet onto the floor.

Trying to get up, he found himself crippled. His legs flailed uselessly at the floor. He tried to grasp a handhold to pull himself up, but his fingers would not work. Howling in anguish, he thrashed across the floor, finally rolling to a stop in a pool of milky moonlight pouring through his single window.

The light seemed to soothe him, yet it beckoned him at the same time. The full moon, a perfect circle of brightness, gazed through the window, and he began to understand his helplessness. The tears of the moon—the glittering chain of bright stars that followed the moon through the sky—blinked cheerily, seeming to mock his plight.

His skin cracked away from his arms and face, but the red wound quickly disappeared beneath a rough coat of brown fur. Sharp, pointed fangs erupted from his gums, and his face distorted in terrible pain. He tried to rub his eyes with his hands, but those appendages had disappeared, to be replaced with padded paws, tipped with sharp, wickedly curving claws.

And as the silvery rays stroked the guard's twisted and aching body, Erian completed his transformation.

xxxxxxxxxx

The Pack awakened to the cold, white glare of the full moon. Gray and shaggy forms emerged from a hundred dens, shaking the weariness of a long hibernation from stiffened muscles and sleep-clouded brains.

A large male raised his voice to the moon in a long, ululating howl. Others joined in, first a few, but then hundreds. As one creature, the Pack raised its voice to the heavens, singing the praises of the goddess.

And then a soft breeze carried to the large male the scent of a stag, somewhere not far away in the misty night. Patches of fog drifted among the towering pines, but bright moonlight illuminated the clearings and the high places as the wolf searched for the source of the scent.

Others picked up the spoor, smelling blood, and meat, and fear. The baying of the Pack dropped lower, and took on a deeper tone of menace. Slowly, like gray ghosts, the wolves began to lope through the forest, gaining speed as alertness returned. The stag turned fear-maddened eyes toward its deadly pursuers, and then fled—a flight that could have only one consequence, as the Pack spread out and began to close upon its prey.

Once again, after a century of sleep, the mighty wolves of the Pack sang to their prey.

The song was ancient and piercingly beautiful. It was a song of the glory of the goddess, and of the might of her children.

But above all, it was a song of death.

BLOODLETTING

4

The boar's stocky head bent forward so that the deadly tusks arrowed straight at Robyn as she knelt by the fungus. With impossible speed, the beast's stubby legs pounded the ground in a blur of acceleration.

Tristan, his stomach churning in fear, spurred his horse into a swift turn toward the boar. Pawldo, Arlen, and Daryth all whirled toward the attack, but they were farther away than the prince.

The hounds, too, were distant. Canthus had led the pack around the shore of the lake, and though the dogs had turned at the sound of the boar's charge, they were still far away.

Except Angus.

The old hound, ambling as always at Tristan's side, sprang toward the boar with fangs bared. Deep snarls rolled from his chest as he leaped between Robyn and the charging beast. The hound's teeth turned and sank into the boar's ear. At the same time, those merciless tusks tore through the dog's flank and deep into its body.

Red blood spurted from the grievous wounds, and the old dog grunted with a hollow, wet sound. His lungs pierced by the tusks, Angus spent his dying strength tearing the ear from the boar's head.

Robyn sprang to her feet as Angus leaped, desperately seeking escape. A bough from a large pine hung several feet overhead. She jumped, barely grasping the limb, and swung her legs upward. At the same time, the boar tossed Angus's body aside and lunged at his original victim. A gore-streaked tusk grazed Robyn's calf, drawing a cry of pain.

His lance sat, useless, back at camp, so Tristan was forced to attack the boar with his sword. Slashing downward, his blade sank deep into the animal's shoulder, but the wound seemed only to inflame the boar's raging bloodlust.

Tristan's horse, whinnying with fear, danced away from the lunging boar. As he broke away from the beast, the prince turned and saw two arrows thunk solidly into the shaggy flank. Arlen and Pawldo were already nocking their second arrows.

The boar turned from its additional wounds, and ducked its head as if to gore an imaginary foe. Confused, it swung its bloodshot gaze from Tristan to the archers, and back again. Lowering its head, it lunged toward the prince. Blood ran luridly across one flank from the gash inflicted by Tristan's sword. On the opposite side, the two arrows were buried deep in the boar's flank. The animal grunted sharply, but showed no signs of weakening.

Suddenly a brown form streaked across the ground and hurtled itself into the combat. Canthus, far outdistancing the other hounds to reach the fight, struck the boar's flank. The force of the great hound's charge sent the creature tumbling across the ground. The arrows snapped off as the boar's weight crashed over them, and the bloody sword wound became matted with dirt and pine needles as the boar staggered to its feet, grunting angrily and ferociously stabbing its tusks into Canthus.

The boar's powerful back legs tensed, and its stocky neck twisted to bring its tusks against Canthus's long flank, but the hound was too shrewd. Turning with his adversary, the dog clamped his powerful jaws onto the boar's snout, above the tusks. The beast bucked and squealed frantically but could not dislodge its attacker's grim hold.

Daryth, his mount galloping across the rocky lakeshore, reached the fight, and reined in with a grim smile of pleasure.

"Kill him, great one," he said quietly, watching the crushing effect of Canthus's bite.

In moments the rest of the hounds had joined Canthus. The killing of the boar was not pretty. Canthus retained his grip on the beast's snout while the other dogs tore at its flanks, throat, and belly. For a full minute the creature stood, invisible under the savage pack, but finally loss of blood set it squatting, and then lying, to the ground.

Tristan sprang from his horse and raced to the limp body of Angus. The old hound looked at him once, and flopped his tail weakly in recognition. Then the brown eyes, already grown dull, closed forever.

For a moment, the prince remembered a hundred carefree outings, Angus bounding eagerly at his side, his own childhood enthusiasm bubbling. Then he ran to grasp Robyn as she swung by her hands. But she let go of the branch before he reached her, and cried out as her gored leg collapsed. Tristan caught her as she tumbled to the ground, and helped her sit on the soft cushion of pine needles.

"I'm fine," she said, pulling her shoulders away from his arm.

The prince felt her body shaking, and heard a quaver in her voice, but he stood up and let her go. She looked up at him, gratitude in her eyes, and then sorrow as she looked at Angus.

Arlen stepped toward them, roughly clearing his throat. "Do not grieve for him—he has died a warrior's death. He would have had it no other way."

They erected a small cairn near the shore of the lake, and Robyn muttered a low prayer for the dog's spirit.

"Let's tend to the game," grunted Arlen.

"Sure," agreed the prince. He turned, with relief, from the cairn and looked at Daryth. "How are the other dogs?"

"Corwyss has a nasty gash on the side, but she'll be all right. The rest are fine."

The prince bent over the ravaged corpse of the boar, drawing his keen hunting blade and sliding the steel edge through the torn remnants of the boar's neck. As he cut down, across the scrawny belly, Arlen began to scoop a pit in the earth for the entrails.

The little group moved from the burial scene back toward their camp. Canthus and the rest of the pack raced around the far shore of the lake as the riders picked their way along the smoother near shore. The dogs had almost rejoined them on the other side when Canthus stopped with a howl. Barking furiously, he refused to come any further. Instead, his attention was directed toward something on the ground, near the shore of the lake.

"I'll have a look," volunteered Daryth, leading his horse among the large rocks of the shore toward the eagerly waiting pack of hounds. He reached Canthus and looked down.

"I think you'd better come over here," he called. "I've never seen anything like this before!"

The others found Daryth standing upon a low, flat rock. Around him spread the shallow waters of the lake in all directions, except at the base of the rock. There, the water was low enough to reveal a small expanse of mud, in the middle of which was a footprint.

The foot that had made the print was wearing a heavy boot, judging by the depth of the mark, with a smooth leather sole. Cleats protruded from the sole at irregular intervals, and the whole boot showed signs of long wear. None of this made the track exceptional, however, for the boot could have belonged to any common woodsman or shepherd—if these were its only features.

But the print was fully two feet long.

xxxxxxxxxxx

Erian awakened in terrible pain. His shoulders and head pounded with agony, and his body was numb from the waist down. He slowly realized that he was naked and lying outdoors.

Lifting his throbbing head, he looked around himself in confusion. He lay upon the muddy bank of a shallow stream. In fact, his lower half was immersed in the chill waters, and this cold had benumbed him.

Slowly, with tremendous effort, the big man pulled himself from the water and lay, shivering, in the mud of the bank. A cluster of tree roots and enclosing bushes gave him shelter. He struggled to remember how he had come here, but his mind furnished him no explanation.

He saw that it was after dawn, yet the whole night had vanished from his memory, leaving a gaping, dark hole. What had happened to him?

Grunting heavily, Erian twisted himself into a sitting position and looked around. The stream flowed from his right to his left, he observed. He heard the caw of a gull, and smelled the salt air of the sea, so he knew that he lay close to the coast. The stream was bordered by a thicket of bushes and small trees, but the land beyond seemed open and rolling.

Looking down, Erian noticed without surprise that he was covered with blood. The mud and the water streaked the crimson fluid into a garish pattern across his body. He did not seem to be wounded, so obviously the blood had come from something, or someone else.

Lurching to his feet, Erian caught sight of Caer Corwell, and knew now that this was Corlyth Creek, which entered the sea just north of the town. Slowly, keeping to the concealment of the undergrowth around the stream, he started staggering toward Corwell.

His mind flashed through bits and pieces of the previous night: the full moon illuminating his cottage, and summoning him, with its cold and unblinking glare. He could remember nothing after that.

The sun had just cleared the peaks of the Highlands, and its harsh light cast long, clear shadows in the crystal morning air. Few villagers were about yet, so Erian was able to slip through the back streets of the town to his own cottage. The door to his home stood open, smashed outward with enough force to break the latch.

Confused, and very frightened, Erian slipped inside and closed the door.

XXXXXXXXXX

"What could have made such a footprint?" demanded Daryth, staring at the massive track.

"Firbolg," muttered Arlen.

Not wanting to alarm Robyn, Tristan said calmly, "Surely it would be very far from home."

"Where do they normally live?" asked the Calishite.

"Usually they stay in Myrloch Vale, north of the kingdom," explained the prince. "I wonder what one would be doing this far south?"

"This explains a lot!" Pawldo interjected. "The sheep disappearing— everybody nervous about something."

"Yes, but it raises more questions than it answers. What could the Firbolg be after in Llyrath Forest?"

"They move, sometimes," explained Pawldo, with unusual solemnity. "At least, that's what the old legends say. " As a halfling, Pawldo's roots were much closer to the original faerie inhabitants of the isles—roots he shared with the Llewyrr, and the Firbolg.

"The Firbolg are held in Myrloch Vale by the firm hand of the goddess, and when her power wanes, the Firbolg can leave the vale. It is," Pawldo concluded needlessly, "a very bad sign."

"We must warn the king!" declared Arlen. "We shall return to the castle at once."

"Not yet," argued the prince, to whom the Firbolg seemed like a remote and adventurous challenge. "We should follow these tracks, find out if there's more than one, and what they are doing here."

Arlen started to argue, but saw the set of Tristan's jaw and knew that the prince would not change his mind. "All right," he grunted. "But one of us must ride back with the lass."

"Forget that idea!" snapped Robyn. "I'm coming with you!" Tristan could not suppress a smile at Arlen's chagrin. As in childhood, the two of them usually managed to manipulate the old warrior into doing what they wanted.

"Then ye'll all do as you're told," grunted Arlen. "We'll move slowly and quietly—if yer seen, yer lives won't be worth a copper piece!"

Daryth had circled the group as they talked, and now called from a short distance away. "Here! I've found another track—and here's another. They went this way!"

Daryth pointed to the southeast, toward a low notch in the rolling terrain of the forest. The land climbed steeply to the south, toward a crest of rock that ran for dozens of miles, high above the surrounding pine, oak, and aspens. Among the ridges nestled numerous swales and valleys, containing hundreds of lakes and many small, isolated pockets of thick woods.

The companions swiftly gathered their gear and scattered any signs of their camp. Tristan felt a thrill in anticipation of battle. He stroked the hilt of the long sword hanging at his side, and examined the mounting of his lance. The thin wooden shaft was smooth and flawless, the head of hard steel razor-sharp.

As the riders mounted, the hounds gathered eagerly, as if they, too, could scent battle. Daryth indicated the spoor, then he gestured sharply downward as the hounds were about to take up the cry, and the canine jaws snapped silently shut. Quietly, as ordered by the houndmaster, the dogs took up the spoor of the Firbolg.

"How old is the sign?" Tristan asked Robyn, whose knowledge of the wild included tracking animals. "Can you tell?"

"No more than a day," she estimated. They started after the monsters, and for a few hours had no difficulty following the spoor. Huge footprints, careless destruction of plants, and, occasionally, offal clearly marked the path of the Firbolgs.

Then the trail crossed a region of smooth rock, and the keen noses of the hounds became the only guide. Shortly, the Firbolgs had again entered woodlands, and the trail grew plain.

For two days the companions rode along the giants' trail, stopping only for brief rests. They pursued long into the night, under the brilliant light of the full moon.

Shortly after they left the lakeshore, the trail dropped into a stream bed, and the dogs lost the scent. It was Robyn who noticed, a hundred paces upstream, the scuffed bark of a pine tree, indicating where the monsters had climbed from the stream. Then, later, as a small storm washed out a portion of the spoor, it was Robyn again who saw the faint impressions in the sodden grass that indicated the passage of heavy bodies. It was as if the ground itself spoke to her, revealing hidden knowledge of those who had passed.

"There seem to be a dozen or more of them," she observed, and Tristan and the others grew silent for a moment. The almost invisible path she followed led them deep into the Llyrath Highlands—the rugged crest of the forest where outcrops of stone became as common as the clumps of pine and oak in the forest's lower reaches.

Tristan rode alert and ready for action. The sight of the giants' tracks inflamed him with excitement. Over and over, he pictured one of the ugly creatures before him, cowering before the deadly thrust of his lance. Then he saw himself, long sword raised, bobbing and ducking with dashing calm through the pitch of battle.

Riding before his prince, Arlen was watchful, leading the party as long as the spoor was visible. Behind him paced the hounds, followed by Daryth and Pawldo.

Tristan walked his horse slowly beside Robyn, at the rear of the party. She had borrowed his knife, and now finished carving a stout oaken cudgel. Her strong hands held the staff firmly as she inspected it for rough spots.

"I don't think it'll be much use against Firbolgs," she admitted. "But it makes me feel a little better to have it."

"We'll see that you don't need to use it," Tristan boasted, enjoying the role of the cavalier adventurer. "How far ahead are they?" he asked. "Can you tell?"

"I don't know," replied Robyn, giving him a sideways look. He thought he saw an emotion strange to her eyes—was it fear? "Tristan, what can it mean? The Firbolg, so far from Myrloch. And the prophecy of the druids—'a summer of peril, an autumn of tragedy.' I can't get that out of my mind."

The prince smiled, reassuringly he hoped. "I'm sure these are just a few renegades out on some kind of raid. As soon as we find them out, and get home, Father'll send out a band of men-at-arms, and that will be that!" For a moment, the prince thought of that war party. He wanted desperately to be a part of it, but would his father let him?

"Remember what Pawldo said a few days ago?" persisted Robyn, still worried. She looked before them, at their companions. "Could he be right about the power of the goddess waning? What if it's true, and the evil creatures take over Gwynneth?"

Tristan turned his gaze to the ground. He groped for words that would calm Robyn's fears, but instead found his own apprehensions growing.

"They can't be more than a few hours ahead of us now," observed Robyn, as they climbed among a series of rocky knobs. "We must be gaining on them fast."

Toward evening of the second day of their pursuit, the trail followed the crest of a long, winding ridge. The rocky spur was the backbone of the Llaryth Forest, though the nearest trees were a thousand feet below the crest. The path was steep, with sheer precipices commonly dropping to one side or another. In places, the slopes dropped away steeply to both sides, offering a craggy path only a few feet wide.

"This is madness!" Arlen finally exclaimed. "We can be seen for miles! I cannot allow us to proceed any farther."

"We must find out what their purpose is!" argued Tristan.

"If they haven't spied us by now, they're even stupider than I think they are! We're walking into an ambush, I tell you!"

"Then we'll just have to be more careful," announced Tristan, fondling the haft of his lance. "We'll be ready if they find us!" Secretly, he hoped they would find the Firbolgs. He yearned to fight one of the brutes.

Finally the path dropped between a number of rocky peaks, and the party relaxed. At least they could not be observed as easily as upon the exposed ridge. They could see ahead of them to where the trail led through a narrow notch between two small mountains, and beyond into a region of tall pines and open meadows.

Arlen scouted the notch, seeking safe passage, while the others waited tensely behind him. A clattering of rock to their rear caught Robyn's attention, and she turned.

"Firbolgs!" she cried in alarm, though her voice was steady. "They're coming."

Whirling, the others saw four of the huge, ugly creatures approaching from a clump of rock that they had passed minutes earlier. The gross figures loomed eight or nine feet tall. Each had a headful of black, shaggy hair and a receding forehead that sloped down to a large nose. They had surprisingly small chins, covered in scraggly and ill-tended beards. Each wore a leather tunic marred by rips, tears, and stains. They carried clubs the size of small tree trunks and hefted large rocks in their massive hands.

Even as the companions turned, the Firbolgs hurled the rocks at the party. The missiles fell short, but clattered and sparked with real menace as they shattered on the rocky ground.

"Quick! Through the notch!" cried Tristan, as the Firbolgs burst into a run.

"Hold!" barked Arlen. "Look before you!"

Tristan looked ahead through the narrow mountain gap to the long slope on the other side and the forest a mile away. From the trees emerged a dozen or more Firbolgs, all loping steadily toward the notch. They were trapped!

For a moment, Tristan froze in panic, his mind groping helplessly for a plan. The Firbolgs to the rear blocked their retreat, and those before them offered certain death.

"My prince, we must attack—there!" called Arlen, speaking firmly and pointing. The Firbolgs behind them had split into two pairs. The pair on the left had moved apart, the two Firbolgs lumbering forward with a wide gap between them.

Instantly, Tristan saw the wisdom of the move.

"Let's go!" he called, kicking the flanks of his mount.

"Follow!" cried Arlen to the others as his own steed leaped forward to gallop beside Tristan's. The pair leveled their lances and charged toward the two Firbolgs to the left. The lances were formidable weapons when coupled with the weight of a charging horse, and Tristan allowed himself a flash of optimism. The baying hounds sang behind him, and a clattering of hooves informed him of the reassuring presence of his companions.

The Firbolgs immediately anticipated their plan. The pair to the right began closing toward their companions, but they were still several hundred yards away. Then, as he and Arlen thundered downhill at breathtaking speed, the two Firbolgs before them stopped, and each grabbed a rock the size of a large melon. As the lancers bore down, the monsters threw the jagged rocks. The first one sailed over Arlen's head and crashed harmlessly among the rocks. The second, however, smashed the right foreleg of Tristan's horse, dropping the poor animal instantly and sending the prince flying from the saddle. The horse shrieked in pain as it collapsed, bouncing and rolling along the ground for some distance before finally breaking its neck and lying still.

The prince managed to tuck his head before he landed, but he crashed into a rocky patch of ground with enough force to stun him.

Arlen's charge struck the second Firbolg with brute force. The point of his lance sheared through the monster's chest and erupted from its back in a shower of blood. As the charge carried him past, the warrior dropped the lance in order to retain his seat, but he instantly drew his sword and looked about.

The Firbolg behind him collapsed, but the one that had struck down Tristan faced the other riders with upraised club. Arlen saw Daryth edge his mount between the Firbolg and Robyn, and he saw the Calishite's sword lash out and cut the Firbolg's hip. At the same time, the club smashed down, striking Daryth on the shoulder and knocking him headlong from the saddle.

In an instant, Pawldo and Robyn thundered past the Firbolg, but the pair quickly reined in their horses and turned. Daryth lay motionless near the Firbolg, while Tristan, moaning, struggled to a sitting position. Bellowing ferociously, the Firbolg that had struck them down turned to confront the riders, ignoring the hounds that raced toward its back.

Robyn stared breathlessly at the monster, her eyes wide and her heart pounding. The heavy cudgel she had carved seemed like a pathetic stick in her hand. Pawldo raised his bow and sent an arrow darting into the Firbolg's chest, but the creature plucked it free and threw it to the ground as it would a small thorn.

Just then the hounds struck the Firbolg from behind like an onrushing landslide. As the monster stumbled and turned back to face this new attack, Arlen urged his horse forward. Striking from behind, he forced his blade deep into the enemy's back, hoping to cut into a vital organ. Another arrow from Pawldo flew over the warrior's head, striking the Firbolg in the back of its neck.

The monster's club smashed into one of the dogs, killing the hound instantly, but the weight of the others, plus the damage of the sword wound, forced the Firbolg to its knees. Instantly the dogs dragged it to the ground, biting and tearing in a frenzy of bloodlust.

Several feet away, Tristan attempted to climb to his feet, but the world began to spin madly and he had to sit back down. Shaking his head to clear it, he looked around.

A bellow of rage caused him to look over his shoulder, and his stomach knotted with terror. Another Firbolg, one they had not seen before, was crashing through the enclosing pines only a few yards away. The monster's club was held high, and its bloodshot eyes glimmered with malice.

Tristan quickly saw that his companions were all occupied and too far away to intervene. So, praying for the best, he groped for his sword. But the dizziness kept him from grasping his weapon. The Firbolg, sensing the vulnerability of his enemy, crept forward slowly, his club raised, ready to smash the prince into the ground. Through the haze in his vision, Tristan vaguely saw that the weapon was studded with rusty spikes. He closed his eyes to block out the sight, hoping it might go away.

"Stop!" Robyn's cry pierced the air like the clarion call of a battle horn.

Something glimmered and shook along the ground, or was it simply imagination? The prince was not certain, but it looked as if the ground itself had begun to throb. The lunging Firbolg paused, confusion and fear at the strange happening clouding its gaze.

Wide-eyed, Tristan saw the trees and bushes around the Firbolg bend fantastically, reaching for the monster and closing hard curls of wood around its huge limbs. The creature uttered a bellow of frustration, and perhaps fear, as in moments the supple limbs held the creature fast.

The pine boughs and sapling trunks wrapped the Firbolg's limbs tightly. The tip of a small pine encircled the giant's neck three or four times. The entire might of the earth was behind the grasping wood, so the creature could barely squirm.

Robyn gasped and clapped a hand to her mouth, but then spurred her horse and galloped toward the prince, whose own limbs still refused to cooperate. He stared in amazement, looking from Firbolg to Robyn and back. She reined in beside him and leaped to the ground, helping him to stand.

"How . . . ?" he gasped.

"I don't know!" she responded, turning to stare at the imprisoned Firbolg. The monster struggled to free itself, but was clasped tight by the knotted limbs and branches.

Tristan grasped the pommel of Robyn's saddle, but could not lift himself. He shook his head, groaning as the pounding in it grew infinitely worse.

Daryth still lay motionless, but the prince could see no blood on him. Little Pawldo was rapidly releasing arrows with enthusiasm and precision into the other two Firbolgs who were fast approaching. Several arrows sprouted from the chest of one, but did little more than annoy the creature.

Tristan glanced toward the notch and was relieved to see that the other Firbolgs had not arrived, though he knew that they would reach the narrow pass soon.

Arlen, Tristan saw, stood over the motionless form of the Firbolg he and the dogs had just slain. The old warrior studied the approach of the pair.

"Fly, my prince!" he called to Tristan, running in his direction. Robyn came up behind him and boosted Tristan into the saddle of her own mount.

"Go! You got us into this—now don't make it worse!" Arlen's visage was fierce.

Tristan, his control returned, saw a look of frantic appeal in Robyn's eyes. Without consideration for his own safety, he urged the mount toward the motionless figure of Daryth.

"Damn!" grunted Arlen, as he strode forward to face the two advancing Firbolgs. The pair closed upon the warrior, wicked grins distorting their bestial features as they approached what they considered an easy kill.

Tristan slid to the ground at his friend's side, staggering slightly but retaining his balance. Robyn joined him in an instant, and they lifted the Calishite's head from the ground. The eyelids flickered and opened, but Daryth, his black eyes sunken in his head, immediately shut them again and groaned in pain.

"For the kings of Corwell!"

The old battle-cry resounded through the valley, and Tristan looked up in time to see Arlen charge the nearest of the Firbolgs. The man's sword darted deep into the creature's belly, and he nimbly ducked the violent swing of the huge club. Again he thrust, and the blade struck home, and again he ducked the savage counterstroke.

But now the other Firbolg leaped into the fray.

Arlen ducked another swing, and thrust home what proved to be a mortal wound against his original opponent, piercing upward through the savage heart. The Firbolg dropped like a felled tree, but before Arlen could recover his sword, a heavy club struck him squarely in the temple. Arlen's skull caved in under the fearsome blow, and his head snapped sideways as his neck broke. The old warrior collapsed over the body of the Firbolg he had just killed.

Robyn screamed in terror, but Tristan stared numbly at the scene, murmuring, "No, no, no, no . . ."

The prince suddenly realized that Robyn was standing by his side, holding his arm. A strange sense of peace flowed through him, and he raised his sword to face the oncoming giant.

Suddenly a black shadow flashed across the prince's vision. A feathered whirlwind struck the Firbolg full in the face, tearing with sharp talons and curved beak. Before the monster could react, the shadow broke away and climbed into the air. Astonished, the prince saw that a huge black falcon had joined the fight.

And then, from nowhere, a sound like the whooshing of a strong wind split the air over the prince's head, and a red arrow slashed toward the Firbolg to thunk solidly into its throat. Giving a gurgling gasp the monster stumbled, clutching at the thick shaft protruding from its throat. Without another sound, it toppled forward, thudding heavily to the ground at Tristan's feet.

XXXXXXXXXX

The mistletoe rustled, spreading apart to allow the great white head to emerge. The head shook, and a satiny mane fluttered through the air and came to rest upon the snowy neck. The branches of mistletoe snapped as the rest of the powerful body emerged from the shady bower.

Hooves, shanked with fur also white as snow, stepped gingerly among the wildflowers, crushing none, as the creature walked to the nearby pool. Bending his neck downward until the long horn broke the surface into a series of ripples, the unicorn drank deeply. Still sleepy, Kamerynn the unicorn raised his head and looked around the grove. The grasses underfoot tasted sweet, and he ate heartily of the most succulent grasses. The beams of brilliant sunlight penetrated the leafy canopy in several places, creating dazzling shafts of yellow.

Slowly, the unicorn grazed and drank, recovering his strength after the long sleep. The goddess had awakened him for a purpose, he knew, and that purpose would no doubt require strength and endurance. With majestic grace, the animal moved through the thick patches of clover.

Suddenly, the waters of the Moonwell swirled, whispering slightly. Kamerynn stared at the milky pool until he understood his task. The unicorn raised his head and trotted toward the pristine and pastoral forests of Myrloch Vale. After several minutes, Kamerynn began to canter, and then to gallop. Soon he raced like a ghost through winding pathways. All the lesser beasts shrank from his path at his thundering approach. His ivory horn held high, and his mighty hoofs carefully avoiding the rarer plants, the unicorn raced to answer the call of the Earthmother.

A BARD OF THE HARP

5

The black horse galloped quickly toward him, so fast that Grunnarch wondered briefly whether the red-robed rider intended to trample him. At the last moment, the rider reined in, flashing his king a tight smile. With a flourish, Laric, Captain of the Bloodriders, dismounted.

"What kept you?" demanded the Red King. "The council will begin without us!"

"I was inspecting my company," commented Laric coolly. The captain regarded the king boldly, subtly challenging him. Angrily, Grunnarch turned away. Damn Laric, anyway! It's too bad the man was such a good leader of horsemen—Grunnarch could not afford to be without his services, or he would have dismissed Laric from his command years ago. Yet no other man could be expected to lead the Bloodriders with Laric's flair and daring.

A servant stepped forward, taking the reins of the foaming black horse, and leading it toward the camp of the Red King's army. Laric ambled toward the king with maddening calm.

"Do you think there'll be war?" asked the captain, slowly licking his lips.

"It's certain," grunted Grunnarch, cheered by the reminder of the night's occasion. They were to meet in the hall of Thelgaar Ironhand to plan the season's campaign.

Laric reached the king's side, and now Grunnarch paused. The king turned and looked at the scene spread below him and could not help but be pleased.

The masts of hundreds of longships bristled from the waters of Iron Bay. Upon the bleak shoreline, and extending along the valley floor for several miles inland, sprawled the tents, stables, and grounds of a massive military encampment.

Rising above the masts and the tents stood Iron Keep, the bleak and towering fortress of Thelgaar Ironhand, Grunnarch and Laric's current destination. Tall granite walls stared down upon rocky ground, and many towers climbed from within the forbidding walls. The pennant of Thelgaar, a crimson dragon emblazoned upon a black banner, flew from the highest tower. Fluttering proudly from lower towers were the symbols of other kings of the northmen, kings who were Thelgaar's guests. The scarlet sword on the banner of Grunnarch the Red, the blue whale of Raag Hammerstaad, and a half dozen banners of lesser kings, all proclaimed an unprecedented gathering of the northmen.

Gray skies glowered over the fortress, and wind lashed at the surface of the harbor, as the kings of the northmen and their chief henchmen prepared for council.

The two northmen climbed the winding stone stairway that led to a gaping doorway in the granite face of the fortress. They created an interesting contrast—men of the same race, yet the king was tall and broad, with a fair complexion and a flowing yellow beard. The captain was short and dark, and walked in a slouch that accentuated his small stature. Yet, should an observer study their eyes, he might come away with the feeling that Laric was by far the more dangerous of the two men. There was something unfeeling, and vaguely inhuman, in his black and emotionless gaze.

"This way, my lords," smiled a buxom wench as the pair passed from the twilight to the bright torchlight of the keep. The woman, swaying suggestively beneath a colorful frock, led them around a corner and into a vast courtyard. Grunnarch had the feeling that she had been ordered to show off Thelgaar's might, for she took them on a round-about route that passed through huge barracks, high ramparts, and thick walls. The Iron Keep was, indeed, impressive.

Finally, the woman showed them into the huge and smoky hall. From the look of the place, the festivities had been going on for some time. The hall was not warm but was brightened by the glow from a huge blaze, laid in a long hearth. The massive fireplace held no less than four tree trunks, sending a hellish glow flickering throughout the chamber. Huge oaken tables, laden with food and drink, lined the room. Hundreds of men sat along the tables, drinking and feasting as the deepening gloom of night settled outside the fortress.

Grunnarch and Laric sat at a long bench, near the men of Raag Hammerstaad. The Red King reached for a massive leg of greasy meat, and tore off a chunk with his teeth, ignoring the juices running through his beard.

"Good to see you," grunted Raag, wiping a smear of ale from his mustache. "Things will start soon—after our host is properly seated."

Grunnarch grunted a response, turning to regard the form of Thelgaar barely visible through the smoke at the end of the hall.

Serving wenches brought more ale, and slaves stoked the fire, as the mood in the chamber grew raucous. The smells of cooked meat, spilled ale, and woodsmoke reeked in the chamber. As the banquet wore on, the odors of vomit and stale sweat added their pungency to the air. Many of the revelers collapsed, unconscious, at the table. Others chased and caught unwilling wenches, having their way beneath the tables or in any other unclaimed space.

Finally, the festivities drew to a close and the Council of Kings began.

Thelgaar the Invincible, mightiest king of the northmen, and host of this gathering, rose to his feet, and the room gradually grew silent. An impressive man, even at his advanced age, Thelgaar took his time in examining his guests. His creased face, hidden behind a flowing white beard, showed no expression as he began to speak.

"My guests ... my countrymen. We stand gathered in a mighty throng. An army, and a fleet, of heroic proportions has gathered unbidden at my doorstep. This is a force capable of making war, or sustaining peace."

Grunts and grumbles of confusion rose from the northmen at the king's last words. Peace was a subject not much in attendance at this gathering.

"Hear me!" roared Thelgaar, and immediately the noise ceased. "We have claimed many parts of these fair islands as our own. We have conquered some places, and coexisted elsewhere with the native Ffolk, until the Moonshae Islands, together, boast a people proud and prosperous—a people that need bow down before no foreign king!

"And now, again, we would embark upon a season of war. With our combined might, we could strike anywhere in the islands, and our triumph would be insured. One more kingdom of the Ffolk would fall before us, and the invincible tide would advance yet further.

"But I say, my people, that this road is the wrong one for us to follow!" A puzzled murmur began to growl throughout the huge chamber.

"With this secure base to operate from, let us prepare our ships for trade. Are we not the greatest sailors in the world? Our vessels can carry goods from any realm known to man, to any other realm. And we shall profit handsomely.

"Let this be the road to our future!"

Gasps of astonishment, mingled with cries of outrage, sounded, as Grunnarch and Raag leaped to their feet, together with many other enraged northmen. "Women's words!" "War!" and many other, less polite, phrases were roared.

Grunnarch leaped to the table, scattering mugs and platters as he hoisted his broad battle-axe over his head. He bellowed for the attention of his countrymen, and gradually the northmen turned their eyes to the fierce, yellow-bearded figure.

"The words of Thelgaar are the words of an old man—a man who has lost the spirit of the warrior! Our destiny leads us to the conquest of the Moonshaes, and fate has given us the tool to fulfill that destiny. Not in the ages of our children, or our grandchildren, but now!"

Grunnarch turned a full circle to regard the others in the room. His words, insolent and treasonous, would have started a brawl, had not he voiced the opinions of so many in the room.

"I say we sail to war before the season grows stale! My scouts have reported to me in detail of the kingdom of Corwell, scarce a hundred leagues south of here. This is a rich and mighty kingdom, yet with the force gathered here today, we could take it! Once Corwell falls, the realms of the Ffolk will have been cut in half, and the rest of the Moonshaes will be ours for the taking!"

Raucous cries of agreement arose from the gathering. The noise gradually coalesced into a single cry: "War! War!" in a chant that filled the vast chamber. Weapons, fists, and boots pounded a martial beat that intensified to a fever pitch. Only gradually did the northmen realize that Thelgaar had stood again, and slowly the tumult ceased enough that the old king could be heard.

"If such is your wish, I cannot stop you. But know this: you shall sail to war without the ships and fighting men of Thelgaar Ironhand!"

X X X X X X X X X

Even as the Firbolg's lifeless body crashed to the ground, Tristan sprinted across the rocky ground to kneel beside his friend and teacher. No second glance was needed to tell him that Arlen was dead. The Prince of Corwell stood and stared numbly at the body of his old friend and mentor. He felt curiously unmoved—as if he should react strongly, but could not summon the tears.

"Look!" cried Robyn, and the prince followed her pointing finger.

A scarlet cloak billowed from a clump of trees across the valley. With a closer look, the prince saw it was worn by a rider on a huge black horse. The mighty steed galloped toward them, and when Tristan saw the huge longbow across the rider's lap, he knew that this was their benefactor. Quickly the prince stole a look at the rocky notch above them. There was still no sign of the other band of Firbolgs.

The rider drew closer, and the companions saw that he was tall and very handsome. His black hair and beard were trimmed neatly. The scarlet cloak, as well as his blue tunic and black leggings, were of the finest silk, and the bow he carried was heavier and longer than any Tristan had ever seen.

The man's face smiled from beneath a wide-brimmed hat. The brim of the hat sported several brightly colored feathers—one each to match the rider's cape, tunic, and leggings. The garish costume looked strangely out of place in the wilderness of Llyrath Forest. Though travel-worn, the man's clothing was clean. His demeanor, as he rode nearer, seemed friendly.

To complete the astonishing picture, a great black falcon swooped low over the rider, gliding in a circle about him. As the rider pulled up before Tristan, Robyn, and Pawldo, the falcon settled to his broad shoulder.

"Ho!" he cried, cheerfully. " 'Twas a fight to make a stirring verse!" For the first time, Tristan noticed the smoothly curved harp slung over the man's shoulder.

The rider leaped to the ground, startling the falcon into an abrupt flight, and bowed with a flourish. He glanced around the scene of the battle, his gray eyes seemingly absorbing every detail. Turning back, he spoke to the companions.

"Keren Donnell, bard of the harp, at your service."

Tristan and Robyn exchanged a look of surprise at the name of the greatest bard among the Ffolk.

"I am Tristan Kendrick, Prince of Corwell. This is my father's ward, Robyn, and our friend, Pawldo." Pawldo nodded his head, studying the man's bow with considerable interest, and Robyn curtseyed quickly.

The prince continued. "Thank you for your help—you saved our lives."

" 'Tis a delight to find I have aided a prince and a lady!" smiled the bard, shrugging off his accomplishment. "And it is always a pleasure to meet one of the small folk," he added, bowing low to Pawldo.

"Your fame has preceded you, sir," added Tristan. "It is an honor to meet the most famous bard among the kingdoms of the Ffolk! But what could bring you from the court of the High King to the wilds of Gwynneth?"

"Ah, Gwynneth—fairest of the Moonshaes, in my own opinion. Your island also holds a wealth of the Ffolk's ancient history. Why, did you know that the Sword of Cymrych Hugh itself is rumored to be hidden somewhere on Gwynneth?"

"It is a fair place, indeed," agreed the prince, "And no, I didn't know that Cymrych Hugh's sword was supposed to be here somewhere—though that is an intriguing thought, I'll admit." Cymrych Hugh, as every child of the Ffolk learned, was the hero who had first united their race under one rule. "Do you travel for your pleasure, then?"

"Alas, no—I'm here on the High King's business. I journey to Caer

Corwell. Am I correct in guessing that is your home?" Tristan and Robyn nodded.

"If my falcon, Sable, and I may be allowed to accompany you?" the bard raised his eyebrows.

"Of course!" Suddenly the prince remembered their surroundings. "But we are not out of danger!" Quickly he explained that there were more Firbolgs in the vicinity. Nervously, he glanced up at the summit of the pass, but as yet there was no sign of further attackers.

"Let's see to your friend," the bard said, nodding toward Daryth, who was beginning to stir. "And the other one?" Keren indicated Arlen's body, lying in a pool of blood.

Tristan had not considered the problem, but knew instantly that he could not leave the old warrior's body to the enemy. "We'll have to strap him over one of the horses. He was the captain of my father's guard, and a loyal soldier who died a warrior's death. He shall be buried in Corwell, in the royal barrow."

The bard helped Tristan secure the body over Arlen's horse. At the same time, Robyn splashed cold water over Daryth's face, and the Calishite slowly regained consciousness. Soon he climbed to his feet, but he could not move his left arm.

Daryth's horse stood nearby, and Robyn, after strapping his arm with her scarf, helped him into the saddle. As Keren finished helping with Arlen's body, he saw the Firbolg, helplessly entangled in the branches of the trees. The monster had given up struggling, but looked dumbly and suspiciously at the humans and halfling before him.

"How did that happen?" the bard asked, surprised.

"Robyn did it," responded the prince, sounding surprised even to himself. "She told me that she doesn't know how, but it happened when she cried out for him to stop."

Keren turned and regarded Robyn with renewed interest, looking from the trapped Firbolg to the lass, and back again. Robyn just lowered her eyes and said nothing. Tristan inspected his hounds, two of which had fallen beneath the Firbolg's club. The others seemed healthy, however, and milled around expectantly.

Preparations finished, Keren, Robyn, Pawldo, and Tristan mounted their horses, Tristan in front of Arlen's body on the dead warrior's horse.

Just then, a thundering shout announced that a fresh band of Firbolgs had crested the pass. With bellows of rage, the monsters raced downhill. Several stopped to throw boulders which fell far short of the companions, who were speeding on their way.

"Too bad we didn't have a chance to bring their heads with us," called the bard to Tristan, referring to an old battle custom of some Ffolk clans. "They make splendid trophies, Firbolg heads!"

"Indeed," replied Tristan, a little sickened at the thought.

Urging the steeds forward, with the hounds loping easily beside them, the little party moved down the valley as quickly as they safely could. Riding hard, they pulled slowly away from the lumbering Firbolgs, who soon dropped out of sight behind them.

"Could they have stopped?" asked Robyn, hopefully, glancing back.

"They might . . . I don't know," answered Tristan. Suddenly he desperately wanted his teacher's advice and realized how much he would miss Arlen. "We can't afford to find out," he finally said, forcing himself to make the decision. "We must move on."

Daryth moaned, slumping weakly on his horse. Tristan, wondering if the Calishite would survive the ride, thought they might stop . . . but would they all die in a Firbolg ambush? . . . Oh, why did Arlen have to die?

The questions brought a weight of misery onto the prince's shoulders. To add to his depression, it soon began to rain.

XXXXXXXXXX

The hours after dawn brought Ffolk bustling into the streets and fields of Corwell. Fishermen took their vessels from the little harbor with the dawn, and farmers busied themselves with a dozen chores. Even the craftsmen were about, tidying and puttering as they prepared for the day's work.

A mile away, the halfling community of Lowhill slumbered on as the sun climbed toward the zenith.

Only in the late morning hours did a few stumbling, bleary-eyed halflings venture forth from their snug burrows. The halflings knew how to enjoy life, and getting up with the dawn was not recommended.

But finally the day brought its quotient of activity to Lowhill—today more than the usual.

Allian, a young maiden of fifty-two years, emerged from her burrow. She was alarmed to feel a sense of urgency running through the community. She saw her fellow halflings hastening to and fro, all looking very concerned. What could all the fuss be?

Halflings of all ages were bustling past the little door leading to her father's burrow, all heading downhill toward the fringes of the community. Following sleepily along, Allian noticed that her people had gathered somberly around one burrow at the bottom of the hill.

As she skipped down the hill in an effort to keep up with the children and young men, Allian grew more and more concerned. The entrance to the burrow did not look right, did not look right at all.

Huge clumps of sod lay strewn about the entrance, and the maiden saw that something had dug furiously at the ground around the sturdy wooden door. That portal, she saw as she moved closer, had been splintered inward by some awful force. The entire tunnel leading into the burrow had been enlarged, excavated hurriedly by some unknown creature with tremendous digging power.

Forcing her way through the crowd that grew steadily thicker and more apprehensive, she looked inside the burrow, and could barely stifle a gasp of horror.

The formerly cozy den now lay in shambles. The neat and sturdy furniture had been smashed beyond recognition, the stove overturned, and all the dishes broken into thousands of pieces. But none of this compared to the horror in the middle of the den.

The bodies, two of Allian's size, and two much smaller, had been gored beyond recognition. Each had been mutilated and torn by a creature of immense, and unbelievably savage, power.

Suppressing her cries no longer, Allian turned, sobbing, and ran from the burrow. Other halflings stood apart from the crowd, breathing heavily, faces ashen. Allian fell upon the ground and shivered. She tried to blank out thoughts of the nearby den, but her mind kept calling up images of huge, fanged creatures. They roared and growled in her head, and she could not drive them away.

×××××××××

Gray clouds and mist gave way to a steady rain as the companions came down from the highest reaches of Llyrath Forest. They pushed the horses hard, eager to put distance between themselves and the Firbolgs. They did not know if the monsters had pursued them beyond the valley, but neither could they risk stopping to find out.

Daryth rode silently, his jaws clenched. Robyn's crude sling held his arm motionless, but the strain of riding had drained his face of color. Tristan knew that they would have to stop for the night, and he prayed fervently to the goddess that the Firbolgs would not follow them into the low country.

The rain alternated between pounding downpour and misting drizzle. Each mile the party covered seemed to drive the dampness deeper into flesh and bone. Robyn located a winding game trail, and the group moved along this in single file, with the woman in the lead. Pawldo followed, with Daryth and Tristan behind him, while the bard brought up the rear. The path twisted and turned among towering pines in a forest nearly devoid of underbrush where the trees themselves provided some protection from the downpour.

Tristan pulled his wool cloak tightly about him, and wore a fur cape over it, but even this combined insulation could not keep the cold at bay. Soon he began to shiver uncontrollably. Before him, he saw that Daryth seemed ready to fall from his horse. At the head of the small column, Robyn slumped miserably in her saddle, wracked by chills.

"We'll have to stop," the prince called over his shoulder to the bard. "If we don't build a fire and warm up, I don't think Daryth'll make it through the night."

"A wise observation," agreed the bard. "Let us look for a suitable spot."

The trail soon began to climb another of the interminable ridges that lined Llyrath Forest. The pines here grew in tight clusters, with patches of meadow between. In one of these open places, Tristan urged his horse up next to Robyn's. The rain had lightened again to a mere mist in the air.

"Let's stop and camp among these pines," he suggested, and she nodded her head wearily. The prince had never seen her look so hopeless and miserable, and a great shaft of guilt pierced him.

"I . . . I'm sorry," said the prince. "I got us into this mess. And I thought following the Firbolgs would be such a great adventure!"

"It's not your fault," said Robyn, sighing. She looked at the motionless body behind Tristan, and her mouth tightened. "We all wanted to go—except Arlen. We are all responsible for the consequences."

She looked up, making a visible effort to shake off her despondency. "Where are we going to camp? I hope it's someplace close."

"Wait here with the others," Tristan said. "And I'll find a place where we can rest in some security."

Relieved to think about something other than Arlen, the prince cantered away from the path to investigate several of the dense patches of pine. He soon found one that was secure from outside view, and contained a large dry area where a soft bed of needles was sheltered from the rain by thick overhanging branches. The rest of the party joined him, and Robyn immediately built a small, smokeless fire. Tristan, meanwhile, rode back over their prints with a sweep made from a thick pine bough. In a few minutes he had erased all sign of their passage, creating the impression that they had continued on up the main trail.

The shelter proved as warm and dry as they could have hoped. They took turns on guard, but there had been no sign of pursuing Firbolgs by the time the gray dawn arrived. Daryth shook with fever and moaned in delirium. They tied him to the saddle and rode on in the cold. The only bright spot was that there continued to be no sign of their enemy behind them.

"They're probably not bold enough to venture into the lowlands," commented Keren. "Even if they are roving—and I fear our halfling friend may be right about that—they will not approach too closely to human settlements in such a small band."

"I hope you're right," replied Tristan. As it was, Daryth's chances of living through the journey to Caer Corwell were slender. If they should have to fight, those chances would be zero.

Toward the end of this day of travel, the party reached a small woodsman's cottage. The homestead lay within a sheltered vale, beside a pleasantly bubbling stream. An assortment of skins covered a rack outside the home, and a small, empty corral stood forlornly beside a dilapidated shed.

"Who are you?" The voice was sour and suspicious.

The speaker stood at the corner of the cottage. He was a middle-aged, work-worn man, dressed in simple clothes. A long-hafted woodsman's axe rested on his shoulder—it looked as if he could swing it into a ready position with a simple flick of his wrist.

The door to the cottage creaked open, and the prince saw a dim shape inside. More clearly, however, he saw a stout crossbow extend through the portal, with a bolt aimed straight at his heart.

"Who are you?" asked the woodsman again.

"I am Tristan Kendrick, Prince of Corwell," said Tristan, swinging boldly to the ground. He flinched as he saw the crossbow quiver slightly, but the bolt did not fly. "We have a wounded companion—he needs shelter and warmth."

The woodsman's attitude was already relaxing. "Yes, of course. I have seen you before, my prince. Please forgive my suspicions—these are dangerous times in Llyrath."

Giving a slight bob, he added, "Won't you come in?"

The cottage door swung open, and the crossbow emerged, followed by a wide-eyed lad of twelve or so. A stout woman bustled out after the boy and hurried to Daryth's horse, where Robyn was already helping the Calishite from the saddle.

"Quickly!" the woman urged, her plump face wrinkling in concern. "Poor lad! Let's get him inside."

Gratefully, the others followed the family into the warm cottage. For the first time in two days, the companions were able to drive the dampness from their clothing and bodies.

"I am Keegan of Dynnwall," announced their host as they entered the little home. "This is Enid, and my son—Evan. Lad, run out and tend to their horses! Be quick, now!"

Evan, still gaping at the visitors, turned and ran toward the horses. The rest of them carried Daryth carefully to the single, large bed. The Calishite had become completely delirious, and the fever seemed to burn him away.

Leaving Daryth to the women, Tristan took advantage of the shelter, and the woodsman's supplies, to wrap Arlen's body more securely. The flesh, clammy and lifeless, seemed to bear little resemblance to the man who had taught and tutored the prince throughout his life. Tristan prepared the body as for a funeral, certain that his father would have such a ceremony when they arrived home. Wistfully, he recalled his old teacher's gruff advice. His compliments had been few, but he had never despaired of Tristan's ability to learn and even excel.

The man had died a warrior's death! And such, among the Ffolk, was the finest way a man could die—at least, this is what the prince had always assumed. This assumption now felt very hollow.

Tristan entered the cottage after dark, welcoming the smells of spices and warm smoke that met him as he passed through the door. Keegan and his family offered every comfort their simple home could supply. After a plain but filling dinner and several glasses of the woodsman's own wine, the company relaxed in the first real comfort they had known in days. Only Daryth's weakened condition, and the unknown threats that might lurk in the forest beyond the sturdy door, prevented the night from becoming a completely pleasant one.

"Your companions tell us that you are Keren Donnell," said the woodsman hesitantly after the meal. "Could . . . could we beseech you to play for us?"

"I'd be delighted," said the bard, rising and crossing to the jumble of supplies they had dropped inside the door. Keren pulled out his harp and as he strolled back to his chair, strummed a few chords, tuning his strings with tender care. Then he began to play.

The Song of the Earthmother floated through the cottage. The words told of the goddess in all her glory, and how she had grown from the balance of good and evil in the world. She and her worshipers knew that neither good nor evil, in a pure sense, would benefit the world. Thus, the goddess was devoted to preserving the Balance.

The song then told of the druids, who were the human children of the goddess. The duties of the druids included preserving the sanctity of her wild places from the depredations of the rest of humankind. They insured that the Balance of the wilderness remained intact—that creatures were born, and died, in a manner pleasing to the goddess.

XXXXXXXXXXXXXXXXXXXXXXXXX DOUGLAS NILES XXXXXXXXXXXXXXXXXXXXXX

But the goddess also had other, even mightier children, and the song next told of these, one at a time.

First came verses about the great unicorn, Kamerynn, who dwelt in Myrloch Vale. A creature of enchantment and power, the unicorn was an unnatural animal, incapable of reproduction. Yet, as the king of the forest, it guarded and protected creatures of the woodland that even the druids did not know.

And the leviathan, the largest of the goddess's children, was charged with the same responsibility at sea. The leviathan slept nearly always, certainly for centuries at a time. When awakened, however, it became a force unmatched in the natural world.

The last of the children was a gathering of wolves known as the Pack. Wolves commonly roamed the wild places of Gwynneth and served their natural role as carnivores, helping to preserve the Balance in this role. Yet, in times of danger, the goddess would summon the wolves, and the Pack would form. Many were its numbers, and formidable its might. Though the distant baying of wolves was a chilling sound to a person alone on a moonless night, the gathering of the Pack was a mighty sign of the goddess's determination to see the Balance maintained.

As the last strains of harp music drifted through the house, Tristan nodded wearily. Druids, and wolves, and unicorns all seemed the stuff of legends . . . He and his friends went to their beds, to dream of Arlen, Firbolgs, and the pleasant tales—the stuff of legend—that had flowed from Keren's harp.

Of them all, only the bard suspected that a new legend had perhaps already begun.

✕ ✕ ✕ ✕ ✕ ✕ ✕ ✕ ✕ ✕

The woodsman, Keegan, had an oxcart, and begged to be allowed to accompany the group to Caer Corwell. Tristan accepted his offer, in the name of the king, since the cart would give Daryth a more comfortable place to ride. For two more days the party moved northward, sleeping at inns in small cantrevs, until they finally emerged onto the moors south of Corwell. In the middle of the next day, the castle came into sight.

XXXXXXXXXXXXXXXXXXXXXXXXX 80 XXXXXXXXXXXXXXXXXXXXXX

The humans continued on the road, and Pawldo gave his farewells. He took to the fields, his pony galloping eagerly, as the halfling rode home to Lowhill.

The bedraggled party slowly climbed the road toward the gates. Their appearance aroused considerable alarm, and as they drew near to the castle, a dozen men-at-arms ran from the gates to see who to help. As the group limped into the courtyard, the king himself emerged from the great hall and stalked toward them.

"What happened?" he demanded, confronting the prince as Tristan dismounted. The king saw the body on the withers of the horse, and his face turned white.

"Father, there are Firbolgs abroad in Llyrath Forest! We followed them, and they attacked us. Arlen gave his life to save us."

The king's face was blank as he looked at the rest of the party. His eyes quickly dismissed Keegan, driving the wagon, but lingered upon Keren, then moved on. "And the houndmaster?"

"He lives," said Robyn.

"Send for the cleric!" called the king to a man-at-arms who immediately mounted a horse and raced for the temple in the village. Robyn started to say something, but stopped as the king's iron gaze challenged her for a moment.

"And who are you?" The king turned his attention to Keren.

"Father, allow me to present Keren Donnell—bard of the harp. He intervened to save us after Arlen died."

"What would you have done if you'd had to rely on yourself?" snorted the king, with stinging scorn. Tristan flinched, but made no reply. King Kendrick turned again to the bard.

"My thanks, sir—though I don't know that the kingdom will be any the better for it. Your fame, of course, has preceded you, and I'm honored to have the greatest bard of the Ffolk as a guest. " He spoke the pleasantries mechanically, as if they were statements to get out of the way. "And what brings you to Corwell?"

"A message, my lord, from the High King to yourself."

"I might have known," grumbled King Kendrick. "It has been a long time since we have felt the hand of Caer Callidyrr in our quiet part of the world."

"I fear that your part of the world is not as quiet as you would wish," commented the bard softly.

"Indeed," muttered the king, looking at Arlen's lifeless form. "Whatever your missive, it must wait for the morrow—we shall have a funeral tonight." He turned his back on the companions, and his voice boomed across the courtyard.

"Gretta! Start cooking for a funeral feast of high honor! Warren—send for a wagonload of ale! You men, prepare the barrow!" Caught up in the preparations, the king marched into the hall to oversee the details.

Tristan, Robyn, and Keren helped Daryth to a bed, and the prince directed the bard to guest quarters. He felt like apologizing for his father's rudeness, but Keren seemed to take no notice of it, so the prince did not raise the subject.

Daryth moaned feverishly as Robyn and Tristan stood beside him. "I wish there were something more we could do," Robyn said, holding a cool cloth to his head.

Suddenly the door burst open, and the beaming, pudgy figure of Friar Nolan waddled into the room. "My poor children," he said. "How awful! I heard about the Firbolgs and Arlen. Dear me!" He bustled to the side of the young man in the bed, and then turned to the pair.

"What are you doing here?" asked Robyn, suspicious. "Do not think you can tamper with the will of the goddess! Leave! And take your new gods with you!"

"That is the farthest thing from my mind," promised the cleric. "I simply wish to see if I can make the young man feel any better. You don't object to that, do you?"

"I don't trust you and your new gods," stated the girl flatly. "But do what you can to help him."

"You two must leave me," countered the cleric simply, as he bent to pull open one of the Calishite's eyes. He clucked nervously as he looked at the wide black pupil that appeared to have lost its sparkle.

"No!" Robyn crossed her arms.

"I must insist," replied the cleric, looking straight into her angry green eyes.

"Come on," said the prince, gently taking Robyn's arm. "We'll wait right outside the door."

She pulled her arm from his grasp and stared unblinking at the cleric for several seconds. He just calmly stared back, and finally she turned and stomped from the room, with the prince springing after her.

"It can't do any harm," he said, quietly closing the door. "And it might even help Daryth!"

Robyn just scowled and turned away to pace anxiously back and forth in the hall. After several minutes, the door to Daryth's room opened, and the cleric emerged.

"Shhh. He sleeps," announced Friar Nolan in a whisper. "He needs rest if he is to recover. You may see him, briefly."

The pair silently entered the room. With astonishment, they saw that Daryth did indeed sleep peacefully, with no sign of the tortured thrashing, nor high fever, that he had displayed throughout the long journey home. His shattered arm looked whole again and rested comfortably upon his chest.

Robyn, her eyes wide with amazement, looked at Friar Nolan with fresh respect as they emerged from the room. The man was obviously more than a sanctimonious busybody.

"Thank you. How did you ... ?" the prince began to ask, but the cleric silenced him with a gesture.

"Not me," he responded humbly. "Such is the power of the new gods. I am merely one of their agents, trying to bring knowledge of them to these islands. It would not hurt you to learn more of them, you know."

"You seek to undermine the power of the Mother!"

"No, my child. " The cleric's tone was patronizing. "There is room in the realms—even on the Moonshaes—for all the gods. I simply seek to spread the words of the gods I worship."

"At what cost to the goddess? And to the Ffolk?"

"Perhaps someday you'll understand. I'm sure your friend will," the cleric added, with a nod toward Daryth.

The bustling cleric left to return to the village, and Robyn, both angry and bewildered, stalked to her room to change. The prince stood for a moment outside Daryth's door, wondering at the miraculous recovery, and then he went to his own chambers to prepare for the funeral.

They had completed changing into fresh, dry clothes just as the preparations were completed, and they joined the procession that emerged from the castle in late afternoon. An honor guard of the king's warriors carried upon their shoulders a bier bearing the body. The king, Tristan, and Robyn followed, and, because the word had spread rapidly, hundreds of residents of the castle and town fell into a column behind. The procession marched down the road from the castle gate, across the commons meadows, and arrived at the great barrows hall that sat upon the moor, a half mile from the castle.

King Kendrick stepped to the forefront of the assembly, where Arlen's body lay upon a raised mound of earth. For a moment, he looked down at the man who had served him all his adult life.

"A brave man, and a mighty warrior has died. Yet, he died as he would have wished—in battle, protecting the family of his king." Did Tristan hear, or imagine, an element of scorn in his father's voice—scorn for his son, who had caused the warrior's death?

"May the goddess take him to her bosom in the earth, and may his spirit fare well."

With these few words, the king stepped aside, and the bearers carried the body into the barrow. Keren, who had been standing near the back of the crowd, strummed a chord, and then gave them the Song of the Earthmother—the ballad that had so lulled the sad companions on the journey back.

Tristan and Robyn stood before the barrow as the rest of the Ffolk filed back to the castle. Robyn sobbed once, and the prince placed an arm around her shoulders. She started to pull away, but then leaned against him as if, for the first time in her life, she needed his strength.

The prince's own vision grew blurry. As they turned back to the castle, he whispered into the night.

"Goodbye, old friend. And thank you."

XXXXXXXXXX

The passage of Myrloch Vale proved to be no more than a minor nuisance as the Beast made its way northward. Soon it left the realms of the dwarves, Firbolgs, and Llewyrr behind, without encountering any of the Vale's occupants. Sometime later, it paused at the rocky shore of a gray and stormtossed strait.

For a moment the Beast reflected. It had gained, already, a potent ally with the perversion of the druid. Trahern of Oakvale would have much to do in following the orders of his master, Kazgoroth. Also, the Firbolgs could be counted upon to perform their special tasks, as the Beast had commanded them. Doubtless, they had already begun. And even the guard, Erian, could prove to be a useful tool, if his own stupidity did not get him killed first.

But these allies would not be enough to carry the attack to the heart of the goddess's strength. The Beast would need more help. Whether it was instinct or distant memory that told Kazgoroth such help could be found across the stormy strait, who can say?

The Beast knew that it would gain its most powerful allies among the northmen, and to this end it now moved.

The waters presented Kazgoroth with no more obstacle than had the magic of the Llewyrr. The creature's shape changed as it entered the water, and in the body of a large shark, it swam easily from Gwynneth to Oman. When it reached its destination, it rose again from the water and walked onto the land. This time, it did not use the guise of a woman, but instead took the form of a tall, blond-bearded warrior, striding forward with all the arrogant confidence of a northman passing through his own domain. Indeed, reflected the monster, this island—as with all of the Moonshaes—would one day be part of its domain.

In time, Kazgoroth reached the northern shore of Oman, there to see the harbor filled with longships, and the tents stretching for miles along the coastal plane and inland valleys. Ignoring the tents and the ships, the warrior strode to the looming fortress that commanded the hill rising above the harbor. It passed through the gates, unnoticed, and moved freely among the dark and drafty halls of the fortress. It knew whom it sought.

The old king, Thelgaar Ironhand, having spoken for peace, rested easily, knowing that what he had done was right. Thelgaar did not know what entered his chamber, that dark and moonless night. He was barely aware of drooling jaws striking at his throat, tearing his heart, still pumping, from his lifeless body.

The monster feasted on the gruesome corpse, licking blood from wherever it had spattered. It then adjusted its shape to match that of the king it had slain. This body, it knew, would serve for a long time.

After dawn had broken upon the camps of the northmen, Kazgoroth emerged from the king's chamber in the body of the slain king. It spoke to the heralds of Thelgaar, and summoned the other kings of the northmen to council.

Word spread fast throughout the camps and across the harbor. The spirits of the northmen soared, as the news brought fresh confidence, and jubilant awareness of their own might.

By noon there was not a single warrior in that vast encampment that did not know that Thelgaar Ironhand had changed his mind. The pennant of the red dragon would fly alongside those of the other northern kings. The fleet, and the army, would march in all its supreme power for the subjugation of Gwynneth.

Thelgaar Ironhand would lead the northmen to war.

XXXXXXXXXX

The funeral feast had been a grand success.

Broken platters, spilled mugs, and sleeping revelers lay strewn about Caer Corwell's great hall. The music of pipe and cymbal wailed through the air, and many dancers still caroused about the hall. Tristan spun Robyn through a wild circle, catching her as she bent back almost to the floor. He thought that the maiden had never looked so lovely as she now did.

Her black hair flowed freely as she spun, before settling down her back as far as her hips. Her slender waist, beneath his hands, seemed supple and strong, and he wanted to be more daring with her, but could not gather the courage. It was odd—he had grappled and groped with a dozen or more maidens who meant nothing to him, but when he tried to show affection to this woman—this delicious creature who had grown, almost overnight, from his childhood playmate—his whole being seemed to freeze. Of course, she was not a mere scullery maid whom he might try to lure into the stables after the celebration. Still, his hesitancy was maddening.

"Excuse me."

The prince turned to see Daryth, looking amazingly healthy, standing behind him. The Calishite cleared his throat. "May I have the pleasure of the next dance?"

Robyn glanced at his arm, which hung freely, and quickly said, "Certainly." She spun away from the prince to settle into Daryth's long arms.

For a second, Tristan watched them whirl away, realizing that his moment had passed. Disgusted with himself, he turned back to the table and sat, pouring another mug of ale. For a moment he almost regretted that Daryth had recovered so completely under the cleric's ministrations.

"Hello, my prince."

Tristan turned to see a somber-looking Pawldo, accompanied by the halfling maiden he had been with at the fair—was her name Allian? Her doll-like face was marred by deep circles under her eyes, and she darted looks about the hall as if she was frightened of something.

"How are you?" asked the prince. "Is something wrong?"

"Trouble in Lowhill," admitted the halfling, as Allian looked away. "Some creature tore into a burrow a couple of nights ago—under the full moon. Killed a whole family."

Keren, sitting nearby, turned at the halfling's words. "The full moon, you say? What kind of creature?"

"Nobody saw it, but it must have been terrifying. It dug the dirt from around the door—left massive claw marks—and tore the burrow apart." Allian covered her face and turned away from Pawldo's description. He lowered his voice, while Daryth and Robyn walked up to listen. The two halflings and humans settled around a small table. Tristan signaled a scullery maid for a fresh pitcher of ale, while Pawldo continued.

"It didn't eat the bodies—just ripped 'em up, and spread the blood around. The warriors followed its tracks to Corlyth Creek, but then lost it. No one had ever seen prints like those before—doglike, but huge."

"The trouble is perhaps worse than we imagined," mused the bard. "First, the Firbolgs, and now this. The power of the goddess seems to be waning rapidly."

"But what does it mean?" cried Robyn, agitated. "What can we do about it?"

"More than you can imagine," replied Keren. "Tell me, what did you do to cause the trees to entangle that Firbolg?"

Robyn looked both embarrassed and puzzled. "Nothing, really. It was going to . . . to kill Tristan, and I screamed—I guess I said 'No!' or something. And it just happened."

"Have you ever done anything like this before?"

"No, never. I mean, I've always felt a kind of empathy with plants—with all wild things. Sometimes it seems as if I can share their joy and sorrow—if plants can know such things."

"Tell me about your parents," persisted the bard.

"I never knew them. My father was an honored captain in the king's regiment, but he died in the last war with the northmen, before I was born. " For a moment, Robyn looked hesitant, but then she continued.

"I don't know who my mother was. The king told me that she died when I was born. I've asked him about her, but he won't tell me more. I, well, I've always gotten the impression that there was some kind of scandal or something—the king gets really angry if I press him, so I've never forced the issue. And no one else around here will tell me anything either!" She scowled as she remembered her frustrations over the years—everyone she asked telling her they didn't know, lying to her! Or else saying it was better she didn't know.

Daryth looked curiously at Tristan while Robyn spoke. "Do you know more?" he said quietly.

"No. She has been here since I was a small boy. For a long time I thought she was my sister."

"But no more. " Daryth winked at him.

Robyn opened her mouth to go on, but felt suddenly that the bard wasn't listening anymore. He stared idly at the ceiling, fingering the strings of his harp. Suddenly he stood, and smiled at her—a smile that lifted her spirits.

"We shall talk some more, soon," he said, and turned to amble toward the hearth.

Gradually, the wailing of the pipes died away as the bard settled himself by the fire. His harp, a golden instrument of grace and beauty, lay in his hands like an object of love. As the room fell into silence, the bard began to strum the wondrous golden instrument.

The music floated through the hall like a magic spell, soothing and calming, bringing peace and contentment. After the raucous chords of the pipes and cymbals, the harp's music was gentle, soft. It was a sound that the Ffolk of Corwell heard only rarely, so all were silent, eagerly anticipating the next notes.

For several minutes Keren played, without singing, and the frenzied mood mellowed easily into relaxed anticipation. When he knew that his audience was ready, the bard began his first ballad.

The Song of the Llewyrr was certainly one of the oldest songs of the Ffolk, yet its haunting beauty flowed freshly from Keren's harp. His voice, strong and deep, caressed each word, and filled the refrains with haunting sadness. Through it all, each listener felt the real power of magic.

The song told of the Llewyrr before the coming of man. Long-lived, and peace-loving, the elves dwelt throughout the Moonshaes in complete harmony with the forces of the land. The first humans to arrive were welcomed and protected by the Llewyrr. Gradually, as the numbers of humans increased, the Llewyrr withdrew from their ancestral haunts. On many islands, they were known only through legend, the song said. But here, on Gwynneth, the Llewyrr retreated to Myrloch Vale, and there they lived, small in number, and shy, but possessing the same carefree spirit and harmonious sense of nature as they had since time immemorial. Humans saw them rarely but knew they were there.

Next, the bard played the Song of the North Wind, a harsh and jarring allegory of the sweeping winter wind that blew fiercely off the trackless sea. Cutting, freezing, and killing, the wind swept over the lands of the Ffolk. All who heard knew that the wind symbolized the coming of the northmen, who had rolled across much of the Isles of Moonshae with the same implacable force as the icy gale. The blood enemies of the Ffolk embarked on frequent raids against their more peaceful neighbors. Tristan knew that his father had joined campaigns against them, but none had occurred within the prince's lifetime.

The bard then raised their spirits with the proud Ballad of Cymrych Hugh—the story of the greatest hero in the known history of the Ffolk. Bearing a silver sword that legends said had been given him by the goddess herself, Cymrych Hugh united all the lands of the Ffolk under one rule for the first time in their history. He became the first of the High Kings, and his legendary battles with Firbolgs and northmen made for stirring verse.

Many stories were still told about the hero—the tale of his death in battle with some fearsome beast was one of the grand epic tales of the Ffolk. After that battle, his sword had disappeared mysteriously. That mighty weapon, forged for the hero by dwarven metalsmiths, from steel forged by the goddess herself, was in itself worthy of heroic tales. Keren's song devoted several verses to the story of the weapon's creation.

Tristan idly dreamed about the sword, wondering what it looked like, what it felt like to wield. Arlen had told him of it many times, and listening to the song was like listening to a tale of an old friend.

Keren continued to play, lifting his audience with tales of hope and heroes, of unicorns, and the children of the goddess. Then he would bring his listeners to the point of despair with a tale of tragic love, or an ancient treasure long lost to the pillaging raiders of the north.

Finally, the bard played a slow tune of rare beauty and exquisite pain. It was the song of a hero, a gentle man who had taught, and served, and earned his peace, but in the end had met his death in battle.

Robyn's head rested upon the prince's shoulder as Tristan listened, enthralled by the piercing strains. He felt Robyn quake, and felt the soft wetness of her tears as they moistened his tunic. He held her to comfort her, and listened, to comfort himself. But he could find no solace in the music.

Such was the Song of Arlen.

The funeral feast faded away with the late hours of the night. Only a few people remained in the great hall, including Tristan, Robyn, Pawldo, Allian, and Keren. Once again, the bard took up his harp, and sang a song of history and legend.

The bard's listeners fought sleep, so they might hear the words and music that so beautifully caressed them. Though they were not altogether successful, those that slept heard the song as part of their dreams.

And who was to say where the song ended, and the dream began?

✗ ✗ ✗ ✗ ✗ ✗ ✗ ✗ ✗

Sated from its gory feast, the Pack sprawled in sleep, the effects of hunger abated.

Already the Pack had grown larger, swelled by a stream of arrivals. Soon the wolves grew restless again. Slowly, one after another, they rose and gathered until the singing cry of their leader drove them to their steady lope. Over heath, and through fen, the Pack moved as if it now had a deeper purpose. Without haste, but also without hesitation, hundreds of shaggy bodies flowed across the land.

Night fell and the Pack did not slow. If anything, its pace took on a sense of urgency as if it flowed toward a nearby destination. As the moon climbed higher into a cloudless sky, illuminating the rugged landscape with a silvery glow, the Pack filed into a narrow gulch, and entered a secluded and rocky glen. Finally, the Pack paused around a bright pool.

Hundreds of wolfish faces gleamed in the reflected light of the pool—light that was amplified more than nature decreed, for this was a Moonwell. More and more of the Pack crowded into the glen, until every foot of space was occupied. And still the Pack grew, spilling out of the glen, and down the narrow valley below it.

For hours the wolves watched the shining waters, until dawn colored the eastern sky. As creatures of one mind, the Pack rose and began to run. Numbering in the thousands, the Pack filled the narrow valley from side to side, rushing like a tide, inexorably toward the sea.

BOOK TWO

MESSAGE AT MIDNIGHT

6

XAs the last to enter, Tristan swung the heavy wooden door shut behind him, and bolted it at a look from his father. The room, even with the great fire blazing, felt cool and dark. Deer and bearskin rugs covered the floor, and the long council table of polished oak dominated the center of the room. A large wolf's head—symbol of the Kendrick clan—glared across the room from its mount above the fireplace. The councilors took seats around the table, the king seated at the head.

The king's council chamber was the most formal room in the entire castle. Located at the center of the keep, it had no windows upon the outside world. Instead, it drew its light from the fire on the broad hearth.

Three cantrev lords sat upon one side of the table. Each of these men presided over a small, rural community, arbitrating disputes, serving as a spokesman between the king and the people, and organizing and commanding a company of men-at-arms in times of emergency. Lords Dynnatt, Koart, and Nowll ruled several of the communities within a few hours' ride of Caer Corwell, and had arrived early in the day for the meeting with the bard. Robyn and Tristan sat opposite them. Keren sat at the foot, and a chair at the king's right hand remained conspicuously empty.

Arlen would have sat there.

"Pardon the lack of formalities," said the king. "But let us get directly to business."

"Ahem," interrupted Dynnatt, a burly warrior whose features disappeared behind shaggy hair and a bushy beard. He nodded toward Robyn, while looking at the king.

"Should the maiden be present?" Lord Koart, a small, vigorous man, asked the question.

"It is my wish that she be here," replied the king. "Robyn may play an important role in our efforts to deal with the crisis. And now, sir?" he concluded, nodding to Keren.

"Thank you, Your Highness," responded Keren, standing. "I only wish I bore happier news.

"A little over a fortnight ago I left Alaron, following a council with the High King himself. Other messengers were dispatched to Moray and Snowdown—the portents indicate that all the lands of the Ffolk are in danger. But the missive of greatest importance is the one intended for Gwynneth.

"The High King's council of sorcerers," continued Keren, "became aware of dark magic growing in the land this winter, pointing toward a summer of turmoil and direst danger to the Ffolk. The danger includes the threat of the northmen, but this is not the paramount danger perceived by the council of mages."

The cantrev lords exchanged uneasy looks. The council of mages earned no love from the Ffolk, who tended to be very superstitious about matters involving sorcery.

"At the time of the Spring Festivals, we learned more about this threat from the circle of druids. The druids have determined that the power afoot represents great danger to the goddess, and thus to our people. Whatever its nature and powers, we know only that it is a supreme menace, of mysterious nature—that it stalks the land even now . . .

"And we know that it is upon Gwynneth."

Keren paused, letting his listeners absorb the impact of his words. The room was silent, until Dynnatt cleared his throat noisily. Tristan cast a sideways glance at Robyn, and saw that her gaze rested intently upon the bard. The sight did not please him.

"We now have confirmation," continued the bard, "that the Firbolgs are abroad. This in itself is a portent of great evil, for the Firbolgs have not left the highlands of Myrloch Vale in over a century. Spies have also reported a great mustering among the northmen. Their fleets, apparently, sail to a rendezvous at Iron Bay, the kingdom of Thelgaar Ironhand. This is perhaps a hopeful sign, for Ironhand has agreed to a peace treaty with the High King. His influence may be able to dissuade the northmen from all-out war, but we cannot count on this.

"Spies report that the northmen gather at Oman's Isle, so Corwell becomes a very tempting target."

For several moments, no one talked. Tristan, who had listened more closely to Keren than he usually did in official meetings, watched his father. He saw that the king looked older, more weary than the prince had ever seen him before. Finally, King Bryon Kendrick looked around the council chamber, studying the eyes of each person seated at the table. Slowly, he rose to his feet.

"I had hoped that the rest of my life would be spent free from the scourge of war. I see now that this is not to be.

"Our course of action is simple, and obvious. My lords—" he spoke now directly to Dynnatt, Koart, and Nowll—"we must mobilize the cantrevs for war. Spare only those laborers most essential to the tending of the flocks and crops. All others must be armed, and the militia units reformed.

"Be vigilant! Send patrols into the hills and forests, seeking signs of the Firbolgs. I shall send word to the farther cantrevs to do the same." The three lords in attendance represented only the leaders of the cantrevs closest to Caer Corwell. Dozens more lay in the farther reaches of the kingdom. Though their lords could not reach Corwell in time for this council, the danger, they all knew, was shared by every community of Ffolk in Gwynneth.

The king turned to Keren again. "Can you stay with us for a while? Your presence is appreciated, and your advice would no doubt be of great aid in our preparations."

"With regret, I cannot," responded the bard. "Having delivered my message, I must return immediately to Caer Callidyrr and inform the High King that I have completed my mission. The fact that the Firbolgs are abroad is no doubt unknown to him."

The king nodded solemnly in understanding. The bard's mission, he had suspected, would call for him to return to Caer Callidyrr on Westshae.

"I thank you for making this journey on our behalf. You are welcome to outfit yourself for the journey with whatever provisions or mounts that I can provide."

"My thanks to you, Your Majesty. I shall make every effort to return under happier circumstances, and next time to accept your hospitality more graciously."

"You shall always be welcome. Beyond common courtesy, I owe you the debt of my children's lives, and this I will never forget!" The emotion in the king's voice surprised his son.

The council lasted for a few more minutes, as details of militia units and patrolling districts were assigned. As soon as they adjourned, the king sent out messengers to the farther cantrevs, while Keren went immediately to the stables and prepared to leave. Tristan and Robyn packed his saddlebags with an abundance of provisions, and joined him at the castle gate.

The bard took the prince's hand in a firm grip, and studied the young man carefully. "You must be strong, Prince Tristan, for the weight of a kingdom, I fear, shall soon fall upon your shoulders," Keren said solemnly.

Trtistan started to smile. "You are worthy of the responsibility, fear not," the bard continued. When Tristan chose not to reply, the bard added, "And remember, above all things, to *think*. A leader must be a man of action, but even more so, a man of thought. And take care of that dog!" Keren smiled, for he had not been shy in his praise of Canthus.

At last Tristan spoke, warmly. "I will. And be careful on your journey!" The prince was surprised to find himself reluctant to say goodbye to the bard—he wished that he would see the man again.

"And you, my lady," Keren said, turning to Robyn. "Keep this headstrong young man out of trouble, if you can. And keep asking questions—there's an answer for you somewhere."

"Now, I must be off!" The bard leaped to his saddle and urged his horse down the castle road. The black, soaring speck of Sable circled over him. The strains of a song wafted through the air, and Tristan and Robyn knew that the bard sang a traveling song, a song of farewell.

XXXXXXXXXX

Daryth resisted all attempts to restrict him to his bed, protesting that he felt fine and only needed exercise to be back in excellent shape. Within a few days, he returned to daily training activities with the royal hounds.

Canthus continued his education under Daryth's tutelage. He learned all the standard guarding and hunting commands, performing to either vocal or hand commands. The Calishite then began to work the dog into more challenging tasks. The moorhound soon learned to knock down a victim without biting, and to stand guard at an assigned place for a long period of time, without his attention straying.

In the meantime, Tristan had worked with the dogs for long hours each day, and came to appreciate more than ever the might and intelligence of the moorhound he had acquired from Pawldo. The dog seemed to grasp tactics, such as silent movement and the importance of surprise, as quickly as a human would, and his keen instincts augmented this intelligence in an almost uncanny fashion.

Canthus forged gladly into icy water, or thorny thickets, with no thought but the completion of his task, be it the retrieval or flushing of game. When retrieving, he brought the game to the prince with nary the slightest toothmark.

Tristan also spent long hours with his bow, striving to gain a mastery of the weapon he had never shown for Arlen. Though he showed marked improvement, he remained far from expert.

As the prince's and dog's training progressed, the Ffolk of Corwell began making preparations for war. Able-bodied young men from the many cantrevs of the kingdom arrived at the castle, swelling its garrison to several hundred men-at-arms. Though many more men and women could be mustered in an emergency, the king did not deem the situation dire enough yet to ignore the tending of crops and animals. The Ffolk of the cantrevs nonetheless were instructed to keep their weapons handy, and the king's army could swell tenfold in a matter of a few days should the situation demand drastic action.

One day as Tristan was practicing shooting from a moving horse, a messenger came from his father, demanding his presence in the king's private study. When the prince reported there, the king gestured to him to enter and shut the door.

Tristan wondered, apprehensively, what his father wanted. He expected a harangue about some irresponsible antic he had committed, or perhaps an admonishment to take his training more seriously.

The king turned to regard the prince carefully. With a sigh, the older man walked to a chair and sat heavily. Tristan felt himself quaking inside, as he always did around his father.

"My son, you have made it clear to me, many times in the past, that you care little for the mantle of royalty that will some day be yours."

Tristan started to respond, but his father held up his hand.

"Let me finish. The current danger confronting the Kingdom makes your cares insignificant. You will have to begin to accept the responsibilities of your position. You have no choice in the matter."

"Father, I have no wish to avoid—"

"Then why is it you have time for nothing more than drinking, wenching, and tending your hounds? And you get my best man killed on a fool's mission!"

Tristan's face stung as if he had been slapped. There was enough truth to the words to bring the hot flush of shame to his cheeks.

"I want you to take command of the town's company. You will train with them, and lead them. This would have been Arlen's task." For a moment his father's voice softened unexpectedly. "Tristan, I need your help."

The king rose and went to a chest in the corner of the room. Opening it, he pulled out a shirt of shining steel mail. He rubbed it gently, then turned, holding it up.

"This was my father's, Tristan, and my own battle armor. Now, I should like to see you wear it. I fear that this summer will again give us cause to test it," said the king. For a moment, Tristan saw the courage and determination that must have been commonplace in his father's character, long ago.

"Thus far," added the king with a smile that did not carry to his eyes, "it has managed to keep the Kendricks alive. May its fortune bless you as well!"

Tristan looked at his father in silence, a mixture of emotions seething within him—guilt, anger at being made to feel guilty, pride that his father was asking something of him, fear that he might not be able to live up to it, and joy at the thought of wearing the beautifully crafted mail armor.

Finally, he could only say, "I shall try to wear it with honor."

"I trust that you shall," said the king.

"Father—everything I have ever done, or tried to do, you have belittled as unfitting of my station. Nothing has ever been good enough for you! I . . . I will try to do as you ask—to command a company of your men. I am just sorry that you don't—from what you say—expect me to succeed."

The king looked genuinely sad, but did not respond, which only increased Tristan's anger. "You will take over the company—mostly swordsmen, a few archers—tomorrow. " His face grew harsh. "Perhaps I should be glad that war is coming—it might make a prince out of you!"

Cursing silently, Tristan left his father's study. He stalked to the stable, and saddled one of the horses.

"Where are you going?" Robyn's voice came from behind him.

"For a ride!" he snapped, and then turned to her guiltily. "I'm sorry. I just had a 'talk' with my father."

"Mind if I ride along?"

"I'd like that."

They quickly saddled a second horse, and cantered together down the castle road. From there, they struck out across the moors, giving the horses free rein.

After several hours of silent, albeit pleasant riding, Tristan turned to his companion. "There's something I've wanted to ask . . . but we haven't had an opportunity to talk for some time."

The maiden turned to him, riding easily, and raised her eyebrows. "Yes?"

"Did you ever figure out what you did to wrap that Firbolg in the trees that way?"

A peculiar expression flickered across her face—Tristan couldn't tell if she was amused or annoyed.

"I've tried to understand" said Robyn thoughtfully. "I looked up, and saw that thing next to you, and all I could think about was how much I wanted you to live. I screamed—I guess I panicked—and the next thing I knew, the trees bent down and grabbed him."

"But how?" the prince persisted. "It seemed like magic, and I've never known you to have any interest in sorcery."

"I don't!" Robyn replied, with a shudder. "I'll leave the sorcerers to the High King's council!

"Still," she continued, "that did not seem sorcerous to me. It was more as if the trees reached out to help me."

She turned to the woods, pensively, and watched a pair of squirrels chatter to each other on a high limb. Then she laughed, and Tristan asked why.

"That fellow ate a pile of nuts that his lady had her eyes on. She's really letting him have it!" Suddenly she looked at him in surprise.

"That's *exactly* what was happening!" she insisted. "I could understand them!" She looked back at the squirrels, and then turned thoughtful.

"Tristan," she asked, regarding him softly. "What do you know of my parents?"

"Not much," he responded, "They wouldn't tell me anything—Arlen, my father, Gretta. You came to the Caer Corwell as a baby, I remember, when I was about two or three. I remember Gretta telling me that your parents had died, and that my father was going to raise you as his ward. I think I asked where you were from, and she told me 'Corwell,' but I couldn't get any more information out of her.

"At the time," Tristan concluded with a grin, "I was just disappointed that you weren't a boy!"

Robyn playfully slapped his shoulder, but then turned serious again. "I have asked Father about this, but he never tells me any more than that—what you just told me. I am convinced that my parents' identity is somehow tied into my . . . trick, or whatever it was."

"Why have you suddenly grown curious about this again?"

"Because of that fight with the Firbolgs. I think what happened with the trees might make more sense if I knew more about myself!" With a grimace of frustration, she lapsed into silence. Tristan did not disturb her thoughts.

Finally, as they neared the castle, Tristan admitted, "You know, it has been nice to ride with you. Perhaps we could try to do this together more often?"

"I'd like that," Robyn smiled, "Except it sounds like you'll be busy training your company."

"Dammit! I'm tempted to ignore his orders!" Tristan scowled. "The king as much as told me he expected me to fail."

"Stop that!" said Robyn, in disgust. "Why don't you try to understand his point of view, for once, instead of thinking only about what you want?"

Angry, but not wanting to spoil the afternoon, the prince turned his gaze to the firth. However, he could feel Robyn's presence, like a moth feels the light, strongly at his back. She said nothing, and they rode the rest of the way to the castle in silence.

That night, Tristan dreamed of Robyn, and of Firbolgs. It was not a frightening dream so much as a frustrating one. Giants stood around the pair, taunting. He moved to protect the lass, and the trees bent around his own limbs, restraining him. As he watched, helpless, Robyn muttered arcane phrases and the Firbolgs fled, shrieking in terror. Long after they ran, the prince heard her voice, speaking as through a cloaking haze.

XXXXXXXXXX

Even the brilliant sunshine could not dispel the shadows that seemed to linger around the Iron Keep. That towering black fortress absorbed the light without reflection, creating a splash of gloomy darkness on the hill over Iron Bay.

The area now bustled with activity, as horses, provisions, and weapons were ferried from shore to the longships anchored in the bay, or loaded onto those smaller vessels that had been drawn onto the beach. Quickly, the northmen struck their camps, carting their equipment to the shore in a long but orderly procession. Columns of troops stretched for miles from the bay as the outer camps straggled toward the sea.

Grunnarch the Red watched his own army mobilize with a deep flush of pleasure. He stood upon a low hill, across the valley from the Iron Keep, and from this vantage point he could see for miles in all directions. Never in his, or even his grandfather's, lifetimes had such a host of northmen mustered to war together.

His men bore Grunnarch's crimson standard proudly as they marched from their encampment to the sea. The Bloodriders, Grunnarch's personal guard, rode their proud horses at the lead of the column, while thousands of footmen marched stolidly behind. The Bloodriders were undoubtedly the finest group of mounted warriors among the forces of the northmen, and Grunnarch's heart swelled with pride as they cantered past.

The armies of the northmen wore little in the way of standardized uniforms, and this fact caused the Bloodriders to stand out distinctly from the rest of the force. About a hundred in number, the Riders wore bright scarlet cloaks over heavy black chain mail. Each rode a powerful warhorse the color of black ink, and carried a double-edged battle-axe that weaker men could not have lifted off the ground.

Suddenly, one horse broke from the file, carrying its redcaped Rider up the slope to Grunnarch. Laric, smiling cruelly, sprang to the ground.

"The men are fit, but they need some killing to keep them so," reported the captain, licking his full lips.

"The loading proceeds well," said Grunnarch.

"The Iron King has asked to see me. I ride now to Iron Keep," said the captain, remounting.

"Why does he want to see you?" grunted the Red King.

"I don't know, but I'm curious."

"Just remember who your loyalty is owed to," growled Grunnarch.

Laric's laugh held a trace of a sneer as he whirled the black horse and raced down the slope.

For a moment, the Red King pondered Thelgaar Ironhand's change of policy. Strange, that. Thelgaar had left the council as the lone advocate of peace, pledging not to lend his considerable force to the summer's raiding. While his refusal had not dimmed the enthusiasm of the other northern kings for war, it certainly had limited their options. Thelgaar's fleet numbered perhaps half of all the other fleets combined.

The following morning, the king had emerged from his chambers and pledged his followers to war. The announcement was made almost in a frenzy, and Thelgaar Ironhand had retained this fever pitch during the preparations that followed.

Thelgaar had driven his troops mercilessly through the necessary outfittings. This was fortunate, on the one hand since his men had not prepared themselves for a summer of war. On the other hand, his intensity had an unsettling effect upon the men, since they had never seen their revered leader behave so.

Grunnarch felt a momentary flash of relief at the fact that his forces had not been ordered to accompany Thelgaar's in the initial phases of the attack. The Iron King had imperiously informed the other northern kings of the plan of attack, and the assembled kings had accepted the plan with little argument. In part, this had been because the plan was sound, but also, the kings had been reluctant to argue with the imposing presence of Thelgaar Ironhand. He had indeed seemed to take on a new and especially warlike personality following his change of heart.

The plan nonetheless served as a fine proposal for the reduction and elimination of the only remaining kingdom of the Ffolk upon Gwynneth: Corwell. A massive fleet, led by Thelgaar in command would sail through the Strait of the Leviathan to Corwell Firth, and there land an army at the very foot of Corwell Castle. This force would be sufficiently powerful to reduce that fortress, and thus shatter any attempt at organized resistance.

The force Grunnarch was to lead would be nearly as big, but would sail down the eastern shore of Gwynneth, landing an army at the opposite end of the island from Thelgaar. Grunnarch's army would then march across the island, taking slaves and booty from each community as it advanced, finally meeting Thelgaar's force at Caer Corwell.

Grunnarch's task would be difficult, for the Ffolk were savage fighters in defense of their homelands. The presence of the huge northern fleet in Corwell Firth, however, should prevent King Kendrick from sending reinforcements eastward. Nonetheless, the terrain was rugged, and Grunnarch's army would need to level many sturdy rural cantrevs in the course of his advance. The prospect of many heated combats, far from dismaying him, caused Grunnarch's blood to race in anticipation.

He stayed upon the hill, watching the loading, for the remainder of the day. A steady stream of men carried the supplies to the beached longships. The horses of the Bloodriders were divided among ten ships, and these vessels would sail at the head of Grunnarch's fleet. The rest of the vessels, some hundred and fifty strong, carried the vast bulk of his army.

By late afternoon, the preparations had been completed, and Grunnarch rode slowly down to the docks. Thelgaar would hold a final council with the kings of the northmen that night, Grunnarch felt certain.

Before dawn the following day, the fleets would ride the outgoing tide from Iron Bay, hoist sails, and begin the journey to war.

X X X X X X X X X X

"Wake up, Tristan! Please! It's important!"

Dimly, he shifted from his dream to real life. He realized that Robyn stood over him, holding a slim candle. She prodded his chest again, and he blinked.

"What is it?" he mumbled, waking enough to sit up in bed. He saw darkness through his window. Robyn stood beside him in a flowing nightgown of white. The cloth made a stark contrast against her black hair, and the prince thought, absently, that she looked alluring. Very alluring.

"Come with me!" Her voice was urgent. "Something's happening here tonight. I don't know what it is!"

Before Tristan had climbed from his bed, she left the room and stood impatiently in the hall. He started to follow her, but she gestured toward his weapon, draped over a chair.

"Bring your sword!"

Without questioning, he strapped the weapon around his waist. As he stepped into the hall, Robyn was disappearing around the corner, so he hurried to catch up.

"What is it?" he whispered, but she did not answer. Instead, she turned into another hall, walking as fast as the flickering candle would allow. In a moment, she stopped before a heavy door and quickly pulled it open.

Inside spiraled the long stairway leading to the platform atop Caer Corwell's high tower. Breathlessly, the pair climbed the stairs, emerging minutes later through the trap door at the top.

The cloudless night sky spread above and around them, sparkling with a wealth of stars. The night air was cool. The moon had not yet risen, so the prince guessed the time at about two o'clock. Robyn extinguished the candle and moved to the parapet, gazing intently into the eastern sky. Nervously drawing his sword, the prince stepped to her side.

"What is it? Should we sound the alarm? Why did you bring me up here in the middle of the night?" The tone of each question grew sharper as the prince's anxiety mounted.

"Please be quiet!" Robyn whispered, and the prince saw that she was concentrating deeply, still staring at the sky.

Puzzled, and a little annoyed, Tristan nonetheless did as she asked. He too stared eastward, and for long moments neither made any sound. Suddenly, Robyn spoke a single word.

"There!"

Following her pointing finger, the prince could see nothing against the starry backdrop. Then, for an instant, a star blinked out, and then on again. Several times this happened, and the prince realized that a flying creature approached. At the same time, he felt Robyn sway slightly and lean against the parapet for support.

"You can put that away," she said finally, gesturing to his sword. "The danger I sensed is distant, and will not menace us tonight."

This time Tristan ignored her, holding the blade ready and squinting to make out the mysterious creature in the sky. In moments he heard the faint whirr of feathery wings, and suddenly the inky form of a huge falcon settled to the parapet before Robyn. The prince recognized Sable, but stifled his announcement as he watched the young woman stare intently into the great bird's unblinking eyes. In moments, she turned to him.

"It's Keren! He's in terrible danger and sent Sable to get help. Tristan, we must go to him! We have to hurry!"

XXXXXXXXXXX

Kamerynn the Unicorn galloped for many days. He thundered across flowered meadows, and raised shimmering curtains of spray as he splashed through shallow streams.

Finally the unicorn entered a region of Myrloch Vale previously unknown to him—a dim region of fens and fetid marsh. He moved more cautiously now, for he knew that his destination was near. Abruptly, he paused, staring intently at a snakelike vine laying casually across his path. Kamerynn's pink nostrils quivered as he checked the air for any menacing scents. His caution turned to alarm as he realized that wrongness was manifest.

Stepping back, the unicorn again regarded the vine. Suddenly, the strand moved, lashing toward his forehoof. Leaping away, the unicorn reared high. At that moment, another vine sailed from the underbrush and a clasping loop settled around Kamerynn's neck.

Now, creatures emerged from cover and attacked. They charged close to throw more clasping vines. Kamerynn's attackers looked like humans, but were much too large.

A sharp hoof lashed out as Kamerynn reared to meet the charge. One of the attackers fell, its thick skull crushed. Another twisted around to the unicorn's flank, but the powerful neck swiveled to meet the attack. Lowering his head, Kamerynn lunged, feeling his ivory horn drive deeply into the creature's body.

But the attackers were too many. They grappled the unicorn's body, first pressing it back, and then bearing it to the ground. In minutes Kamerynn was securely hobbled and blindfolded.

THE FENS OF THE FALLON

7

"There he is!" Robyn's voice called Tristan's attention to a small black dot, soaring among the clouds ahead of them. The maiden kicked the foaming flanks of her steed, and the gray gelding sprang forward.

"Isn't she ever going to rest?" gasped Pawldo, struggling to retain his seating upon his lurching pony.

"I hope so," answered Daryth, cantering smoothly alongside. "But I doubt it will happen while there's a glimmer of daylight left!"

The great falcon soared eagerly eastward, and then circled slowly as the riders below tried to keep up.

"I can't believe we're following a bird!" muttered Pawldo.

"Are you sure she knows what she's doing?" asked Daryth, indicating Robyn. The king's ward was galloping ahead, oblivious to the grumblings of the other riders.

"I trust her," replied Tristan.

Before dawn, they had awakened Daryth and outfitted themselves for the journey. Canthus and several other hounds accompanied them. They had brought four extra horses in order to hold to a rapid pace. Leaving a message for the king, they had ridden forth, delaying only to pass through Lowhill, where Pawldo had not hesitated to join the group.

Now they rode steadily in the saddle the whole of each day, from the first glimmerings of dawn through the final darkness of night. They stopped for the night where sunset found them.

The coat of chain mail rested comfortably on the prince's shoulders, reminding him of his father's wish. Idly, Tristan wondered who would command the Corwell company now. He tried not to think about his father's anger upon his return. But he had to trust Robyn; somewhere, Keren was in deep trouble.

They paused, late in the afternoon of the fourth day, to exchange horses and stretch their stiffening muscles. While the men grunted in anguish and painfully tried to work the kinks out of their legs and backs, Robyn stared silently skyward. Finally, as they mounted again, she spoke.

"He's turning to the north. He means for us to follow up one of these valleys. I think he's leading us to Myrloch Vale."

"Hold it a minute!" Pawldo's voice squeaked with indignation despite his fatigue. "Myrloch? That place smacks of sorcery! Best leave it to the Llewyrr—it's no place for humans or halflings."

"I shall follow Sable," Robyn announced quietly, mounting and kicking her horse forward.

"And so shall I," said the prince, though Robyn's mention of Myrloch had brought a chill to his own heart.

"I think sorcery is kind of interesting," admitted Daryth. "Do you really think we'll see some magic?"

"We'll be lucky to ride out in the same bodies we take in!" grumbled Pawldo, but he nonetheless mounted and accompanied the others. The three had to gallop for several minutes to catch up with Robyn. They found her, halted, in the center of the road, examining a narrow trail to the side.

She looked up at their approach. "This looks like a trail. With luck, it'll take us over the highlands into Myrloch."

"Some luck," grunted Pawldo softly, as they left the road, passing along the path in single file.

The narrow path wound among vast trunks of oak, hickory, and yew—a place with the look of a forest that had never felt the woodsman's axe.

For the rest of the day they moved steadily along the shaded path. Ever upward it climbed, moving among great piles of boulders, fording shallow streams, and always holding the general bearing of north. In places the forest opened into small meadows, and they caught sight of the great falcon, circling impatiently as it waited for the time-consuming passage of the earthbound humans.

Finally darkness provided them a respite from the long hours in the saddle. The moon, nearly full, cast glaring shadows among the huge trunks surrounding their camp. They built a small fire, taking care that it smoked little and that its light was screened.

"We'd better keep watches," suggested the prince. "This is still part of the Kingdom of Corwell, but with Firbolgs and whatever else abroad—"

"Who lives here?" asked Daryth, looking around at the pristine wilderness of their surroundings.

"Very few people—mostly Ffolk who are hunters, or shepherds—people who like the wild places more than they like companionship," answered Tristan.

"Aye. And we're not far from the lands of the Llweyrr!" declared Pawldo, looking over his shoulders and suppressing a shudder. "I sense magic!"

"There is no danger here," Robyn said quietly, staring into the small campfire.

"Still, I'll vote with Tristan to keep guard. I'll take the first watch. " Daryth climbed stiffly to his feet and looked around.

"As you wish," replied Robyn, shrugging. "I'll take a turn at guard, too."

The others exchanged uneasy glances, but no one said anything.

They remained vigilant, in shifts, but the night passed without disturbance. They ate cold bread and cheese for breakfast, but even before they finished, the black falcon had launched himself northward from his perch in a tall pine, decreeing that his followers quickly take to the trail again.

Their route climbed steadily, toward the crest of the ridge separating the kingdom of Corwell from the realms of the Llewyrr—Myrloch Vale. As the morning progressed they encountered patches of snow still lying in shadowed places throughout the woods. The higher they climbed, the more snow-covered ground they saw. By noon, they plodded through wet, slushy snow with every step. In places, melting drifts still three or four feet deep covered the path.

After several hours, they finally emerged from the trees onto the rocky upper slopes of the highlands. These rolling mountaintops, subjected to the continual light of the sun, had long ago lost their snowy mantle. Now the companions made good time as the trail wound even higher. Still the falcon soared far ahead.

Robyn rode beside Daryth for much of the afternoon, talking and, occasionally, laughing. Tristan rode at the rear of the party, with Pawldo. He wanted to join them, but felt reluctant to intrude. Robyn and Daryth seemed to share some private agreement. Pawldo was good company, but the hours passed very slowly.

By nightfall, they could see their destination: a high pass in the jagged ridgeline. The trail twisted treacherously among lower peaks before emerging along a sheer cliff and following a narrow ledge to the summit. Sable, an almost invisible speck, hovered over the pass.

They camped in a small clump of miniature pines that somehow managed to survive at this high altitude. The pines sheltered one end of a small lake in a narrow valley. Great sheets of ice floated in the water, and a freezing wind howled through the small vale, but this scant shelter seemed to be the only place not exposed directly to the elements.

The pines provided enough wood for a small fire, and a three-sided niche among the boulders gave respite from the persistent wind. They ate without enthusiasm, and sat quietly staring into the fire. Finally, Daryth broke the silence.

"What is it about this Myrloch Vale? Why do I feel you all just oozing apprehension? It's as if you don't expect to come out of it again!" His bluntness took the party by surprise.

Tristan thought back to the tales he had learned as a child, surprised to realize that he had taken them so seriously. "Well, it's more legend than fact," he said. "When humans first came to the Moonshaes, the Llewyrr—the elvenfolk—lived on all of the islands. As humankind spread, the Llewyrr retreated eventually to the valley just beyond this final ridge—Myrloch Vale."

"The Llewyrr do not brook trespassers lightly," added Pawldo. "The small folk have tales that'll shrivel your ears—the Llewyrr have a ring of magic around the place that'll fry anyone trying to pass it. Their wizards! No one knows what dark secrets of sorcery they practice! They'll turn us into snails, or worse—if the barrier leaves any parts of us to turn!"

Robyn laughed—the first laughter any of them had heard this long day. "It's really a little less harmful than all of that!"

"Since when are you such an expert?" Pawldo shot back, insulted that the veracity of his exaggerations had been questioned.

Robyn looked surprised. "I don't know where I became such an expert, but I don't think we have much to worry about—not from the Llewyrr, anyway."

"What *should* we worry about?" asked the prince.

"That I'm not so sure of . . . although Firbolgs come to mind, as a place to start."

"At least Firbolgs we can see!" grumbled Pawldo, turning his back to the fire and curling up to sleep. "I'll take the middle watch," he added.

"I'll take the first," volunteered Tristan, climbing stiffly to his feet and poking into the trees for more firewood. The others soon slept, and the prince stood a lonely vigil. Soon Canthus joined him, and the two paced steadily around the camp. They seemed to be the only living creatures in this barren stretch of highlands—at least Tristan hoped they were.

The moorhound never seemed to sleep. He paced with Tristan as the prince paced, or sat alertly next to him when he rested. Canthus sat as an equal, however—he never rested his head upon the prince's knee, or flopped carelessly at his feet, as would any other dog. His posture erect, he perked his ears at any faint sound, and constantly sniffed the faint breeze for information.

Tristan sighed, and turned to look at Robyn. She slept soundly, nearly buried by a massive fur blanket, her black hair spread like a veil across her face. Then the prince's gaze shifted to the slender, swarthy Calishite, tossing unevenly on the other side of the fire.

What did that wonderful girl—woman!—think of these men, her closest friends? Which did she prefer? Desperately, Tristan wanted to know. Robyn stretched, luxuriously, and slowly rolled over, and for a moment Tristan was tempted to wake her and take her in his arms. He chuckled wryly as he pictured her reaction, and turned away to resume his watch.

Each of them took their turn at the watch, and Canthus accompanied them all, but the night passed without incident. They broke camp with the dawn, picking their way slowly up the last treacherous slopes leading to the pass. Fortunately, the slope faced primarily south, and the snow had long since melted away. Though the path was still treacherous, at least they had the security of walking along solid ground.

"We'd better dismount and walk the horses over this part," called Tristan.

Robyn reined in and turned, as if to argue, but then she studied the terrain before them.

"All right," she answered. "But hurry!"

Moving as quickly as possible, which still meant picking footings with great care, they moved along the narrow ledge, often kicking free stones that seemingly tumbled for minutes before striking the jagged rocks far below.

Finally, at midday, they turned from the narrow ledge and walked into the high, windswept pass. Behind them stretched miles of rocky highlands and dense forests. The pastoral farmlands of Corwell were invisible in the haze of distance.

And ahead of them, seen by each for the first time, lay Myrloch Vale.

The glimmering blue waters of Myrloch itself were barely visible. Many smaller lakes dotted the nearer landscape, and rows upon rows of craggy peaks stretched away to the right and left. The trail to the north of the pass descended steeply across a wide, snowy slope, into a lush forest of aspen and pine.

Broad meadows, bright with flowers, broke the green canopy of the forests. Sparkling waterfalls, too numerous to count, spilled from the highlands into the vale, feeding the many brooks that created a silvery network of waterways connecting the many lakes.

In one place only, below them and to their right, did Myrloch Vale seem unhealthy. A sprawling region of spindly, leafless tree trunks surrounded a marshy fen. Numerous ponds spotted the area, but did not seem to sparkle with the sunlight as usually did the water elsewhere.

Much of the fen was obscured by thick growths of tangled brush, and slumping, mossy trees.

Sable circled away from the pass in a long dive. The falcon glided straight toward the boggy fens.

As the companions passed over the summit, staring in awe at the scene before them, each felt a little prickle across the scalp, as if lightning was prepared to strike nearby. Yet the sky was cloudless.

"Magic!" barked Pawldo, nervously scratching the back of his neck. "Mark my words—we'll all be salamanders if we take another step into this accursed place!"

Nonetheless, he accompanied his friends through the pass, looking suspiciously about, as if expecting an attack at any moment. Nothing happened, however, and he joined the inspection of the slope before them as the group searched for a way down. The sun had not yet cleared the north-facing slope of the ridge of its snow cover, and a white carpet lay thick across the highlands. Tristan could easily imagine the deep drifts they would encounter when they reached the woods.

Robyn started boldly forward, leading two horses, and the others fell into file behind her. They alternated as leader, and for several hours they made good time, dropping across the slope toward a steeper area where the highlands fell to the timberline.

Tristan, hurrying up to join Robyn, said, "All of you wait a minute while I check this snow."

"Wait!" cried Robyn. "It's too weak to hold—"

Before she had finished her warning he had already felt the snow shift under his feet. With a loud crack, the surface slipped to the side and crumbled onto the long, steep slope, carrying Tristan with it. The great slab of wet snow picked up speed rapidly, and Tristan lost the reins of his horse as he fell. The slab began to break apart, and the prince fell between the huge chunks of soggy snow, struggling to keep his head free of the choking mess.

Like a plummeting sled, the snow began to pick up speed, gathering more wet snow as it fell. The prince caught a glimpse of the shelf of snow above him cracking free, dropping his companions into the avalanche behind him.

Snow smashed into Tristan's face, blinding him, and filling his mouth and nose. Desperately, he scraped it away, still kicking madly to stay on top of the stuff. He got a quick look at the smooth slope before him—at the bottom, a clear blue lake glimmered placidly.

Conscious for the first time of the real weight of his chain mail, Tristan knew that the lake meant a freezing, suffocating death, for there was no way he could swim in the metal garb.

He tried to scramble to the side, but the rolling surface gave him no footing. Clawing at the snow with his bare hands, he felt his skin scrape, and he cried out in pain as a fingernail was torn off.

Twisting, he pulled his sword, and drove the tip deep into the snow, cursing as the blade snapped off at the hilt. But gradually, the momentum of the slide slowed as the slope grew less steep. Finally, he managed to stick the broken blade of his sword deep enough into the subsurface to drag him to a halt. Snow still tumbled past him, and he heard it splashing into the lake below.

Tristan's gray mare slid past, screaming in terror and scrambling for a foothold. The creature splashed into the icy water and disappeared under tons of heavy snow. The slide had narrowed, and the prince now lay just outside its path. Exhausted and barely conscious, he saw Robyn tumble limply past. As the snow carried her into the lake, however, she sprang free and splashed into the water, well away from the avalanche. Swimming strongly, she made her way to shore.

And then his other companions passed, seemingly in a single mass of horses, humans—and halfling. Pawldo clung to the neck of his pony as the animal hit the water and swam away. Daryth and the other horses stopped close to the water's edge as the slide's momentum finally dissipated.

"Are you all right?" called the Calishite up the hill.

"I think so," replied Tristan. He saw Robyn climb from the lake, and the rest of the horses swim to shore, Pawldo still clinging desperately to his pony. "Have you seen the dogs?"

"No," answered Daryth, concerned. "Wait—look up there!"

Tristan turned to see the hounds bounding down the slope, next to the path of the slide. They had somehow managed to break free of the avalanche while it was still high upon the mountain, and now made their way to the companions.

They had lost only one horse—Tristan's—in the slide, but all of the prince's extra clothing had been strapped to the unfortunate steed. Robyn pulled several woolen cloaks from her saddlebags. Though the material was still sodden, they were able to huddle underneath them and gradually feel warm.

"One thing's for certain," announced the prince, looking up the slope they had descended so precipitously. "If we're going to leave Myrloch Vale, it'll have to be by a different route!"

The others, too, looked up the steep slope and were silent, until Robyn, sounding almost cheerful, said, "At least not until the snow melts. And that won't be for a couple more months."

"Cheerful thought," moaned Pawldo. "I knew we should—"

"There's Sable!" cried Robyn, cutting short the halfling's lament. "He's not far away!"

Tristan realized that their slide, while dangerous, had carried them in several minutes over ground that would have taken the rest of the day to cross by more conventional means. The great falcon circled several miles away, still over the fens they had seen from the summit.

"Let's go," the prince suggested, and they quickly adjusted their gear to resume the march.

The snow cover diminished as they picked a steadily descending trail among a lush forest of aspens. In several hours, they dropped more than a thousand feet, and soon walked along a dry dirt trail. But soon the aspens withered and thinned, and the wildflowers became nonexistent. The path dropped farther, finally ending at the edge of a murky pond. All around sprawled a wasteland of fetid pools, rank grasses, and soggy turf. Occasional copses of stunted trees broke the landscape, but even these looked scraggly and unhealthy.

"Let's stop and camp," suggested Tristan.

"Hear, hear!" agreed the halfling. "You won't get me into those fens at night! I smell sorcery."

"We must go on," pleaded Robyn, "for Keren's sake! It can't be much farther!"

"They're right," said Daryth, nodding to Pawldo and Tristan. "It would be madness to enter that swamp in the dark of night."

Robyn turned away, and for a moment they wondered if she would plunge into the fens without them. Then, she sighed and looked back.

"You're right. Why don't we try to build a little fire and dry out? But we move at first light, all right?"

The others agreed, and they set about making camp. Tristan built a small fire to dry out soggy clothes and warm chilled bones. As always, they divided the night into watches, and Tristan again took the first shift.

His nerves on edge, the prince called Canthus to him and walked slowly around the perimeter of their small camp. Tristan had always felt that, somehow, he led a charmed existence, that he need fear nothing—except his father. But now, more than ever before, he felt a sense of apprehension—a certainty that something, or someone, watched from beyond the circle of light.

And he didn't like it!

Gripping his knife, Tristan strode back and forth, staring into the encloaking darkness. Even the stars seemed dimmed, as if a thin haze filtered their light on this nervewracking night.

Then he saw a flicker of movement.

Freezing, he stared at the spot, and again saw a glimmer of light. Canthus, too, saw it, and growled deep in his chest. Tristan, his knife drawn, moved toward the spot, feeling a strange attraction. As stealthily as he could, he picked his way across the wet ground. He seemed to draw close to the light, but then it moved away, drifting deeper into the fens. Hurrying, he followed. The light dipped and floated through a thicket, and the prince tore at the brush in his eagerness to get through. Canthus, whining, followed.

Tristan burst free from the thicket and lunged into a clearing, Canthus bounding beside him. Suddenly, he felt clutching mire close around his ankles, then his knees, then his waist. With a strangled gasp of panic, the prince turned to flee, but felt the clutching muck rise across his stomach toward his chest.

Canthus, surprisingly, bounded across the surface of the mire, only to pause and look back curiously at the prince. Dropping his knife, Tristan tried to swim, clawing desperately with his hands, but they moved too slowly to help. The apprehension he had felt had changed abruptly to fear, fear that the charm of his life had ended. Choking, he felt cold slime enter his mouth.

The prince's mind noted, as if it were a matter of no import, that the muck had no taste, nor could he smell it. Squeezing, he felt it slide through his fingers, and then fade. He reached around freely, and realized that he was not sinking in some stinking bog. Instead, he lay upon a patch of dry ground.

Suddenly a chittering voice, sounding only a few feet away, broke into a volley of giggles. Overcome with laughter, the creature nonetheless managed to spit out a few words.

"Oh my . . . that was splendid! Hee, hee—Oh, perfectly marvelous!"

Looking around, the prince could not see the speaker.

"Oh, oh! If only you could have seen the look in your eyes! I say, I have never seen anything so funny in all my seven hundred and eighty four-years!" With a soft *pop*, the creature suddenly exploded into view, still convulsed with laughter.

"Can you do it again? Oh, I'd love to see it again!"

In shock, Tristan stared into the eyes, less than an arm's length from his face, of a tiny dragon. The creature's toothy mouth was spread into a wide grin.

XXXXXXXXXX

Grunnarch looked with foul temper at the Iron Keep. Whatever business one of his captains had meeting Thelgaar Ironhand, it was now getting in the way of the loading.

"Send Laric to me when he returns," the Red King commanded.

The men of Thelgaar Ironhand, meantime, spent the day desecrating the sleek lines of their longships by attaching heavy iron rams to the prow of each ship.

Grunnarch heard that Thelgaar himself would inspect the attachment of each ram. Already there were rumors of the Iron King caressing the rusted metal, muttering some sort of mysterious chant as it was affixed to the hull. Who could see the point of such long and heavy beams, sure to throw off the balance of the seaworthy longships? Perhaps, if the Ffolk possessed a fleet capable of resisting the invasion, the rams might render some useful purpose. But the Ffolk would choose to fight on land, so no one could see the point of naval armament.

Nonetheless, Thelgaar gave his orders with a fiery intensity that allowed no man to question his authority, and so the men mounted the rams, and the grumbling came only in whispered huddles.

And still Laric had not returned from the Iron Keep.

Grunnarch made his way to a large bonfire at nightfall, for there Thelgaar had summoned the kings of the northmen for a last council of war. He found Raag Hammerstaad and the other kings present. Laric, too, stood beside the great blaze, but he ignored his liege lord. His attention remained fixed upon the person of the Iron King.

Thelgaar stood before the fire, flames casting orange and red flashes of light over him. As Grunnarch reached the circle of kings, Thelgaar fixed him with an intent gaze. Grunnarch suppressed a shudder, thinking that the bonfire paled in companson to the raging intensity of the Iron King's stare.

"You, King of Norland," began Thelgaar, "have a most important task in this undertaking."

Grunnarch noticed that Thelgaar spoke to him as he would speak to a vassal, not a peer. He nevertheless listened quietly, for something about the Iron King's manner forbade resistance.

"Here is Gwynneth," announced Thelgaar. Grunnarch saw that he had sketched a crude map into the sand at his feet. "The men of Norland and Norheim shall sail here," he ordered, pointing to a spot on the eastern coast of the island.

"You will land here, and here, and here—ravaging all of the communities of the Ffolk along that shore. This will certainly send a crowd of refugees fleeing west, along the road. " Now Thelgaar drew a line across the waist of the island from the eastern coast to Caer Corwell itself.

"You will send enough warriors to maintain the pursuit. The rest of your force will circle around to the north, passing through the mountains to get before the refugees, trapping them here."

Grunnarch's mouth went suddenly dry. The path Thelgaar had indicated passed through Myrloch Vale—a fell place indeed for an army of northmen.

His protest was anticipated.

"There will be no danger!" Thelgaar's voice rang triumphantly. "In fact, as you enter the Vale, you shall be joined by an army of Firbolgs. I have arranged for a spy to show you the hidden pathways of Myrloch. With his aid, you will pass safely."

Grunnarch's superstitious nature prickled with alarm, but he suppressed the urge to object. Thelgaar continued.

"All the Ffolk of eastern Gwynneth will be caught in this trap. You will slay the men and old Ffolk. The rest you shall take as slaves."

All the kings gathered around the fire stood in shocked silence. The wars with the Ffolk had been bloody, savage affairs, yet never had they set out with the objective of annihilating a population. Still, Thelgaar's commanding presence brooked no argument, nor was any made.

With a grim half-smile, the Iron King looked around before continuing. Grunnarch had trouble believing that this was the same king who had counseled peace less than a fortnight earlier.

"You will then resume the march, joining me here, at Caer Corwell. If we have succeeded in reducing the fortress, our task will be completed at this point. If not, your forces will join with mine in the destruction of the last stronghold of the Ffolk upon Gwynneth!"

The plan was exceedingly bold—far beyond the scope of the usual raiding expedition. Yet it seemed solid, in so far as Grunnarch could see, try though he may to spot a flaw.

"Who is this spy?" he asked, for this was the weakest part of the plan.

"He is . . . a druid."

Gasps of astonishment arose from the group. "How can you expect us to trust one of that sinister circle?" Grunnarch expressed their doubts. "The druids are the very heart of the Ffolk's strength!"

Thelgaar Ironhand smiled—a cold, cruel grimace that bore no hint of humor. "That is why this one makes such an excellent spy. And, I assure you, he is quite worthy of your trust."

Grunnarch now had serious misgivings, but a look from the Iron King silenced him before he could speak. Again the Iron King went on.

"He is called Trahern, and you need not worry about his loyalty. He is quite devoted . . . to me, personally. He will place a series of cairns along the trail you are to follow, revealing the secret ways into Myrloch Vale."

Grunnarch's misgivings passed unspoken as the meeting ended. Something about Thelgaar Ironhand had projected such unassailable confidence that any argument would have seemed futile even had it been uttered. Yet it was with vague discomfort that he left the bonfire to join his men.

Kazgoroth, in the body of the Iron King, watched Grunnarch leave, and was pleased. That one, it felt certain, would perform as expected. The eastern cantrevs of Corwell would burn to ashes beneath the might of the northmen's invasion.

It also watched Laric, captain of the Bloodriders. That one, Kazgoroth felt sure, would not fail. Even if the Red King did not accomplish his objective, the red-robed horsemen most certainly would. Across the fire, Laric looked back at Thelgaar. The red gleam in his eyes seemed to come from more than simple reflected firelight.

Slowly, Kazgoroth swiveled its gaze to the vast, placid sea. Great swells rolled softly beyond the cozy protection of Iron Bay. Tomorrow Kazgoroth in the body of Thelgaar Ironhand would lead a second fleet of longships southward, directly toward Corwell. The long rams would slow the progress of the fleet, and increase its danger. Yet they would serve a necessary purpose before the end.

For Kazgoroth knew with certainty that the Leviathan awaited them.

XXXXXXXXXXX

A low, deep growl rumbled from Canthus's chest as the great dog regarded the dragon. The hound did not attack, however, because the prince remained too astounded to issue such a command. Surprise mingled with annoyance, at the rude trick the dragon had played on him, and amusement at the dragon's appearance.

For this dragon was only a little over two feet long.

Fluttering daintily on gossamer wings, the bright blue creature hovered before him. His little paws were clasped together before his chest, his eyes sparkled with intelligence and humor, and a thin, snakelike tail wriggled behind him. Suddenly the little creature disappeared, but a few seconds later he popped back into sight. He repeated the process erratically, becoming invisible briefly and then blinking back and forth.

Finally the prince burst out laughing. The little creature reacted with glee, clapping his forepaws quickly and giggling in a high-pitched voice.

"Oh, I say, this is simply splendid. You have a sense of humor, too! Why, everyone else I play a little prank upon seems to get all twisted about! They really, sometimes, say the nastiest things! Why, if you only knew—"

"Hold," cried the prince. "Who, or what, are you? And why did you lure me out here?"

"Why, I'm Newt. I thought you knew. I thought everybody knew. Oh dear, I thought I was much more famous than all that!" The dragon looked deeply distressed, but then just shook his head and continued.

"And why? Well, for the fun of it, of course. Don't you know anything? Still, I should say, you don't look like you live around here. The ones that live here are much bigger than you—and a good sight uglier, I might add, if you won't get a big head. I mean, it's not like you're the most handsome—"

"Wait!" The prince finally interrupted the flow of chatter. His mind whirled from keeping up with the dragon. "*Who* lives around here? Where?" The dragon's description had naturally reminded the prince of the dread Firbolgs.

"Well, now," the dragon began, obviously pleased at having a partner in conversation. "They live in the Big Cave—here in the fens. They look like you, as, of course, I said already, except they're much taller and broader and, well, hairier, and their noses are huge, I mean they just hang out of their faces like a limb hangs off a tree, and, well, they smell bad, and—"

"I think I understand," Tristan blurted, trying to stem the flow of words. "Can you show me where this Big Cave is?"

"Why, certainly," Newt said proudly. "Just follow me!"

In an instant, the little dragon disappeared.

"Wait!" cried the prince, afraid that Newt was gone forever. In a like instant, however, the creature returned to hover before him, regarding him with pity.

"My, but you are slow. If you want to creep along, well, it'll take us all night to get there, and I'll just have to have a bite to eat before we go because, you see, flying like this is very hard work, very hard work indeed. If I don't eat, well, I'll just collapse in a heap, and then I won't be of any use to anybody, least of all you or me, who are the people I could be of some use to if I had something to—"

Tristan burst out laughing, to Newt's obvious chagrin. The little dragon sniffed, hoisted his scaly snout into the air, and turned his back on the prince.

"I'm sorry," the prince said. "But my friends are camped over . . ." He turned, and realized he hadn't the slightest notion of where he was.

"Oh, them," the dragon said, obviously disappointed.

"I thought that perhaps the two of us . . ."

"They are my companions on a quest to save a man's life!" Tristan said sternly. "I cannot abandon them, though we would welcome your company. I have a feeling that the Big Cave will hold the answers to several of our questions."

"Very well. " The little dragon heaved a massive sigh of resignation. But he proceeded to lead Tristan swiftly through the fen, forcing the prince to stumble often in the darkened thickets. Nonetheless, the dragon followed a path over dry ground, allowing the human to avoid the many ponds and marshes sprawling across his path.

Tristan ran, stumbled, and crawled forward for nearly half an hour. He grew more and more amazed at the way the dragon had drawn him away from the camp. He had assumed that it was at most five minutes away. Finally, he crashed through a thicket of thorny branches into the circle of firelight. All of his companions, awake, stared at him in astonishment.

"What in the world happened to you?" cried Robyn in a mixture of relief and alarm. "We were just getting ready to start searching."

Pawldo, meanwhile, jumped backward and drew his sword. "Dragon!" he cried, confronting Newt with the steely tip. For his part, the little dragon blinked out of sight, reappearing behind the prince and staring huffily over his shoulder.

"This is Newt," Tristan explained, and introduced his companions in return.

"Newt sort of played a joke on me, and the next thing I knew I was out somewhere in the middle of the fens!"

"I knew it!" Pawldo's voice quivered with righteous indignation. "Sorcery!"

"Well, I've never been so insulted in my life!" It was Newt's turn for indignation. "Sorcery my scales! It's nothing more than a little visual-tactile illusion, and perhaps some minor hypnosis, but *not* sorcery! Why, I've a good mind to make you find the Big Cave yourselves, or maybe I'll just go tell those big ugly people that you're here, and let them come and take care of you!"

"Wait a minute," interjected Tristan, turning to his friends. "Newt has told me about some creatures that have built a 'big cave' around here. I bet they are Firbolgs and that is where Keren is!"

"Who's Keren?" asked Newt.

"Our friend—we're here to try and rescue him. He's the greatest bard among the Ffolk!" said Tristan.

"Oh, the bard!" Newt squealed with excitement at the recognition. "I saw them bring him in—he's probably dead by now. I hope that doesn't mean you'll go home, does it? Oh, I would hate that—and just when we're starting to—"

"Dead?" Robyn's face went white. "Are you sure?"

"Well, no," replied the dragon, miffed at the interruption. "He might be alive, but when they dragged him into the Big Cave, he didn't look too good."

"We must find out!" declared Tristan. "Will you show us the cave?"

"Not if you keep up this talk about sorcery and sordid stuff like that!" With remarkable conciseness, Newt stated his point.

"We're sorry," Tristan said. "We won't do it again, will we . . . Pawldo?"

The halfling looked about to object, but instead he grunted his agreement.

"Well, after a little bite to eat, I'll show you." Newt came to rest next to a saddlebag of provisions, and curiously looked inside. "Hmmm, cheese . . . oh my, and sausage! How splendid!"

In a second, the little dragon had pulled forth a link of sausage as long as himself and begun to devour it. He followed it with two loaves of bread, a massive cake of cheese, and a flask of red wine. He was about to delve back into the saddlebag when Tristan seized upon the excuse of the approaching dawn.

"Could you show us the cave now? It really is most urgent."

The little dragon looked reluctant, but then contemplated his swollen belly, and decided he would not starve in the next few hours.

"It's not far," promised Newt, proceeding to lead them through a horrible entanglement of branches, thorns, and vines. In several places Tristan or Daryth had to hack a path through the growth with their swords. The dragon proved as good as his word, however. As they crossed a flat and marshy clearing, Newt looked over his shoulder and whispered conspiratorially. "The Big Cave is right up here, through these bushes."

Silently they tethered the horses in the thicket, and carefully probed forward. Tristan and Robyn advanced side by side, with Newt fluttering along above him. Soon they reached the shelter of a low hummock, and looked around it into a great clearing. Before them stood the Big Cave. It was some sort of large stone structure—perhaps a temple, or fortress. Above the great building soared the black falcon, Sable.

× × × × × × × × × ×

The leviathan sensed the presence of the fleet as soon as it broached the waters beyond Iron Bay. Dimly, the creature understood the threat these ships posed to the goddess. It resolutely turned toward the longships, still many miles away.

Slowly, the great tail propelled the creature through the sea, occasionally sending the great body to the surface to breathe. Then its head would dive again, the sinuous body rolling across the surface behind it for an impossibly long time.

Finally the great tail would lift above the waves. The leviathan raised it high, perhaps in a gesture of challenge, and then slapped it against the surface to propel itself deeper and deeper.

For many days it rolled thus, breaking water to breathe, and then plunging far beneath the surface to swim. As it moved, it sensed the threat far before it. A perversion had entered the water, befouling a Balance of the clean sea, and laying a clear challenge before the leviathan.

The befoulment grew stronger as the leviathan moved northward. It spread across the sea like a cancerous poison, clogging the creature's breathing hole, and stinging its eyes. Resolutely, however, the leviathan advanced.

Soon would come the time for killing.

THE BIG CAVE

8

Once again the full moon poured its irresistible rays over the sleeping village of Corwell. Erian, alone in his cottage, dreaded the rise of the moon, but as its light washed across him he had no choice but to succumb to the summoning force.

As the first twinges of change wracked his body, he smashed open the door of his cottage and ran through the quiet, moonlit streets. The shadowy bulk of Caer Corwell loomed to his right as he splashed through Corlyth Creek at the ford just north of town.

His feet pounded the turf in panic as he sprinted, trying to get as far away as possible. Abruptly, a convulsion wracked his body and he tumbled to the ground, rolling in agony across the grass.

Landing on his back, he lay helpless because his limbs did not respond to his command. Instead they twitched and thrashed with a will of their own. He tried to avert his face, to bury it in the darkness of the earth, but the glowing orb of the moon called to him with such force that he could only gaze skyward. His eyes wide, he felt the stabbing force of the moon burning into his skull.

His body contorted through the changes wrought by the bite of Kazgoroth two months before. Hair, fangs, claws all sprouted. His limbs twisted and shrank. Finally a tortured howl broke from his lips, ringing across the moor and silencing every creature within hearing.

Erian climbed to his four feet and padded softly forward. His tongue lolled heavily from gaping, fang-studded jaws. His sensitive nostrils searched the air, soon catching wind of a fat cow. His path took him inland, away from Corwell. He broke into a lope, drooling in anticipation of the kill.

This time he would eat very well.

✗ ✗ ✗ ✗ ✗ ✗ ✗ ✗ ✗

"I told you!" boasted Newt.

"What is that?" whispered Tristan.

"It's an affront to the land!" The prince turned, startled at the vehemence in Robyn's voice. Her jaw was clenched tightly shut, and he saw tears welling in her eyes.

"What do you mean?"

"Can't you see?" She talked as if he were being very stupid.

Tristan looked. He saw huge stone walls, running for a hundred paces to the right and left of where they lay. Much of the surface of the walls was streaked with green moss or climbing tendrils of weeds—but in other places the stone was bare and gray. For the most part the walls were smooth and featureless, but the top of the structure was lined with a row of hideously grinning gargoyles. The stone creatures looked down upon the approaches to the structure, their crystalline eyes seeming to glitter with malevolence.

Tristan, Robyn, and Newt lay behind a fallen tree trunk. They stared in awe at the massive structure.

Directly before them, a pair of huge wooden doors at least ten feet high stood between several wide columns. A deep pathway led from the doors into the depths of the fens, passing very near to their hiding place.

"But what is it? Why is it here?" Tristan could find no clue in the building's appearance. All he knew was that he felt a very definite threat from the structure.

"Its purpose is to menace the goddess," stated Robyn.

The stout walls seemed fortresslike in their strength, yet they contained no apertures through which defenders could fight.

Noiselessly, Daryth slid forward until he was alongside Tristan and

Robyn. The Calishite pursed his lips in a silent whistle as he looked at the building.

"Pawldo and I will slip around behind it," he whispered.

"Be careful!" the prince urged. He saw that the halfling was nearby, and then all of a sudden Pawldo and Daryth were gone—vanished into the underbrush with scarcely a sound.

"Um," said Newt after a few minutes. The little dragon had been visibly restraining himself and could manage no longer. "Maybe I'll go keep an eye on the foo—I mean, the horses. " He quickly blinked out of sight.

All day—Pawldo and Daryth from the rear and the prince and the maiden from the entrance—observed the strange structure. Once, the great doors opened and several Firbolgs emerged, tromping heavily down the path. Later, toward the end of the day, a score of the misshapen monsters marched back up the path. The leader pounded the doors with his club, and they quickly opened to admit the column.

Each time the door opened, Tristan strained to see inside the black hole. No guards were visible, but it would have been foolhardy to risk an approach. Their little band would not stand a chance against an army of Firbolgs.

Finally, Tristan and Robyn wriggled back along the ground to the small clearing where they had tethered the horses. There they found Pawldo and Daryth, as well as Newt. The little dragon was busy putting a large dent in a massive slab of cheese.

"What did you find?" Tristan asked.

"There's another set of doors at the rear—even bigger than those at the front," Daryth replied. "Must be some kind of back door or escape route. I heard all kinds of noise behind 'em."

"You went up to the doors?" Tristan was appalled.

"The fellow sneaks pretty well, let me tell you," Pawldo said, amused. "I was right behind him, and I didn't know he was there!"

"And what did you hear?" asked Robyn.

"I'm not sure. It sounded like some kind of digging, or maybe chopping. They might have been building something or excavating, but there were a bunch of those monsters in the next room! Nobody came in or went out, though, not while we were watching."

"There seems to be no way around it. " The prince spoke low. "We'll have to go in through the front door."

Tristan did not feel very heroic at the thought. What would a true hero—what would Cymrych Hugh have done at a time like this?

"We might wait for nightfall. Maybe they'll all go to sleep." But there wasn't much hope in Robyn's voice even as she made the suggestion.

"Well, all this seems very silly to me!" announced Newt. "Why don't you just go in through the tunnel?"

"What tunnel?"

"Naturally, the tunnel that leads into the Big Cave. Why, what other tunnel could I possibly be speaking of? My, but you all are a little short on brains sometimes!"

"Why didn't you tell us about this tunnel?" demanded the prince through his teeth.

"Because no one asked me, of course!" sniffed Newt. "Why, I should think that would be obvious even to such, well, dimwits as yourselves— no offense, of course, but you people could really stand to do a little more thinking!"

Tristan began a sharp reply, but quickly bit his tongue. Perhaps there was some truth to the dragon's words. After all, they had seen that he knew his way around the fens, and yet it had not occurred to him, or any of them, to ask him what else he knew.

"Maybe, if you show us where this tunnel is, even we dimwits can find a way to help our friend," the prince said. "That is, if you're quite finished eating."

"Well," said Newt, looking wistfully at the last saddlebag of provisions. "It'll keep. Now follow me, and try not to do anything really stupid."

Tristan signaled Canthus to "guard," knowing that the other hounds would remain with him. The dogs should provide some discouragement to anyone or anything who stumbled on the horses. They each selected weapons. Pawldo carried his bow and shortsword, while Daryth fingered his dagger and wrapped a long coil of rope about his shoulders. Tristan took his longbow and knife, while Robyn still carried the stout oaken cudgel she had made in Llyrath Forest.

Shortly, Newt led them to the tunnel, and the prince immediately felt more optimistic. The opening proved to be a scum-lined drainage pipe, emptying water from the building into a fetid marsh several hundred yards away. Measuring nearly six feet in diameter, it emerged from the building into the wall of a shallow gulley.

"Let's make some torches," suggested the prince upon seeing that the passageway swiftly disappeared into darkness.

They found many dried reeds near the entrance, and swiftly bound the stalks into effective torches. Each burned with a nearly smokeless, yet very bright, flame. The torches seemed to burn rapidly, however, so they carried several extras.

"I wonder if they'll have anything for us to eat," asked Newt, eagerly buzzing around as they prepared.

Tristan paused, carefully considering his objections. For a moment he thought about bringing the dragon along. Perhaps that would be safer than leaving him with the supplies. But he discarded the idea as impetuously rash. There was no telling what the unpredictable Newt would do in the midst of a battle, or when they were trying to move very quietly.

"Newt," the prince said, seriously. "We need someone brave and very, very smart to stay and watch the dogs and horses. Of course, that one will have to keep an eye on all our food, and supplies. Would you consider performing this important service for us? I don't think any of these other 'dimwits' could handle that."

For a moment, he thought that the little blue creature would argue, but Newt quickly reconsidered the prospect.

"Well, all right, but you'll have to tell me all about what it's like in there. I've always wanted to go in, but never really had the time in my busy day before."

"We promise!" answered the prince. "Wait with the horses, and we will see you very soon!"

"Good-bye!" called the dragon, already heading toward the saddle-bags.

The prince turned to his friends. "Be careful," he cautioned. "And be prepared for anything!"

Robyn and Daryth took burning torches and followed Tristan into the tunnel. The passage widened enough immediately that Tristan and Robyn could walk side by side in the lead, while Daryth followed them and Pawldo brought up the rear. The little halfling walked carefully backward, keeping an arrow nocked and ready.

As Tristan walked deeper into the tunnel, he felt his feet sink into clutching mud. The stuff came up to his ankles, making each step hard work. In several places a pool of chilly water spread across the tunnel, splashing as high as his calves. Pawldo was forced to hold his bow horizontally at shoulder height.

Soon the thin rays of light filtering in the tunnel entrance disappeared behind them, and they advanced by the dim light of the flickering torches. Fortunately, the tunnel was straight, and the footing even.

Looking around, the prince saw that the tunnel was supported by a network of overhanging roots, many as broad as oak limbs. Occasionally a creeping tendril draped from the ceiling or wall, but for the most part the framework seemed quite secure.

Soon they entered a larger chamber, where the tunnel walls fell away to the bare limits of their vision on either side. The room seemed to be a good ten paces wide. The far end was lost in darkness, and water covered the entire floor.

Rank smells seemed to rise from the stagnant pool. It smells like death, thought the prince, or maybe not quite death, but close. No sound stirred in the tunnel except for the quiet sloshing of their feet moving through the water.

"Oh!" Robyn uttered a sharp cry and fell.

The prince turned to see her slip downward as if she had stepped into a deep hole. Water splashed as he grabbed her arm. Sputtering and splashing, she managed to regain her footing on the lip of the underwater hole. Somehow she had kept her torch out of the water during the mishap.

"Look out!" hissed Daryth, and the prince saw the flash of a scaly body in the center of the pool. Whatever it was, it swiftly disappeared underwater.

For seconds the room was absolutely silent. The only movement was the steady growth of the rings of ripples on the water's surface. They spread outward, sloshing against Tristan's legs. Still there was no sign of their maker.

Suddenly a gaping mouth, bristling with white teeth, burst from the water at Robyn's feet, followed by most of a scaly body. She lurched backward as Pawldo released his arrow and Tristan stabbed with his knife. The prince felt the blade bite home, but the creature immediately vanished under the water again.

Pawldo quickly readied another arrow as Daryth pulled Robyn back. The Calishite brandished his torch, moving toward the hole.

For a moment the chamber resounded with no sound other than their heavy breathing, which rasped with fear and excitement. Tristan felt the thrill of challenge tingle through his body, and had difficulty holding his blade steady.

Again, water exploded before them and a large body rushed toward Daryth. Scales gleamed in the torchlight, but Tristan could not tell whether the monster was reptile or fish. Limbs that could have been fins or feet thrashed through the water, and those vicious teeth drove toward the Calishite's face.

Pawldo loosed his arrow instantly and saw it lodge in the monster's neck. Tristan hacked mightily with his knife, opening a deep gash in its head. And Daryth brought the torch around in an instinctive effort to ward off the attack.

Light flared in the dingy chamber as the torch rushed through the air and plunged into the monster's mouth. The smell of seared flesh spread through the air, and the creature whirled around frantically in the water. A final thrust of its huge tail knocked the prince headlong, and then the monster was gone.

For long moments they waited, slowly catching their breath.

"Is everyone all right?" asked Tristan, regaining his feet.

"I think so," replied Daryth.

"What was that?" asked Robyn, trying unsuccessfully to suppress a shudder.

"I don't know," admitted the prince. Like Robyn, he felt a nameless, crawling horror in this place. He wanted very badly to run into the light of the sun, but instead he gestured forward.

As Daryth climbed carefully to his feet, he spoke, his eyes wide.

"I've heard of things that live deep in the earth, half fish, and half serpent. They are used by the mountain sultans of Calimshan to guard their most priceless treasures and the secret passages of their palaces. They are large and fast . . . and mightily evil. Their fangs drip with venom. " The Calishite paused, remembering something unpleasant.

"I almost met . . . "His voice trailed off and he looked up, as if suddenly remembering his surroundings. He shook his head and remained silent.

Not certain whether he wanted Daryth to say more or not, Tristan led the group as they carefully picked their way around the hole that had caught Robyn unaware. She carefully probed the ground before them with her cudgel, and they soon waded through the large chamber into the shallower water of the tunnel.

As they continued through the long tunnel, the prince noticed that the floor had begun to slope a bit. The water flowed around their feet toward the large chamber behind them. Then, for several minutes the water level decreased steadily, until soon it had dropped to a small stream running down a gutter in the center of the tunnel. With some relief, they walked upon dry ground again, and their progress quickened.

Soon they reached an apparent end to the tunnel, as bare dirt walls capped the passage before them and to either side.

"This looks like a dead end," said Tristan, inspecting the walls with his fingertips. "We might have known that Newt's solution would have a drawback."

"Hold on a minute," cautioned Daryth. "Give me a boost. " Looking up, Tristan saw that they stood below some kind of drainage pipe. About four feet in diameter, the pipe appeared to go straight up, outdistancing the range of the torchlight.

The prince lifted his friend to his shoulders so that the upper half of Daryth's body extended into the pipe. He grunted in pain as the Calishite climbed to his feet, resting muddy boots against each of the prince's ears.

"This doesn't look too bad," grunted Daryth, his voice echoing from the pipe. In moments he found a handhold, and his feet disappeared into the pipe after him.

"Stand back" he warned, as mud and unidentifiable muck fell from the pipe to splash upon Tristan, who had been looking upward in amazement. The prince ignored the mess on his face, continuing to marvel as Daryth forced his way up the pipe using little more than the sheer sides of the passage as hand and footholds. His progress was slow, but he soon moved into the darkness above.

"Hsst!" The voice filtered down from the pipe. "Come up after me!"

Immediately, an uncoiling rope emerged from the pipe. One end of the rope dropped to the ground at Tristan's feet.

Pulling the line to test its security, Tristan then climbed hand over hand up into the pipe. For several minutes he strained steadily upward, feeling numbness creep into his shoulders and arms. The passage here darkened to inky blackness.

He almost started to panic, but then he heard a voice from above him say, "It's all right. Come on up. You're almost there." And soon he felt a presence near him, and Daryth's welcome hands reached out to pull him sideways. With relief he collapsed onto a narrow ledge next to his friend.

Soundlessly Tristan willed his arms to stop trembling.

Gradually they obeyed, and he became aware of a very dim light filtering down from above. Robyn reached them on the ledge by the time his eyes made out the faint outlines of a metal grate low over their heads.

Finally Pawldo ascended, grunting and cursing under his breath the whole way. He reluctantly refrained from any loud objections as he joined the companions on the ledge. As a precautionary measure, they had extinguished all the torches down below. Thus, they now crouched in near total darkness. Only that faint, eerie glow illuminated the heavy iron grate above them.

"Can you slip through that grate?" Daryth asked, in a faint whisper. Pawldo quickly nodded in understanding, and squirmed easily through the metal bars over their heads. The humans down below could barely make out the shape of their small comrade.

"Now, look for some way to open it," ordered Daryth, again in an almost inaudible whisper.

Waiting in the dark below, they heard a quiet scurrying on the grate, then nimble fingers located a pair of small catches, and they heard the slight sound of metal moving on stone.

"Push up!" Pawldo ordered, and the three humans strained upward against the grid. Slowly, the heavy metal lifted from the hole as they stepped to the floor above. As they laid the grate back onto the floor, it clanged noisily and unexpectedly against a stone floor. Tristan gasped, and then they were all silent, frozen, listening for a response. No sound broke the silence of the dank passage. Finally, they began to breathe again, and silently they eased the grate back into its place.

Tristan's eyes, grown accustomed to near total darkness, now served him well in the dimly lit passage. He saw that they stood in the middle of a wide corridor. The grate in the floor seemed to be some sort of drain, for gutters in each side of the corridor carried a steady flow of water to the tunnel.

They saw walls, ceiling, and floor all constructed of smooth stone. The craftsmanship, though crude, seemed very solid. The corridor reached perhaps fifteen feet from side to side, and twelve feet to the ceiling. The only illumination was a light at one end of the corridor and seemed to be coming from far away, as if the light traveled around several corners before reaching the companions.

"Let's have a look," suggested Tristan, nodding in the direction of the light.

The others agreed, and they assumed their original formation, now without torchlight. They walked for several minutes, Tristan and Robyn cautiously leading. They passed a darkened corridor leading to the right, and another, but wordlessly agreed to continue forward.

A snort erupted from the second side passage just after they passed it, and they whirled toward the sound. Daryth and Pawldo seemed to disappear as they crouched in the darkened shadows of the gutter.

The scrape of heavy footsteps announced the appearance of a stooping Firbolg. It lurched into the corridor and then stood, swaying from side to side. Suddenly, he gave forth a tremendous belch, and blinked at Tristan and Robyn, standing side by side before him.

The prince, smelling strong spirits on the stumbling Firbolg, realized that the creature was drunk. But the reason didn't matter when the filthy creature grunted an unintelligible oath and leaped at Robyn with an upraised fist.

Tristan quickly drew his knife and slashed upward at the Firbolg's fist. At the same time a figure darted from the shadows and hurtled itself at the Firbolg's side. A gleaming dagger was thrust, and suddenly the creature's throat exploded in blood. Soundlessly, it dropped to the ground.

The prince stared at Daryth in awe, realizing that his friend had slain the Firbolg with one blow—cutting the creature's neck by surprise.

"Quick! Let's get him out of sight!" Pawldo urged. "Pull him into the gutter."

They dragged the heavy corpse to the side and concealed it as best they could in the shadowy depression.

When they moved on through the darkness toward the unseen light source, Tristan saw that Robyn walked a little closer to him than before.

They neared the corner, where they paused, noting that the light was brighter now, as if it were just around one more corner.

"Stay here," cautioned Daryth.

They did as he suggested while he advanced silently, finally lying down on the floor and peering around the corner at ground level. In seconds, he returned to them.

"There's a big iron door in the wall," he explained. "It's got a big lock on it, but I might be able to open it. Oh, and there's a giant asleep in a chair outside the door."

"Some afterthought," grumbled Pawldo.

"This could be a cell," whispered Robyn excitedly. "I'll bet that's where Keren is!"

They each moved forward and looked around the corner. Twenty feet away, a Firbolg slouched in a huge chair, snoring contentedly. A large jug lay on its side at his feet and a smoky torch flickered in a wall socket above the chair.

Next to the Firbolg stood the door Daryth had described, and that portal seemed formidable indeed. A surface of dull black iron dotted with heavy bolts, the entire thing hung from three massive iron hinges. In the center of the door was a small keyhole.

Daryth stealthily crawled past the sleeping Firbolg while his companions breathlessly marked his progress. The Calishite reached down and seemed to fumble with his belt. In moments, he withdrew a curiously shaped metal object and inserted it into the keyhole. Carefully, he began to wiggle it around, holding his ear next to the keyhole.

The sharp click of the latch suddenly echoed through the corridor, and the sleeping guard grunted and smacked his lips. Daryth's hand darted to his dagger, but the Firbolg soon sank into the depths of slumber again.

Slowly, the Calishite pulled on the door. The hinges squeaked in protest as it started to swing outward. Again the Firbolg did not awaken, and soon the door stood wide enough for them all to see within. The light of the wall torch spilled through the door and into the room, which was obviously no prison cell.

The small light of the torch was reflected again and again, lighting up the entire chamber in gleaming dots of many colors. Gold coins lay strewn over the floor. Jeweled bracelets reflected a rainbow of colors. Crystal chalices and steel swords lay scattered casually about the room, as if left here and forgotten.

The fortune was greater, Tristan felt certain, than even that stored in the coffers of the High King's treasury. And here it was, locked away in a Firbolg dungeon.

XXXXXXXXXXX

Groth stood upon the low hummock and watched the Firbolgs—*his* Firbolgs—at work. A column of twenty marched stoically past him. Each carried a basket upon his head containing some four hundred pounds of coal. Grimly purposeful, the Firbolgs trudged down the trail into the thickness of the fens.

Smiling—if a gap-toothed, drooling grimace could be called a smile—Groth stepped from the hummock and followed the column down the trail. He decided to oversee the other part of this operation as well.

Soon the procession reached the shore of a murky pool. The dirt along the water had been trampled into mud, and the plants within fifty feet of the pond were broken and dead. Here, the coal-carriers emptied their loads into the water, and then turned along the trail to the mines.

Groth stood alone, after they left, admiring their handiwork. The chunks of coal bubbled and hissed as they sank into the water, dissolving quickly into a murky cloud of pollution. Groth could tell that the enchanted and pure water of the Darkwell was gradually being destroyed by the steadily increasing grime. Every day, as the coal fed the waters, the violence of the reaction increased.

Groth's dim mind pondered the potentials.

Though he had assumed rulership of the Firbolgs by his shrewd mental ability, such ability among the Firbolgs was no great testimony.

Still, Groth knew that Kazgoroth would be pleased.

Groth recalled his fear when the Beast had risen from the Darkwell on the night of the spring equinox.

Kazgoroth had ordered the trembling Firbolg to feed the well with coal, as the Firbolgs had done in centuries past in answer to their master's command. Before winter, Kazgoroth would return to the Darkwell—and Groth would see that it was ready.

Groth had used his acute—for a Firbolg—mind to separate the work into two tasks: first, they collected a massive stockpile from the mines around the vale. Now they were on the second stage: adding the black, dusty coal to the festering waters of the Darkwell, pouring in tons of the stuff every day.

Groth noticed that the sun had dropped below the level of the treetops. He turned and lumbered toward the temple, eager to shut the heavy door behind him before nightfall.

Overall, Groth felt pleased—in fact, very pleased. His Firbolgs worked diligently to pollute the well. Perhaps it was time they had a reward.

A line of thick spittle ran from Groth's widespread lips as he considered the possibility of entertainment. Of course, he could not afford to slay the unicorn yet—he did not understand why the Beast had told him to capture it, but he would not risk Kazgoroth's wrath by slaying his prisoner. Still, there was that other one who would provide grand titillation as he suffered a gory death in the Pit. Yes, indeed—Groth licked his lips in anticipation.

It was time for the bard to die.

XXXXXXXXXX

Flickering torchlight glittered on gold coins, silver bracelets studded with jewels, and shining wealth in a thousand forms. Robyn caught her breath in astonishment, and Tristan failed to suppress a low whistle. Pawldo, meanwhile, sprinted soundlessly forward and darted into the treasure room before anyone could react.

Tristan muffled a curse and held his knife ready in case the sleeping Firbolg awoke. He showed no sign of leaving his grunting dreams, however. Before the prince could react, Robyn too slipped past him and into the room. Sighing in resignation, the prince watched the guard for any alarming movement.

Through the door, he could see Pawldo kneel down amid a great pile of coins and jewels. His nimble fingers picked up and discarded object after object, until he found something of worth to slip into his backpack. The leather sack quickly grew heavy with valuables.

Daryth and Robyn walked slowly around inside the room, awestruck, touching nothing. Finally, Tristan could contain himself no longer, and he followed the others into the treasure room.

Daryth knelt down and pulled a curved scabbard from the shadows. Its plain leather surface belied the worth of its contents, as he whisked forth a gleaming scimitar. Seeing that Robyn still carried only her oaken cudgel, he bowed with a flourish and offered the weapon to her. She looked down, considering the offer, but then she smiled shyly and shook her head. The Calishite, instead, buckled the weapon to his own waist. It was clear from the way he easily demonstrated the skill of pulling the blade from the scabbard that he was no neophyte with the weapon. He held the scimitar at the ready, moving silently to the door to watch the Firbolg.

Robyn suddenly knelt and picked up a large silver ring. Tristan recognized it as a torque, a druidic ornament to be worn around the neck. The maiden shook back her hair, separated the band at its clasp, and then placed it around her smooth throat. The silver shone coolly against her tanned skin.

Tristan, disturbed at the sight of Robyn, looked through the treasure at his feet. Suddenly his eye was caught by something. "Look!" he whispered harshly, almost crying out. "Here's Keren's bow!"

Indeed, the bard's longbow was unmistakable. The polished black wood, stretching through an arc as tall as a man, looked like no other weapon. The prince remembered the bard's description of the weapon, which had been carved from a hefty bough of the Callidyrr yew. It was one of a dozen or so such weapons, crafted by the High King's own bowyer.

He carefully picked the weapon up, noticing that the bard's quiver, containing some dozen arrows, still hung from the stout shaft. As he lifted the bow, he caught a glimpse of something brown and dull, lying in stark contrast among the glimmering metal.

Kneeling, the prince saw that it was a leather pommel, almost buried under a mountain of coins. He brushed the gold and silver coins aside as if they had no more importance than dirt. And, though he couldn't have said why, that was so, because everything in him was drawn to another piece of dull, unadorned leather. He lifted a plain, dirty, worn scabbard from among the jewels. From it projected an ancient, battered sword hilt.

In a swift gesture, the prince seized the hilt and pulled, drawing forth a silver long sword. He whispered a gasp of awe as he saw that it glowed with a light all its own, a light that had a purity that outshone all the other treasure in the chamber.

Slowly he lifted the sword, feeling the contours of the hilt fit naturally into his palm. The blade was emblazoned in a crest and motto, written in the Old Script. Squinting, he could make nothing of the words. Their very presence, however, told him that indeed the weapon was ancient. Suddenly, the sleeping Firbolg snorted outside the door of the room.

XXXXXXXXXX

Kamerynn paced restlessly around the dirty pen, snorting and pawing the floor. Stone walls rose to a height of more than thirty feet on each side—even the unicorn's powerful legs could not jump such a barrier. The wooden gate set in the wall was constructed of layer upon layer of wood and was too solid to smash.

All around, the scents and sounds of the Firbolgs assailed Kamerynn, driving him frantic with disgust and rage. In a frenzy of frustration, the unicorn kicked the door. As before, he bounced off. After pacing restlessly for a minute, he smashed the stubborn portal again. This time, his ivory horn sent splinters of wood flying, but did not weaken the door.

Again and again the mighty unicorn smashed shoulders, horn, and hooves into the wood. Finally the wooden barrier shuddered, bouncing slightly as strained timbers began to break.

Now Kamerynn turned and kicked the door with his powerful rear legs. It strained, and finally burst outward in a shower of splinters. Turning, the unicorn leaped through the opening.

Four Firbolgs, clubs upraised, stood waiting, glee in their bestial eyes. Kamerynn charged forward, bowling over two of the Firbolgs with his broad shoulders. The others leaped and grabbed, but could not stop him.

Kicking off the last grasping hands, Kamerynn galloped down a wide stone corridor, illuminated by flickering torches. Somewhere ahead, he knew, he would find the door.

THE LEGACY OF CYMRYCH HUGH

9

X**T**he companions froze in the treasure room. The Firbolg grunted and stirred in his chair. Finally, he settled back to a deep pattern of snoring. The incident made them realize how precarious their position was, however, and they gathered by the door.

"Come on." Robyn signaled to them. Holding her handmade cudgel ready for action, she led the party from the room.

Tristan strapped the silver sword to his belt while he waited for the others to leave the room. He noticed that Pawldo's pockets and pouches bulged with treasure, yet somehow the halfling didn't make any clinking noises as he moved. Daryth carried the scimitar. In addition, the prince saw that the Calishite had bedecked his fingers with an assortment of gem-encrusted rings. Robyn had taken only the torque—even in the dim light, Tristan could see that the silver band enhanced her beauty.

On impulse, the prince reached down and scooped up a handful of gold coins, realizing that he held in his hand more wealth than most humans ever came across in a lifetime. Carefully, he left the room and pushed the door shut. It latched with a barely audible click, but the sleeping Firbolg snorted in irritation and lurched in his chair. For a moment they feared that he would awaken, but he soon lapsed into deep slumber again.

They looked about, realizing that they could return from the direction they had come, or advance farther into the Firbolgs' den. Torches flickered up the corridor, holding the promise of more—and probably dangerous—activity if they continued ahead. Still hoping to find Keren, they chose to continue on into the stone structure.

Behind them, the Firbolg snorted a few times and went on sleeping.

X X X X X X X X X

Groth returned to a scene of mass confusion, rage, and panic. Giants ran to and fro, brandishing weapons and crying an alarm.

"Hold!" cried the Firbolg chief, in a voice that reached into the very depths of the earth. Instantly, his minions paused and turned to face him. None spoke.

"What is the meaning of this?" Groth demanded, fixing one Firbolg with a glaring eye.

"The unicorn, yer greatness—it seems to have, well, escaped!"

"Seems to have *what*?" asked the chief, very softly.

The Firbolg paled, for the chief spoke softly only when he was very angry indeed. "It seems to have escaped!" he finally blurted. "But it is still in the temple. We were just about to catch it when—"

"Fools! Blundering idiots! Can I not leave the temple unattended for a brief afternoon without you bringing disaster down upon our heads?" Groth's voice now rattled the foundations of the temple with its strength.

The other Firbolgs met his outburst with silence. "Find the unicorn!" he bellowed finally, triggering his minions to frantic action. "And return it to me, unharmed!"

Giants raced in all directions, as anxious to escape the presence of their wrathful lord as they were to locate the wayward unicorn. Soon Groth stood alone in the entry hall, contemplating the situation.

Groth was not particularly worried about the unicorn running loose through the temple. The structure only had two exits, and both were heavily guarded, so the creature did not seem likely to escape. Nevertheless, Groth gathered a few more of his warriors to him, and took them around the outside of the building to the exit from the coal bin. He would wait here, with a reinforced guard, in case the unicorn proved tricky.

Any enemy loose in the temple of the Firbolgs was a potential threat, reflected Groth with a grimace. He thought of the treasure room and its valuable stores.

There would be no telling what kind of trouble could result if the Sword of Cymrych Hugh should fall into the wrong hands.

XXXXXXXXXX

Robyn ran down another of the long stone corridors, her companions following quickly. They passed several branching corridors but continued straight ahead, hoping to find some clue to the whereabouts of Keren's prison.

"Shh!" called Daryth, and the whole party lurched to a stop. "I hear something up ahead. Sounds like quite a commotion. " The others, straining their ears, also heard the sounds of shouting and bellowing.

"Something has the Firbolgs riled up," offered Pawldo. "Maybe they found that one we left in the gutter."

"I don't think so," countered Tristan. "We left that one behind us, and all of the noise is coming from up ahead."

They approached a four-way intersection of corridors, and Tristan advanced to peer down the right and left paths. They were both empty.

Suddenly a loud clattering emerged from the corridor before them, and they saw a huge white creature galloping toward them. Freezing momentarily, they stared at the magnificent beast in surprise. Apparently sharing their shock, the fabulous creature stopped suddenly before them and tossed his head in frustration. A milky white mane billowed from his neck, but their attention collectively focused on the animal's forehead.

"A unicorn!" gasped Tristan, saying what the others were thinking.

The beautiful animal reared high and then stomped his forehooves upon the stone floor. For several seconds he stared at them, as if thinking. Then, he tossed his head to the left before turning and galloping down the corridor to the right.

Tristan started after the unicorn, but paused as he felt Robyn's restraining hand on his arm. At the same time, he noticed the sounds of pursuing Firbolgs far down the corridor. Obviously they were chasing the unicorn.

"He wants us to go this way," declared Robyn firmly, tugging the prince into the left-hand corridor.

Too surprised by her assertion to argue, Tristan mutely followed Robyn. Daryth and Pawldo did likewise, and they all ran down the passage as fast as they could. Finally they ducked around a corner and paused, gasping for breath and listening for sounds of pursuit.

The bellows and cries of the pursuing Firbolgs built to a crescendo and then faded again, so they knew that the creatures were chasing the unicorn down the opposite corridor. More slowly, but understandably vigilant, they continued to advance.

Suddenly Robyn stopped by a door and held up her hand. Immediately, the others halted behind her. She concentrated—not as if she were listening for something, thought Tristan. It was more as if she sought a faint scent in the air.

"Keren!" she called, in a loud, clear voice.

Tristan gasped at the sound, looking nervously behind as if he expected hundreds of Firbolgs to leap upon them from ambush. Before he could urge Robyn to silence, however, an answering voice was heard from beyond the door.

"Robyn!" The voice, though muffled, could belong to none other than the bard.

Quickly Daryth knelt beside the door and examined the lock. He removed an odd tool from his pouch and began to pick carefully at the mechanism, as Tristan and Robyn pressed to the door. Pawldo sensibly maintained a watch up the corridor.

"Are you all right, Keren? What happened?" Robyn and Tristan began to ply the door with questions, but Daryth silenced them with a curt gesture. Keren seemed to understand, for no further sound emerged from the room.

Minutes passed like hours, and still the deft fingers of the Calishite could not spring the stubborn lock. Sweat beaded on Daryth's forehead, and his brow furrowed in concentration. In the distance they could still hear the bellowing of angry Firbolgs.

Daryth cursed in frustration, wiped his palms on his shirt, and returned the tool to the lock.

Tristan developed a cramp in his fingers, and only then did he realize that he held his hands clenched tightly into fists. With an effort, he forced himself to relax, breathing in a long, deep rhythm as Arlen had taught him.

Then the lock clicked, a loud sound among the tense companions. The door creaked eerily as Daryth pushed it open.

A figure staggered toward them from the darkness. Its face was gaunt and haggard—its clothing torn and tattered into rags. Around the eyes spread dark, bloody circles. Yet those eyes held the light of humor and wisdom they had come to know and appreciate in the bard.

"Keren!" Robyn sprang forward to embrace the bard in a hug. He held her for a moment, smiling at the others over her shoulder.

"You don't know how good it is to see you!" he exclaimed, his voice shaking.

They said nothing for several moments, until Pawldo's voice brought them sharply back to reality, "Save the tea party for later," groused the halfling. "Let's get outta here!"

"I'm comin' too!"

The sound of a strange voice brought Daryth, Robyn, and Tristan around immediately. They stared in wonder at a bedraggled figure emerging from the dark corner of the cell.

"What's the matter?" demanded the obviously female, if not feminine, voice. "Ain't you guys never seen a beard before?"

The stubby figure emerged into the light and glared belligerently at them. She (if the voice was to be believed) stood perhaps four feet tall, with a stocky body, short legs, and long arms. Her shoulders were broad and sturdy, and her legs ended in surprisingly large feet, protected by huge leather boots.

The face of the stranger disappeared completely behind a bristling beard that dropped past the beltline. A sloppy hat could not conceal an equally unruly mass of hair atop the rounded head.

"Allow me to present Finellen," said Keren, hastily intervening. "My dear, these are the young heroes I was telling you about . . ."

"Hmph!" muttered Finellen, as Tristan recognized her nature.

"You're a dwarf, aren't you?" he said. "I consider it a high honor to make your acquaintance, my lady." Finellen seemed slightly mollified, deigning to give the prince a quick once-over.

"Finellen had the misfortune, as did I, to be taken prisoner by the Firbolgs," explained the bard as they moved into the corridor.

"I suppose I owe you my thanks," admitted the dwarf. She hastily continued. "But don't go gettin' any ideas about takin' advantage of my gratitude! It won't work!"

Tristan, taken aback by the dwarf's rudeness, ignored it and said, "Here's your bow, Keren. We found it in the treasure room."

"Why, thank you!" A surprised Keren quickly inspected the weapon, stringing it in one powerful motion. "Have you an extra weapon for Finellen?—I saw her fight these brutes, and we would do well to have her aid."

"I don't have much use for this anymore," said Daryth, extending his dagger, hilt first, to the dwarf. "This scimitar will do me just fine."

Finellen snatched the dagger quickly, studying the workmanship and running a callused thumb along the blade. "Thanks," she grunted. "I'll give it back when I'm through killing Firbolgs."

"Let's get out of here," urged Pawldo. "I've a feeling some giant is looking to turn me into a pancake!"

They rapidly retraced their steps, this time with Pawldo and Finellen in the lead. Certainly there were Firbolgs ahead of them. One deep voice in particular commanded their attention, and it sounded as if the Firbolgs had been ordered to begin a systematic search of the area.

Pawldo signaled a halt from his position in the lead. They stopped and heard distinct sounds of heavy footsteps. A party of Firbolgs was coming their way!

"What are we stopping for?" barked Finellen.

Pawldo, looking irritated, began to answer. Simultaneously, a trio of hulking Firbolgs turned into the corridor ahead of them. The Firbolgs saw them immediately.

"Hoorrgghh!" All three of the creatures uttered the cry, and charged. Their huge boots, studded with hobnails, cracked against the stone floor, sparking. Two of the creatures held clubs, while the third brandished a monstrous sword, held in both of his hands. Bloodshot eyes gleamed wickedly at them, while their thick-lipped mouths split into wide, drooling grins of anticipation.

Pawldo loosed an arrow, and immediately backed up to leave an opening for Tristan. Daryth and Robyn followed the prince, but with a gesture he cautioned them to remain behind.

Finellen, however, took the prince by surprise. He had planned to stand next to the dwarf and meet the Firbolgs' charge, but she raised the dagger Daryth had given her, and uttered a bloodcurdling shriek. Even the Firbolgs seemed momentarily taken aback.

"Outta my way, you overgrown bags of blubber!" Finellen darted forward to attack. Tristan gaped at the incongruous sight for a second—the dwarven warrior came not as high as the waists of her antagonists—and then leaped forward to support her valiant attack.

A long arrow whooshed past the prince's ear. Keren was shooting now, but unfortunately the missile skittered off the wall and bounced harmlessly down the corridor.

In seconds, Finellen reached the Firbolgs. Instead of stopping to fight, she tucked herself into a ball and rolled between the legs of one of the creatures. As soon as she had passed him, she straightened with a motion too fast to see and thrust upward with the dagger. Her victim howled in pain and whirled to try and club the dwarf woman.

The Firbolgs bellowed together, in a noise like thunder, and pushed each other about in their eagerness to attack. One separated itself from the others and lunged for Tristan, who saw vividly the rage in its face and smelled its hot, stinking breath.

Tristan leaped to the side, dodging a heavy club, and struck quickly with his new sword. The blade bit into the chest of the advancing Firbolg.

And, as he fell back, he heard flesh sizzling. Tristan looked with horror at the wound he had just inflicted. The Firbolg's skin burned away from the cut, and the creature tumbled backward, screaming. The giant flopped onto the ground heavily, kicked a few times, and lay still.

For a moment, the other two Firbolgs and the companions stood frozen in shock. Then a Firbolg bellowed, and Finellen whirled into another attack. In a second, the melee raged anew.

Daryth and Robyn sprang forward to aid Tristan, as the Firbolg with the huge sword took a swing at the prince. Spinning away from the attack, Tristan desperately raised the new sword, and the two blades met with a ringing crash. The force of the blow smashed the prince into the wall, where he slumped slowly to the floor, his sword still clasped in his stinging hands.

The sword of the Firbolg, meanwhile, had shattered into hundreds of shards.

Still stunned, the prince barely rolled in time to avoid a thudding blow as the last Firbolg's club broke flagstones from the floor. The prince still held the strange sword—almost as if the weapon would not leave his hand. The crushing attack seemed to shake the very ground, but the prince avoided it by a scant inch. He saw Finellen tuck and roll again, this time biting into a Firbolg's hamstring with the small dagger before reaching Tristan's side. The dwarf's victim howled in pain as his leg collapsed, and then crashed heavily to the floor.

"Hey, ugly!" she cried, momentarily distracting the Firbolg who had nearly crushed the prince. Tristan scrambled to his feet and stood beside the dwarf. Two Firbolgs now lay on the floor, but the remaining monster threw away his broken sword and picked up one of the clubs. It advanced cautiously, now prepared to take this fight seriously.

None of them heard the clattering of hooves, but suddenly the advancing Firbolg gasped and tumbled forward. A great ivory horn erupted from its chest in a shower of gore, and now they saw the proud form of the unicorn, extracting itself from the mortally pierced Firbolg.

For several seconds the companions regarded the unicorn. The great beast returned their stares impassively. Its snowy flanks were lathered and flecked with blood, though the unicorn did not seem to be wounded.

"Thank you, ancient one," said Robyn, very quietly.

The eyes of the unicorn softened, and it tossed its proud head. With a short whinny, it turned and looked back the way it had come.

"Let's follow it," cried Robyn.

"Wait," said Keren, in an urgent whisper. His eyes were fixed upon the prince. "Tristan, where did you get that sword?"

"I found it, in the same room where we found your bow."

"Let me see it, please."

Tristan instantly handed the weapon to the bard, who peered quickly at the script on the blade. When he looked back at the prince, Tristan saw that his eyes held a new emotion. It could have been respect, or even awe.

"Can you read it?" the prince asked.

"My prince," said the bard. It was the first time he had ever used the honorific in speaking to Tristan. "You have found the Sword of Cymrych Hugh!"

Robyn gasped and stared, wide-eyed, back and forth between the prince and the weapon. Tristan, stunned, could think only of the mighty weapon he held in his hand. Slayer of Firbolgs, and bane of the enemies of the Ffolk, the Sword of Cymrych Hugh was certainly the most fabled weapon in his people's history. Tristan still recalled Keren's long ballad about the hero that he had played at Arlen's funeral.

"What's going on?" Daryth asked. "Who was Kimrick Hue? I'm not from these parts, remember?"

" 'Cymrych Hugh' was the first of the High Kings—the man who united all of the Moonshae Islands under a single strong, wise rule," Tristan explained, recalling his most basic history lessons. "Never before or since have the Ffolk been as strongly united. I remember fables telling of his death, at the hand of some nightmarish beast. At the same time, his sword was lost . . ."

"It is said," Keren interjected, "that his sword will be found again, so that the wielder can challenge the beast that slayed him!"

Tristan looked at the weapon in Keren's hand, and thought of the bard's fighting prowess. He felt frightened and weak by comparison. "You keep it," he said. "You can do it—"

"The sword must be wielded by he who finds it," said the bard with a shake of his head. "And besides, you are more fit to carry that weapon than you know."

Tristan wanted to argue, but the weapon seemed to beckon him to take it. "I don't know," he replied, but nonetheless reached for the simple leather hilt and took the sword.

As they continued down the long passage, Tristan saw the others glancing at him and the sword occasionally. He hoped they weren't as puzzled—and amazed—as he was. Why had fate decreed that *he* should be the one to pick it up? And what was he going to do with it now that he had it?

Tristan was paying little attention to their surroundings, as the little party moved cautiously forward, soon passing several wooden doors but no branching corridors. Suddenly Finellen called out.

"Wait a minute!" She turned to regard a huge pair of oaken doors. They noticed that one of them was slightly ajar. "I smell fresh air—let's have a look in here!"

Before anyone could disagree, she pushed the slightly opened door with the point of her dagger, and it swung freely inward. Before them they saw a huge room—by far the largest chamber they had yet seen in the Firbolgs' complex. In the center of the room, towering perhaps forty feet into the air, rose a black, hulking mass, like a small mountain.

Sunlight streamed into the room from cracks in a pair of massive wooden doors at the far end. They noticed that no torches burned here.

With a sudden snarl, a Firbolg sprang from the darkness to the side of the door. Another emerged from the same area, bearing a massive pickaxe in its uplifted arms. They had apparently been surprised at their work. The unicorn reared back and crushed the skull of one with his slashing forehooves, while Tristan leaped at the other, stabbing quickly. Again the blade sizzled into Firbolg flesh, and the howling creature fell over and died.

Seeking any other foes, they cautiously advanced into the chamber.

"Look—we can bar these doors for a while," exclaimed the prince. Quickly they swung the portal shut. Their combined strength could barely lift the heavy crossbeam, but they finally dropped it into place against the inside of the double doorway.

"That'll slow up anyone, including Firbolgs!" Tristan said with satisfaction.

As a group, they turned toward the doors through which streamed shafts of sunlight. Skirting the black mass in the center of the room, Tristan studied it curiously. Pawldo made the first guess as to its nature, however.

"My prince!" he cried, holding a clump of black rock. "It's just coal!"

Tristan thought the discovery interesting but insignificant and continued toward the doors across the room. Keren, however, paused immediately and appeared to lose himself in thought.

"Indeed!" the bard finally cried, snapping his fingers. "Quickly! Help me gather these wooden benches! And those tools over there—someone grab the ones with wooden handles. And hurry! There's no time to lose!"

"What? Why?" asked Tristan, turning back.

"We can destroy this stronghold!"

Instantly, Tristan understood Keren's plan. He stumbled upon some loose boards in a corner of the room and eagerly tossed them against the massive pile of coal. Benches, and tools, and several unlit torches discovered upon the walls, all increased the size of the pile.

As they worked, they heard a heavy thud against the door. Again and again the sound rocked through the chamber, and Tristan thought that he heard the creaking of a hinge as the timber barring the door slowly threatened to give way. The great unicorn heaved stalwartly against it, holding with the strength of his body against the press of Firbolgs.

But now the pile was ready. Daryth, Tristan, and Pawldo all carried flints, and each knelt down and struck sparks into some shavings they had trimmed from the heavy boards. The door creaked noisily, nearly opening, as three small fires began to spread through the shavings. Soon, tongues of flame licked across boards that had been soaked with oil, apparently to preserve their life. Now, the treatment only hastened their destruction.

Robyn, Keren, and Finellen, meanwhile, ran to the double doors leading outside. They threw their weight into lifting the huge crossbar.

In less than a minute, three raging bonfires had already begun to pop and sizzle. Sparks flew onto the coal, but they knew it would take a great deal of heat to ignite the stuff. The door creaked alarmingly, but still the great beam held.

"Let's get out of here," called the prince, as choking clouds of black smoke began to fill the room. Already the fire seemed dangerously out of control.

Coughing, the companions stumbled toward the doors leading out. Tears welled from their eyes as the smoke stung. The clouds grew thicker every second. The great unicorn raced ahead with them, and Tristan knew that the Firbolgs would soon smash the doors.

Keren threw open the huge portals and they all staggered forth into sunlight and fresh air. A stream of black smoke poured from the doorway, but rose over their heads until dispersed by the breeze.

"We made it!" cried Robyn.

"Not so fast, deary," grunted Finellen, pointing.

Between the forest and the temple, standing close before them, stood some twenty Firbolgs. They were arrayed in battle formation, which they maintained as they began to advance.

Smoke poured from the doors behind them, and the gray walls of the stronghold spread to either side. They were trapped.

XXXXXXXXXX

The enemy was very close now.

The cool, gray waters of the Sea of Moonshae rolled past the great body, as the leviathan began to move with a new sense of purpose.

A rank pollution spread through the water, offending the senses of the mighty creature, child of the Earthmother. The leviathan had killed many times, but never had it sought out its victims with such determination.

The leviathan emerged from the strait and broached, rolling its serpentine form among the great swells of the sheltered sea. Gray skies glowered overhead, and many thin patches of mist and rain spread across the horizon.

The leviathan turned slightly, as it sensed its prey somewhere to the left. Soon, many long, narrow shapes came into view, scuttling across the surface of the sea like tiny waterbugs. The pollution of the water became so strong that the mighty creature choked on its own bile. Its rage grew unstoppable.

The leviathan opened its great jaws just before its head broke the surface. Spray erupted as the powerful tail drove the creature from the water. Higher and higher the leviathan rose. At the same time, those awesome jaws clamped together.

The leviathan tasted wood and blood in its mouth. Splintered bits of the narrow shape fell to either side, but the great bulk of it remained within that terrible maw. The creature crashed back to the surface, and then dived deep, carrying the shapeless mass of wood and men to a permanent grave. Finally it opened its mouth, letting the wreckage float free.

Turning toward the surface, it again began to rise.

There still remained a great deal of killing to do.

FLIGHT

10

The monsters spread into a thin line, advancing to do battle. They held an assortment of deadly weapons—swords, clubs studded with vicious spikes, long battle-axes. Their most effective weapon was their sheer size, and the inexorability of their march toward Tristan and his companions.

The fire roared higher behind them, belching smoke from the double doors.

"Any ideas?" the prince asked, half-heartedly.

"Not me," replied Daryth, looking grimly at the monsters.

This last group of Firbolgs had obviously been posted to watch the stronghold exit. They did not seem to be as stupid or undisciplined as the others. A great bull of a Firbolg, with a high, bulging forehead and a horrible red scar down his cheek, commanded them, and led their charge.

Keren launched an arrow from his mighty bow. The missile tore into the thigh of one of the Firbolgs, dropping the creature in its tracks. The bard's second shot thudded solidly into the Firbolg leader's shoulder, but the creature ignored the wound. Pawldo also fired, but his arrows seemed to be little more than pinpricks to the hulking attackers.

Robyn was standing beside the proud unicorn, oddly calm. Tristan saw Finellen fingering her dagger and starting to slip forward. Yet their chances of winning the fight appeared slim, until, suddenly, something glimmered in the field before them.

"What's happening?" Before he could think of an answer to Robyn's question, Tristan realized that many of the Firbolgs had stopped advancing. Some fell thrashing to the ground, while others swung their weapons viciously against something unseen in the air.

The scar-faced Firbolg leader turned and bellowed orders at his minions. Then he, too, seemed to lose his mind, striking at nothing, and grunting in fear. For a brief second, the prince's mind reeled with confusion. Then he understood what was happening.

"Come on!" he cried, leaping forward toward the half dozen or so Firbolgs who had not been affected by the strange madness. Tristan knew that he and his companions had been given a fantastic opportunity, but they needed to capitalize upon it quickly.

The white unicorn thundered past him, its ivory horn zeroing in on the chest of a Firbolg. Finellen, uttering a bloodthirsty yell, sprinted along at his side. Her eyes, he noticed, glowed with a savage joy.

Twin streaks flashed over his head, and he knew that the two archers had gone to work. Keren seemed to have recovered his aim, for his bolt lodged deep in the throat of one of the Firbolgs, striking it, gasping and dying, to the ground. Pawldo's missile lodged in the eye of another Firbolg, triggering pain. Berserk, the Firbolg bolted into the thickets.

Two Firbolgs stood before Tristan, but the unicorn's charge knocked one flat. The tough horn turned the creature's chest into a splintered mass of blood and bone. Tristan ducked under the blow of the other Firbolg and drove his potent blade upward. With a blood-curdling scream, the Firbolg swooned backward and died.

For a brief moment the prince paused in wonder. He had slain a Firbolg with a single blow! Then, another of the monsters charged toward him, and he raised his guard.

A flash of brown crossed the periphery of his vision, and Canthus led the hounds into the fight. At the same time, a shrieking black shadow dived from the skies to scratch at the eyes of another Firbolg. Crying shrilly, Sable rose quickly to make another attack.

"Hey, you guys!" The high-pitched voice, Tristan knew, could only belong to Newt. Sure enough, the little dragon popped into view in the midst of the melee.

"Boy, I sure played a trick on them! Did you see the way they rolled around and stabbed the air and looked so silly? I laughed so hard I could hardly stay invisible!" Newt clasped his forepaws, almost as if he were applauding himself, which he probably was.

"Thanks, little friend!" said Tristan. I thought I detected your . . . unique touch!"

"Look!" Robyn cried, pointing to the rest of the Firbolgs. They saw that Newt's enchantment was wearing off. Though groggy, the Firbolgs were looking in stupefaction at the companions, standing among the dead bodies of their comrades.

"Run!" shouted the prince. "To the horses!"

As a group they bolted into the thicket. Daryth led the way, forcing his way through the woods to the small clearing where they had left the mounts. The steeds, unharmed, nickered in welcome at their approach.

Tristan followed the party in the rear, keeping an eye on the Firbolgs. They seemed not entirely recovered, and he guessed—at least he hoped—that they would not be able to organize a pursuit for several minutes yet.

The companions mounted quickly, thankful that they had brought extra horses. They turned to ride from the area when the building behind them shuddered and groaned. Smoke billowed heavily from the door they had emerged from. The ground shook with the force of a heavy crash, and suddenly the smoke blossomed from the top of the temple.

"The roof is collapsing!" shouted Keren. "Look!"

The smoke trails emerging from the door immediately reversed course as a tremendous cloud rose into the air. The fire built to a roaring intensity as its air supply improved. They heard a tremendous sucking noise as air was pulled into the building, feeding the flames.

The force of the sucking draft uprooted small bushes, and created a forceful wind. Orange flames towered into the sky.

This fire would burn for a long time.

XXXXXXXXXX

Kazgoroth sensed the presence of the huge shape as it passed far below the surface of the sea. The Beast could feel the massive body rising—could sense the awesome might of its attack, as it rose toward the fleet. Kazgoroth even guessed, correctly, which longship would be the creature's first victim.

In the guise of Thelgaar, the Beast had led the fleet of longships from Iron Bay on a journey south, along the coast of Gwynneth. The heavy rams had indeed proved troublesome, as three ships had foundered in moderate seas during the voyage. Now, however, Kazgoroth knew that the potent enchantments laid on the beams would give them their only chance of dealing with the leviathan.

The massive creature erupted from the water like lava from a volcano. One entire ship, and fifty men, met an instant end between the crushing jaws. As the huge shape, bigger than anything living in the world, crashed back to the water, another longship capsized from the monstrous waves.

"To your oars!" the figure of Thelgaar bellowed, from the bow of his longship. Somehow the voice carried clearly across the churning sea, to the ears of every northman in the fleet.

And with the voice came a deadening of fear and thought.

The northmen heard the words, but mostly they felt the power of Kazgoroth's unnatural essence. And the power enchanted them, so that they became capable of nothing more than following the orders of their king. Certainly, without this enchantment, the appearance of the leviathan would have driven them mad with terror.

But now the longships surged forward as callused hands took the oars. Transfixed by the awesome sight of their leader, the northmen ignored the deaths of their comrades, seeking only to hear and obey the next command.

"Swing starboard!" The next order rang out with the same clarity as the first.

Like choreographed dancers, several hundred longships swung gracefully to the right. The frothing surface where the leviathan had disappeared melted back to the dark gray of the rest of the sea. The longships raced ahead, as sails were trimmed and oarpower gained momentum.

Kazgoroth again felt the leviathan climbing, and calmly watched it destroy another longship in the same manner as the first. The massive tail smashed another vessel to splinters as the creature crashed back to the surface.

The Beast waited again, pleased with the effect of its enchantment. The northmen rowed like automatons, showing no signs of panic. Kazgoroth knew that the leviathan would soon change its tactics, for the leaping and diving attacks would sap its strength too quickly.

And then, when it attacked from the surface, the poisoned rams would work their own magic. The crewmen on his ship saw Thelgaar stoop down and open a long crate that he had stored in the bow. From the crate he extracted a harpoon—one such as these sailors had never seen before. Thicker than a giant's wrist, it seemed nearly as long as one of the oars. The head of the weapon was a wicked barb of black, corroded steel. The air around the barb shimmered from the effect of its putrid essence.

The leviathan attacked again, and again, diving deep and then crushing a ship between its awesome jaws. Often, its tail, or the huge splash created by its body, would crush or swamp another vessel.

Kazgoroth watched perhaps a score of his vessels die thus, before the leviathan began to tire. Now, instead of diving, it swam just below the surface among the longships. Its great back rolled above the water like the coils of a snake. It turned suddenly and caved in the hull of a longship. It capsized another with a flip of its tail.

"Attack!" Thelgaar's voice boomed forward, propelled by the power of Kazgoroth. "Ram the beast!"

The longships now veered toward the monster, triggering dozens of collisions as the sailors, their wits slowed by the enchantment, could not take proper care with the maneuver. Nonetheless, a hundred longships closed in on the creature.

Several died from the powerful strokes of the tail, or the crushing bite of the massive jaws. While making one of these bites, however, a ram plunged through the leviathan's jaw. Roaring with pain, the creature bucked backward, sinking several more ships with the frenzy of its agony.

Kazgoroth felt some small dismay, for the fleet suffered greater losses than the Beast had anticipated. It cared nothing for the dying sailors, only for the loss of valuable tools in the master plan.

Still, the northmen's persistence began to tell. As the leviathan thrashed, another of the wicked rams plunged into its flank, tracing a long and bloody wound before breaking from the ship. Now the sea creature's thrashing became more frantic, and a dozen longships suffered accidental destruction or damage. Several more of the rams slashed into the slippery flanks, and the creature's struggles began to weaken.

"Forward!" cried Thelgaar, in a voice intended for his own crew alone. The longship darted forward, the figure of the white-bearded king standing proudly in the bow. His upraised arm held the impossibly large harpoon.

The ship drove close to the leviathan's massive head, which now rolled listlessly at the surface. Thelgaar's powerful shoulders flexed, and the harpoon rocketed forward to plunge deep into the shiny black shape, just behind one of the massive eyes.

The leviathan twitched convulsively. A long column of bubbles arose from its mouth. The huge creature struggled to keep its eyes open as it sank into the dark and frigid depths.

×××××××××××

"That was some fight, wasn't it? I haven't had that much fun in, oh, I don't know how many years!" The little dragon chattered incessantly, as they slowly left the Firbolg stronghold behind.

"Say, I've got a great idea! Let's go back and do it again! There must be a few Firbolgs left for us to torture!" Newt giggled with excitement at the thought of additional pranks.

"Um, maybe some other time," said Tristan, gently trying to dissuade their enthusiastic comrade.

"And where did you come from, friend?" asked Keren, as the little dragon remained visible for several seconds at a stretch.

"Why, I'm Newt, of course, and I live around here. Your friends had gotten themselves into terrible trouble, but lucky for them I happened to come along when I did. If I had been just a little later, well, who knows what would have happened? But there's certainly no point in dwelling on that!"

"Well done, Newt," said the bard, laughing. "It seems we owe you our lives!"

"Well, of course you do. I mean, really—what did you expect? Say, aren't you that bard fellow they dragged in awhile back? I thought you were dead, but, oh dear, it seems that you're not. Oh, this really is too bad—"

"Why is it too bad that our friend is alive?" demanded Robyn.

"Well, I do so hate to be wrong, and I told them all that you were probably dead, but you had to show up, alive as a hive of bees, and now—oh, but don't get me wrong. I think it's really quite splendid that you're alive—really I do."

"Indeed," nodded Keren. "Well, I'm quite relieved to hear that, Newt."

"Me too!" snorted Finellen. "I've always wanted to owe my life to a blue worm!"

Newt just said "Hummph!" and turned invisible.

The companions rode hard, paying little attention to direction, only seeking to put much distance between themselves and the Firbolgs. The horses flew eagerly across the rugged terrain, forcing their way through dense thickets of thorns and creepers.

After some miles, the unicorn gave a signal and they all reined in, briefly. Robyn dismounted and walked over to the magnificent animal who regarded them with huge eyes. She stroked its neck, and Tristan would have sworn that words exchanged between them, though he heard nothing.

Then, with a proud toss of its head, the unicorn turned and galloped away. The sleek white coat was visible among the tangled fens for some time, and they all watched until it had disappeared from sight.

Robyn said nothing, so they returned to their flight, riding now without panic but covering ground very quickly. Though Tristan wasn't certain, he thought their course was carrying them generally toward the east, away from the direction they had entered the fens.

Behind them, rising higher and higher every minute, a thick black pillar of smoke billowed into the air.

XXXXXXXXXXX

Grunnarch the Red selected his first target with care. The shock of the landing caught the large fishing village nearly by surprise. Many of the Ffolk fled inland but they were forced to leave all their possessions behind. Those who did not flee the raiders swiftly enough fell dead beneath swinging battleaxes or were taken as slaves and felt the bite of cold chains.

The northmen torched the village after collecting everything of value. The fishing boats at anchor in the sheltered cove were sunk or burned, and much livestock was slaughtered. Even before the flames climbed from the roof of the last cottage, the Bloodriders had disembarked their horses.

"Go," ordered the Red King. "Make haste, and show no mercy."

Laric smiled, the expression stretching the pasty skin across his cheeks into a grotesque mask. The captain's eyes smoldered with blood-lust, and Grunnarch fancied that they grew brighter at the thought of the killing to come.

"Do not worry," said Laric, swinging into the saddle of his sleek black stallion. "Mercy will not be a concern of mine. " Laric swung his arm forward, as his red cape made a fluid arc around him. Behind him, one hundred frenzied Riders struck out for the next cantrev.

In the ruins of the village, the bulk of Grunnarch's army feasted and drank well into the night. Many of the slaves—young women—suffered horribly, as objects of pleasure for the raiders.

The following morning, the northmen reembarked, sailing down the coast to strike at another fishing cantrev. Again and again they struck the small, isolated communities of the Ffolk, burning, killing, and enslav-ing. The Bloodriders rode miles inland, paralleling the progress of the fleet as it sailed southward along the coast, taking particular pleasure in wreaking destruction and death upon the inland Ffolk.

After several raids, the alarm was carried throughout the countryside. The word of the depredations traveled even faster than the scourging advance of the Bloodriders. The deeds of those scarlet-garbed horsemen exceeded the horrors of their seaborne countrymen. The Bloodriders could not burden themselves with slaves, so survivors of their raids were rare.

As pandemonium spread in the land, however, the northmen found village after village abandoned before they had reached it. Valuables and livestock had been removed, and the inhabitants had fled further inland.

Finding a large and sheltered bay in the center of Corwell's eastern coastline, Grunnarch ordered his fleet beached. As planned, here the Bloodriders reunited with the army. A few of the older men were detailed to watch the slaves and the ships, while the rest of the warriors prepared to march.

It was time, Grunnarch knew, to begin the second phase of Thelgaar's master plan.

XXXXXXXXXX

"Where's Newt?"

Robyn's question brought the companions up short.

They reined in their mounts and looked around, realizing that there had been no sign of the little dragon for some time. They did not risk calling aloud for him—they could not take the chance of advertising their position.

"He must have gone back home," surmised the prince. "Wherever that is."

"He's quite a character," observed Keren. "We owe him a lot."

"Indeed," the others agreed. The diminutive serpent—Finellen described him as a faerie dragon—had saved their lives with his timely "prank."

"But our food will last a little longer now," observed Pawldo, ruefully contemplating his almost empty saddlebags.

"We're better off without him," observed Finellen. "You can't trust a faerie dragon as far as you can see him—when he's invisible."

By nightfall they emerged from the fens, and found a dry and grassy clearing for their camp. The ground had climbed slightly from the lowlands of the swamp, and they could look back on their path of the last few days.

"Look at that," remarked Daryth in awe. The towering column of smoke still dominated the sky behind them.

"How many Firbolgs do you suppose we killed?" asked Tristan.

"A lot, I'm sure—but a lot of them got away, without a doubt," replied Keren.

"And every one of 'em is looking for us," muttered Pawldo, dismounting stiffly as they halted for the night.

They decided not to risk building a fire, and the warm summer night made this no discomfort. Still tense and jumpy from the intense combat and flight of the day, the companions sat quietly in their grassy bower. The light of a half moon, pouring from a clear sky, gave them illumination and some small comfort. The crimson glow in the western sky added a surreal effect to their surroundings.

"You haven't told us how you came to be the guests of the Firbolgs," said Robyn, after a long period of silence.

"Well, it was foolish, actually. I decided to take a short cut—through Myrloch Vale—on my way to the coast. " Keren smiled, sheepishly. "It was the long way around, to tell the truth, but I couldn't pass up the chance to see Myrloch again, when I was so close.

"Anyway, I got ambushed practically as soon as I came over the pass—a bunch of them got me surrounded and tackled me. Sable put more than one eye out, but they almost got him too."

"It's lucky he got away. He told me about you," Robyn explained.

"Well, isn't he a smart bird!" laughed the bard. He sobered quickly. "I owe you all a lot, and I thank you. You know, there might even be a song in this!" Keren leaned back thoughtfully, humming a bit of melody.

The dwarf snorted. Scratching her ear with a dirty finger, Finellen looked around. Her whiskers twitched irritably. "You know," she said suddenly, her rich female voice emerging incongruously from the bushy beard. "For humans—and a halfling—you folks are not all that bad. I'm proud to have fought with you."

The simple statement, they all realized, meant a great deal. The dwarves were traditionally aloof and haughty toward the shorter-lived races, rarely deigning to involve themselves in human quarrels.

"We're honored by your praise," responded Tristan. "We, too, look highly on the chance that brought you among us as a companion."

"Where are your people?" asked Robyn. "Do you live near here?"

"My people live wherever we want, within the borders of Myrloch Vale. It happens that, this year, we've taken residence in a comfortable group of caves, a few days north of here, in the Highlands.

"It was there that we saw the signs of Firbolg activity. The fen country, down there, wasn't such a bad place in the past. We knew of this Firbolg stronghold, but it's never been a problem before. Lately, though, they started hauling coal here from the mountains. I was sent to investigate. Now," she said, chuckling wryly, "I can tell my people that the problem has burned itself out."

"Perhaps one part of the problem," observed Keren, "but not its core. Gwynneth is in dire danger, and the help of your people would aid greatly in the thwarting of this threat."

"Oh no!" objected Finellen, with surprising vehemence. "We're not about to get entangled in a bunch of human problems! It's like my mother used to tell me—if you see a human coming, you see trouble coming!

"I owe you my thanks, for getting me out of that cell. But don't go expectin' us to bail you out of another of your big messes!"

"But this is not a problem that threatens only the humans," argued Tristan. "All the peaceful Ffolk of Gwynneth—including those of Myrloch Vale—are in danger. Can't you convince your people of that?"

"I couldn't even try!" shot back the dwarf. "I'm sorry, but this is a problem you'll have to work out for yourselves."

They tried for several hours to get the stubborn dwarf to reconsider, but she was adamant. Finally, they dropped the topic, as tempers on both sides neared the breaking point.

In the morning, Finellen was gone.

✕ ✕ ✕ ✕ ✕ ✕ ✕ ✕ ✕

For many days this time, Erian remained locked in the body of the wolf. Only gradually did his human form return, in a process of nearly unendurable pain. He finally awakened far inland in an area of near wilderness. As before, he was naked and covered with blood.

Horror gripped his mind with icy fingers. He knew now that he could not return to the world of men. Choking out sobs of agony and fear, he staggered through the wilds.

For tendays he ate only such food as his bare hands could gather. Nuts, berries, grubs, and even mice all passed his smacking lips—he cared not for taste, nor appearance. He only craved enough food to stay alive. Once he stole a chicken from an isolated farm, giving him the best meal since returning to his human body.

He moved aimlessly, or so he thought. Driven on by the consuming horror in his mind, he staggered through the wilderness, first moving north, and then east. He paid no attention to his location, but his direction was guided by an instinct deeper than his consciousness.

Gradually, night by night, the moon faded to black, and then slowly grew. It fattened over his head, passing from sliver, to crescent, to half moon. And still it kept growing. Behind the moon, came the Tears of the Moon, growing brighter and more distinct each passing night, a glittering necklace of light.

A consuming fear gripped him with the approach of the next full moon. That one, he knew, would be the summer solstice—the brightest full moon of the year. What effect this would have he could only guess, but all his guesses led him to stark nightmares.

Several times he resolved to take his own life, before the nightmare could become real. But always he lacked the will. Driven by his fear, madness slowly took his mind from him. Always he kept moving, as if toward some unknown destiny that had been planted within him by Kazgoroth's bite.

And every night the moon grew larger.

XXXXXXXXXXX

"You know a lot, for a man who has trained hounds all of his life." Keren's comment was casual, but Daryth sat bolt upright, staring at the bard.

"Yeah—I've picked up a few skills here and there," he said, shrugging.

The small fire created an island of warmth in the cool forest. The two men sat on either side of the blaze. Tristan and Robyn had gone for a walk, and Pawldo slumbered within a nearby mountain of furs.

"It's almost as if you had been trained by masters in your craft—say, those masters who teach at the Academy of Stealth—the Pasha of Calimshan's school for spies?"

Daryth was silent for a moment. Finally, he chuckled. "You are well-traveled, indeed.

"Yes, I attended the sultan's 'school'—I was trained as a spy, or a thief, or assassin, however you choose to describe it. I have also," he added, defensively, "trained desert racers and other dogs for many years!"

"Then, why are you here?" The bard studied Daryth's eyes very carefully as he asked the question. For a moment, the Calishite looked away.

"I ran away from the Pasha, the school, everything. I got into some trouble with the Pasha over rights to . . . some property I had acquired, and became a sailor the same night. Corwell was the first port of call, and I jumped ship there."

The bard leaned back again, satisfied. "You fight very well. You must have been a good student!"

Daryth laughed, and then grew serious. "You know, I've done a lot of fighting against things in my life, but I've never fought *for* anything before."

"Indeed," replied the bard. "Well, you're fighting for Corwell now."

xxxxxxxxxxx

Tristan and Robyn walked slowly together in the cool night. Neither of them felt like sleeping—at least, not right now. As the moon illuminated her exquisite face, the prince wanted to take her in his arms, but his courage failed him.

"You did very well, back there," said Robyn, quietly, "Your father would have been proud of you."

Tristan froze, surprised by the compliment. He recovered his voice quickly, enough to say "Thank you," then turned toward the maiden.

They stood together on a rocky lakeshore, gazing at a world that appeared to have never known violence or death. The moon, half full and followed by her glittering Tears, stood near the zenith. Thousands of stars—more than he had ever seen before—glittered from the black sky. Though their camp, and the small fire, was just a few steps away, the screening rocks hid it perfectly. It might have been very distant, as far as Caer Corwell, for all they could see of it.

Tristan reluctantly thought about his father. The king must now be bitterly disappointed in his son—leaving in the middle of the night, ignoring the command of the company his father had given him.

"We all did pretty well," reflected the prince. "But if my father were here, I'm sure he'd point out a few mistakes." He did not try to hide his bitterness.

"Don't be so hard on him!" Robyn whirled, surprising him with her intensity. "Why do you two have to fight all the time? It's not your fault—alone—but neither of you is willing to admit that the other has a point of view."

"I don't know why we do it. He's always wanted me to be better at whatever I do—and, maybe, I do some things to annoy him. I will not be his servant!"

"I don't think he wants that," she said, a gentle smile softening her face. "I think he just wants his son to be a worthy prince of the Ffolk. And if he'd been with us today, he'd know that you are!"

The praise from Robyn overwhelmed all other emotions. Tristan felt that he would fight a Firbolg barehanded if she would smile at him afterward.

"We needed you there as well," he said. "It was remarkable the way you understood the unicorn."

She smiled. "When something like that happens, it surprises me that no one else can hear—the message was so plain! It was like the desecration of the ground under that building—I could sense the evil there, and it surprised me that you didn't see it."

"Robyn," the prince began, awkwardly. He turned to the maiden and reached out for her. Her eyes met his, and she deliberately leaned into him so that their lips met. There was nothing tentative about their kiss. It was as if each moment of their separate lives had been racing toward this moment. He pulled her to him, his blood pounding at the feel of her body against him. She met him eagerly, and for a moment their nerves and muscles and bones melted into each other. . . . Then Robyn gently pushed Tristan away.

"When we get back home," the prince started to speak in a rush, "I want to—I mean, will you—"

"No."

The simple word brought him up short. For a moment, jealousy surged through him again. "What! Is it because of Daryth?"

"Don't be a child," she rebuked him. "It isn't—at least, not that I know of. He means a lot to me—he is a good friend. And so are you."

The classification, as a 'good friend,' came like a bucket of ice water poured over Tristan. He turned away, not knowing whether to cry out in rage, or to sob in despair. After a second, he turned back.

"I want you to know that I love you."

She smiled, her eyes moist, and kissed him quickly again. Then she turned and walked slowly back to the fire, leaving him standing in the forest that seemed, suddenly, to grow very cold.

xxxxxxxxxx

Pain wracked the giant body. Grayness clouded its vision, and it was not the grayness of the darkened sea. Its great muscles flexed violently, then relaxed. Slowly it sank, knowing only that burning pain.

And then the pain disappeared, leaving behind a warm, comfortable glow. Grayness became bright, and the arms of the goddess beckoned.

Thus the leviathan died.

xxxxxxxxxx

More than a hundred longships had been scattered across the steel-gray Sea of Moonshae. Splinters of wood, survivors, and bodies all bobbed in the cold waters. Many of the remaining longships wallowed low in the water, nearly foundering, or they listed to the side with damaged hulls. The battle was won, but not without cost.

A low rumbling sound bubbled from the depths, and the water around the center of the fleet churned, steamed, and frothed. Then gouts of fire erupted from the depths. Two dozen ships vanished immediately, and twenty-foot waves rolled across an equal number, swamping or capsizing them.

The sea boiled for many minutes. When the roaring finally subsided, the surviving vessels regrouped slowly, delayed by broken masts, missing oars, and torn sails. Finally, the vessels limped toward the nearest shore.

xxxxxxxxxx

The goddess feared that her pain would drive her mad. An aching despair grew inside her. Even through the curtain of her grief, she recoiled in terrible awareness of the increased power of the Beast.

The stabbing sore of the Darkwell inflamed her skin, sending poisonous tendrils crawling throughout her being. The passing of the leviathan unleashed potent venom from the black pool, and the Balance shifted dangerously. The numbness—the urge to sleep—penetrated the goddess more deeply than ever.

Suddenly she felt very tired.

XXXXXXXXX

Roaring flames rose high into the sky as the cantrev burned. Wails rose from the pyre in a hopeless, keening chorus of death. Ringed around the little community, and with blood-stained spears prodding back into the flames any villagers attempting to save themselves, the Bloodriders observed the carnage.

Strangely motionless, they stared into the fire as if mesmerized. The hellish glow reflected from their crimson cloaks, and seemed to glow unnaturally in the eyes of the bloody Riders and their black, shining horses.

And all at once the fire surged upward, and the Bloodriders raised their voices in a throaty chant. The words seemed meaningless, and yet carried dire portent in a language so ancient that it should not have been known by any of the sinister horsemen. Yet now they spoke.

And they understood.

BOOK
THREE

GAVIN

11

A black tentacle slithered toward Robyn, wrapping tightly around her calf, searing her skin with venomous suckers. Screaming, she tried to crawl away, but the tentacle dragged her along the stony ground.

Another grasping tendril reached around her waist, squeezing the breath from her lungs in a painful vise. The ground shifted and cracked, as a great fissure opened beside her. It seemed bottomless—within its bowels seethed an orange tumult, rumbling slowly.

She turned and grabbed at the ground, uprooting small plants as the tentacles dragged her toward the abyss. Suddenly, from the black smoke that seemed to swirl everywhere, a pair of white slender arms emerged. Even in that foul setting, the arms were wrapped in the whitest satin, with soft hands that promised comfort and safety.

But then the tentacles pulled, and the arms, and finally the hands, vanished into the black smoke.

With a low moan, Robyn awakened, drenched with perspiration. Sitting up, she held a hand to her mouth as if to stifle any further sounds, and looked around.

The camp was quiet. Tristan and Daryth slept quietly by the fire, while Pawldo snored under a mound of furs in the shadows. The fire had died so that only an occasional deep red flicker showed among the coals.

Canthus, lying next to the prince, kicked and whimpered in his sleep, Twitching, he rolled almost into the coals.

Then Robyn saw Keren, standing alone in the shadow of a great rock. The bard faced her, the light of the half moon casting his face into eerie shadows. Still, the shock and pain written across his features were plainly visible.

"What is it?" Robyn asked, getting to her feet. "I'm frightened."

"I do not know. Never have I had such a nightmare! This is a portent of something dire, indeed."

"I had a nightmare, too." She shuddered. "It was the most frightening thing I could imagine!"

The bard put a comforting arm around Robyn, and they sat before the coals. She threw several small sticks into the embers, and they quickly crackled into light.

Suddenly Canthus leaped to his feet, growling nervously into the darkness. Stiff-legged, he walked about the camp, finally settling nervously behind Robyn and Keren, alertly studying the woods to their backs.

"He senses it, too," Robyn said.

"I can only guess, but I think the goddess has been struck a cruel blow. Perhaps, even, the loss of one of her children."

"Kamerynn! The unicorn!" For a moment, Robyn felt truly forlorn, as she imagined that magnificent creature killed.

"Perhaps, or the leviathan—there is no telling."

"Look!" cried the woman, as her gaze crossed the sky.

Above them, a hundred streaks of light flashed briefly between the stars, and then blinked away. Still other flashes followed, thousands and thousands of tiny blinking lines in the sky, as if the moon herself wept.

Keren's arm was warm around her shoulders, and Robyn drew some hope from her friend's presence. The two of them remained thus through the long hours until morning.

XXXXXXXXXX

The men of the cantrev spread across the field before the Red King's northmen, and Grunnarch smiled at the thought of the approaching combat.

"To the kill!" cried the king, and the line of northmen surged forward. A deep bellow rumbled from the raiders, and the men of the Ffolk wavered.

Nonetheless, these farmers and craftsmen stood hard against the charge. Outnumbered four to one by the bearded, howling attackers, the cantrev men fought for time to allow their women and children to escape.

Grunnarch cut open the chest of a farmer, casually stepping on the dying man as he sought another victim. Around him, his men took a bloody toll of the Ffolk. While some of the raiders closed in to wipe out the last pockets of resisting fighters, Grunnarch led the bulk of his force into the cantrev.

Most of the inhabitants had left, but some still emerged from their cottages, terror-stricken, as the raiders swarmed through. For these, there would be no escape.

Bloodlust seemed to pound in his temples as the Red King bellowed his challenge. An old woman turned to face him, giving her daughters a chance to escape, but Grunnarch, giving a sharp laugh, cut off her head in a single stroke. Others of his men grabbed the daughters—barely young women—and dragged them screaming into the cottage.

For a moment Grunnarch looked around, realizing that his vision had grown hazy and red. Panting, he gradually became aware of a pounding headache.

He watched numbly as two children running in terror were spitted by his men upon a long spear, first one, then the other, and cast casually aside. The Red King felt suddenly nauseous at the sight, and turned to vomit against the cottage.

He turned again to regard the scene of battle, and he could barely recall its details. Bodies, most belonging to the Ffolk, lay scattered throughout his field of vision.

Somehow, the war seemed to have lost its thrill.

× × × × × × × × × ×

For two more days they continued the journey to the east, finally entering the pastoral cantrevs of Eastern Corwell. Tristan had rarely visited this part of the kingdom, connected as it was to the rest of the realm by a narrow corridor of land between Myrloch Vale and Llyrath Forest—a corridor which could be traveled only with difficulty.

In fact, the prince was not altogether certain that they had, in fact, reentered the kingdom until late one afternoon when they finally stumbled across an actual road.

"We'll certainly come upon a fishing cantrev soon," said Tristan to Keren. "And there you should have no trouble finding passage to Callidyrr. We'll accompany you until then."

The bard looked wistful. "It galls that I've been ordered to return to the High King, for it seems certain that the adventure, and hence the tales, of this summer will occur here on Gwynneth."

Idly, the bard strummed a few notes upon his harp. He tried several variations on the tune, until he found one that he liked. He repeated this one several times, and gradually a look of contentment grew upon his face.

As darkness began to creep into the eastern sky, they came upon a small hollow where a little campfire twinkled cheerfully, and a string of donkeys stood patiently nearby. A figure shuffled slowly around the fire, silhouetted in its glow, and from its size the prince worried that they had stumbled across a renegade Firbolg.

Then a booming voice, unmistakably human, rumbled up the road to them.

"Well met, travelers! Would you come and sup with me? A fire is always warmer with the kindling of conversation to feed it!"

The silhouette turned into a great bear of a man as he moved into the dusky clearing, greeting them with exaggeratedly widespread arms and a huge, ear-splitting grin. He certainly was the largest human the prince had ever seen. A flowing black beard combined with thick, curling hair of the same color all but concealed his broad face. His smile, which made his eyes sparkle, revealed an array of chipped and broken teeth. His garments were heavy and serviceable, albeit worn and grimy.

"I am Gavin, smith of Cantrev Myrrdale," explained the stranger, in a voice that thundered through the night.

"Thanks for your welcome," responded Tristan, dismounting before the smith. The prince introduced himself and his companions. If the smith recognized the Kendrick name as his king's, he gave no notice of the fact.

The companions relieved their horses of the burdens of saddles and bridles. Tristan noticed the hounds gathering eagerly around the fire, and he saw for the first time a large kettle, bubbling and steaming in the coals. A truly delightful odor rose from the pot. Even considering the size of the cook, the pot held far more than one man could eat.

"Now, won't you join me for a bite?" called the smith, when their horses had been tended. "There's plenty for all!"

"Why did you cook such a large batch?" asked Robyn, looking at the simmering stew. "Did you know we were coming?" Her question, Tristan sensed, was only half facetious.

"Why, not you in particular," replied the smith, chuckling heartily. "But this is the last night of my journey, and I had a full haunch of mutton left. I have often found that the means to be generous will often result in an opportunity for the same arising!" He threw back his shaggy head and roared with laughter, as if he had just made a great joke.

"And here tonight," he continued, gesturing expansively, "I have good company, and enough food for us all."

"Indeed," observed the bard, "though the good fortune would seem to be our own."

"Let it be all of ours! Many a night I've been on the road, and camped beside a small fire with nought but me asses to keep me company. Oh, and it's nice enough that they are, but very short on conversation!" Again, the smith convulsed himself with hilarity, and the others could not suppress smiles of amusement.

The mutton stew tasted fabulous after the dry trail fare that had sustained them for a tenday. Gavin produced a flask of biting rye whiskey that added a smooth glow to the meal. All of the companions ate like starving wolves, and the smith like a starving bear, but the pot was still only half empty when they could eat no more. In a flourish of generosity, the smith then saw that the hounds had plenty to eat.

They fed the fire with large logs, and built it perhaps higher than caution warranted. Still, no one complained—it just added to the pleasurable atmosphere.

Tristan leaned back against a tree, enjoying the blaze. "It almost feels like we're home again," he said, stretching leisurely.

" 'Again'?" asked the smith. "And where is it ye've been?"

"Through Myrloch Vale," replied the bard, "from Caer Corwell."

"I've been to that place, I have," boasted the smith, "in the service of our king himself, against the northmen on Moray. That would be yer father, I'm thinkin'. " Gavin looked toward the prince.

"Yes, I am Prince of Corwell."

"And how fares our king?"

"He was . . . fine, when I left him. He has ordered the gathering of companies from the cantrevs—we have had reports of a great mustering of northmen."

"Indeed?" Gavin sat up straight. For the first time, a look of concern came over his face, "Perhaps I should not have left my home. " Nervously, the giant smith looked toward the east.

"Myrrdale . . . is that on the coast?" The prince could not remember the town.

"No, some twenty miles inland. It should be safe enough, even if war comes to the eastern cantrevs. I doubt the northmen would strike very far inland. And we'll be there early tomorrow, anyway . . . No, no, I've naught to worry about. " Still, the big smith cast many glances toward the east, and they knew he wished to be home.

"It's my little girls I'm missin' the most," Gavin said, wistfully staring into the flames. "They're the cutest little mites this side of Myrloch, if I do say so myself. The spittin' image of their mother, my dear Sharreen."

"I'd like to meet them," Robyn said, smiling wistfully at the thought of the man's love for his family. She wondered if her own father had loved her the same way.

The second flask of rye finally worked its effects upon the companions, and they fell asleep around the fire. For the first time in many days, they did not bother to post a watch, and their camp was not troubled during the night.

They rose early, sharing the smith's infectious enthusiasm for a new day. The smith strung his donkeys together, and the companions helped him load the heavy crates which had been lying among the trees.

"Iron and coal," he explained. "The fodder of my forge. Twice a year I journey to Cantrev Thorndyke for supplies."

"That's one of the mountain cantrevs, isn't it?" recalled Tristan.

"Indeed—they mine the best iron in the Moonshaes up there, apart from the dwarves, of course. And what human could buy iron from the dwarves?" The smith chuckled deeply at the thought of the reclusive dwarves selling to humans.

"It's not that I couldn't hire me a carter to make the trip instead," explained the smith, as loudly as if he spoke to a gathering of several hundred. "It's just that—" His voice dropped to a conspiratorial bellow—"I like the mountains so much that I give meself the trip as a little reward."

"They are beautiful, these mountains," agreed the prince, wishing he had paid more attention to his surroundings during their flight.

"But again," the smith continued, looking eagerly toward the low ridge that would be their first landmark of the morning's journey, "there's nothin' like gettin', home again afterward. And with any luck, we'll be there in time for lunch!"

A pleasantly warm breeze rose from the lowlands, and the sun smiled from a cloudless sky. Light of heart, the six of them set off down the road. The smith led his string of donkeys on foot, but he had no difficulty matching the pace of the others, who were mounted. As they rode, Keren worked some more with his tune, finally developing it into a delightful melody.

"What is that?" asked Robyn.

"Just a sort of a ballad I'm working on. Perhaps I'll play it for you when I've finished."

"I'd like that," she answered, humming a piece of the tune as he went back to work. The hounds bounded through the fields and forests to either side with energy Tristan had not seen in them since their flight from the Firbolgs' lair.

The road wound easily up the low ridge, with a scarcely noticeable grade, and soon they came upon a wide, grassy field at the crest. Before them, the ground dropped gently through a series of broad valleys. Narrow streams sparkled amid orchards and pastures. The horizon vanished into the haze, where, Tristan knew, the sea lay about thirty miles to the east.

But all this detail faded into insignificance as they perceived one stark and painful fact: Columns of smoke rose into the sky from several places—thick pillars of darkness, each marking a cantrev of the Ffolk, a burning cantrev.

Gavin groaned—a strangled, inhuman sound incongruously

emerging from the smith's barrel chest. Tristan knew, without asking, that the nearest of the columns marked Cantrev Myrrdale.

X X X X X X X X X X

"Blast and damn! You are all idiots!" Grunnarch the Red ordered his men to assemble outside the ruined cantrev. Food, drink, and wenching seemed to have driven most of the worthless scum to the brink of unconsciousness. Those who did not stir readily enough felt the thud of the Red King's solid boot.

Stomping among the wreckage of people and homes, he cursed with renewed vengeance as he considered the true reason for his irritation.

Where were the damned Bloodriders?

For a tenday he had had no direct word from Laric, the captain of the Riders. Rumors trickled back, about villages scourged until they were nothing more than black splotches on the ground, about acts of unspeakable cruelty.

Grunnarch recalled, uneasily, his last meeting with Laric. The man had seemed determined to go his own way. He had barely listened to Grunnarch talk, yet something forbidding in his simmering gaze had stopped the king's rebuke before it reached his lips.

Now, it seemed that Laric's negligence was jeopardizing the whole plan.

The Bloodriders were to have met the rest of the army here, at Cantrev Macsheehan, three days ago. Macsheehan was a large and wealthy cantrev, and the army had been able to provision an entire supply train for the march on Corwell.

As Thelgaar had predicted, the tide of refugees flowing westward had grown to a flood. If the army could be ready to march within another day, they could strike through Myrloch across the refugees' route of retreat, and massacre them.

A dull thundering finally caught Grunnarch's attention, and he looked down the road. His anger vied with relief, for the Bloodriders were thundering into the great field at full gallop. The black horses gleamed with sweat, their flanks and legs caked with dust. The fur cloaks of the Riders were also travel-stained.

Laric reined in before Grunnarch and leaped from the saddle. The king prepared a rebuke for his henchman, but the oaths died on his lips, as his eyes locked with horror on the face of the approaching man.

The Bloodrider's skin had lightened to a pasty gray hue, and his bright red lips stood out in awful contrast from the unnatural face. The man's eyes were sunk deep into his head, but seemed to stare from their cave-like sockets with fiery intensity. Grunnarch thought fleetingly of a skull, upon which someone had painted garish red lips.

Laric walked passed the king without saying a word, and Grunnarch the Red, a man not known for reticence, could not command him to stop. In fury, the Red King returned to his task of organizing his army, kicking and lashing out with renewed fury at anyone and anything that failed to hop to.

As he moved about the camp, the king saw that his troops universally reacted to the appearance of the Bloodriders. The rest of the army collected uneasily, with many nervous glances at the cadaverous Riders. The horsemen ignored the other northmen, preparing a simple camp in an area they claimed for themselves.

Grunnarch, wishing he could ignore the Bloodrider, sent a messenger to summon Laric to his meeting of officers. The captain of the Bloodriders arrived silently, joining the ring of leaders gathered around Grunnarch. The group shifted apprehensively for a moment. When movement ceased, no one stood within five feet of Laric.

"We will march with the dawn!" declared Grunnarch. "Raag Hammerstaad will take half the army and the supply train, and advance along the main road toward Corwell. He will make certain that bands of refugees cannot slip around through our onslaught and return here."

"We will spread the force across the entire valley!" declared Hammerstaad. "A rabbit will not be able to slip through our lines!"

"Good. The rest of us will strike out due west, through a pass in that ridge." Grunnarch pointed to a skyline of rock some twenty miles to the west. It looked sheer and unclimbable from their current vantage, and a rumble of surprise arose from the men.

"We will be met by a guide," the Red King assured them, hoping that Thelgaar had spoken the truth about the treacherous druid. "He will reveal the pass to us.

"The Bloodriders will precede this column," he continued, looking at Laric. The captain looked on, his mind clearly elsewhere. "For the rest of us, speed is the major requirement. We take only enough provisions for five days. We march steadily, from dawn until dusk.

"And we come out of the mountains directly in the path of those refugees. The whole mob of them will be pinched between the two armies!"

The thought of the massacre that would ensue brought the blood pounding to his brain. He could see the same excitement shining in the eyes of the assembled warriors.

In the eyes of Laric, that excitement seemed to shine like the coals of a hot forge.

XXXXXXXXXX

Gavin abandoned the string of donkeys and lumbered down the road toward the blazing village, which still lay in the distance behind another low ridge.

Tristan immediately galloped forward to join the smith. "Wait!" he cried. "Take one of the horses—we'll ride with you!"

Gavin ran stolidly, as if he hadn't heard, and Tristan repeated the plea. Finally, his lungs heaving from exertion, the big man stopped. The pain in the smith's eyes struck the prince through the heart. He quickly dismounted and gave the smith his horse. The big gray gelding was the largest of the mounts. The prince remounted on an extra horse as the others began to gallop down the road. The dogs raced along in the ditch, while the donkeys, unled, plodded steadily along, falling quickly to the rear.

They slowed to a canter shortly, and less than an hour later they looked down upon a wasteland of ravaged farms, burned buildings, and trampled fields. In the center of the wasteland lay the smoldering wreckage of Cantrev Myrrdale.

Not a single building remained standing upon the site of the small community. Most of it had been burned, but some smaller buildings had apparently been trampled into the ground with ruthless determination.

Spurring their mounts, they neared the ruins. Now they passed some of the burned farms, and occasionally saw human or animal remains lying in the fields or along the road. From the appearance of the bodies, it seemed that the carnage had occurred at least twenty-four hours earlier. No living creature entered their sight during the entire ride, except for the crows that climbed, squawking, from the corpses as the riders passed. Reining in at the edge of town, they all dismounted. Gavin lurched forward, stumbling down a charred and devastated main street, while Tristan motioned the others to wait.

"What could have done this?" asked Daryth, after a long minute of silence. Beside him, Robyn choked and turned away from the scene.

"I don't think this is the work of Firbolgs," Tristan muttered. "It's too thorough."

"Northmen?" Pawldo asked the question through clenched lips.

"Something far more sinister, I fear." The bard spoke very seriously. "The earth itself has suffered a desecration."

Robyn, moaning quietly, took the reins of her mount for support. Tristan stepped to her side and took her arm. He shook violently.

"Let's spread out and look around," suggested the prince. "Look for clues as to who did this—I'd hate to think that the Firbolgs are numerous enough to garrison a stronghold like that and still have enough to ravage the countryside!"

Robyn stayed outside the village, while Tristan, Daryth, Pawldo, and Keren spread out and moved among the ashes of the town. Here and there, a smoke-blackened shape that could have been a corpse lay like so much grotesque wreckage.

Sickened, the prince walked numbly. He felt as if a deep wound had been struck into his own vitals. His stomach knotted with pain, he forced himself on.

Tristan finally found Gavin, kneeling among the splintered ruins of a small cottage. The building had not burned, but instead had been flattened by some powerful force. Looking carefully at the ground, Tristan saw many horses' hoofprints among the shattered boards.

Gavin did not look up from the pitifully small, wrinkled form he held in his massive arms. The smith moaned softly, and Tristan's throat choked. Tears stung his eyes as he turned away.

Daryth ran over to join him, his smooth leather boots carrying him soundlessly through the mass of rubble. He slowed as he approached, and Tristan pulled him beyond Gavin's hearing.

"Northmen!" the Calishite announced, pointing toward the far side of the village. "They're about a mile from the village and they're coming this way."

"How many?" asked the prince, suddenly aroused. Perhaps this village could be avenged!

"About a score," answered Daryth.

Tristan looked at Gavin, who tenderly deposited the body next to another tiny form on a smooth patch of ground.

"Gavin, the enemy approaches your village. Join us in vengeance!"

The big man stared dumbly at the ground, making no sign to indicate he had heard. Instead, he poked again into the rubble. They watched as he gently cleared the wreckage from the last body—this one full grown—crushed beneath a wall.

"Leave me," grunted the smith, turning to look Tristan in the eyes. Though tears streaked the smith's broad visage, he looked rational and firm. "I will die here, where I should have been yesterday. Let the enemy come to me alone."

"Would you have them burned, with the rest of this town?" Tristan snapped, pointing to the bodies. "Would you kneel here and have your head struck from your shoulders?

"Or will you stand and fight beside companions who would offer their lives in a battle to avenge your village? Answer me, man!" Daryth and Gavin both looked at the prince in shock. The prince stared coldly into the eyes of the smith.

"Yes, of course, you are right," mumbled Gavin. Kneeling in the wreckage again, the smith pulled great sheets of wood from the pile, tossing them casually aside. Reaching the remains of a trampled bed, he threw that away as well, finally revealing a long, flat box.

He slipped the latch and opened the lid. Reaching into the box, he pulled out the largest hammer that Tristan had ever seen. Its haft was fully six feet long, and the massive head of cold, black iron could not have weighed less than fifty pounds. Yet the smith twirled the massive weapon through the air with feathery ease. Gavin looked toward the edge of town, from where Pawldo now ran in their direction.

"So tell me," he said calmly. "What do you want me to do?"

X X X X X X X X X X

"Would you care for some pudding?" The thin but sturdy old woman held out the wooden bowl with almost childish eagerness. Her visitor looked up, smacking his lips with the last of the quail, and nodded.

Gwendolynn, druid of Dynloch Pass, got few visitors to her remote grove, high in the Synnorian Mountains. Thus, when Trahern of Oakvale had arrived, she had persuaded him to join her for hot tea, then dinner. Now, of course, it was far too late for him to begin a journey home.

Oakvale was a distant grove, but Trahern was known to Gwendolynn from councils over many decades. She felt girlishly pleased at his visit.

Dynloch Pass lay so high in the mountains, with approaches so convoluted, that few besides the Llewyrr, dwarves, and druids knew of its existence. Gwendolynn had tended this region for more than half a century. Trahern must have some purpose for his trip, but she asked nothing, being respectful of the druid's privacy.

She chattered happily into the evening as they sat before the hearth, talking of the wild places that were her mountains. Finally, rocking cozily in her favorite chair, she nodded off before the fire. She did not see the fiery glow that consumed her guest's eyes. Nor did she see him rise as she dreamed of eagles, loftiest of her flock.

Nor did she see the steely dagger or the treacherous thrust that, together, ended her life.

Trahern wiped the blade clean, and then lay down to sleep. The next morning, he left the old druid's body to the scavengers, as he started across the secret trailways of Dynloch Pass. His progress was slow, for every fifty paces he stopped to build a large cairn, clearly marking the trail.

X X X X X X X X X X

The twenty or so northmen marched wearily toward the wreckage of Cantrev Myrrdale. Tristan saw that these men had no wounded with them, nor did their clothing show signs of recent battle. Nor did these northmen have horses. They were certainly not the band that had ravaged the village.

Yet they were here, deep within the borders of the kingdom of Corwell, and they were outfitted for war. The prince had no doubt that they were the enemy.

He saw the trudging column move wearily among the smoldering buildings as it entered the village. Suddenly, from the swirling smoke, what seemed a shower of arrows struck them, as Pawldo and Keren fired one after another with rapid precision.

The northman in the lead pitched forward, killed instantly by an arrow in the back of his neck. Another gasped and died with a feathered shaft sticking through his chest. In an instant, another pair screamed and stumbled to the ground.

One of the northmen shouted something, and the survivors charged toward the archers. Several cursed or bellowed animal noises as they attacked.

As they advanced, however, five snarling moorhounds burst from the smoke on their left flank. The dogs were led by a great hound that ripped out a man's throat with its first leap, an iron collar deflecting a thrust of the dying man's sword.

"Let's go!" cried Tristan.

With a grunt, Gavin spurred the gray gelding forward, and thudded toward the northmen.

Tristan, Gavin, and Daryth surged from the smoke to strike the northmen from behind. Mounted, they held their formidable weapons high. The Sword of Cymrych Hugh, gleaming in Tristan's hand, smashed an enemy's sword as if it were an icicle, and clove the warrior from forehead to collarbone.

Gavin's long-hafted hammer crashed about him vengefully, and the raiders fell back in fear from its deadly blows.

Daryth rode quickly at the enemy, slashing with his scimitar and leaving gaping wounds before his nimble mare sprang away.

Tristan, Daryth, and Gavin each struck a northman dead, and the rest began to flee madly through the smoke, taking the only path between dogs, riders, and archers.

The dogs snapped and snarled in pursuit, and Daryth and Gavin lunged after them as well. Tristan reined in to look around for Robyn but did not see her.

Suddenly, speaking in a strange language, her voice cut through the air. Tristan's heart nearly stopped as he saw her step from the swirling smoke into the path of the fleeing northmen. She stood before them and repeated the strange phrase. Tristan, his heart in his throat, gasped at her power and beauty.

The raiders, as one man, screamed and threw down their weapons. The prince could see the blades smoldering, glowing cherry red and shedding sparks, as they struck the ground. Howling in complete and abject panic, the northmen scattered and disappeared into the distance.

Tristan rode up to the girl, looking at her in amazement, wondering what she was. "Are you crazy? They could have killed you—or worse!"

"I would not let them kill me," she replied, coldly. "And now they have no weapons to kill with!"

"Yes, I see," answered the prince. "What . . . what did you do to them?"

"I *heated* them. It's something I have done for fun, when no one else was around. I have never tried it on so much metal at once. " Her brows narrowed. "I think my anger gave me the strength."

"Indeed," said the bard as he joined them. "The Balance has been badly disrupted. Evil has grown very powerful, and power for evil must be balanced by power for good."

The bard studied Robyn curiously. "All that is needed is a vessel capable of wielding that power."

xxxxxxxxxxx

The goddess tried to marshall her strength, but the Beast had grown so strong, that she feared this time her utmost efforts would be to no avail.

It was time to intervene directly.

She called, softly, to a favorite of her creatures. High in the Synnorian Mountains of Myrloch Vale, her call was heard. A great white stallion perked his ears, and stared into the night around his corral. The goddess spoke slowly, and the horse understood.

With a terrific burst of speed, the stallion hurled himself into the gate. Though the barrier was Llewyrr-crafted, of supple but strong vines and branches, it crashed apart before the heaving white breast. With a kick of his heels, the stallion galloped into the night.

AVALON

12

Gray dawn spread across the sea. Kazgoroth, through the eyes of Thelgaar Ironhand, surveyed the fleet as it crawled toward the protected beach of a sheltered cove. Fully a third of the longships had gone down during the battle with the leviathan. Half of those remaining had suffered enough damage to make every additional mile fraught with peril.

Precious time would be lost as the crews repaired the damaged vessels, but the only other choice was to leave behind much of his strength.

This Kazgoroth would not do. Forcefully, the Beast restrained a more violent display of its emotions. For the dead northmen, thousands of whom now floated in the Sea of Moonshae, the creature had no regard. They, like all humans, were tools who either served the Beast's purpose, or attempted to thwart it. The former were used, the latter destroyed, with equal dispassion.

The death of the leviathan provided a great boost to the Beast. The limitations of the body of Thelgaar made a prison as this new power begged for release. Kazgoroth stalked the deck of the longship, fighting for control.

Finally the fleet reached the beaches, and sailors dragged each vessel onto the sand beyond the reach of the highest tide.

The figure of the king strode angrily about the beach. "Begin the repairs at once!" He watched the sailors leap to the damage, eager to avoid Thelgaar's wrath.

"Remove the rams," he added. "They have served their purpose."

As soon as the work began, Kazgoroth stalked into the forest surrounding the beach. Inland, it found a stagnant swamp, surrounded by flat marshes. Here it removed the clothes of Thelgaar, and allowed its skin to assume a more comfortable form.

The Beast lay upon the ground and stretched, reveling in its freedom. Scales began to form and soon coated the body that grew longer, and more serpentine. Kazgoroth stretched its jaw, and felt an almost sensual pleasure in the forked tongue stroking hundreds of sharp teeth. It reached forward with massive claws, snapping tree trunks for the simple joy of destruction.

The Beast slipped into the water of the swamp, slithering along a trough six feet deep. Still, the crested plates of its scaly back broke the surface. Finally, the channel flowed into a lake, and here the Beast dived. Its whiplike tail thrust from side to side, and its powerful hind legs kicked tirelessly.

Kazgoroth found a boat and attacked in a frenzy, killing and eating three fishermen. The feast did not serve to calm its unease, and, in fact, drove it to even greater restlessness. Finally, the Beast forced itself to lie still, lying in the cool mud of the lake bottom, restoring its energy.

Its agile mind swirled with plans and ambitions, and the Beast knew that it could not maintain its identity as the Iron King unless it brought these chaotic impulses under control. The northmen were a very important part of those ambitions and so it could not risk driving them away in panic. And this was sure to happen, should Kazgoroth's base urges transform it into its true form before the eyes of the northmen.

For three days the monster lay below the surface of the lake. The massive heart slowed its tempo, and the great body cooled. Finally, it emerged. With great control, the body bent again into that of Thelgaar Ironhand. Kazgoroth retrieved its clothes, and returned to the fleet.

It arrived there at nightfall, to see that the work on the longships had progressed considerably. Many more days of labor would still be required to complete the job, however.

Resolved to retain control, the Beast went into its tent. Brusquely, Thelgaar called for wine, which was swiftly delivered. And Kazgoroth spoke no more that night.

XXXXXXXXXX

Gavin claimed one of the slain northmen's swords, and raised the weapon over the body. He then dropped the weapon with a short, quick chop. The head rolled from the corpse, and he tossed it to the side where he had assembled a pile of heads. Grim and expressionless, the smith threw the sword aside and returned to the companions.

The party started out immediately, though night already was on them. No one felt any desire to spend the hours of darkness in the ruins of Gavin's village. The smith accompanied them, silently marching behind.

They followed the path of the horsemen who had destroyed Myrrdale. A large body of riders had carved a swath of ruin across the face of the kingdom. Often, bodies that lay in their path showed signs of disfigurement or, slow, cruel torture which only death had ended.

The land that had fallen to these riders was devastated. Fields of crops had been trampled to mud, buildings smashed or burned. Any animal that had not been taken for food had been butchered and left for the crows.

The moon was nearly full, and they followed the plain trail throughout the night. Near dawn they stumbled upon another ruin.

"What town was this?" the prince asked the smith, biting down on the pain that had been growing with each scene of tragedy and destruction they had come across.

"Cantrev Macsheehan," said the smith.

After scouting the area, Robyn and Daryth came riding back to the prince.

"Many northmen gathered here," explained Robyn. "The riders were joined by two, much larger, groups on foot."

"When they left," Daryth added, "many of them went southwest, toward the Corwell Road. That group took all the wagons and carts."

"The others moved due west," Robyn broke in, and the prince could hear the scarcely controlled rage in her voice. "This group included the riders that destroyed Myrrdale. They go toward Myrloch Vale."

"I suggest we go west, after the riders that destroyed Myrrdale," said Tristan. The others nodded, and the decision stood.

They paused only long enough to eat a meal and rest their tired mounts before again resuming the pursuit. The tendays of hard travel had toned Tristan's muscles, and he felt no discomfort with the rapid pace. His companions seemed equally unaffected. Their provisions were nearly exhausted, but that was a secondary importance to not losing time.

For the length of the hot summer day they pursued the army of northmen, gaining steadily over the large column. By nightfall, they reckoned themselves to be less than six hours behind. Twenty-four hours of combat and marching had worn them all to the point of collapse by this time, and they were forced to pause for the night.

They selected a secluded grove of evergreens surrounding a placid pool, and sprawled wearily to the ground. As they unpacked the horses, a panicked deer suddenly burst into the grove, pursued by the five hounds. Keren, who never let his bow get very far from him, put an arrow into the unfortunate creature, and they ate well that night.

Because of the nearness of the northern army, they built only a small fire, its glow shielded carefully by tall boulders. Still, it served to smoke the rest of the meat sufficiently for them to carry it along with them. Robyn gathered some nuts and an assortment of huge mushrooms, so they again had enough food for a few days.

Tristan, having drawn the middle watch, slept gratefully for several hours, until Pawldo awakened him for his shift. The prince climbed the great boulder they had selected as their watchpoint, leaning into the shadow of another huge rock so that he could not easily be seen, and settled down to watch. Periodically, he shifted around, stretched, and even pinched himself to stay awake.

The full moon rose high above him, its silvery beams pouring straight down, and lighting up the forest like daylight. Tristan calculated quickly, realizing that this was the third full moon since the spring festival. No wonder it seemed so bright tonight—this was the summer solstice, the brightest moon of the year.

For an hour he let his gaze wander across the towering crags of rock to either side, or to the lush blanket of evergreens that filled the valleys, or to the silvery ribbon of water that fed the pool beside their camp. Remembering Gavin's words, he looked at the scene with a renewed appreciation. Sadly, he wondered about Gavin and whether the smith would ever again be able to open his eyes to the beauty of the land.

The summer solstice—Midsummer's Eve—traditionally meant a festival and a celebration among his people. The druids held the night to be the time when the goddess's power—the power of all life on earth—pulsed most strongly. Tristan wondered if the Midsummer Festival were being held this year at Caer Corwell. It seemed like years since he had last seen his home, although in reality it had been only tendays, but that prince who had left home seemed to be a different, unknown person.

He wondered how much his father knew about what had befallen the eastern half of his kingdom. Had messengers reached Corwell with news of the raiders?

His attention focused on the trees before him. Solstice, friends, home all fell forgotten from his mind as he stared keenly at the rustling branches of two giant spruces. He had just seen those branches rustle, and there was no wind to cause such a movement.

Slowly, he slid from the rock to the ground, cursing to himself as his feet made a crunching noise in the pebbles. Why could he not move soundlessly when he needed to, like Daryth? The prince left the sword of Cymrych Hugh in its scabbard, worrying that its inherent light would attract attention if he should draw it.

As he moved forward, he felt as if every footstep carried the snapping of dried twigs, or the rustling of dead leaves, echoing into the night air.

Before he reached the spruces, the branches parted, and a huge shape stepped forward, glowing in the moonlight. At first, the prince thought the unicorn from the Firbolgs' fortress had returned to them, for the satiny white shape, proud head, and graceful bearing all suggested that mighty creature. But a second look found no horn upon this creature, and Tristan realized that it was a little smaller than the unicorn.

What he saw, in fact, was simply the most magnificent horse he had ever imagined. The stallion stood still, breathing slowly in the warm summer air, and looking at the prince with large, intelligent eyes. Its clean coat was an even white in color. Pink nostrils flared slightly as Tristan approached, curiously seeking his scent. When this was confirmed, the great horse stepped forward and nuzzled the prince's shoulder.

The prince stood still, awed, for several moments, and then looked more closely at the horse. It was larger than any of the steeds in his father's stable, with a broad chest and long, muscular legs. The stallion had a flowing white mane and tail.

Hesitantly, wondering if the horse would let him mount, Tristan gathered a handful of the silky mane. When this provoked no resistance, he leaped onto the broad back with a swift, fluid motion. Holding his breath for a second, he waited for the creature to rear or buck in objection. But the stallion stood still, breathing easily, as if waiting for a command.

Grasping the mane firmly with both hands, Tristan nudged the great flanks with his heels, merely brushing the smooth fur. The horse reacted like a rocket, springing forward so quickly that the prince nearly lost his balance.

The white horse galloped across the clearing and through the camp. Tristan saw Robyn sit up in surprise, and the dogs awaken, barking. With a tremendous leap, the steed cleared the pool and vanished into the woods. A whistling blur of trees, rocks, and meadows passed across the prince's vision as the horse raced like the wind through the enclosing woods. How the steed managed to find a path, the prince could not imagine, but soon they rode even more swiftly along a narrow and winding trail.

The prince rejoiced in the feeling of powerful horseflesh below him. Each time the steed leaped an obstacle, the prince held his breath, almost fearing that they were about to take to the air. He wondered, not yet concerned, where they were going.

Only his desperate grip on the creature's mane kept him on its back, for the horse turned so nimbly, and accelerated with such power, that he came within inches of falling to the ground many times.

As far as Tristan could tell, from the confusing scene racing past his eyes, the horse galloped up a branching valley near their camp—not the one taken by the northmen's army.

Finally the magnificent horse slowed to a trot, carrying the prince through a spruce forest into a flower-filled clearing, high in the narrow valley. As the moonlight struck him, Tristan felt curiously exposed here in the middle of the clearing.

His fears materialized then in the form of a rider emerging from the trees before him. He whirled the stallion about, but saw several more riders approaching from behind him. In another moment, a ring of proud knights, perhaps a score in number, had emerged from the trees to surround him.

Brilliant moonlight reflected from the riders' silvery helms and tall, metal lances. Proud pennants fluttered from the tips of these lances, but the weapons were now lowered to point at the prince's heart. That heart almost burst as, slowly, the riders approached, their full attention focused on him alone.

As the last of them stepped into the moonlight, Tristan saw that every one of these mysterious knights rode a mount as pure white and sleekly powerful as the one beneath him.

❌ ❌ ❌ ❌ ❌ ❌ ❌ ❌ ❌ ❌

Grunnarch began the journey with the Bloodriders, riding at the head of the column as was his right as king. Laric followed, and behind him came the rest of the fur-cloaked horsemen, as they began the arduous trek up the Dynloch Pass.

Every fifty paces, as promised, they found the trail clearly marked with a cairn of rocks. These guideposts were essential, for the mountains here were so tangled and convoluted that the trail would otherwise have been invisible. Side valleys, box canyons, and sheer dropoffs all provided pitfalls for the ignorant traveler. Even with the markers, the Bloodriders found the pass tough going.

The riders had to dismount for most of the way, leading their steeds through narrow niches among the rocks, or across treacherous ledges above roaring streams. The twisting passageways were often so narrow that the horses had to be physically pushed through the gaps.

Grunnarch cursed with frustration as his army's pace slowed to a crawl. Laric, meanwhile, remained strangely silent and aloof from his leader's concerns. Grunnarch thought, stealing a glance at him, that Laric looked even more frightening than he had upon his arrival at

Cantrev Macsheehan. The rider's eyes now glowed madly from sockets sunk deep within his skull, and his pasty skin had drawn more tightly across his face.

The Red King also noticed that the horses of Laric, and all the Bloodriders, had grown gaunt and skeletal.

Their ribs showed clearly against their black skins, and their eyes seemed clouded with some mysterious ailment. These signs of exhaustion, however, did not carry over into the mounts' endurance. If anything, the black steeds of the Bloodriders seemed immune to fatigue, pain, and fear. They plodded stolidly along with their masters, seeming to care little for their surroundings or their condition.

At last, Grunnarch could stand it no longer, and he paused by the trail as the file of Bloodriders slowly marched past. All of the men had the same dying look of Laric's countenance which had so chilled him. Though he could not quite accept the fact, in the back of his mind Grunnarch knew that the Bloodriders, the pride of his army, had slipped from his control into the clutches of something far mightier, and even more menacing. Something that he might need to fear.

After the Bloodriders had passed, Grunnarch stepped into the column and marched at the head of the footsoldiers. Cursing his reluctance to confront Laric, to accuse him of double-dealing, the Red King marched fiercely, kicking at any stone that stood in his path, tugging mercilessly on the trailing reins of his unfortunate horse.

Thus, Laric was the first of the northmen to come upon the summit of Dynloch Pass, and see the long, descending route into Myrloch Vale. Here, the trail opened enough for the men to mount, and the black horses and red-robed warriors filed through the barren and windswept rocks.

Night closed in before the bulk of the army reached the summit. Grunnarch, new to mountain tactics, had not ordered the column into camp early enough. Confusion and accidents resulted from the late bivouac in the hostile environment. Still, the moon shone brightly, and for the most part the men were able to find shelter from the howling wind. Nevertheless, the raiders suffered a very uncomfortable night.

Under the harsh light of the full moon, Grunnarch sat before a small fire and worried about his army. Frustrated by the time lost climbing the pass, he pondered with deep foreboding the strange sense of sorcery that now separated him from his Bloodriders.

A shadowy figure emerged from a crack in the rocks and approached. The brown robe muffling his features testified that he did not belong to the army, yet he had somehow managed to pass the pickets without raising an alarm. Grunnarch resolved that some guard would pay for his negligence, and his hand came to rest upon the stubby shortsword beneath his own robe.

The figure sat down on the other side of the fire, and the king saw that he wore simple, woodland garb. A deep hood cloaked his face, but two eyes gleamed wickedly from within the hood. Suppressing a shudder, Grunnarch looked the figure in the face.

"Who are you?"

"I am Trahern, a druid of Myrloch Vale. I am here to show you the path."

XXXXXXXXXX

The ring of knightly riders slowly closed about the prince, and he saw fine, shining armor protecting each of them. Even in bulky plate mail, the riders seemed small atop the huge horses. They carried themselves and their weapons with the smooth competence of professionals.

"Who are you?" The accusing voice shot at him from one of the riders before him. Startled, the prince realized that the speaker was female. She had a high, almost musical voice that seemed oddly distorted by her rude question.

"Silence, Carina!" spoke another, in the voice of command. This one, too, was a woman.

Tristan sat still astride the great stallion, watching the knights close in. The Sword of Cymrych Hugh lay in its scabbard at his waist, but it would be folly to draw the weapon.

He considered turning the giant horse and leaping away through the ring of riders. But one of them, the one who had silenced Carina, moved from the ring toward Tristan. She held her lance aloft, unthreateningly. The prince looked at her, and with a corner of his mind, noted the exquisite workmanship of her smooth plate armor. She carried a slim sword at her side, and wore a tall helm that exaggerated the unusual narrowness of her face.

Her horse stood a full hand shorter than the stallion, but was equally sleek and well-muscled. Breast and faceplates of the same silvery metal as the rider's armor protected vital areas of the horse. The prince saw that the saddle was deep and heavy, providing a secure seat for the rider, as well as sturdy flank protection for the horse.

The narrow visor in the helm was open, and he looked at the rider's face with interest. Exceptionally slender and fine-boned, it was accented by a pair of huge, luminous brown eyes. Tendrils of golden hair framed her face, emerging haphazardly from the confining helmet.

"How came you to be riding Avalon?" she asked in an accusing voice.

"He came to me by my camp in the forest. I mounted him, and we rode up the valley to this spot. Now, why do you accost me?"

"He let you mount him, then?" she asked.

"Yes, he did."

"What is your name, please?" asked the female knight, visibly shaken.

"I am Tristan Kendrick, Prince of Corwell."

The reaction this statement drew from the riders was not what Tristan expected. All of the knights, their movement fluid despite the heavy armor, lowered their pennants and dismounted. The prince noticed that the one called Carina, unlike the others, seemed to hesitate before dismounting.

Suddenly, the knight before him drew her sword and knelt at his feet. She held the blade before him and spoke. "My lord, I am Brigit. I present my company, the Sisters of Synnoria. We are warriors of the Llewyrr, and we are at your service."

XXXXXXXXXX

Pawldo nearly drowsed while holding the last watch before dawn. Suddenly, he jerked upright, astonished at the figures that emerged from the darkness.

"He's back! And he's still got the horse! And——!" Pawldo's announcement choked away in his astonishment as a file of riders emerged from the forest behind the prince and collected in the small clearing.

"—and he's brought an army," he finished lamely, as Robyn and Keren gathered around. Daryth held the dogs silent, although their hackles bristled at the approach of the strangers. Even Gavin looked up alertly at their approach.

The prince dismounted before his companions. Smiling, he gestured toward the female knights and said simply, "This is Brigit, and her lieutenants, Carina and Maura."

Carina still scowled suspiciously, regarding the companions with disdain, but the other two greeted them with apparent sincerity.

"They are knights of the Llewyrr, from Synnoria.

They will aid us against the northmen."

"Not bad," muttered Pawldo, impressed. Indeed, the knights looked battle-worthy. Their armor was both beautifully crafted and fully protective. Their slim lances and long, narrow swords looked almost fragile, but again master craftsmanship suggested inner strength in the metal.

The knights took off their helmets as they started to make camp, and Tristan for the first time got a look at their features. To a person their hair was long and golden, framing slender faces and huge, brown or green eyes. The tips of pointed ears broke through the tresses of many of the knights. They were almost childlike and beautiful to gaze upon.

Tristan had not fully digested the events of this midsummer's eve. Brigit, her manner cool and polite but every inch the resolute warrior, had explained things on the ride back to camp. She had told him that the company became pledged for a year's service to a person of royal birth who rode the stallion. The great horse was called Avalon, and had crashed through the gate to his stall two nights earlier. The knights had ridden in pursuit of him.

The prince, it seemed, had found the horse first. Or perhaps, thought Tristan, recalling how the horse had emerged from the woods at the very rock on which he stood guard, the stallion had found him. That is what Brigit and the others believed.

Also during the ride back to camp, Tristan had described his friends' experiences of the past tendays and summarized their current mission. The sisters, he found, knew about the raiders and were aware of the branch of the army that was even now crossing into Myrloch Vale.

The prince gathered Robyn, Daryth, and Keren in the moonlit clearing and joined Brigit and her two lieutenants for a council.

"The army we follow includes a large band of horsemen and many thousand footmen. It seems they now intend to violate Myrloch Vale," the prince began.

"We discovered this army yesterday," announced Maura. She was the smallest of the sisters, not a great deal larger than Pawldo. Her voice was so soft that the others had to lean forward to hear.

"The horsemen number perhaps a hundred—strange-looking men in fur cloaks, to a man mounted on black horses. There is something foul and unnatural about them. They are to be feared."

"Someone had blazed the trail over Dynloch Pass," growled Carina, almost accusingly. "We discovered the fact too late to divert them."

"By now," concluded Brigit, "they have probably reached the pass and entered Myrloch Vale."

"What will that allow them to do?" asked the prince. "I am not familiar with the terrain of the Vale."

"They will have two choices," explained Brigit. "Since travel west is blocked by the highest mountains on Gwynneth, they can turn north, in which case all of Myrloch Vale is open to them. Or, by turning south, they can cross a low pass and, in a few days, occupy all of central Corwell."

The strategic possibilities did not escape the prince. "Should the army enter Corwell, as you suggest, it could cut the kingdom in two. Corwell Road is the only easy path between the eastern and western halves of the kingdom, and they could close that road!"

"Don't forget the other army!" exclaimed Robyn. "It's moving down Corwell Road from the east—they'll trap thousands of refugees between them if these riders reach Corwell Road before we do!"

"It would be a massacre such as the Ffolk have never suffered," said Keren, quietly.

Tristan's mind groped for a solution to the problem. This small force could never hope to halt the northern army, yet somehow the fleeing populace must be helped to escape.

"Is there any other way into Corwell from here? A way that doesn't involve travel over Dynloch Pass?"

The sisters looked at each other nervously for a moment. Glaring at Brigit, Carina shook her head, silently arguing with her about whether to speak. Finally, however, the captain of the sisters turned back to the prince.

"There is such a way, shorter even than the route through Dynloch Pass. Yet it passes through Synnoria, and our people do not brook lightly the passage of outsiders."

The prince's heart leaped. "You *must* take us that way!" He looked Carina squarely in the eyes. She bit her lip, fighting the temptation to retort furiously, and her huge eyes seemed to blaze with suspicion and distrust.

Brigit, giving an awkward glance at her sisters, finally answered for them.

"It shall be as you wish."

As they turned to their bedrolls, they heard a faint cry, carried by the wind for an impossible distance. The noise increased in volume, haunting and joyful at the same time. Together, the sister knights and the prince's party listened to the song of the wolves.

xxxxxxxxxx

An unearthly chorus rolled across the moors, carrying mystical notes through the midnight air for miles. The full moon, brilliantly spilling the radiance of the summer solstice, illuminated the Pack. Individual wolves sat upon every high crag and plateau of rock for miles, joining all other wolves in raising their voices in praise of the Mother.

Woodland creatures, and all the animals of the wild, cringed at the sound. Dogs throughout the isle howled an answering cry, as the call awakened some primeval instinct within them.

The goddess heard the praises of her children, and her pain grow more tolerable.

SYNNORIAN RHAPSODY

13

Not all of the notice wrought by the full moon was benign, or heralded the greatness of the goddess. In a filth-strewn cave not very many miles from the Pack, Erian awaited the summer solstice with a tormenting mixture of dread and longing.

After tendays of living like an animal, emaciated and covered with grime, the man now bore little resemblance to a human being.

Now, as the beams of the moon thrust mercilessly against the stone walls of his cave, reflectively lighting up the interior, Erian crawled forth. Outside, exposed to the full illumination of the full moon, he begged for the body he now craved. He wanted the powerful legs and teeth, the keen nose and ears, that were his as a wolf. As a human, there remained nothing of himself that he wished to keep.

And so he changed, under the light of the silver moon, for the third and last time. The wolfish body and the wolfish senses would remain his until he died. The change was like a blessing of comfort, laid upon his brow, for he now sensed a purpose and a power to his life.

His ears, keener by far than those of the man he once was, heard ever so faintly the mournful lament of the Pack. Leaping to his feet, Erian set off across the moor at a steady, loping gait.

Soon, now, Erian would be home.

×××××××××

The approach to Synnoria followed a mazelike pattern of connecting valleys, canyons, passes, and forest trails. Though the trail in all places was wide and easily passable, the routes were so cleverly camouflaged that Tristan knew he could never retrace their steps without a guide.

After a full day of climbing, the trail entered a box canyon with no apparent access other than the trail the companions followed.

"We'll camp here tonight," announced Brigit. "Tomorrow morning we will enter Synnoria."

"I see why you don't get many outside visitors," Tristan remarked. "I know that I'm lost!"

Brigit looked at him. Her huge, serious eyes seemed to be gauging him, trying to determine his reaction to what she was about to say. With a deep breath, she spoke.

"Tomorrow you will all have to be blindfolded."

Tristan began to protest, while the rest of his companions looked suspiciously at the sisters. Brigit cut off his arguments before he could make them, however.

"Partly, you will be blindfolded for our security, and I will not pretend otherwise. " Her voice was feathery, but as firm as iron. "But also, this is for your own protection.

"You see, the beauty of Synnoria far exceeds that of the world you know. An outside visitor, it is said, would be driven mad by the sights and sounds of our little valley. One who enters Synnoria for the first time, and sees the land in the light of day, will never be able to leave!

"This is a risk I will not take, neither with my land nor with the sanity of you and your companions.

"You must agree to be blindfolded, or we will not take you through Synnoria. " With a note of finality, Brigit regarded the prince.

The prince found it hard to believe the woman, but saw no alternative. "It shall be as you wish."

The sisters arose before dawn began to lighten the sky. Stars still twinkled brightly, though the first traces of sunrise colored the east, as the sisters firmly tied blindfolds across the eyes of Tristan and his companions.

The women helped them to mount, and took the reins of the companions' horses. Tristan silently cursed the imposed blindness, feeling strangely disoriented astride Avalon's broad back.

He could tell when they passed through a very narrow corridor in the rock. Echoing sounds offered clues as to the surroundings, and every once in a while he felt a chill in the atmosphere. Once he reached out and felt a shelf of cool, fragmented rock, confirming his suspicions. He felt himself slide toward the rear of his horse, and consequently deduced that they journeyed primarily upward.

When the party finally emerged from the corridor in the rock, a warm breeze caressed the prince's face, carrying fragrances that made him think of Brigit's warning about the beauty of the valley. The sun spilled its lifegiving heat onto his skin and spread a comforting warmth through his body after the clammy morning ride.

Nearby, a waterfall trilled across rocks with a musical tinkle. The sound was so delightful that he would have halted Avalon to listen if he held his own reins. He felt his throat choke with sorrow, and tears sprang to his eyes, as the soul-soothing sound faded into the distance.

Now he heard the wind rustling through leafy branches with a pleasant sigh. The branches whispered with a seductive tone, and birds trilled a calling song. They crossed a bridge, hoofs clattering on the wooden beams like the chiming of a massive bell.

The sound arose so rich and throaty that the prince forcibly pulled back on the stallion's mane, for he could not bear to ride on. Someone tugged firmly upon the reins, however, and he was carried unwillingly forward. Weeping unashamedly, he tore at the blindfold frantically, but the heavy cloth was wrapped tightly around his face. In anguish, he turned his head to savor the last, hypnotic sounds arising from the bridge.

Suddenly he heard, again, the musical chimes of a waterfall. This one sounded larger than the other, and its notes carried more force and a wider gamut of tones. If such a thing were possible, the prince thought, these sounds were even more beautiful than the other.

He made up his mind. Never again would he know happiness in the mundane world. His future lay here, in Synnoria, whether or not the beauty of the place would drive him mad. He swung a leg across Avalon's back and started to drop to the unseen ground below.

A jangling noise struck him in the face like a bucket of ice water, stopping him just before he let go of the horse's reins. Dissonance crashed into his ears again, and still a third time.

"No!" he cried. "I can't hear the waterfall!"

But the jarring notes continued—the strings of a harp, plucked without tuning or harmony. Dimly, the prince heard other voices raised in protest, but the chords kept coming. Painful to the ear, absent of any musical worth, they only served to mask the sounds of the lovely waterfall.

The prince recognized the sound, if not the tone, of Keren's harp. "Stop!" he ordered. "Stop that instrument!"

Futilely, he shouted at the bard, railing against Keren until his voice grew hoarse. And all the time, Keren played the harp loudly and constantly, so that he and his companions could not enjoy the sounds of the waterfall, and the trees, and all the things that made Synnoria so . . .

Seductive.

Suddenly the prince stopped shouting and felt very foolish. His resentment toward the bard quickly changed to gratitude, for he knew that without the timely sounds of the nearby harp, he would have leaped from the saddle, determined to spend the rest of his life listening to the distant harmonies in Synnoria.

The prince could still hear the waterfall in the background, but the sound now arose only as minor accompaniment to the music of the bard's harp. Keren soon ceased the tuneless strumming and began to play a little ditty, quite profane, about an amorous barmaid. The tune displayed none of the mastery and craft that the prince had heard on other occasions, but it was such a simple and catchy melody that Tristan could not get it out of his mind.

For the rest of the day, the bard strummed his harp and sang the simple little song. The others joined in, occasionally, as his voice began to crack and waver. Yet the chords he struck from his harp never wavered in their clarity. Tristan felt no regret when cool walls again pressed in from either side and they entered a region of deep shadows. He knew that the seduction of Synnoria now lay behind them.

Finally Brigit called a halt, and the sisters removed the blindfolds. Once again they found themselves in a narrow canyon, surrounded by sheer rock walls. Canthus jumped against Tristan, licking his face as the prince dismounted. With a squawk, Sable settled to the limb of a scraggy tree that somehow grew in the barren cleft. Robyn swung quickly to the ground, then weakly leaned against her horse. Daryth and Gavin dismounted stiffly, while Pawldo leaped from his pony to kiss the ground. "I've had enough sorcery to last me the rest of my life!" he declared, lacking his usual vigor.

Keren remained mounted as he slung the harp over his shoulder. With a pained look, he held up his obviously stiff fingers. The fingertips were cracked and bleeding.

"It'll be a few days before I want to play my harp again," he admitted.

"Thank you," said Robyn as the bard finally dismounted. She stepped to his side and kissed him on the cheek. "Without your harp, I would now be a permanent resident of Synnoria."

"I agree," said Daryth, while Pawldo nodded. Gavin grunted, noncommittally, and turned to look back, toward Synnoria.

"Let's camp here," suggested Brigit. "It's all downhill to Corwell. With luck, we'll make it in two more days."

The captain of the sisters turned to Keren. "That," she said with a rare smile, "was a very impressive performance."

Exhausted, the prince collapsed into his bedroll, delighted, for a change, to leave their safety to someone else. He quickly fell into a deep sleep, and dreamed of trees that sang a vulgar song about a tavern wench.

✕✕✕✕✕✕✕✕✕✕

The army camp sprawled along the shore of a formerly clear mountain lake. The green fields along the lake had been churned into a sea of mud by the tread of thousands of booted feet. The waters had turned brown and dirty.

Grunnarch looked over his camp with ill-concealed unease. It had taken the force more than two days to cross through Dynloch Pass, and he knew that he had fallen behind schedule. Near the summit of the pass, a sudden rockslide had claimed the lives of a hundred of his men. To lose a hundred with a single blow was a bitter pill. And finally, the army of Firbolgs that was supposed to meet him here was nowhere to be seen.

At least his men, famished and exhausted from the grueling passage, would be able to rest for a few hours and eat a hot meal at this camp. The druid Trahern had assured him that the passage back into Corwell presented far less of an obstacle than did the pass they had just crossed.

Thoughts of sustenance reminded him of another cause of unease, the Bloodriders. They seemed to suffer from the fatigue of the march as much as any of the other men, but they showed no inclination, at the end of the march, to eat, drink, rest, or any of the other activities that insured recuperation. Instead they stood or squatted in their own area of the camp, waiting with barely concealed impatience to strike out on the trail again.

"Perhaps," thought the Red King grimly, "they now survive on blood!" He avoided entering the Bloodriders' camp, preferring to remain near his own tent. Accompanied by Trahern, the druid, he watched his army slowly recover its spirit.

A commotion at the edge of camp attracted his attention. With Trahern at his side, Grunnarch hurried toward it. A young warrior ran up to him, pointing toward the forest.

"Firbolgs, my lord! They're coming this way!"

Grunnarch saw a band of perhaps five dozen Firbolgs trudging toward him. They moved listlessly, as if they were the remnants of an army. Indeed, many of them wore stained bandages over moist wounds. The Red King was not prepared for the filthy appearance of the Firbolgs, nor for their smell. The odor preceded them by several hundred yards, carried by an unfortunate breeze, and was offensive even by the northmen's uncritical standards.

"This is the army?" Grunnarch muttered in disgust, looking at Trahern. The druid, too, seemed puzzled.

"I expected a much larger band" he admitted. "Though they do look formidable, those that there are."

Indeed, the Firbolgs, even in this condition, looked like fierce fighters, with powerful legs and arms. Their low, sloping brows made them look very stupid, which was a quality Grunnarch praised in his soldiers. But they looked decidedly useful.

The largest of the creatures gestured the others to halt, and approached Grunnarch and Trahern. He stopped before them, and the king realized that the brute was not as tall as he had first seemed. He towered perhaps a couple of feet over Grunnarch's head, no more.

"Groth," grunted the creature, chucking a squat thumb at its barrel chest. "Corwell," he added, pointing to the southwest.

"I am Grunnarch the Red, commander of this force," the king declared. The Firbolg only looked curious, spreading his hands.

"Grunnarch," grunted the king, pointing to himself, and then turned to the druid for help. "Can you talk to him?"

"I can try," Trahern said, sounding reluctant. He grunted something short and harsh at the Firbolg, and the creature replied loudly, making violent gestures in the air. Then the Firbolg turned its back and stalked away.

"He says they had some trouble with humans," explained the druid. "He also says not to bother him."

"That's great!" Grunnarch spat. "A lot of help they'll be, I'm sure!"

Trahern shrugged. "We cannot know the nature of their role in the Iron King's plan. It is better not to question." The druid walked slowly back to his seat by the fire.

Grunnarch cast an angry look after the druid. He wondered, briefly, how Thelgaar had convinced the man to betray his land and his goddess. He looked back at the Firbolgs, who were claiming a great section of the lakeshore as their own. His army was demoralized—nervous about the presence of both the Bloodriders and the Firbolgs. This land—Myrloch Vale—seemed to sap their spirit. The king grimaced as he remembered his own nightmares. Nevertheless, Grunnarch knew that he had passed the point of no return. His force was committed to the plan, and he would do his best to lead it into the battle that Thelgaar had described to him so long ago.

Grunnarch and his army slept that night on defiled ground, haunted by bad dreams. Many struggled to remain awake, no matter how many hours till the dawn.

The next morning, a serpentine column of troops snaked away from the lakeshore toward the low pass that Trahern indicated. If they could make good time, the druid assured Grunnarch, they would be astride the Corwell Road by nightfall.

Above the marching army, the day started ominously. Heavy clouds gathered along their route of march. Even before the last troops marched out of the camp, the rain began to fall.

× × × × × × × × × ×

Genna Moonsinger, Great Druid of Gwynneth, knew of the army violating the sacred protectorate of Myrloch Vale. She watched, brokenhearted, as her animals died before the merciless invaders. She noted with revulsion that a band of Firbolgs had joined the northmen. She felt the earth itself recoil from the tread of the Bloodriders.

Genna had no army to send against the invaders. In the body of a little sparrow she observed the sprawling encampment along the lakeshore. She was not emotional, but part of her wanted to rain a shower of rage against the enemy.

Yet the great druid was not without recourse. In another guise, that of the tiniest of mammals, the shrew, she slipped into the camp at nightfall. Seeking the tent of the leader, she listened carefully for several hours to meaningless and offensive debate.

Finally, however, she learned what she sought: Grunnarch's objective.

The northmen would march south, into Corwell, instead of continuing their sacrilegious march through Myrloch.

The Great Druid resolved that the raiders would be hampered every step. The rest of the night was spent in preparations, as she raced with dawn to work her own brand of sorcery. Steam climbed from the surface of every body of water within the radius of her power. Winds bent from their natural path, seeking and collecting clouds in the sky.

All night, her powers increased the weight of water vapor hanging above the camp, and the path, of the northmen. Gray clouds dropped low over the mountain valley, and the pressure of heavier clouds above forced them lower still.

As morning began to gray the eastern sky, Genna finished her spell. As the northmen broke their camp and began their march as yet unaffected, the great druid smiled patiently, for hers was not the magic that strikes in a single, dramatic blow.

The rain began as a light sprinkle, annoying the marchers but causing no great impediment. Soon it was a steady shower, making footing treacherous on the narrow trail. More and more marchers passed over that stretch, churning it into a morass of mud. Finally, the showers became a downpour, washing out sections of the trail and creating a bottomless mire of the lowlands.

When four of the Bloodriders, horses and all, collapsed and disappeared into a frothing torrent that had, minutes earlier, been a splashing brook, Grunnarch could deny the signs no longer. Cursing the ill favor that seemed to accompany his expedition, he ordered the army to bivouac until the storm subsided. And with this order went the realization that he would not reach the Corwell Road that night.

XXXXXXXXXX

The great wolf loped steadily across the moor, ignoring the passage of time. The moon set, and the sun climbed into the sky, but still the great creature ran with steadfast purpose. Finally, Erian reached the area where the Pack had spent the night.

From here, the trail led eastward. Sniffing eagerly, Erian conjured clear images of hundreds of yearlings and pups, of an old male, gamely keeping up, of a bitch in heat. And one scent, finally, his supernatural nose identified. The largest male seemed to lead the Pack, but Erian knew himself to be larger, and stronger.

He started along the trail, still loping. He intended to conserve his strength for the encounter, and knew that the great population of wolves would travel far more slowly than he would alone. And indeed, the spoor grew steadily fresher as he followed the trail.

The wolves had taken a winding path, leading through shallow mountain valleys and over low ridges. Sometimes they passed through forest and thicket, while other times the Pack broke onto the open moor.

Finally Erian reached the top of a low hill and saw the Pack below him. Thousands of wolves nearly filled a small valley, where the Pack was in the process of crossing a shallow river. Many wolves, having already made the swim, shook themselves or rested on the far side. Others bobbed steadily across, swimming resolutely against a mild current.

His bloodshot eyes glittered with hate as Erian searched among the wolves, seeking the big male. Finally, he found him, still lolling comfortably on the near bank.

Raising his face toward the sun, Erian howled, a long wail that ululated through the valley, and pulled the attention of every wolf to the great beast standing atop the hill. Erian howled again, masterful and evil, as the wolves cringed.

The big male, he noticed, bristled aggressively and began to move forward, but even his bearing bespoke fear. Erian loped down the hill, arrowing straight for the big male. The other wolves scampered out of his way, then turned, intent on watching the fight.

Erian grinned with pleasure. "Now, my wolves," he thought, "your master has arrived."

XXXXXXXXXX

Again the companions awakened early, this time driven to activity by the icy breath of the high mountain air. The barren canyon provided no wood for a fire, so they gulped a cold breakfast and mounted.

As Tristan swung into the saddle on Avalon's broad back, Brigit and another knight rode up alongside.

"This is Aileen," introduced the captain. "She is very familiar with these valleys. I suggest we send her ahead to scout for signs of the enemy."

Aileen, the prince saw, had masked her shining armor with a woolen tunic of green, earthen tones. Instead of a lance, she carried a bow, along with her slim sword. She smiled and nodded to the prince as he met her eyes.

"That's a good idea. Arrange a rendezvous for this evening, with alternate sites if we get held up." The prince wondered if the raiders' army had left Myrloch Vale yet. Perhaps, even now, the army lay across Corwell Road.

Once again they had entered Myrloch Vale, and this time Tristan enjoyed his surroundings. For the rest of the day, they descended through a series of rocky canyons and valleys, which soon gave way to sparse groves of cedar, and then thicker forests of spruce and aspen. The beauty of the mountains, and the pristine purity of the wilderness, made the day pass swiftly for Tristan, who found himself enjoying the land in his kingdom for the first time.

By late afternoon, they left the higher elevation permanently behind. Their trail followed a meandering river through many flat, flower-filled meadows.

"This is the place Aileen described," cried Brigit, pointing to a jagged finger of rock jutting from a small clearing. "She'll meet us here at sunset."

They broke to form a small camp there. Shortly after dark, the green-clad scout slipped into camp.

"There's no sign of them in front of us," she reported. "They must be farther north. It's strange—I saw an awful thunderstorm up there. It just hung over one place for the whole day. If they got caught in that, they'll be moving very slowly tomorrow!"

"Excellent!" said Tristan. "With a good day tomorrow we should beat the northmen to Corwell Road. We can at least warn the refugees!"

"Yes," agreed Robyn. "But then how do we stop the northmen?"

Grimly, the prince acknowledged that he, as yet, had no plan. And none of his companions had any ready solutions either.

For a moment they lapsed into silence, glumly realizing the depth of the problem. Suddenly, a bush rustled across the camp, and they saw a faint movement.

"I mightta known I'd find you here!" The gruff voice, bursting from the darkness, brought the group to its feet. Canthus, with a growl, leaped from the fireside to face an approaching figure.

"Finellen!" cried Robyn, as the others gaped at the approaching dwarf. "What are you doing here?"

"Those dolts did you a big favor when they invaded Myrloch Vale," Finellen replied, pointing in the general direction of the northmen's army.

"How did they do that?" asked the prince, confused.

"They made the dwarves mad!" answered another gruff voice, this time male, from the darkness. Suddenly Tristan noticed a number of figures, all roughly similar to Finellen in size and shape, emerge from the forest and join them in the clearing. Perhaps fifty or sixty stout figures—all with bushy beards, darkened metal armor, and shorthafted battleaxes—soon stood around the fringes of the camp. The Sisters of Synnoria, the prince saw, regarded the newcomers suspiciously.

"I see you're not too particular about the company you keep," grunted Finellen to Tristan, nodding across the fire at Brigit.

"Dwarven scum!" The fiery Carina leaped to her feet, and her slim sword snaked from its sheath to dart toward Finellen's beard.

But its strike rebounded from a broad axehead that somehow had appeared in Finellen's gnarled hands. For a second the two stood frozen, sending currents of tension through the gathering. Then Tristan leaped to his feet.

"Stop it!" he cried, stepping between the two women. "Our homeland is in jeopardy. We cannot afford to fight among ourselves—our enemy is far stronger than we to begin with! Do you understand?"

Carina glared at the dwarf, and Finellen sneered at the Llewyrr warrior. Slowly, the two relaxed and backed away from each other, continuing to glare until they had seated themselves.

"We welcome your help," said Tristan to Finellen and the rest of the dwarves. "Why don't you establish a camp, right over there?" He indicated a smooth, grassy expanse, well removed from the sisters.

Finellen hawked and spat noisily into the fire. "By the way, them Firbolgs we got mixed up with, they joined up with the humans. Quite an ugly lot of 'em there are."

Digesting this unpleasant bit of news, Tristan asked, "Are your friends as good at killing Firbolgs as you are?"

Finellen's eyes sparkled with pleasure, but she gruffly cleared her throat and spat again. "Well, we kind of like to make a hobby of it."

XXXXXXXXXX

The Pack watched the monster racing down the hill. Fear convulsed the wolves, but something more powerful prevented them from fleeing. The big male, grizzled and scarred from countless battles, moved forward to meet the threat.

He had led the Pack for many centuries, as had his sire before him. Of a bloodline born from the goddess herself, the male had always risen to meet any challenger. Now, he sensed, his reign had come to an end.

Compelled by every instinct in him to fight, the wolf raced forward to meet the attacker.

He leaped, but his jaws snapped on air as the great beast sprang from his path with astonishing quickness. Before he sprang clear, those awful jaws slashed against his foreleg, and the male felt pain lance from his leg to his heart. Knowing it was his last act, the wolf hurled himself at the enemy and fastened his powerful teeth in its stinking, shaggy flank.

But the enemy's flesh resisted the teeth with the strength of steel, and before the male could break away, his neck was clasped by those drooling jaws. Mercilessly, those mighty jaws tightened their grip. The big male kicked weakly, and there was a sharp snap.

Erian flung the body aside with casual strength.

His red eyes did not blink as he slowly circled, making sure that his gaze passed over each of the thousands of animals that returned his look. He compelled each of them to accept his mastery, and they did so without question.

Erian, Master of the Pack, could now begin to fulfill his destiny.

 CORWELL ROAD
14

Finally Kazgoroth judged the fleet seaworthy enough to meet its fate at Corwell. Sails had been sewn, hulls patched, and the rams removed. Precious time had been lost, but the Beast hoped to reach Corwell within a few days. The delay need not prove fatal to the grand scheme.

The northmen left a dozen ships, or parts of them, behind as they sailed. These hulks, too badly damaged to repair, had been picked over for materials to repair the other ships and then abandoned to become driftwood.

The morning tide rushed away, pulling the throng of longships from the cove into the open sea. Scarcely a breath of wind arose, so Thelgaar ordered the men to the oars. Propelled by powerful strokes, the fleet resumed the journey to Corwell.

For a time, Kazgoroth wondered about the other army, Grunnarch's command. The plan had been sound, if only that blustering old fool could execute it. Kazgoroth remembered, with hot pleasure, the corruption he had laid upon the Bloodriders. If the fiendish cavalry could find a way to strike the huge mass of humanity that must be fleeing the invasion, there was no telling how much their power would soar!

✗ ✗ ✗ ✗ ✗ ✗ ✗ ✗ ✗ ✗

"My prince! Wait!" A musical voice called for the prince's attention. Turning, he looked back upon the column. Daryth, Pawldo, Keren, and

Gavin rode abreast behind him. After them, in a double column, rode the Sisters of Synnoria, except for Aileen and another of the knights, who were scouting up the valley. Finally, also in pairs, marched sixty axe-wielding dwarves. Their short legs pumped steadily as they kept pace with the rest of the party.

The prince saw that Aileen, coming rapidly up on the rear of the column, galloped swiftly, gliding like a ghost along the side of the trail.

"We've done it!" she cried, her light voice carrying the length of the column. "They're only now coming out of the 'Vale."

A spontaneous cheer arose from the sister knights and the dwarves. Tristan himself raised his voice in a yell of triumph.

"I can't believe it!" exclaimed Daryth, with a grin.

"We'll beat them to Corwell Road for certain!" agreed the prince. "But how do we stop them? I still don't see a way that we can keep them from seizing the road and trapping the refugees."

"What would Arlen have done?" asked Robyn quietly as she rode up behind them.

The prince suddenly recalled his teacher's advice with a clarity that amazed him. "He always said to study the ground—to choose your fight carefully. Good terrain was worth an extra army!"

But now that he and his tiny force had succeeded in seizing this vantage, how could they hold it against the thousands of northmen? Tristan considered the terrain of the broad river valley that opened into rolling farmland. If he took his force any farther, the prince realized, the raiders could easily out-maneuver him among the open farmlands.

Calling the column to a halt, Tristan studied their current position. The northmen would have to march down this valley, and perhaps, with a little assistance, this small force might be able to bottle them up in the valley long enough for most of the refugees to escape westward.

The prince stood upon a low hill. Several hundred yards away, the river flowed past, too deep to cross easily. The far side of the river, and the land beyond this hill, were cloaked with tangled undergrowth. The only good terrain for such an army, Tristan realized, was a flat field, about two hundred yards wide, stretching between the river and the hill.

He looked again at the tiny specks inching along the Corwell Road and finalized his plan. If several elements of his force could work smoothly together, they just might have a chance.

Brigit dismounted beside him and removed her helm. Her red-gold hair spilled about her shoulders in a huge cascade. The tops of her small, pointed ears poked through the tresses. Finellen, too, clumped up to them, seeming still fresh even after the dwarves' long and rapid march.

The prince nodded at the distant road as he started to speak. "We've got to try and keep the raiders from reaching the road. The longer we can delay them, the more of our people will have a chance to escape the trap."

He looked at each of his companions. "I've been thinking of a plan. The best place to try and hold them is here—if we move any closer to the road, we'll lose all benefit of terrain.

"I'm going to take Gavin and Daryth and ride to the road. I'll try to enlist as many people as I can to aid us. If I can gather enough, we might have a chance at stopping the raiders in battle."

They all considered this, silently, for a moment. The prospect of meeting the veteran raiders in battle with a hastily recruited mob of refugees did not seem like a sound battle plan to any of them, but they were willing to listen to this new, young "general" who spoke with such confidence.

"Finellen, can you deploy your company across the crest of this hill?" Tristan went on.

The dwarf eyed the low hilltop and the surrounding terrain. She seemed to approve of his choice, and grunted her assent.

"Brigit, I need you and the sisters to harass them all the way down this valley. See if you can make them think they're under attack, and force them to deploy for battle. The more time you can buy, the less time we'll have to stand them off when they get here."

The captain looked at him quietly, no emotion visible in her huge brown eyes. She thought for a moment, and nodded. "I understand."

He looked at Robyn. "Remember that trick with the tree?" The lass nodded, puzzled. "While the sisters ride up the valley, I'd like you and some of the dwarves to do whatever you can to those woods, and the field, to make it difficult for an army to pass.

"And," he added, "be sure and let Brigit in on your plans. I suspect the sisters might be in kind of a hurry when they get down here, and we'd hate to delay them."

The prince pointed now to a shallow ditch he had noticed. Its purpose, apparently, was to carry rainwater from the hill to the river. Thus, it neatly bisected the field where Tristan planned to make his defense.

"If I can recruit some troops, I'll station them along that ditch. They'll be anchored by the dwarves here on the right and by the river on the left."

"What if you don't get any volunteers?" asked Robyn, deeply concerned.

"Then we will go it alone," answered Tristan, with more fervor than confidence.

"Here," Robyn said, with a serious look. She removed a scarf she had worn around her neck. Emblazoned upon it, the prince saw, was the Lone Wolf crest of his family. She tied the scarf to the tip of a lance and handed the weapon to him. The scarf fluttered bravely from the tip, billowing out in the faint breeze.

"If you're going to try and raise an army," Robyn explained, "you might as well try and look like a prince!" He carried the memory of her departing smile all the way to the road.

xxxxxxxxxx

Grunnarch sat morosely beneath a hastily erected canvas tarp. He watched the water flow around his shelter, small rivulets in the dirt that soon merged, and merged again, to create torrents and flooding. The Red King longed for the feel of a rolling deck beneath his feet, for the kiss of the salty sea air. Instead, he could look forward only to many more days of this exhaustive campaign.

The rain finally ceased at sunset, but Grunnarch's army was then compelled to spend the night where it had halted. Heavy, lowhanging clouds blocked out any hint of light from moon or stars, and to attempt to march in the dark would have been sheer folly. Thus, it was not until the day after the storm that Grunnarch's army finally managed to resume its pace.

But as they embarked on the sodden and muddy trail, a swarm of biting and buzzing insects erupted from the woods, stinging the northmen like a scourge. The army scattered to avoid the plague, but not before many a soldier had been stung to death.

As Grunnarch tried to assemble the force, vines and creepers that bristled with thorns sprouted from the ground between his men. They laboriously hacked through the imprisoning vines, but their progress was further hindered. And they began to whisper darkly of magic, and their step slowed further.

As the king ordered the army to move again, a wall of hot fire sprang from the ground in its midst. Dozens of men died from the searing heat of the flames, and the rest broke in panic to race headlong down the trail.

All along the trail, that day, strange disasters befell his men. A group, walking across a slab of solid bedrock, suddenly found themselves sinking in a bog of mud. Before a man could escape, the sucking mire pulled the little band under. Grunnarch watched, sickened, as the dying men's hands reached above the mire, twitching and grasping before they finally grew still.

"It is the druids of Myrloch Vale," explained Trahern, paying little attention to the calamities suffered by the northmen.

"How can we stop them? Where are they?" growled the Red King. He hated this unseen enemy more than any normal foe, no matter how fierce.

"They could be anywhere," shrugged the traitor. "Perhaps there is only one—the great druid could muster such power by herself!" Trahern looked around. "She could be in the guise of the tiniest mouse or insect along our trail. There is no way to tell."

"We must stop these attacks! How, man? Tell me!"

Again, the druid shrugged. "Simple. We have to leave Myrloch Vale."

Cursing the useless advice, the Red King turned back to his army. The attacks seemed to lessen and the panic gradually gave way to fatigue among the raiders. They trudged listlessly until at last they emerged from the wilderness empire of Myrloch Vale. Ahead of them, once again, lay the kingdom of Corwell.

Grunnarch allowed his hopes to rise slightly. The skies, by the end of the day, had cleared.

Slowly the winding column moved south. Through the mud and mire of the ravaged trail, the Bloodriders led the way. Grunnarch watched them pass, these curiously altered warriors that he had once known. He could see that they staggered with fatigue. Riders and mounts both looked haggard and emaciated. Though the troop had been given plenty of food, Grunnarch realized with a shudder that the Bloodriders required a different kind of sustenance.

The army on foot, slogging through the mud in the wake of the Bloodriders, covered ground steadily, yet the men seemed fearful and nervous as they looked at the deadly Riders ahead of them, or at the band of Firbolgs behind. No longer did Grunnarch's army have any heart to complain.

And finally, the Firbolgs plodded past. They seemed to pay no attention to the sucking mud that reached halfway up their massive calves, nor did they acknowledge the presence of the Red King as they slogged by.

More worried than ever, Grunnarch fell in with Trahern at the rear of the long column. He fervently prayed for the weather to remain kind during this day. If it did, he felt quite confident that they would reach, and block, the Corwell Road before it was too late.

Suddenly, an urgent cry brought him back to reality. Picked up and passed down the line by agitated troops, the message was unmistakable.

"We're under attack!"

xxxxxxxxxxx

The Prince of Corwell, seated astride the great white stallion Avalon, blocked the Corwell Road with his presence. The long lance, with the Lone Wolf pennant flickering proudly from its tip, stood next to him. About fifty of the Ffolk, all refugees from the eastern cantrevs, stood about him in the road, or alongside it. More refugees joined them steadily, as those coming down the road hurried to see what the gathering heralded.

"Citizens of Corwell," Tristan called again, for the benefit of the new arrivals. "Hear me, in the name of our king!" He hoisted the banner high, as the Ffolk watched him impassively.

Immediately in front of him, two ragged little girls, wearing the tattered remains of filthy dresses, held hands and looked up at him with open, trusting smiles. Immediately behind them, a young woman hovered, trying bravely to restrain her tears.

A number of Ffolk had an animal or two—a prized goat, or pair of chickens—tightly leashed and jealously guarded. Some had managed to carry a few possessions, such as tools, pots, or, rarely, a weapon.

Some of them had a numbness in their eyes that told of unspeakable loss. Tristan knew, for this was the look he saw in the eyes of Gavin the smith. Others of the Ffolk met his gaze with a stare of determination and courage. Others showed anger, as if he, their prince, were responsible for the terrible events that had befallen them.

As he started to speak, he saw again the searching stares of those who were not abjectly defeated—those who were still willing to stand up to the invaders. All they needed was a spark, and the prince knew that his words must provide that spark.

"I ask you all of able body for help. I also offer an opportunity to any who would strike back at the invaders who have sullied our land and killed our loved ones!" The prince was encouraged to see many listeners straining to hear.

"The enemy comes soon, from there!" He pointed to the low hill, six miles away. "I will meet him there, with a company of knights, and others of seasoned foot!

"Now, I seek any man—or woman," he added, thinking quickly of Brigit and Finellen, "who will stand with us against the northmen."

He paused to give the people a chance to confer hastily among themselves. He saw many looks of enthusiasm, but more of fear and shame. The crowd had grown enormously, and dozens more hurried down Corwell Road from the east.

"The army of the northmen stands poised!" cried Tristan, raising the pennant of the wolf. "We must hold them here, until those of us who cannot fight have escaped safely to the west. If you can hold a weapon, join me now! Give those who are weaker a chance to live!"

Lightly, he tapped Avalon's flanks with his knees.

The stallion sprang from the roadway into the field, where the prince reined him in and turned to face the collected masses.

"All of you who will join me, form up here!" He drew the Sword of

Cymrych Hugh, and slashed an imaginary line along the ground.

And the Ffolk ran to their prince.

XXXXXXXXXXX

Grunnarch finally reached the scene of the attack that had thrown his entire column into disorganization. There, he found one man dead of a single arrow wound. The Red King could see no sign of attackers, nor reason for disrupting the army.

"Fools! Imbeciles! A single archer has thrown you into panic! Now, move!" The raiders automatically resumed the march. Angrily, Grunnarch rode beside the column until he reached Laric, who was at his customary position at the head.

"Send some outriders into the woods! We can't have woodsmen taking shots at us every league of the march!"

Laric regarded him passively for several seconds, and the king saw with numbing horror that the Bloodrider's eyes had lost all semblance of humanity. Dull and cold, they seemed to be deep, and opaque, at the same time. They were no livelier than the empty sockets of a deaths-head.

Desperately, Grunnarch struggled for an idea to bend Laric to his will. The gaunt, weakened appearance of his lieutenant suddenly inspired him.

"You must kill!" He spoke the words slowly, clearly. "There, in the woods—you must ride there, and kill those you find!"

The hot flare in Laric's eyes was the most frightening thing that Grunnarch the Red had ever seen. Yet the Bloodriders climbed into their saddles. Lurching forward, the horsemen spread across the valley, seeking something, anything, to kill.

XXXXXXXXXX

Aileen rode lightly in the saddle, letting the supple mare select the swiftest path through the cloaking pines. Like a white ghost, Osprey carried her mistress past the enemy army, sliding easily through the shadows and tangled places so that they avoided discovery.

She held her bow ready across her lap, but knew that her primary mission was intelligence, not attack. Still, she had not been able to pass up this easy shot into the middle of the column. The ensuing chaos made the risk well worthwhile . . . and left her chuckling.

Suddenly black death exploded from a thicket, and Aileen barely ducked the savage thrust of a Rider.

The attack came from so close that even Osprey's lightning reactions could not anticipate it. As the attacker swung, Aileen got a look at the skull-mask and screamed aloud in horror.

The skull was his face! The Bloodriders no longer needed masks to create their horrible aspect. Aileen imagined she felt the sheer, reeking evil of the creature's breath against her face. Whether it was her imagination or not, the young warrior could do nothing but clutch her reins in terror.

Osprey's instincts were all that carried her mistress from danger. The mare leaped from the high bank into the stream bed and splashed into the opposite bank. Flying as only a Synnorian steed can fly, Osprey streaked down the valley, toward the company.

Several more of the black Riders tried to pursue them, but Osprey easily outdistanced the sinister horsemen. Finally, Aileen broke into a clearing and found Brigit and a dozen of the sisters. Gasping, she quickly told her story.

XXXXXXXXXX

Laric led all the Bloodriders, pursuing the morsel of life with tightly focused energy. He wanted, in fact needed, to kill. The white mare and its tiny but vibrantly strong rider would yield considerable sustenance.

Though several of the Bloodriders stayed close to Laric, most of the rest fell away with distance. Fueled by his lust for blood alone, Laric was the only one, finally, who managed to keep the white ghost in sight.

Finally, the Bloodrider emerged from the woods and halted. Even the bloodlust pounding in his skull could not compel him to suicide, and further pursuit would be such.

The white ghost had joined a band of similar mounts. They regarded him cautiously as he studied them, until finally Laric turned back to the forest. As he stepped into the shadow of the trees, he turned and studied the group of knights. His burning gaze sought, and found, his original quarry—the knight dressed for scouting.

He recalled the feeling of the quarry when his blow had almost struck home. Warm and succulent—he wanted that one.

And he would get her.

× × × × × × × × × ×

Tristan felt a knot of worry grow in his stomach, and turned to pace nervously. He stood atop the low hill—a local farmer had called it Freeman's Down. From here, he could see the entire length of his line. The view also carried up a shallow slope about five hundred paces, toward the forest from which the raiders would emerge.

The dwarves squatted around him, resting and talking quietly. They projected an aura of routine, and the prince envied their calm demeanor. From the base of the hill to the river, lined up along the ditch, four hundred men and women of the Eastern Cantrevs stood, carrying an assortment of weapons that included pikes, spears, pitchforks, axes, and sharpened stakes.

Every twenty paces, for the length of this line, the prince had appointed a cantrev lord, or respected elder, or veteran soldier, with instructions to steady and lead the others.

Some distance behind this line, Gavin stood with another group of similarly armed Ffolk, the reserve. Many of Arlen's lessons had drilled home the importance of a reserve, and the prince had determined with the creation of his plan that one of every three volunteers would form such a unit.

On the far side of the hill rested another group of Ffolk that Tristan had been happy to recruit. About two score in number—mostly woodsmen and hunters—each of them carried a longbow and several dozen arrows. The prince kept his archers out of sight for the time being, the desirability of surprise being another of Arlen's oft-repeated tactical lessons.

A file of white shapes emerged from the trees, and Tristan then heard the sound of dwarven axes biting into timber. The sound had been a common one all afternoon, as Robyn and the dwarves had worked to make the forest a difficult passage for the army of raiders. Two final crashes completed the task, and Robyn and several dwarves followed the sisters from the woods.

The tangled maze of felled trees created a nearly impassable obstacle for Grunnarch's force. The northmen had to chop and hack their way through the forest like a band of woodsmen—ignominious work indeed for proud seafarers. Drawn and dispirited, the army's pace slowed to a crawl. Ranks of men in the forefront took ten-minute shifts with axes, striking at the broad trunks until they collapsed with exhaustion.

"This is the work of a druid," Trahern remarked, observing the tightly woven branches that blocked their path.

"A druid, eh? Well, that one'll die like all the rest," observed Grunnarch.

"Perhaps," commented the druid, turning his dull eyes to look about the forest. "The work is crude, amateurish. Still, there is a 'strength' here that disturbs me."

"Druids give me no cause for alarm," grunted the king, "At least they are human enemies, and can be slain!"

The axemen maintained their chopping rhythm. The Red King sensed the toll that Myrloch Vale had taken on his army. Now, with the vale behind them, the men displayed a palpable eagerness to press on. Yet they did so more out of fear for what lay behind them than any willingness to strike ahead.

"Your Highness!" Another messenger ran up, clumping heavily in his leather boots. "We have broken through the woods. There is a line of Ffolk—peasants, I think—that would block our way!" The messenger seemed more surprised than alarmed.

Word spread quickly through the army of the northmen, and morale improved noticeably. The king heard joking and cursing again. Raiders strained to get a look forward through the tangled forest. Finally, the axemen opened several passages into the clearing for the raiders.

Grunnarch strode forward, glancing at the sun. It was low in the western sky, offering perhaps two hours of fighting time. Then he looked across the field. In the distance he could see the thin ribbon of Corwell Road. Between him and it stood a rank of peasant rabble.

It was time to set the plan in motion.

XXXXXXXXXX

Like a growing tumor, the Darkwell burned the goddess. Each outrage seemed to inflame the thing, adding weight and venom to its poison. The cruel theft of the Pack cut deeply after the loss of the leviathan.

Kamerynn the unicorn, now the only child remaining, heard the summons as he restlessly patrolled the wild places of Myrloch Vale. He sensed that the mission was a hopeless one, and he felt the depths of the Mother's sorrow. Nevertheless, he obeyed.

Galloping once again with a clear goal in mind, the unicorn turned back toward the fens of the Firbolgs. The smoldering coal fire still marked the Firbolg building, sending aloft a permanent smudge over Myrloch Vale.

The goddess thought again of the Pack, but she could not speak to them. The power of the Beast held them firmly in its grip.

She knew that the true might of the Pack had never been truly revealed. It, of all the children, would perhaps prove to be the mightiest. In the service of the Balance, the Pack might provide the strength needed to hold the cause.

But if the Pack were allowed to serve an evil end, the goddess knew that the cause of the Balance was lost.

FREEMAN'S DOWN

15

 The army of evil seeped from the woods, gathering just beyond the shelter of the trees. The raiders overbalanced the little force standing before them by at least three to one. The broad field between them, covered in a sea of colorful blossoms, lay open to bear the attack.

Tristan noticed the vibrant colors in the petals of the wildflowers, and he smelled the pollen-laden air wafting past his nostrils on a gentle breeze. The scent was one of peace, not war.

Then the wind died away, and he heard flies buzzing in the suddenly heavy air. He looked across the field, and watched as more northmen emerged from the woods. For several minutes the only sound was the droning of the plump insects. Several hundred yards away, he could see the northmen gathering for a charge, but they made no sound.

Then the host of northmen raised a great cry, thrumming a deep chorus against the walls of the valley. Voices thundered and pounded against the Ffolk, as thousands of voices roared their primitive challenge.

But from the line of the Ffolk, clashing notes sang an answering challenge. The peasant warriors cheered lustily, knowing for a fact that a greater bard stood with them, and that the dwarves and Sisters of Synnoria were joined in rare common purpose. The notes smote, impossibly loud, upon the ears of all who were present.

The northmen charged in a great, howling mass. Their bearded faces grimaced as the berserk rage took them.

The prince signaled the longbowmen. The archers sprang to the crest of the apparently empty hill, and sent showers of arrows onto the center of the charging line. Dozens of the missiles found a mark of flesh, but the losses seemed to make no difference to the horde. Leaving the fallen where they lay, the howling northmen rushed forward.

Avalon carried the prince along behind the two ranks of Ffolk lined up at the central ditch. Canthus raced at his side, and Tristan still carried the lance with the Lone Wolf pennant aloft. His hastily recruited troops seemed determined, their leaders working to steady and calm them as the northmen drew closer.

Rays of sunlight slanted sharply across the field, highlighting the flowers for a last glimpse of beauty, before the blossoms disappeared under the trampling charge. Now, the weapons gleamed in the late afternoon sunlight.

The first raiders to reach the ditch slipped and fell in surprise. Ignorant of the obstacle, their companions to the rear swept onward, and the entire momentum of the charge vanished in the steep slope and muddy bottom of the trap. As the fallen attackers regained their balance and struggled out the far side of the ditch, the Ffolk met them with a line of stabbing and slashing weapons.

A tall farmer thrust with a pitchfork against the broad axe of a stumbling northman. The raider nonetheless lifted his weapon to deflect the blow, and the clash of metal rang out across the battlefield. In seconds, the noise melded with thousands of similar sounds. Crashing and clanging, the armies met in a fight to the death.

The Ffolk fought like veterans. A young farmwife cracked a stout staff across the face of a leering northman. He fell, and she reached down to claim his sword. Daryth and Pawldo, together, stabbed the raiders crawling from the ditch before them, until a pile of bodies collected.

The Ffolk had been given cause to fight in the last tendays. They all harbored burning hatred for the northmen after the outrages of the Eastern Cantrevs. Spears, forks, and stakes all thrust the slipping raiders back into the ditch. Many of the Ffolk fell to fatal thrusts from the attackers, but the line reformed quickly under the commands of the lords and veterans.

And then the farmwife fell, dropping her new sword into the mud of the ditch. The man behind her died, gurgling over the shaft of a spear in his chest, and suddenly the front line broke. A dozen raiders burst through, turning to strike the Ffolk from the side in an effort to expand the breach. Desperately, the prince spurred Avalon toward the scene.

But Robyn was already there. The woman had been pacing behind the line, standing firm for just such an eventuality. Now she stepped forward, raised both hands, and shouted those arcane words the prince had heard only once before. The northmen screamed and dropped weapons suddenly grown red hot, and then fled back to their own as they saw the approach of a thundering white stallion and a rider bearing a Lone Wolf pennant.

"Well done," the prince congratulated Robyn.

"My prince," she acknowledged, smiling, oddly peaceful in the midst of the chaotic setting.

"Look," called Tristan, as the line of the Ffolk stretched and cracked in another place. Robyn leaped to Avalon's back and they galloped toward the threat. By the time they reached it, however, a young cantrev lord had shifted the line to fill the gap and drive the attackers back to the ditch.

They came upon Keren, who paced behind the line. His harp and songs of valor were of more value than his sword.

"Even so," said the bard grimly, "more than once I've had to sling my harp in favor of my blade. The line holds, but barely, my prince."

"Perhaps 'barely' will be enough!"

The bard grinned and started another song. As always, the music and words rang out clearly, impossibly loud, above the din. The prince saw Daryth and Pawldo, standing at the ditch, drive several stumbling raiders back into the mud and blood at the bottom.

Avalon's flanks heaved with excitement, and the great stallion tossed his head proudly, as Tristan scanned the field for developments.

Suddenly the line of Ffolk vanished in the center, as several northmen struck fatal blows. Trampling the bodies of the defenders, a hundred raiders surged into the breach. The tall farmer who had been the first to strike a blow in this battle stepped into the charging mass and lay about with his pitchfork. He soon went down beneath the press of attackers, but the sacrifice had bought a few precious seconds.

Tristan and Robyn raced for the breach, even as the hole in the line grew broader. The Ffolk began to stream away from either side, panicked by the sudden breakthrough. The prince turned to see Gavin watching him intently, waiting for some sign.

The Lone Wolf banner dipped toward the breach, and with a throaty yell, Gavin led the reserve forward. Two hundred Ffolk rushed toward the rupture. An even greater number of northmen plunged through the hole, sensing victory.

X X X X X X X X X X

Grunnarch had remained behind when the bulk of his army charged across the field, although such a rear-echelon role raised a bitter taste in his throat. Still, he could not trust the Firbolgs or the Bloodriders to choose an appropriate moment to attack. Even with his presence, he knew that he could not hold the two bloodthirsty bands out of the fight for long.

Yet he knew that if the infantry could blast a hole through the feeble line, a timely charge by the riders around the open flank of the Ffolk would send the entire force into a chaotic rout.

Then, the killing could truly begin.

Even before such an opportunity arose, however, Laric took matters into his own hands. As Grunnarch attempted, through Trahern, to hold back the anxious Firbolgs, the Bloodriders spurred their gaunt steeds and thundered toward the battle. Turning with a fiery oath, the Red King shouted his frustration at the backs of the charging horsemen. Before he could realize his mistake, the Firbolgs had also rushed forward, and Grunnarch was left with no reserve.

The battle would now proceed out of control, and the Red King grimly strode forward to exact a few blows of his own before the carnage ended. At least he saw the Bloodriders rushing toward the bare hill—Laric had obviously seen the same weakness in the enemy position that he had. The Firbolgs lumbered behind the Riders, also making for the hill.

Still annoyed, Grunnarch held no doubts as to the outcome of the battle. He would have preferred the fight to go a little more according to plan, but knew that his army would soon crush the amateur defenders. The enemy included a few able knights, but the Bloodriders would soon find and destroy these. The peasants would be scattered.

Then he saw the enemy riders, silvery force astride their white mounts, riding over the crest of the hill to meet the Bloodriders' charge.

"Ah," he chuckled to himself. "They ride forward to bring on their deaths that much more quickly."

And he paused for a minute to watch the fight.

✗ ✗ ✗ ✗ ✗ ✗ ✗ ✗ ✗

Aileen, lying in the grass at the crest of Freeman's Down, saw the Bloodriders break into the field. She waited only long enough to ascertain the direction of the charge, and then scuttled to Osprey. The mare grazed patiently a dozen yards downhill of her mistress.

The sister knight scout sprang to her saddle as the horse broke into a gallop. She cut several circles in the air with her sword, and the rest of the company, already mounted, charged up the hill toward her at the signal. Aileen shed her tunic of brown and green, and seized the lance she had thrust into the ground. In another second, she fell into her position on the left flank.

The Sisters of Synnoria charged in brilliant formation.

The great white horses cantered gracefully, a precise six feet apart. The line of twenty silver lances, gleaming righteously, the knights held aloft. From the tip of each, the gaily colored pennants still trailed into the air.

The knights rode with visors down, metal armor gleaming. Each matched the movement of the others so exactly that they might have been one knight and nineteen shadows.

Laric, leading the charge of the Bloodriders, saw the pennants, and then the silver lances, arise from behind the crest of the hill, and he knew that the riders would follow. His cracked and bloody lips moistened at the thought of the one he sought. The horsemen thundered on, each Rider grimly silent atop his snorting, pounding steed. They did not alter their course, but thundered directly toward the oncoming horsewomen.

The savage fighting along the ditch faded slightly, and then paused, as northmen and Ffolk alike turned to watch the clash of the mounted riders.

The breastplates and faceplates of the horses, and the armor of the sisters, all gleamed flawlessly in the sun, casting long shadows across the rolling down. Sharp, hot reflections of silver flickered like beacons over the rest of the battlefield.

The white horses broke into a gallop as the line rumbled down the gentle slope of Freeman's Down. The momentum of the steeds built, aided by the weight of metal each horse carried. The Bloodriders had them outnumbered five to one, but the Sisters of Synnoria had the advantage of downhill speed.

As she rode, Aileen felt her lance nestle comfortably beneath her shoulder, and she sighted the tip upon the chest of a leering Bloodrider. The ghoulish figure raised his sword and cracked open his mouth. Then the lance splintered through his chest, breaking his body and slamming him to the ground. Around him, many of his comrades met the same fate—in all, about twenty Bloodriders crashed to the ground in the first instant when the forces met.

The remaining Bloodriders spun their more agile steeds to swarm like sharks around the sisters, hacking with weapons while the black horses kicked and bit. Aileen, alone on the left end of the line, deflected blows from in front and behind her. Her lance became useless in this close combat, but she did not want to drop it.

"Forward!" cried Brigit. "Don't slow!"

And in seconds the speed of their horses carried the sisters clear of the savage Riders. Aileen, however, felt the searing thrust of cold iron tear her shoulder. Somehow, one of the frightening horsemen, desperate for blood, had stretched out and cut her.

The pain of the wound rushed through her body, blurring her vision and sending the horizon reeling. She felt the world growing black, and she slumped in the deep saddle. Osprey held her place in the line, even as Brigit ordered the company about, while her mistress rode, unknowing, into another charge.

XXXXXXXXXX

Laric's blood pounded in ecstasy as he pulled the dripping blade from the wound. His eyes glowed with unearthly fire, and he raised his voice in a piercing yowl of triumph. Heated and vitalized, he turned toward the silver riders.

He thirsted for more of the enemy's hot blood. Even around the rush of pleasure, Laric could sense his strength failing. The loss of so many of his Riders had exacted a toll that could only be paid in blood.

Steeds snorting angrily, the Bloodriders turned in pursuit of the sisters, even as the elven knights turned to strike again. Watching the charge form, Laric vowed that this time, they would prevail.

XXXXXXXXXX

Gavin's bellow of command electrified the reserve. With screeching war cries, the Ffolk rushed forward. The great smith led them all, his huge hammer swinging easily above his head. Northmen poured through the breach in the line before him, raising war cries of their own. The momentary lull that had fallen over the field when the riders clashed vanished as suddenly as it had occurred.

"Miserable scum!" snarled the smith, splattering the brains of a raider with a vicious, curving blow.

"Die, northman!" The word was a curse.

Another dropped like a felled tree as the smith recovered instantly from his swing, reversing the momentum of the hammer to tap this one on the forehead, that one on the shoulder. The Ffolk of the reserve struck the charging northmen to either side of their leader, and the line ebbed and flowed as the two forces vied for the ground.

And slowly, inspired by the strength and heroism of the smith, the Ffolk drove the northmen back through the breach. Scores of fighters on each side lay dead or dying, but the press of Gavin's reserve finally sealed the line.

The smith looked up to see the prince, upon Avalon, wiping the bloodstained sword of Cymrych Hugh. Tristan had ridden to the breach and helped to close it.

"Splendid charge!" the prince cried.

The praise brought the first trace of a smile to Gavin's face since he discovered the massacre at Cantrev Myrrdale, and that thought stood out in Tristan's mind amid the death and pain surrounding him.

The prince looked around and saw Robyn kneeling beside a wounded young man. Keren still stirred the force with his harp, while the Ffolk stood firm all along the line. Daryth and Pawldo paused, amid the bodies of dead raiders, and the halfling waved at the prince.

"Send more northmen!" he cried, brandishing his bloodstained blade.

The prince smiled, and then saw the Firbolgs lumber onto the hill. He prayed fervently that the next part of his defensive plan would work. He looked toward the field, beyond the lines, and saw the Bloodriders and the Sisters of Synnoria again ride together. This time, the black horses swerved from the path of the frontal assault, and the knights struck only a few from the saddle. Many of the sisters had lost their lances by now, and the battle quickly turned to a close melee, sword against sword.

And here the odds would work against the sisters, as each knight faced four or five Bloodriders. Tristan realized, suddenly, that the battle was nearly won, and the sisters could be dying needlessly. He must call them back!

As soon as he made this decision, he nudged Avalon's flanks, and the great stallion sprang through the line at the ditch, easily leaping the muddy obstacle. Canthus accompanied his master, streaking like an arrow along the ground.

Before him, the swirling mass of horses, swords, fur capes, and silver armor spread chaotically. He heard the screams of wounded horses, and the sharp orders of Brigit that still seemed to float like music through the horror that was battle.

And then he was a part of the melee.

✕ ✕ ✕ ✕ ✕ ✕ ✕ ✕ ✕

Groth led the Firbolgs in a heavy charge toward the bare hilltop. Let the humans fight the dirty battle in the ditch, thought the Firbolg king to himself. His giants would seize the high ground and then take the enemy in the rear!

For the first time since the destruction of his stronghold, Groth felt happiness again swell within his monstrous heart. Today he would get the chance to exact revenge for that defeat. He caressed the knobby head of his club, imagining it covered with his enemy's gore.

Suddenly his right leg collapsed beneath him, and Groth hit the ground with a thud. Sharp pain lanced through his thigh, and his nose struck the ground sharply. Dazed, he raised his head and looked around, seeing others of his troop tumbling down. Then, a small shape darted from the grass, a wicked battle-axe upraised. A dwarf!

Groth desperately rose and slashed out with his club, crushing the dwarf's skull. Yet that was only one. The dwarves, blood enemies of the Firbolgs, attacked with cruel efficiency, hamstringing many of their giant opponents with the first attack. Now they swarmed over the rest, hacking with those murderous axes, or scuttling and ducking away from the Firbolgs' return blows.

Panic clutched at Groth. He fought off another dwarf, climbing to one knee. More of the Firbolgs fell as the dwarves—merciless and cunning—closed in for the slaughter. In moments, the Firbolgs who had not fallen beneath the weapons of the dwarves lost heart—their fallen leader, and the surprise of the attack by the wily dwarves, had quickly shattered what remained of their morale.

"Help me!" groaned Groth, as the fleeing Firbolgs trundled past. He finally persuaded a pair to support him. Thus, ignominiously carried, the mighty Groth left the field of battle.

XXXXXXXXXX

Laric rode through the tumult, constantly seeking the knight he had struck. He drooled at the thought of finishing the job. Should she already be dead, he did not want her body to escape him.

His charcoal eyes sought eagerly, peering closely at each of the sisters he saw. The dried, rotted flesh of his nose crinkled and dropped away as he sniffed her delicious scent.

And then he found it.

The wounded knight slouched motionless in her saddle, closely protected by a comrade to either side. Her silver armor, from left shoulder to left foot, was tarnished by bright blood. The slender body, even concealed by metal plate, seemed to call Laric with undeniable force.

Spurring his black stallion, Laric drove toward the motionless sister. A Bloodrider charged close at each side, skillfully distracting the two knights guarding their wounded sister. Reaching forward, his clawlike hand concealed by a heavy gauntlet, he seized the reins of his victim's horse and pulled.

Startled, Osprey lurched ahead. A moment later, Laric's captive knight and her horse vanished into a group of Bloodriders.

⨯ ⨯ ⨯ ⨯ ⨯ ⨯ ⨯ ⨯ ⨯ ⨯

Avalon carried the prince into the fray with thundering speed. Tristan slashed the Sword of Cymrych Hugh, and struck a Bloodrider from the saddle with his first blow. The sword surged through the corrupt body, eagerly. A hot wave of pleasure tingled in the prince's hand, as if the sword itself had enjoyed the killing.

A vicious cut assailed the prince from the right, and suddenly Tristan was fighting for his life amid a circling cluster of skull-faced Riders. Desperately, the prince sought Canthus.

The great hound had stayed with his master in the long charge across the field, and now fought with him among the pounding hooves and clashing steel. A Rider lunged at him, and the prince got his first good look at one of the hideous faces. He saw the bones of the skull showing through cracked and rotted flesh, sickening him. He nonetheless parried the creature's wild swing, and thrust sharply with his own weapon, grazing his opponent's side.

The Rider leered at him from those glowing, hot eyes. The prince could see no white, nor pupil—just a liquid pool of red heat, and lust for killing. The Rider's face, so pasty white that it might have been the bone of his skull, remained frozen in a hideous grin. His lips were bright red strips of skin stretched taut and cracking around his mouth.

A spittle of drool, pale pink in color, trickled from the Rider's grotesque mouth to run, unnoticed, across his chin. As the creature struck again, the prince saw the hellish eyes glow with increased intensity. This time Tristan's response proved more effective, as he dodged the blow and then struck his attacker's sword arm off at the elbow. The Rider displayed no pain, but continued to lunge and strike at the prince with the gory stump.

The prince saw that no blood flowed from the wound. And then that antagonist vanished in the chaotic motion of the melee, and Tristan thrust and parried with three horsemen that attacked together.

Avalon skillfully twisted to prevent more than one of the attackers from striking at the same time. Canthus dodged nimbly among the pounding hooves, striking at the rear legs of the black horses. Once, the moorhound fastened his teeth into the leg of a Rider. Canthus held on, growling, as the pitching and bucking of the horse jerked the dog around. With a savage pull, the hound tore the Bloodrider from his horse to crash heavily to the ground. With one savage bite, the dog tore the rest of his face off.

Now the Riders realized that they could not ignore the snarling hound in their midst. Several attempted to strike him down, slashing thin air as the agile dog sprang away, though one swordcut left a bleeding slash along his back.

Suddenly the prince saw a flicker of white through the Bloodriders, and saw one of the enemy leading a white mare with a sister knight slumped, unconscious, in the saddle. The woman's captor pulled free of the melee, tugging sharply on the reins of the reluctant mare.

A nudge of Tristan's heels sent Avalon springing after the helpless captive, leaving his three attackers to find a new opponent. Tristan had recognized the mare as Osprey. The thought of the lively and spirited Aileen in the hands of a ghoulish Rider inflamed the prince.

Another Rider reared into Tristan's path, and his gleaming sword nearly severed the neck of the black horse. The steed dropped like a stone, and Canthus tore out the Rider's throat before he could recover. Avalon smashed into the steed carrying Aileen's captor, and the Bloodrider's grip on Osprey's bridle broke. The white mare skipped away, carrying her unmoving rider to safety.

Never had the prince seen such an unearthly, or hateful, fire as he now beheld in the eyes of the Bloodrider. The man's sword flew blindingly toward Tristan's face, and the prince lurched backward with a clumsy parry. Again the lightning attack, and though the blade did not strike home, the Bloodrider's savage horse managed to knock the prince to the ground.

The wind exploded from his chest as he landed on his back, and he lay helpless among the bucking and screaming horses, gasping for breath. His opponent's steed reared over him, and the prince struggled through the churned mud to avoid the hooves that sought to shatter the life from his skull.

And then Canthus leaped between them, springing so high that his jaws tore at the shoulder of the Rider. The man knocked the moorhound aside with a blow from the hilt of his sword, but Canthus immediately crouched for another spring. The black stallion twisted as it reared, and as the hound sprang, those heavy hooves met the dog in mid-air, driving into the broad skull. Soundlessly, Canthus dropped to the ground and lay still.

"No!" cried Tristan.

The Rider charged forward again to strike at the now standing prince. Before the charge could connect, however, a silver shape interceded and one of the sisters met the attack.

The Bloodrider hacked viciously, with superhuman strength, at his tiny opponent, as Tristan leaped again to Avalon's back. He spurred to the aid of his rescuer.

Just as he reached the pair, he saw the Bloodrider's stained sword strike underneath the sister's guard, cut through the hard metal of her armor, and sink into her heart. She slumped, mortally wounded, in her saddle.

"Monster!" growled the prince, but now the swirling course of the battle took the killer away from him. Still, he marked that one, remembering well the deathshead grin and crimson eyes of this Rider.

And then the Bloodriders streamed away from them, galloping as a group into the protective cover of the nearby forest. Only now did Tristan look around, beyond the limits of the battlefield, and see the upraised arms of the Ffolk.

He heard their throaty cheers and saw Gavin, still swinging his gory hammer, striding up, followed by the reserve. The smith had led another charge, and this one had driven the remaining northmen to the trees.

The prince saw the hillside, the strip along the ditch, and the field where the riders had battled, covered with bodies of the dead and dying. He leaped from Avalon's back to the side of the sister who had saved his life. Ignoring the blood that now coated the white horse, as well as the rider's body, he released the belt that held her in the saddle and lowered her gently to the ground.

Carefully, he lifted the silver visor. Carina's eyelids flickered once, as the prince stared in shock.

The slender, elfin face broke into a smile—the first that Tristan had seen there—and then Carina died. Gently, he laid the elf upon the grass, and Robyn and Keren joined him.

Next he sought Canthus, lying somewhere on the muddy battlefield. Night was falling rapidly, however, and he failed to locate the dog. The northmen prepared a camp only a few hundred yards away, and finally his companions persuaded him to pull his troops back to the relative security of their line.

Brigit joined them as they slowly rode toward the bloody ditch. She looked somber, and tears welled within her eyes. She spoke to Tristan with no trace of emotion, however.

"We've lost Carina, as you know. Aileen, I fear, will not live through the night. She has lost much blood, and the wound of the Bloodrider's sword seems to fester unnaturally."

"And the rest of the sisters?"

"They live, none of them seriously wounded."

"The Ffolk fought well," observed the bard. "But losses were very heavy . . . as if they had not had enough already."

"We cannot fight here again," said Robyn. "The carnage has been too great!"

"You're right," said the prince. He looked at the woods, where the northmen had withdrawn, and then toward the Corwell Road, where the tide of refugees was already slowing as most of the Ffolk had passed this point already.

"Still, we whipped them today, didn't we?"

× × × × × × × × × ×

The thick, black water bubbled slowly. Normally snow-white, the shanks around Kamerynn's ankles trailed, black and grimy, along the muddy shore. At the outflow, the unicorn stepped carefully across the high log dam that maintained the level of the Darkwell.

The dam was small, perhaps half the height of Kamerynn, but the trunks that held it together measured a foot or more in girth. The Firbolgs had stacked several dozen of the felled trunks across the small stream that had flowed from the Moonwell, and then bolstered the dam with an earthen dike to either side.

Kamerynn's keen eyes surveyed the nest of logs, finally selecting a weak point. He reared and struck the rotted timber with a backward kick.

Again and again, he pounded the log, finally splitting it. One half fell from the face of the dam, and Kamerynn kicked it aside. Selecting another timber, exposed by the loss of the first, he destroyed it, and then another.

The dam began to crumble. Great logs broke free, tumbling into the growing stream, and the rest of the timbers shifted violently. Kamerynn's footholds rolled completely, and suddenly the unicorn's forelegs slipped into the churning trunks. Bones snapped, as tons of wood crushed even the sturdy legs of the unicorn.

Black, polluted water splashed into Kamerynn's face, choking and gagging him. The liquid seared like acid against the unicorn's skin, destroying his eyes and driving him into a frenzy of pain.

But the weight of the logs held him down, and black water surrounded him, and soon he knew only blackness.

BOOK FOUR

HOME

16

A flickering shadow dipped over the battlefield, rose, and dipped again. Darting low, the small shape swept from body to body, seeking one specific one. Finally, with a delighted chirp, the swallow settled to the ground next to the one it had sought.

The tiny bird hopped across the churned, muddy turf, to peck with concern at a shaggy ear. It tilted its head and focused black, shining eyes on the great black nostrils inches from its face. Again, it chirped, this time as it observed those nostrils flaring slightly with passing breath.

The shadow shimmered, or perhaps it was the moonlight itself that wavered. Then the swallow was gone, and where it had been stood the plump form of an elderly woman.

"There, my puppy," she said, stroking the bloody head. "Such a brave dog."

Genna Moonsinger called the power of the goddess, and brought it welling from within her heart, flowing through her fingertips into the still form of the great moorhound. Slowly, the long slash in the animal's side closed. The broken skull mended, and the dog's shallow breathing grew deeper and stronger. The long, shaggy tail slowly thumped against the ground.

With a low whimper, Canthus rolled stiffly onto his belly and tried to lift his head from the ground. He gave up quickly, when throbbing pain resulted, but moved his tail slightly as a gesture of enthusiasm. He looked up at the great druid, then his eyes closed and he fell asleep.

"Good dog," Genna whispered, smiling sadly. "You sleep now. We'll talk tomorrow."

Canthus's low, steady breathing was his only response. Sadly, she stood, wishing she could simply leave the dog to return to his master.

But she needed him.

XXXXXXXXXX

Six sister knights cantered beside Corwell Road, as the little army marched along. The armor of the knights was tarnished and dented, and only three of them still held lances. The white horses were mottled with grime and blood. One of the steeds had a bloodstained bandage wrapped across its shoulder.

Still, the sister knights rode proudly, as if their dents and dirt were badges of honor. The outriders broke into pairs, and spread out to the flanks of the column.

Tristan sat upon Avalon, watching the long column wind away from him toward Corwell. The dwarves trooped steadily past him, three score minus eight that had fallen upon Freeman's Down. They marched stoically. Some of the whiskered faces turned up to regard the prince as they passed, but Tristan could read nothing in these gazes. Finellen, bringing up the rear, plodded grimly past without looking up. Yet, they marched to Corwell to fight in a human war.

Gavin stepped to the prince's side while the company of the Eastern Cantrevs marched past, five hundred strong. Another hundred would remain, forever, at Freeman's Down.

"Any word of pursuit?" asked the smith.

"Three hours past dawn, and they still haven't broken camp!" exclaimed Tristan.

"Good. These Ffolk could not wage another battle now."

The fighters of the Eastern Cantrevs walked past steadily. Fatigue and pain were writ on the duststreaked faces. Yet many straightened their shoulders and wore looks of pride as they passed the prince and the smith.

"Soon, they will have no choice. But by then we should have the companies of Caer Corwell behind us!"

"Perhaps," muttered Gavin, with a long look to the east. He nodded curtly to the prince, and stepped back onto the road as the last of his company passed. His shoulders, too, were straight as he marched toward Corwell.

Tristan spurred his stallion forward, and Avalon galloped along the side of the road, past Gavin's company, and then Finellen's, until he reached a stretch of clear road. The white stallion leaped a stone fence and landed in the road, stretching low as his rider gave him his freedom to run.

For a minute they thundered down the road, and then the prince saw a pair of horses before him, grazing quietly in a small meadow. He reined in beside them and saw Daryth and Pawldo lying in the shade of a broad oak tree. Swinging down from the saddle, Tristan released Avalon to graze, and stretched out beside his companions.

"Where's Canthus?" Daryth asked.

"He fell, fighting those Riders," Tristan said, fighting back tears. "I searched for his body, but found nothing before dark."

"Damn them!" cursed the Calishite, spitting. "That hound was worth five of those horsemen!"

"And that's nearly how many he took with him," exaggerated the prince.

"We should have taken them again!" growled Pawldo, looking to the east. "Then they'd not be following us!"

"I wish we could have," said Tristan, sincerely. "Still, we hurt them, badly, I think. By the time we get to Corwell, they'll be in no shape to fight a battle!"

"There's an enchantment laid on those Riders on the black horses," grunted Pawldo. "I can smell magic a mile away! We should have wiped 'em out when we had the chance."

"All too soon we'll get another chance." Tristan suddenly felt very weary. He climbed to his feet. "Is Robyn riding with the wounded?" he asked.

"Yes," replied Daryth. "She's in the wagon with Aileen. I was up there most of the morning—that's an evil wound she's suffered!"

"Sorcery!" interjected Pawldo. "I told you!"

"I'm quite sure that you're right," answered the prince as he mounted Avalon. "I saw the eyes of the creature that struck her. Whatever it was, it was not human!"

Now Tristan let Avalon amble down the road. He wanted to see Robyn, to talk to her, but he wanted some time to sort out his thoughts. He did, indeed, want to confront the ghoulish horsemen again. The Sword of Cymrych Hugh felt light against his thigh, as if the weapon too had the desire to renew the attack.

Instead, he turned at the sound of another rider, and saw Keren riding up to join him. The bard's harp was slung over his shoulder, but as usual he was absently humming a tune.

"Are you still writing that song?" asked Tristan.

"And nothing else! You've given me several splendid verses over the last few days, I must say. You handled yourself and the rest of us very well indeed!" The bard's bantering tone could not mask the genuine respect in his eyes.

"I am honored by your words," responded the prince. "But there is no measuring the spirit you gave to our troops with the music of your harp. Without it, I doubt the battle would have been won."

"The spirit was not mine to give, but perhaps to awaken. Nevertheless, I thank you."

"Awakened it enough to give us a smashing victory!" said the prince.

"Hardly!" disagreed Keren, sharply. "We met a small, demoralized army at the end of a hard march, and held it up for a few hours. We did that, and we did it well! But this enemy is far from smashed, my prince. And you endanger us terribly," he continued, "if you think otherwise!"

XXXXXXXXXX

The waters of Corwell Firth placidly guided the narrow hulls. After the rolling swells on the Sea of Moonshae, the smooth bay might have been a pond for all the challenge it presented to the veteran sailors. To the north and south of the fleet, the green hills of Corwell climbed into the hazy sky. Sea birds soared behind the ships, dipping toward the fish churned up in the wakes.

Thelgaar Ironhand stood in the bow of the leading longship. His gaze locked to the east, he searched the horizon for the first sign of the town and castle of Corwell. The Iron King had been unusually patient in the last few days, but his men sensed their leader's tension.

The steady stroking of the oars drove the longships forward. The air had remained still since the fleet had taken to sea following the enforced stop for repairs. Consequently, the northmen had been forced to row much of the distance. Now, as they approached their destination, the time for rowing would soon be over.

But, as the fleet pushed its way through the long, sheltered neck of Corwell Firth, a fickle offshore breeze arose, as if attempting to drive the northmen away. The sailors leaned into their oars and the ships tacked back and forth, but the wind fluctuated in its course from northwest to southwest, delaying passage through the Firth for several days more.

Then the fleet approached close enough for Thelgaar to see Caer Corwell, high on its rocky knoll.

Soon afterward, the raiders could discern the town sprawled along the shore below the castle. Crouched behind its low wall, the town seemed to cower in fear before the approach of the raiders. And they were cheered by the sight. But as the fleet drew closer, the winds sprang even more strongly from the shore. The raiders strained at the oars, the longships advancing slowly against the growing force of the breeze. Steadily, though, they inched closer and closer to the port.

"More wind!" The King of Corwell's bellow rang out across the Corwell docks, and the three druids bent to their task. Gusts of wind exploded from the little port to roar across the firth, pushing against the invading longships with relentless force.

Then, the youngest druid—a woman of two score years—clutched her throat. With a strangled gasp, she toppled forward to lie motionless.

"My lord!" Quinn Moonwane, druid of Llyrath Forest, turned to King Kendrick and spoke harshly. "We cannot maintain the wind much longer! If you do not let us rest, we will be useless when they finally land, as they will do!"

The king stood very still, staring at the druid. Murderous rage seethed within, but finally he turned away and stalked off along the waterfront.

He passed the men of the Corwell Company, which was led by the

Lord Mayor Dinsmore himself. That pudgy captain, a shiny brass helmet perched ludicrously upon his bald head, waddled after the king.

"My lord! We cannot let them enter the harbor! We simply must have more wind! You must speak to the—"

"Be quiet, you imbecile!" roared King Kendrick, sending the mayor scurrying back to his company. "Ready yourself to drive them away when they land!"

One of the king's loyal lieutenants, a lean swordsman called Randolph, approached. Frustration showed everywhere in the warrior's mien.

"Damn these shortsighted fools!" Randolph snorted, "They have no sense of the stakes of this battle—all they can think about are their petty territorial squabbles."

"Koart and Dynnatt?" asked the king, staring at the clear waters of the firth.

"Yes. They are here with their companies. Now, they argue as to who will strike the first blow when the raiders come ashore. Each seems certain that the battle will end there, before the other can share in the 'glory'. " The captain's voice was heavy with disgust.

"The halflings?"

"They have evacuated Lowhill. A small company of archers came to the town—the others have fled past Caer Corwell with the refugees from the east."

But the king had ceased listening. He squinted into the haze of the firth and stared. "They're coming," he said. "It will not be long now."

As if on cue, the mist seemed to part, and sleek, dark shapes emerged from the haze. More and more of the looming objects appeared, and soon Thelgaar Ironhand's entire fleet, released by the inhibiting breeze, swept toward Corwell. The sails of the longships remained furled upon the masts, but the long banks of oars dipped and rose with deadly precision. As the druids marshaled their strength for battle, the wind died completely away, allowing the fleet to glide across calm water.

King Kendrick climbed to the top of a wooden bulwark that had been hastily erected on the dock. It masked two slender catapults and their crews.

"Have you got the range?" demanded the king.

"Aye. We've sighted on the harbor mouth, sire," replied one of the band.

The king sprang down to the dock, and came to another bulwark, this one made of straw piled to shoulder height.

"Are the archers ready?" he asked, spying a bowman peering over the straw.

"Yes, my lord! We've a hundred of us back here—and half that number of small folk have arrived with their bows from Lowhill."

"Good. Send them to me."

The longships drew steadily closer, as the king installed the halfling archers on the roof of a small warehouse beside the docks. By the time the last defenses had been prepared, the enemy vessels had narrowed into a column, and the leading ship neared the narrow gap in the breakwater that gave access to Corwell Harbor.

The lead vessel advanced quickly, her rowers driving her forward with rhythmic strokes. A white wave foamed from her bow, and the tall prow loomed higher and higher as the ship darted through the gap. The king could see a northman—probably the enemy king—standing at the prow. The raider was a huge man, bristling with a white beard and long hair of the same color. Even at this distance, the fanatical intensity of his gaze made him look like a madman.

"Now!" cried King Kendrick.

At his command, the artillerists released their weapons. The long beams of the catapults cracked forward as each weapon launched a fiery bundle of pitch-soaked straw into the air. The missiles climbed through a shallow arc, leaving thick trails of black smoke to mark their trajectory, and then sizzled to the water at either side of the longship.

"Missed, dammit!" cursed the king. "Again! Fire as fast as you can!" Before the second volley of missiles was launched, the king had left the catapults and hurried to the archers.

A second longship followed the leader through the breakwater, but this one took a flaming bundle in the center of the hull. The oily pitch spattered across the boat, and in seconds the fire had claimed her midsection. Northmen leaped overboard, struggling to the breakwater, or else sinking like stones from their weight of weapons and armor. The boat drifted against the breakwater as the fire spread throughout the vessel.

Yet a steady stream of longships approached the harbor mouth. The artillerists kept a steady rain of flaming pitch upon them, igniting three more, but an equal number slipped through the firestorm.

"Archers!" called the king. "Now!"

Showers of arrows soared from behind the straw bulwark and the ridge of the warehouse. Many of them found marks among the rowers of the enemy king's longship. King Kendrick stared in disbelief as several of the missiles struck that leader himself, only to be jerked from the wounds and cast scornfully away. The pace of his driving advance slowed, however, for many of his crew suffered hits from the arrows.

Black smoke now obscured the mouth of the breakwater as the burning longships drifted aimlessly. A fifth, and then a sixth longship emerged from the smoke as the raiders drove steadily closer to the docks.

Leaving the archers to their own commanders, the king ran back to the druids. Only two remained at the ready. Quinn Moonwane looked up at the ruler's approach.

"We have marshaled our strength as best we can," Quinn Moonwane stated grimly. "Dierdre of Dynnatt Grove is lost to us."

The king noticed that the druid who had collapsed while creating the windstorm lay, pale and unmoving, at the rear of the docks. For a moment, a pang of anguish crossed the king's face, but he turned to Moonwane with authority.

"Do your best. Try to damage the longships in the harbor. We'll have a better chance if we can force them to land outside of the town."

"Very well," sighed the druid. He and Edric of Stockwell—a stout druid of middle age—stepped to the edge of the dock. The king could now see five longships driving toward them—the sixth had caught fire. These five were within a hundred yards of the waterfront.

Quinn stood facing the approaching vessels while the other druid moved several paces to the side. The dark-haired druid raised his hands, closing his eyes in concentration. He called upon the might of the goddess, marshaling her strength from within the earth, turning it to magical energy. Selecting one of the ships as a target, he unleashed the power of the goddess through the tool of his magic spell.

The enchantment seized the long beam of the longship's keel. The wood bent to the will of its Mother, warping and twisting along its entire length. Nails sprang from the oaken boards of the hull. Shrieking and groaning in protest, the twisted keel broke loose from the longship, destroying the vessel. In seconds, the ship became a spreading circle of wreckage and swimming bodies on the surface of the harbor.

The other druid called forth a storm of fire that surged across the water to spill against the hull of the longship carrying the northmen's king.

That king still stood boldly at the prow of his vessel, and as the fire licked against the sides of the ship, he cut his hand through a curt, chopping gesture. Instantly, the flames sizzled away. At the same time, the druid who had cast the flaming spell clutched at his chest and doubled over. With an earsplitting shriek, he toppled off the dock and splashed into the water. Quinn started, turning to stare at his comrade in growing anguish and fear.

"That one!" cried King Kendrick, pointing to the white-bearded northman standing at the prow of his ship.

Quinn Moonwane—the most powerful of the three druids who had come to fight in Corwell—regarded the raider king. His eyes, trained to see the good and evil within nature, saw that the enemy king was not human. The druid knew that he faced something corrupt and very powerful, but he could not understand its omnipotent nature.

Quinn took up his staff and pointed it at his foe. From the deepest wells of his strength, he called forth the might of the goddess. His enemy turned to regard him, and the druid looked into those hellish eyes for a split second.

King Kendrick saw the druid's body explode into a shower of red mist. His robes, boots, and belt, soaked with blood, fell to the dock, in the middle of a spreading pool of gore. The King of Corwell turned in rage.

"Destroy them!" he bellowed, calling the artillerists to direct their fire against the leading longship. The archers sent their deadly missiles raking the two other vessels that had not caught fire. Both of those soon drifted to a halt, with no one alive to man the oars.

But the leading ship resisted all attempts to incinerate it. A curtain of protection appeared to surround the vessel, as fiery missiles that seemed destined to strike her suddenly veered away to hiss, uselessly, into the water of the harbor.

Yet the raider king knew that he would not be able to land his force

XXXXXXXXXXXXXXXXXXXXXXXXXXXXX DOUGLAS NILES XXXXXXXXXXXXXXXXXXXXXXXXX

on the docks. The fleet beyond the breakwater already steered toward
the gravelly beach beyond the town, and the lone longship in the harbor
turned to withdraw.

King Kendrick snorted, momentarily satisfied at the withdrawal.
"Randolph? Where are you, man?"

The captain stepped up quickly, smiling at the scene of destruction
in the harbor. "We've slowed them up, sire."

"Indeed. How fares the organization of the companies?"

"Badly, my lord. Your presence is required, I fear, before Dynnatt,
Koart, and the Lord Mayor will listen to reason."

"Damn their pettiness!" The king turned to look at the retreating
longship. "Very well. I'll find you as soon as that one clears the harbor.
And blast my son again for disappearing when I most need him!"

Randolph hurried back to the lords, while King Kendrick stared at
the lone vessel. He saw the white-haired enemy ruler, now standing in
the stern. For a moment, their gazes locked, before a swirling cloud of
smoke swept between them. The king felt, saw, the explosive force of the
enemy's magic erupting toward him.

Then, the building behind him erupted in a shower of broken stone.
The high wall collapsed forward, burying the King of Corwell beneath
a tumbling curtain of jagged rock.

XXXXXXXXXX

Laric rode hungrily across the ruined farm, ignoring the blazing building and torn, muddy field. His gaze remained fixed toward the west.

His eyes glowed red with pleasure at the memories—the slaying of
the sister knight had been an exciting thing, fueling him for the battles
to come. The rush of that memory could not compare, however, to his
hunger for the knight he had almost taken. That one, somehow, beckoned irresistibly to him.

Laric did not know if that knight still lived, for the spirit had flickered
very weakly within her body when he had seized her reins. Yet, he had
discovered no sign of her body, and he had searched diligently through
the bloody fields for it. Therefore, it seemed that she must have accompanied the army toward Corwell.

XXXXXXXXXXXXXXXXXXXXXXXXXXXXX 254 XXXXXXXXXXXXXXXXXXXXXX

And if so, Laric knew, they would indeed meet again.

But until then, the other Bloodriders needed to eat, and this was one reason the farm Laric rode across burned now. Many other such dwellings had become ashes during this long day of riding, and occasionally the Riders had been fortunate enough to find Ffolk within that had not had the sense to flee with the rest of the population. The killing of these poor fools had made a hot and nourishing feast for the scattered Riders. As Laric rode from detachment to detachment, he was encouraged to see that most of his horsemen were slowly regaining their strength.

His company preceded the combined army of Grunnarch and Raag Hammerstaad down the Corwell Road. Ostensibly, the Bloodriders would scout for pockets of enemy resistance and engage the rearguard of the retreating Ffolk. Laric had his own priorities, however, and the sustenance of his company was highest among them. Thus, the Riders let the Ffolk retreat unmolested, and Laric remained confident that the enemy would not again offer battle until they reached the imagined safety of Caer Corwell.

So, instead of scouting during this long day of riding, the Bloodriders found nourishment, and grew mightier.

XXXXXXXXXX

Tristan finally caught up with the wagons and carts carrying the wounded to Corwell. Cantering beside the road, he passed a large wagon, thinly padded with hay, carrying nearly a score of bloody Ffolk. The wounded warriors, men and women both, sat or lay listlessly while their transport jolted along, pulled by six massive oxen.

Several similar wagons preceded this one, but he finally reached a small cart pulled by a single horse.

Here, stretched on a bed of hay, lay Aileen, the sister knight. Robyn sat beside her.

"How is she?" The knight's slender face was exceptionally pale from beneath the woolen blanket. Her eyes were closed.

"She suffers horribly. The wound is not deep, but it festers unnaturally—like those horsemen themselves."

"The Riders on black horses—are they the scourge you sensed, in Cantrev Myrrdale?" asked the prince.

"Yes. They leave a trail of corruption in the earth, wherever they pass. It is very easy for me to see. It seems that others have more difficulty." Robyn answered quietly, as if she were concealing some deeper emotion.

"Could these Riders be the evil warned against by the prophecy?"

"I don't think so. They are more like a spawn of some great evil." Robyn looked him squarely in the eyes. "I accompanied the knights when they buried Carina, and I heard how she died. Why weren't you there?"

The prince could not meet her gaze. "There were too many things to attend . . . I was looking for Canthus . . . " he trailed off, appalled at having neglected such a duty.

"She died to save your life!"

"I know that!" he snapped.

"Don't you feel anything? Did you see how many of our people died in that field?"

"Of course I feel! But we fought—and won—a battle. The dead are the price of that vic—"

"Price? Now you're talking about them like pieces of gold!" Robyn's anger brought a flush of color to her cheeks. Her green eyes bored into his mercilessly.

"You may be able to fight a battle, but being a prince is more than that!" Robyn stopped, suddenly.

She bent over Aileen and mopped the sister knight's forehead with a soft cloth, before turning back to the prince. "Tristan, you can lead these people through a war, I think. But you must be worthy of leading them in peace, as well. You *must care!*"

The prince cleared his throat, feeling suddenly very responsible for the bad things that had happened this day. He thought of Carina's heroic death—of the farmer and his wife who had fallen trying to close the breach at the ditch. And of a hundred other pairs of eyes that would never again see the light of the sun.

"Robyn, I do care. It's hard for me to show that, but I want very much to be a prince and a man you can be proud of. " He could think of nothing else to add, and so rode quietly behind the wagon for several minutes.

Suddenly, a clamor of noise attracted their attention to the west. The prince could see a rider, galloping beside the road toward them. With a sudden eagerness, he realized that the man might bring news from home.

"Take me with you," called Robyn, reaching out. Avalon trotted to the wagon, and the young woman slipped nimbly onto the broad back of the horse. Together, they raced the stallion up the long road.

Tristan saw a haggard rider, feebly lashing a foamflecked horse. With a start, he recognized Owen, a castle guardsman.

"My prince!" cried the messenger, reining in at Avalon's approach.

"What is it?" he asked, fearing the answer.

"Northmen raiders! They have landed at Corwell. Even now they fall upon the town!" The words spilled from the messenger in a chaotic tangle.

"When did they land?" asked Tristan, fighting panic.

"Yesterday! They landed beyond the town—at least a hundred long-ships! I set out to find you as they approached the harbor, but saw them land before I rode far inland."

In a clatter of hooves, Daryth and Pawldo galloped up to them. The halfling's face grew pale as he heard the news.

"What of Lowhill?" he asked.

"It has been evacuated, the halflings sheltering in the castle or the town," explained Owen.

"We must go there!" urged Robyn, as Tristan sat, frozen, upon his horse. A graphic picture formed in his mind of the grim rendezvous of two armies of northmen at Corwell.

"Come on!" cried the woman, digging at his ribs.

"Yes, of course," the prince replied. His mind spun, and he had trouble grasping a single thought.

"Get word to the sisters," Tristan said to the Calishite. "Tell Brigit that Robyn and I ride to Corwell. She should follow with her company, if the rear of the column continues to remain secure."

Turning to Pawldo, he said, "Find Finellen, and tell her to get the dwarves to Corwell as fast as she can. Gavin and the Ffolk will have to defend the column from the rear, if need be."

The two friends nodded in understanding, and turned to gallop

XXXXXXXXXXXXXXXXXXXXXXXX DOUGLAS NILES XXXXXXXXXXXXXXXXXXXXXXXX

eastward. Robyn's grip tightened about the prince's waist as he urged Avalon to speed in the opposite direction. The white stallion leaped a low hedge and took to the fields.

Avalon seemed not to notice the additional rider, carrying them both with easy grace, toward the home that had suddenly become very precious. The prince did not know what he could hope to do when he arrived—he only knew that he had to get there as quickly as possible.

"Idiot! Bumbling oaf!" Grunnarch's temper raged, now that he had found a victim for his wrath.

"You call me names, when it was your army that was stopped by a band a peasant rabble?" Raag Hammerstaad's voice returned the Red King's rage with equal measure. The two kings rose to their feet, shaking their fists at each other across the campfire.

"If you had maintained pressure on that road—"

"If you had attacked with an army, instead of this band of vermin, you could have taken that road! Look at these men—I challenge you!" Raag gestured dramatically at the camp.

In an instant the rage left Grunnarch, depression again pushing other emotions into the background.

"Aye," he grunted, sitting again. Puzzled and frowning, Raag sat also.

"The spirit has been drained from this army, I tell you, like the juice might be sucked from a lemon." Grunnarch paused, and then pointed roughly toward Myrloch Vale. "That place up there is a place I'd wish on no man! I'll not enter it again, were it worth my life to do so!"

"I, however, shall return to the Vale," said Trahern. Until now the sullen druid had been ignored by the kings.

"I thought you were accompanying us to Corwell!" objected Grunnarch, but the druid waved away his arguments.

"I have things to do here. " The druid rose and quickly disappeared into the darkness.

"Well, you're back in the realms of men, now," grunted Raag, looking curiously at his old friend. The two kings had embarked upon many a raid together, and never had Raag heard Grunnarch sound so worn and out of control.

"Aye," agreed Grunnarch, forcing himself to lift his head. "This malady must certainly pass from us, now that we have passed the

XXXXXXXXXXXXXXXXXXXXXXXX **258** XXXXXXXXXXXXXXXXXXXXXXXX

borders of that nightmarish place!" He tried to convince himself of the fact.

In another part of the camp, red, glowing eyes looked over the sleeping army.

Hungry eyes.

X X X X X X X X X X

In a half day's travel, Avalon carried his two riders over land that would take the refugees half a tenday to cross. Shortly before sunset they crossed the last rise east of the town, and began the long descent to the sea. Caer Corwell, resting proudly atop its rocky hill, stood out clearly against the sinking sun. The pennant of the Lone Wolf fluttered bravely from the high tower.

They saw with relief that the town lay pristine and intact beside its sheltered harbor. But, as the road slowly dropped and they drew nearer their destination, they saw other, more disquieting, signs.

The skeletal hulks of several ships jutted from the waters of the harbor, and wreckage floated among the hulks. Then, as they came around a low hill, they saw the longships of the northmen, drawn onto the beach a mile beyond the town. Like a creeping plague of insects, the raiding army was swarming across the moor toward Corwell.

The refugees from the Eastern Cantrevs bypassed the town and castle entirely, moving on to the north and west, toward more remote sections of the kingdom. As long as Caer Corwell held out, the raiders would not be able to risk a force in pursuit.

Seemingly tireless, Avalon increased his speed as they approached. Now the prince could see encampments around Caer Corwell. From them fluttered the pennants of lords Dynnatt and Koart. Still, the fighters of the Ffolk were vastly outnumbered by the horde of raiders.

Finally, the stallion rode under the very shadow of Caer Corwell, and Tristan guided him onto the long, climbing road toward the gatehouse. The exertion of the long run now took its toll, and Avalon slowed to a trot. He carried them steadily upward until they passed through the open gatehouse. Several guards, shouting cries of welcome to their prince, ran to spread the word of his arrival.

A young stableboy ran forward to take the white stallion's reins. "Welcome home, my prince, Miss Robyn," he cried.

Robyn swung to the ground, followed by the prince as the boy led Avalon away. For the first time, Tristan noticed how fatigued the horse was—he held his head low, and his flanks were covered with lather.

"It's good to see you, my prince," said Randolph, one of the officers of the guard, as Tristan dusted himself off and turned toward the great hall. The guard's manner was hesitant, welcoming, and relieved.

"It's the king," continued the man. "He was wounded during the fight on the docks. He is in his study now. My prince, you must see him!"

"Of course," replied Tristan. He felt a flash of fear for his father's welfare that surprised him with its depth.

xxxxxxxxxxx

Bobbing like a corpse in the rush of water, the unicorn's body disappeared into the oily liquid, then popped to the surface again. Kamerynn's snowy coat had vanished. In most places, black and sticky mire covered the broad body in grotesque patterns.

In other, uglier places, the caustic water of the Darkwell had burned away the hair and some of the skin. Great pink wounds lay exposed to the poisonous and stinging touch of the unleashed torrent.

The waters of the Darkwell flooded far beyond the banks of the little stream as they erupted from the crumbling dam. Hissing poisonously, they destroyed all vegetation in their path. The ground they flowed across blackened—it would be lifeless for many years.

Yet even as the water flowed, the power of the Darkwell waned. The poison lost its potency as the flood dissipated across a broad marsh, and the unicorn's body floated to rest against a broad oak tree. As the waters drained away, Kamerynn lay still upon a muddy bed of dead grass.

For a full day the unicorn did not move. Kamerynn's eyes, burned to senselessness by the Darkwell, could see no glimmer of light, even from the direct rays of the sun. The useless forelegs throbbed with pain, and slowly Kamerynn's awareness drifted away.

IDENTITY

17

X**B**e very quiet!" warned Friar Nolan. "You must not agitate him!"

Tristan paused outside his father's study and took a deep breath. "Well, let's go," he said to Robyn. Nodding, the maiden quietly opened the door into a firelit room.

Hesitantly, Robyn approached the huge couch where the king lay nearly buried beneath a pile of quilts. Large blue-black bruises marked his face, and one eye was swollen shut. His lips were cracked and bloody.

Tristan, disbelieving the sight of the vulnerability of his father, stood awkwardly behind Robyn.

The good eye fluttered open as the woman moved closer, and the king held out a bandaged hand. "My child, come here," he croaked, clasping Robyn's hand as she stepped to his side. She matched his tight grip, and for a moment they remained silent.

"You are strong," the king said, finally. "Your mother would be very proud of you."

"Who is my mother, sir? Please, you must tell me!" The need to know had grown within her during the last tendays as her powers became more apparent. Her tension caused her voice to shake slightly.

"Yes, it is time you knew," said the king in a low, weak voice. "It was only for your own protection that we kept it a secret for so long."

Robyn waited, surprised, as the king caught his breath.

Tristan watched the two. He was painfully aware that his father had not so much as greeted him.

"Your mother was Brianna Moonsinger, Great Druid of all the Isles of Moonshae. You were her only child."

Robyn sat upon the edge of the bed, feeling strangely calm. The news no longer had the power to surprise her.

"What happened to her?" she asked.

"You were a year old when she brought you here. Your mother and I had fought together against the northmen—she trusted me. She told me that she had to travel to Myrloch Vale, to one of the Moonwells. Some sort of perversion grew there, and she was going to cleanse it.

"She felt that it would be very dangerous, and she wanted you cared for in case she did not return. I . . . I never saw her again."

"And my father?"

"I am sorry, but I do not know who your father was. Brianna never said anything about him."

"Why did I need to be protected—my identity a secret?"

"Your mother warned me that potent evil gathered strength in the land. It could be a generation or more before it was released, but if her mission failed, such a catastrophe would become an inevitability. The druids are the most potent force we have, to cope with that evil. Your mother sensed great power within you, even as a baby, and she feared for you, should this evil presence become aware of your existence.

"She felt that on reaching adulthood, you would take on the mantle of the druids and would play an important role in the struggle. She hoped, as did I, that you would be much older when this became necessary.

I see that you have matured much, in the short months of this summer—you are as ready as I could have hoped. Now we need your help in the battle against the accursed enemies of our people!" The king collapsed backward, exhausted from telling the tale.

"I have seen the might of that enemy, sir, and have already fought it," replied Robyn, clasping the king's hand. "I will fight it as long as I live!"

"I admire your spirit, my chi—my lady. The Ffolk have always resisted this evil, but we have never completely defeated it. Even Cymrych Hugh failed, in his final battle, to—"

"Father!" Tristan interrupted, stepping forward.

"We . . . I found the Sword of Cymrych Hugh! I brought it to Corwell, and carry it now!"

The king's eye clouded. "Don't joke about such a thing." But his outburst was half-hearted, and he looked at Robyn for confirmation. "Of course, he is not joking."

"He's not," she agreed, shaking her head slowly. "You underestimate him, I think."

"Perhaps. " The king was not convinced. "In any event, he is fortunate to have a companion like you at his side."

Tristan bit his tongue and turned away, stung.

"We were fortunate to have a man like him as our leader during the last tendays!"

The king forced a smile from his cracked lips but did not acknowledge her comment. Robyn rose to take her leave. "Here," said the king, reaching to the side. "You are to have these now. They were your mother's."

King Kendrick picked up a long staff of white ash and handed it to Robyn. "This is the Staff of the White Well. Your mother made it. " She took a deep breath and touched the smooth wood. She could almost imagine her mother's hands—strong, but gentle—caressing the shaft.

"And this. " The king handed her a heavy leather tome, clasped with a brass lock. It was the largest book Robyn had ever seen. A tiny silver key stood in the lock.

Robyn, fearing she was going to cry, clenched her teeth. All these years she had hoped for an answer to a single question. Now, she had that answer, but it only raised a thousand more imponderables among her whirling thoughts. The king cleared his throat, and she looked at him.

"I'd like to talk to my son."

XXXXXXXXX

A waterfall tinkled across a sunlit face of rock to splash musically into a clear pool. A brook, alive with trout, foamed from the pool, through a broad clearing bright with wildflowers. A surrounding forest of pine and aspen provided security and shelter.

The power of the goddess flowed here, and this was where the Great

Druid of Gwynneth brought Canthus, the moorhound, to recuperate. For days, the great dog rested on the grass or upon a thick shelf of moss on the bank of the pool.

The old druid chattered pleasantly to the dog, surprising Canthus by speaking his language. The hound would lie peacefully for hours as she talked of hunting, and chasing, and running—things Canthus understood very well.

"And how is my puppy today?" she greeted him, one morning, after he had spent many days under her care.

The huge tail thumped Canthus's response, as he sniffed to see what she had brought him. This morning, however, the druid offered him nothing to eat.

Her mood seemed unusually serious.

"See how strong you have grown," she told him, stroking the smoothly mended skull, and the scarless spot where the Bloodrider's sword had cut him.

"And your coat, and your eyes—how shiny they are!" Lovingly, she brushed her fingers through his long coat, picking out a few last tangles.

"My puppy, you must help me," she began finally, speaking very slowly. For a long time, she very carefully explained to him the task he needed to perform, keeping her glittering, clear blue eyes upon the dog.

Canthus returned her stare. He waited for the command. But she paused, a tear growing in the corner of her old eye, and she fumbled within her baggy pouch. Finally, she found what she sought, bringing a silvery band of metal into the sunlight.

"But wait. Let me put this on." She held in her hands a silver torque, such as a great warrior might wear into combat. Stretching the springy metal apart, she placed it over Canthus's head to lock firmly about his sturdy neck. The thin strip of silver vanished beneath the studded iron collar.

"There," Genna said, "that might help—anyway, it certainly can't hurt. Now, begone with you! Get busy, do you hear?"

If Canthus understood that he had just received the benign blessing of the goddess herself, he did not give any indication. He sprang up, bounded across the field, and disappeared.

XXXXXXXXXX

"How are you, Father?" Tristan asked awkwardly after Robyn had touched his arm lightly and left.

"I fear I shall live," replied the king hoarsely. His manner was brusque.

"So you've found the Sword of Cymrych Hugh," continued the monarch. "Let me see it."

Tristan slid the blade from its scabbard and showed his father the gleaming weapon. The king's one good eye widened, and he reached a hand forward to stroke the silver sword, lightly tracing the runes inscribed into the metal.

"Where did you find it?" There was sudden energy and life in his voice.

"In a Firbolg stronghold, in Myrloch Vale. It was the same place Keren was held—we rescued him as well!" The memory gave Tristan more confidence.

The king leaned back, and closed his eye. For a moment the prince wondered if he had fallen asleep, but then the wounded man sighed heavily and again looked at his son.

"How I searched for that blade! My entire youth, and much of my manhood, was devoted to discovering the Sword of Cymrych Hugh. All across Gwynneth, and Alaron, and Moray, and all the rest of the isles. Twenty years—no, more than that—I spent on that quest. And you find it by accident!" The prince could not tell if the irony amused or angered his father.

"The goddess wants you to have it, that's certain," continued the king. "And these other reports I've heard . . . Do you really have dwarves and Llewyrr elven knights fighting with you?"

"And a company from the Eastern Cantrevs—more than five hundred strong."

Tristan told his father about the army closing in from the east. He described the battle at Freeman's Down, but did not elaborate on his adventures. He was still bothered by his father's cool reaction.

When Tristan finished his tale, the king merely said, "As you can see, I will be of little use in the coming battle. If Arlen were here, I would entrust my army to him. " The prince felt a sudden surge of guilt over his teacher's death, as well as anger at his father's failure to respond to his story.

"But of course he is dead, and the commanders of our forces bicker incessantly. I do not know that you are ready . . . " He shut his eyes in frustration and unrelinquished bitterness. "But *you* must take command of these companies and compel them to fight together!"

"The town is a lost position. You must convince the Lord Mayor to evacuate everyone to the castle before the raiders cut them off. We do not have much time, so you must make haste!

"My son," the king said, his voice fluttering. "You are a Prince of Corwell. You must not fail me in this. I will not allow it!"

"You will not?" Tristan rose quickly, trying to control his annoyance. "Father, *I* will not allow it!" He turned and stalked from the room. A few minutes later, riding Avalon, he thundered through the gatehouse and raced down the road toward Corwell Town.

✕ ✕ ✕ ✕ ✕ ✕ ✕ ✕ ✕

The Pack had never eaten so well. The wolves had been introduced to an assortment of new tastes—mutton, pork, beef, horse, and human— by their new leader.

The rolling tide of death would race through quiet streets, smashing through windows, or pressing against doors and walls until they collapsed, pouring into the buildings to drag screaming Ffolk to a gruesome death. Those that fled would be run down and savaged in the fields.

Erian led the Pack through many cantrevs, always leaving a wasteland, devoid of animal life. Gradually, the spawn of the Beast moved his fearsome band into more heavily populated areas of Corwell. These cantrevs, along the northern border of the kingdom, had not known the cut of the northmen's steel, but found themselves faced with an enemy every bit as merciless and implacable.

Now the great band of wolves set enthusiastically upon entire communities. One such cantrev attempted to screen itself with a massive ring of burning timder. The Pack waited until the fire burned itself out, and then lunged in to slaughter everyone within the enclosure.

Gradually, as he saw that the Pack was bent completely to his power, Erian began to lead them toward his true objective. They loped steadily southward, their voices raised in cries as they crossed the moonlit moors.

Now, Erian led them past rich cantrevs and farms, forcing his wolves to ignore the tantalizing aromas of all the foods their leader had taught them to love. Erian allowed them to attack only when hunger became a critical concern. Behind them they left a wealth of carrion for the scavengers.

Erian did this intentionally, for when the wolves reached their destination, he wanted them to be very hungry indeed.

XXXXXXXXXX

Tristan looked around, appalled. He tried desperately to understand the plan behind the town's defenses, but concluded that there was no plan. Three separate companies of troops, under three separate commanders, were trying to defend the town three different ways.

Lord Mayor Dinsmore met him as he passed through the north gate in the town wall. This gate, the most crucial in the link between town and castle, was lightly garrisoned. Most of the town militia were spread along the length of the town's south wall.

"Oh, thank heavens you're here, my prince!" exclaimed the old mayor. His ridiculous brass helmet still perched atop the crown of his shiny head, restrained by a thin strap under one of his many chins.

"Such folly, I can hardly describe!" wailed Dinsmore, as soon as the prince had entered the town walls. "The Lords Dynnatt and Koart would not stand within the walls. They form in the field, each seeking to outdo the other in glory!"

"Damn!" Tristan urged the stallion through the crowded streets to the low wall at the town's southern border. He was about to leap the barrier and gallop into the field to confront Lords Koart and Dynnatt, but he saw that there was no longer any point.

The remnants of the two companies, led by their esteemed lords, streamed chaotically toward the town. The northmen gathered threateningly behind them, prodding the retreat.

The prince looked around and saw that Lord Mayor Dinsmore had caught up with him. Tristan dropped quickly to the ground, holding Avalon's reins, and confronted the pudgy mayor.

"My Lord Mayor, we must evacuate the town! Within the palisade of the castle we stand a much better chance of stalling the attack!"

"Impossible!" the mayor wailed. "We cannot give them the town!"

"They will take it, regardless," snapped Tristan. "Do you see how many of them are out there? Do you think that low wall is going to slow them up?"

"I will die here, even if you choose to leave!" The mayor's brass helmet bobbed frantically as he made his pronouncement, which seemed to startle even him.

"And how many of our people will your vanity drag down?" Tristan resisted the urge to grab the man's shoulders and shake him. "Don't be a fool! You will doom everyone within these walls to certain death! Can you die with that on your conscience?"

The stout mayor sighed, as he appeared to deflate. Even the helmet seemed to rest more solidly upon his bald crown. "I cannot. Very well, what must we do?"

"We must make a plan. Where can we meet the lords?"

Tristan had Koart and Dynnatt summoned to the mayor's small cottage, where together they leaned over the mayor's dinner table to study a map the prince had rendered on parchment. The two burly competitive lords clumped into the room, leather armor creaking. Neither of them had suffered a wound, though their companies had fought hard.

"We've got a dangerous situation here, with the number of people in the town," the prince began.

"We will move these people, as fast as possible, to the greater security of the castle. Therefore, it is imperative that we keep the castle road, from the north gate of town to the castle's gatehouse, secure!" He looked around. Gruff Lord Koart seemed about to argue, but then changed his mind.

"We should have the services of a company of horse, and of dwarven axemen, within another day at the most, as well as a company of militia from the Eastern Cantrevs. Until then, my lords, I ask you to place your companies along the road. Lord Mayor, your militia and any recruits we can muster within these walls should continue to hold the town."

"My prince!" called a swordsman, pounding on the door. "Someone to see you—a knight! A *female* knight!"

Tristan sprang to the door, quickly pulling it open.

"Brigit! Thank the goddess you have arrived."

The slender knight stepped through the door, nodding curtly to the men gathered in the cottage.

Her gelding was still blowing from the ride, and the dust of the trail coated the knight's armor.

"The company has remained outside the town walls, to the north. The dwarves," she added, managing to say the word without distaste, "should be here within two or three hours."

"Excellent!" cried the prince, pounding his right fist into his left palm. "Lord Mayor, let's get these people moving to the castle as fast as possible!"

XXXXXXXXXXX

Kazgoroth viewed the collection of life within the castle and town of Corwell, and drooled at the prospects. Forcefully, the Beast brought these hot bursts of emotion under control. The plan needed to be a careful one.

The Beast knew better than to try and reduce both pockets of resistance—the town and the castle—at the same time. Instead, they must be divided, and then destroyed one at a time. Not only would the defenders suffer the misery of watching their comrades' deaths, but the attackers could concentrate most of their strength against a single position.

The Beast focused the eyes of Thelgaar Ironhand upon the castle road—the slender thread connecting the town to the castle. Immediately beyond the road glittered the blue waters of the firth. If he could sever that thread, the Ffolk in the town would be trapped within those low walls.

The Beast took note of defensive preparations, watching the two companies march into position to defend the road. Kazgoroth felt little concern, recalling the slaughter those same companies had just suffered in their first encounter with the northmen of Thelgaar Ironhand.

Smiling, Kazgoroth thought of the killing still to come.

XXXXXXXXXX

Daryth and Keren each embraced the prince heartily. They stood before the north gate of the town—the key link between castle and community. The long stretch of road leading to the castle gatehouse seemed a tenuous link indeed.

"Where's Pawldo?" asked Tristan, pausing in the maddening pace of preparations.

Daryth nodded at the company of halflings forming before the road. "He's joined up with some of his kin. What do you want me to do?"

"Can you stay with me? Both of you? I would welcome your counsel."

"We are at your service," said the bard.

A huge gray horse galloped toward them. Behind it marched a long column of troops—the Ffolk of the Eastern Cantrevs. Tristan recognized Gavin astride the horse.

The giant smith slowed to a trot, and then stopped before the gate, swinging heavily to the ground. His face was covered with dust, which lines of sweat had turned into muddy rivers running into the tangled thicket of his massive beard.

"What is the plan, my prince?" he asked brusquely.

"We are beginning to evacuate the town," explained Tristan. "I have two companies of Ffolk and the dwarves and halflings protecting the road. I would like to hold you and the sisters in reserve. I think the northmen will attack as soon as they realize what we're trying to do."

"Very well," said Gavin. "I shall assemble my company before the gate."

"Good!" exclaimed the prince. "We'll start the evacuation within the hour."

XXXXXXXXXX

Robyn's door remained tightly shut, though a glimmer of faint candlelight flickered through the keyhole and underneath the door throughout the long night. Even with the arrival of dawn, the door did not open, nor did any voice respond when Gretta called to the maiden, inviting her to breakfast.

Finally, the old housekeeper burst into the room with a tray of hot tea and bread. The young woman sat at her reading table, staring at the opened book before her. She did not acknowledge the interruption. Sniffing indignantly, Gretta set the tray noisily on the dressing table and stomped out.

Robyn did not even notice the door close behind her old friend. The book held her firmly to its pages, compelling her to turn one after the other, as she carefully devoured each word of every sentence.

The Staff of the White Well lay comfortably across her lap. The wood seemed to glow with an unnatural, positive warmth. Each page of the book that she read seemed to create for her a new vista onto the world, a new point of view.

The book contained her mother's thoughts. The inscription stated that it was written to "Robyn, my only child. " The pages of the book told of Brianna Moonsinger's life as a druid, and of the importance of the druids to the Ffolk, the goddess, and the Moonshaes.

But her mother wrote as well about the land and she wrote about the goddess with a special reverence that brought tears to Robyn's eyes. She savored each page, spending many minutes reading and rereading every phrase. The long day passed again into night, and Gretta entered again, quietly this time. She set fresh candles in the holders, and saw that the room was well lit, before she tiptoed out.

Through another night Robyn read the book, unmindful of the battle menacing the town. Her vision blurred with weariness, and her head nodded occasionally from fatigue, causing her to jolt upward and begin reading with renewed interest.

Finally, she read the secrets of her mother's craft. And now her eyes widened, and the need for sleep vanished. The book drew her attention even more deeply, quickening her pulse and sending vibrant ripples of energy through her body. She now read the last part of her mother's book. She had passed the words of greeting, of wisdom, of history and theology.

Now, she read the words of power.

xxxxxxxxxx

Canthus raced tirelessly across the rolling downs of central Corwell. His objective glared sharply in his mind. Though he had never seen it, its foul stench burned like a familiar enemy in his nostrils. Unerringly, he raced toward that enemy, instinctively changing course to home exactingly upon his foe.

He killed and ate as he ran, never deviating from his course. Some benign fortune seemed to send a rabbit scampering in his path, or a pheasant squawking from a bush just as the moorhound loped past. In these instances, he killed and ate quickly, and then slept for a few hours, before again resuming his quest.

As the dog ran, he held his head low, swinging slowly back and forth, trying to scent the quarry still a hundred miles away. Those broad nostrils would quiver as they identified an odor. His hackles would rise instinctively into a bristling collar, and a low growl would rumble from his cavernous chest.

The moorhound's pace quickened slightly, as his long legs carried him easily over mile after mile, climbing the hills as easily as he went down them.

More days passed, and the scent grew stronger. Once, he caught and ate a plump goose, sleeping briefly as was his custom. He awakened soon, alarmed by a wayward breeze.

Canthus knew that his enemy was very close.

xxxxxxxxxx

The throaty roar that rumbled across the field was very different from the hollow cries of the northmen at Freeman's Down. Tristan barely noticed the fact, for by then he could see thousands of northmen charging across the field in an avalanche of assault against his thin line.

The evacuation had not properly begun, for as soon as the prince had posted the companies to guard the road to the castle, the enemy had attacked.

Lord Koart's company, to the left of the line, had already lost a fight to these northmen this day and had no stomach to fight again. One, and then another, man broke from the lines, and suddenly the whole company, some four hundred men, ran in rout toward the castle.

And the northmen were still two hundred yards away.

Seeing Koart's men run, Lord Dynnatt's men, though shaken by the exposure of their flank, stood firm against the charge. From the north gate of the town, Tristan could see the company surrounded by a horde of berserk attackers as the northmen poured through the gap left by the flight of Koart's men.

The halflings, beside Dynnatt, fell back before the press of the attack, as did the dwarves to their right.

Dynnatt's troops were wiped out to the last man, and hundreds of northmen charged across the road, down to the shore of the firth.

The town was cut off from the castle.

XXXXXXXXXXX

The last candle flickered wildly as the short wick finally reached the brass holder. The flame spurted high, and then went out, to leave only the probing beams of the waning moon spilling through the wide window to outline in silver the flowing tresses of black hair that covered the lone table.

Finally, her mind sated, Robyn slept. Her cheek lay upon the smooth leather cover of her mother's book. She breathed easily and slowly.

Her long, thick hair covered her back, her sides, and her arms, as well as most of the table, blanketing her against the cool evening.

The smooth staff still rested across her lap. In the sudden darkness when the moon disappeared behind a cloud, it seemed to flicker and shimmer with an inner light that vanished as moonlight again spilled through the window.

As she slept, Robyn dreamed, more vividly than she ever had in her life. She dreamed that she was a small, furry animal, and she saw the world as that animal might. Then she became a wolf, and looked at the world through his shrewd and hungry eyes. A fish, and a bird, all gave her dreams, and each dream seemed to strengthen and vitalize her.

She dreamed next of hot light and frigid darkness, and of the warm gray that resulted from a balanced mix of the two extremes. And finally she dreamed of the goddess, resplendent in a soft, gray gown and simple ornaments of silver. Her face was the face of serene beauty, but her eyes had been tempered by tears.

And the goddess looked at Robyn, and smiled.

×　×　×　×　×　×　×　×　×　×

Erian looked across the ravaged field, suddenly concerned. His crimson jaws dripped with gore, and he stood astride the corpse of a half-eaten man. The pleasure of the feast was forgotten as his sensitive nostrils searched the air for the source of his worry.

The frenzied feeding of the Pack surrounded the werewolf with a chorus of growls and snarls. But then the wolves, sensing their master's unease, slowed. One after another, the gray heads raised from the kills, to look across the field as they followed his gaze.

Erian saw the newcomer first. A huge moorhound, loping easily, as if on a routine hunt, came toward him. The dog's head hung low, swinging patiently from side to side in rhythm with his long, surprisingly fleet, strides. His yellow eyes searched among a thousand wolves on the ruined farm. Finally the gaze locked with Erian's.

Erian did not feel fear—though the dog was even bigger than the wolf Erian had slain to take the leadership of the Pack, Erian himself was still bigger. And the Darkwell-bred wolf knew that no normal weapon, no mortal flesh, could strike a wound into his hide.

Still, there was something strange and unnatural in this hound's singleminded determination. Already the werewolf could hear the creature's deep and rumbling growl and see its shaggy hackles bristle menacingly.

Erian did not hesitate to spring forward to meet the intruder. His own deep growl rumbled, and he bristled for battle. Black lips curled upward to reveal long fangs, slippery with drool and hungry for the kill.

THE ATTACK

18

Rain lashed the town and its gathered armies throughout most of the night, fading to mist several hours before dawn. The perimeter of each force was marked by a ring of blazing fires, creating pockets of life in the miserable night.

Tristan walked uneasily from fire to fire along the town wall, leading Avalon by the reins. He knew that it was nearly dawn, but no streak of light penetrated the overcast sky.

"Good morning, my prince," greeted a young man-at-arms as the prince walked up to the fire. A dozen of his fellows all nodded a greeting, and Tristan saw that not one of them was old enough to grow a beard.

"Good morning, gentlemen," he answered. I need to warm up a bit."

"Do you think they will attack?" asked one youth, his voice cracking.

"Probably. Are you ready?" responded Tristan.

The youths nodded seriously, and most of them looked into the misty night as if they could see the northmen assembling. Tristan wondered if they knew how acutely dangerous their position actually was. The town wall, varying from four to six feet high, would create only a minor obstacle for the attacking raiders. And once they breached the wall, the fall of the town would follow shortly.

He walked on, stopping to chat briefly at each fire. He wondered if his presence really did anything to bolster the fighters' morale.

Finally, he reached the south gate. This was a crucial point, since the largest body of northmen was massed beyond it. Daryth and Keren stood at the gate itself, looking up soberly as the prince approached.

"How does it look?" asked Tristan.

"We're doing all right," said Daryth, looking around. "But a lot of these people don't have much spirit for battle. I'm not optimistic about stopping them here."

"There are no more troops I can give you," admitted the prince. "So do what you can."

"Where's Robyn?" asked the Calishite.

"In the castle. I haven't seen her since she talked to the king right after our return."

"You sound worried. Do you think something's wrong?"

"I am worried," the prince admitted. "But I can't do much about it now."

"We'll laugh about this come winter," said Daryth, clasping the prince by the shoulder and looking him in the eyes.

"I certainly hope you're right. " Tristan returned the gesture, and then swung into the saddle of his stallion. "See you at daybreak!"

As Avalon trotted up the street, the prince noticed a crowd sitting or lying upon the ground around Friar Nolan's chapel. The prince dismounted and entered the building, noticing that all the people gathered here had been wounded.

Within, he found a floor covered with miserable humanity, as a hundred Ffolk, the seriously wounded, lay everywhere in this makeshift hospital. The prince saw, but did not call to, Nolan. The stout cleric was covered with sweat, his shiny crown reflecting the light from the many candles. His arms, to the elbows, were red with the blood of the wounded.

Slowly, Tristan left the chapel and remounted Avalon. The day was still black. He tried to focus his mind on the battle, but he kept remembering the hospital and the wounded. The warrior's death should be a clean, precise thing, thought the prince angrily. Why were there so many ugly problems?

Next he visited Lord Mayor Dinsmore at the west gate. The mayor commanded this section of the defense, which included much of his militia, as well as Finellen's dwarves. The mayor had readily agreed when Tristan suggested that the dwarves should guard the gate.

On the north wall, the situation looked more encouraging, if only because of Gavin's presence. The big smith had deployed his company of easterners along the wall, and grouped a strong reserve by the gate.

"Let 'em come," was the blacksmith's response to Tristan's report. After his tour, Tristan moved the Sisters of Synnoria from their position in the central square closer to the south gate. Though the large and heavy horses would have difficulty maneuvering in the enclosed streets of Corwell, they were the prince's last recourse in the event of a breakthrough.

Dawn came slowly on this windswept morning. Faint light, diffused by the heavy overcast, gradually replaced the darkness. Even after the sun rose, however, the day remained very dark. Occasionally, a sharp spatter of rain would lash downward from the clouds, but most of the time the glowering overcast just threatened.

XXXXXXXXXX

Grunnarch watched Thelgaar Ironhand pace around the fire, whirling in agitation to pace in the opposite direction. The Iron King behaved very strangely. Grunnarch had heard rumors, in the hours since he had joined the army at Corwell, of Ironhand plucking arrows from his body with impunity. Eyewitnesses swore that there was no way his longship could have survived the inferno in Corwell harbor and emerged without so much as a scorched board.

The kings and lords of the northmen slowly assembled around the high fire. The sky was still inky black, but Grunnarch sensed that dawn was near. Laric, ignoring his own king, strode arrogantly past the group to stand beside Thelgaar Ironhand.

The Iron King looked around, staring at each of his lieutenants. Grunnarch felt a numbing sensation of terror as that gaze passed over his own, and he forced himself to look away.

"We will attack at first light," stated Thelgaar. "We will hit the south and east gates, making a feint against the north gate.

"I want the men of Norheim to strike to the south. Grunnarch, the men of Norland will attack from the east." Groth the Firbolg grunted something in his bestial tongue. The giant, a dirty bandage around his thigh and dirty stains upon his person and crude tunic, looked foul even by the northmen's standards. Thelgaar spit some phrases back at the Firbolg in his own tongue, and Groth turned away from the fire, sulking.

"You will all have the chance to fight!" said Thelgaar, his eyes lingering on Laric. "The attacks to the south and the east will force them from the town. When they try to reach the castle, the Bloodriders and my own legion will destroy them!"

×××××××××××

A ragged, bloodthirsty yell rose from the length of the raiders' position, and the thousands of northmen hurled themselves against Corwell Town.

At the south gate, Daryth and Keren exchanged quick glances of apprehension, for the greatest volume of the noise seemed to come from directly before them.

"Remember," said Daryth wryly, as a ferocious horde of northmen charged from the mist, "we're supposed to do what we can!"

Keren grinned, but did not respond. Drawing his bow with mechanical efficiency, he sent arrow after arrow soaring into the charging mass. Several dozen other archers also inflicted losses upon the raiders, but the missile fire did not seem to slow the attack.

Seconds after the charge began, Daryth faced a yellow-bearded berserker who leaped from the ground to the top of the four-foot wall, then dived onto the defenders. The Calishite's scimitar disemboweled the attacker, but another took his place. This time the strike of Daryth's blade sent him falling backward into the mass of his fellows.

All along the length of the wall, steel clashed against steel, and flesh strove against flesh. Many northmen fell during the initial charge, but once they reached the wall, the toll of dead came quickly from both attacker and defender.

A man fell beside Daryth, and several northmen poured over the wall. He turned to face them, his silver scimitar flickering like lightning into the group, cutting off an arm on a foreswing, and slicing a neck on the recovery.

"Look out!" the bard called from behind Daryth.

The Calishite turned to see a spear-carrying northman poised upon the wall, ready to drive his spear into Daryth's back. Before he could throw the weapon, however, he gasped and toppled back over the wall, one of Keren's arrows jutting from his throat.

But the attackers' numbers were just too high. More and more defenders fell, mortally wounded, or simply turned and ran from the onslaught. Hundreds of raiders poured through the breaches in the walls.

"I think we'd better retreat," grunted Daryth, holding off three northmen with his flashing blade.

Keren, now wielding his sword, backed against the Calishite as he fought two more northmen. Already, the two of them stood virtually alone among the sea of enemy fighters.

"Now!" cried Keren, finishing his opponent with a lightning thrust. "This way!"

Daryth lunged once, throwing his opponents off balance, and then turned to race after the long-legged bard. They darted through the mass of the enemy, dodging attacks, or slaying those who stood in their way.

"I didn't know we got left so far behind," panted Daryth, as a dozen northmen suddenly appeared to block their path.

"Behind!" cried Keren, turning back to face an equal number.

Their bloodstained weapons upraised, the northmen closed upon the two defenders, caught far from their own troops. None of them heard the clatter of approaching hooves.

Suddenly a silver blade dropped between Daryth and the enemy, and he looked up to see the Prince of Corwell ride into the fray. The heavy hooves of the white stallion Avalon, and the slashing cuts made by the Sword of Cymrych Hugh, killed three northmen in the first rush, and warned the others off.

"Over here! Run!" Tristan gestured to Daryth and Keren with his sword. The pair saw the Sisters of Synnoria advancing behind the prince and quickly ducked between the nervous white horses.

They saw that their respite was a brief one, for the few knights—brave as the elven women were—could not hold back the press of raiders for long. As soon as the fighters were safe, the knights fell back, holding the fanatical attackers at bay with the tips of their lances. The crush of the onslaught slowly forced them back through the town square, and the defenders were cornered in the northern end of the town.

And still, the enemy kept pushing.

XXXXXXXXXX

Canthus watched the great wolf race toward him without fear. He ignored the ruined cantrev and the thousand wolves watching him with yellow-eyed stares. Never before had the moorhound hesitated to face danger, nor did he do so now.

The wolves of the Pack felt neither hope nor dismay for the outcome of the fight—they would always follow the mightiest of their number.

As the wolf and the dog came together, Erian hurled his body through the air in an effort to knock his opponent to the ground. Any other dog would have been flattened by the leap, but Canthus managed to swerve to the side a split second before collision. Drooling fangs lashed at each other as they passed, but neither struck home.

Stopping and whirling quickly, they crashed together as each sought to sink sharp teeth into the other's neck. Their heads thrust like swords, and their chests pressed together. Back legs still churned the creatures forward, so their heads and forelegs gradually rose from the ground until they stood, as if wrestling, on hind legs alone.

Now the greater weight of Erian asserted itself, and Canthus tumbled backward. Somehow the moorhound managed to flip away, springing before his foe's drooling jaws found their mark.

For a second the two animals regarded each other. Each curled his upper lip back to display many white, pointed teeth. And then they crashed together again.

This time Erian leaped upward, to come down upon the great moorhound and bear him to earth. Twisting, Canthus managed to deflect the wolf's bite from his throat to his shoulder. Even so, he could not suppress a yelp of agony.

The pain gave him a momentary burst of adrenalin, and he sprang free from the heavy wolf. Even as he turned to face his opponent again, however, Canthus's wounded shoulder failed to support his weight, and he stumbled.

The blood drove the werewolf into a frenzy, and he leaped forward with little caution. Canthus slipped to the side easily, and then repeated the evasion as Erian made several more frantic attacks. Soon the big wolf calmed himself, and closed in with more precise menace.

Noticing that Canthus was forced to treat the injured shoulder with care, the wolf continued to feint attacks, forcing the hound to leap out of the way again and again. The many evasions began to sap Canthus's strength, and each time he leaped he felt pain lance his foreleg.

Finally, the unnatural wolf pressed his attack home. He charged, and twisted, and rushed to follow each of Canthus's evasive maneuvers, forcing the dog into more and more desperate leaps and dodges.

And then the wounded shoulder collapsed, and Canthus tumbled to the ground. The spawn of the Beast dived upon him triumphantly before the hound could begin to twist free. The force of the heavy body drove the dog's breath from his lungs.

Before he could inhale, the bloody fangs of the werewolf closed upon his throat.

×××××××××

"We've got to try and break out!" announced Tristan, after he had finally caught Brigit's attention and joined her in a desperate attempt to form a plan.

With the south wall breached, the town rapidly fell into the hands of the enemy. Ffolk of the militia fought bravely, defending each house, cottage, and shop, but the northmen could not be stopped. Unless they could reach the safety of the castle, the entire force, Tristan knew, faced annihilation.

Already the corner of the town held by the Ffolk was crowded with people. The prince could sense emotions rising to panic, and knew that they must try something, however desperate, immediately.

"I'll gather the sisters," agreed Brigit. She nodded to a knight, visor down, who rode up to her. "Pass any further orders through Aileen."

The knight lifted her visor, and Tristan suppressed a gasp of shock at Aileen's gaunt, pale visage. Still, she held her head high, and met his gaze evenly.

"Take word to Gavin at the north gate—tell him we're going to attempt to reach the castle. The sisters will lead the way, and his company is to follow!"

Nodding, Aileen galloped up the street. The prince, with one more order to give, rode off to find the mayor. He first encountered Friar Nolan, leading a caravan of stretcher-bearers up the street. The cleric turned toward Tristan.

"The butchers!" he cried with a steely, murderous look upon his face. "They broke into the hospital—it was a massacre!"

The cleric looked very gravely at the prince. "These men are driven by something far more evil than their own nature."

"I know," replied the prince simply. Then he added, "We shall try to reach the castle. Bring your wounded into a column, and we'll try to cover them."

He rode on, watching the column form up behind the north gate, and he soon found Lord Mayor Dinsmore. To Tristan's surprise, the mayor was covered with the sweat and dust of battle. His ridiculous helmet actually displayed a deep gash, where it had apparently saved his life.

"We have to get out of here," Tristan told him. "The knights will open a path to the castle. I want your militia to serve as a rear guard."

The mayor's eyes widened in surprise, but he thought for a moment before responding, and seemed to realize that this was their only hope. "As you wish," he agreed, looking at the prince with his watery eyes. "Tell me when to go."

"We'll charge out of the north gate in five minutes. Gavin will follow, protecting the weaker citizens. As soon as everyone's out, you follow, holding the raiders away from the rear of the column."

"Excellent plan!" said the mayor enthusiastically.

Avalon next carried Tristan to the north gate. He found the sister knights already assembled in a long column, ready to charge through the portal the moment it opened. Seizing a lance, the prince took a place beside Brigit at the front of the column.

"Are you ready, my prince?" Gavin asked, standing to the side with his heavy hammer resting easily upon his shoulder.

"Let's go," Tristan answered.

Gavin raised his hammer, and a hundred archers sprang from cover to send a shower of arrows into the northmen gathered at the north gate. He had stripped bowmen from every other portion of the perimeter to raise this concentration, but it proved effective.

The raiders' attack on the north gate, already listless, broke into panic as dozens of raiders fell dead from the rain of missiles. Those that remained could find no shelter, and as their companions continued to fall, they turned and bolted for the safety of their own lines.

"They're running," called Gavin, after leaping to the wall. "Go!"

Eager hands pushed the wide oaken gates apart, and the column of knights raced from the town. Tristan and Brigit slowed after they emerged, allowing the others to fill out the line to either side. In line abreast, the Sisters of Synnoria charged.

The area immediately before the gates had been cleared by the archers, and they raced among the bodies of many dead northmen. As they reached the limits of bow range, small bands of raiders stood to oppose them. The lances of the knights, and the hooves of the steeds, turned each of these groups into piles of bloody corpses.

Quickly, the northmen realized that they could not stand against the charge of the heavy cavalry, and they began to flee from the sisters' path. Tristan risked a quick look behind and saw Gavin leading his company from the gate to protect the ground captured in the charge. His heart soared with excitement as he saw the raiders fleeing in panic before them, opening the path to the castle.

He did not see disaster approaching from the right until it was too late.

Laric had been waiting many days for just such an opportunity. The black and threatening skies of this day had seemed a fitting omen. Patiently, standing with the Bloodriders, he waited through the morning hours in the shelter of a small grove of trees north of the town. If the Ffolk attempted to break out, as seemed very likely given the battle in the town, he knew that the silver knights would lead the charge.

And the Bloodriders would be waiting.

Finally they got their chance. The sweeping charge of the white horses sent raiders scurrying before them, or falling dead in their tracks. Closer they rumbled, but still Laric delayed. He wanted his attack to surprise, and would not advertise the presence of his company by breaking from the trees prematurely.

But now the time was right, and he spurred the great black horse forward. Behind him thundered the rest of his troop, racing toward the right wing of the sisters' line. The knights passed so close to the trees that the Bloodriders struck them before any of them saw the threat.

Laric saw one Bloodrider strike the head from a sister knight, and felt the resulting rush of power infuse the troop. One of the white horses fell heavily, knocked to the ground by the crush of the attacking Riders. In seconds, a dozen of the ghoulish horsemen had leaped upon the immobilized horse and rider, hacking with their cruel swords.

A minute later, the Riders were still hacking, though little besides blood now lay on the ground beneath them.

As the black horses carried their Riders around the sister knights, Laric smiled grimly to see the momentum of the enemy's charge broken. The white horses swerved in confusion as the knights tried to restore some order to their line. Thelgaar's legion of northmen, Laric could now see, attacked the rear of the column, driving to shut it off from the north gate and the dubious shelter of the town.

The Bloodriders swept across the front of the charge, forcing the knights to turn. In minutes, the path to the castle had been securely closed again. "We have them!" exulted Laric. The enemy was trapped!

And then a wayward breeze wafted a familiar scent past Laric's decaying nostrils, and the fire surged in his eyes.

She lived! With a sweet rush of pleasure, he sensed that the knight he had nearly slain was now within the formation. Like her companions, she was caught in the trap.

Finally, she would be his.

xxxxxxxxxx

Robyn walked slowly from the cool gray gloom of her bedroom through the hallways of Caer Corwell. She had awakened, feeling a vague, unidentified concern. As she stepped from her bed, her legs nearly failed her, but soon she could walk.

She felt herself grow stronger with each step, and then realizing that she carried her mother's staff, she leaned on it for support. Dimly, she wondered what had happened to the world outside her room while she had read the book.

Some great purpose prodded at her, but she could not fathom its nature.

The book . . . it had given her many clues, but little direct knowledge.

The goddess smiled upon Robyn, and held her arms open for the young woman. Falling into the embrace, Robyn continued to walk blindly through the hallway as the goddess spoke to her.

Unknowingly, Robyn opened a door and began to climb the steep and winding stairway leading to the high tower. All the while, the goddess comforted and instructed her. She dried Robyn's tears, and hugged her when she wept for her mother, and supported her body when it might have slipped upon the stairs.

But mostly, she convinced Robyn that, within her mortal flesh, lay the power of the immortal earth. The druid within her needed confidence and wisdom for her task. For Robyn already possessed the strength.

XXXXXXXXXXX

The clouds pressed, black and menacing, over the battlefield. Gusty winds whipped through the air, lashing waves onto the shore of the firth. The wind churned the clouds as if trying to match the violence on the ground below.

Avalon leaped and kicked through the melee, carrying his rider from one foe to another. Many Bloodriders felt the keen bite of the prince's blade. But still they swarmed, more thickly than ever, and he knew there would be no breaking through to the castle.

Avalon whirled and the prince saw that retreat back to the north gate was blocked by charging northmen. Gavin, at the front of his company, swung his massive hammer through a deadly pattern. The smith had cleared a wide area around himself, but beyond that circle the Ffolk fell under the attacks of the savage raiders.

Nearby, Tristan saw a knight dragged from the saddle by the press of northmen on foot. The sister vanished into a slashing maelstrom of swords, axes, maces, and spears.

Suddenly a crimson robe flashed past the prince, borne by a streak of black. One of the Bloodriders was dashing among the knights, ignoring most and seemingly seeking one victim in particular. Suddenly Tristan realized that the target must be the one knight who was not looking at the crazed menace. Aileen.

Avalon sensed Tristan's command, leaping toward the charging Rider. The macabre figure turned and raised his sword. With a shock, Tristan recognized the Bloodrider who had momentarily captured Aileen earlier at Freeman's Down.

His enemy seemed to share the memory, for a ghastly grin split his horrible face, and he reined in to meet the prince's charge. Vowing to slay the creature, Tristan slashed the Sword of Cymrych Hugh savagely downward toward the grinning deathmask, as all the horror and rage in Tristan's body unleashed itself in that one blow.

And the blow whistled harmlessly through the air, for the Rider had used a simple feint to dodge the prince. As Tristan struggled to regain his balance, he saw his enemy's black stallion crash into Osprey. The creature held his long sword in his heavy gauntlet, extended toward Aileen's armored back.

The point of the sword split the silver armor, causing it to fall away. Then, it cut mercilessly through the soft body beneath it. The Bloodrider struck with such force that the tip of his sword burst through the front of the hapless knight's body and breastplate.

And as the sister died, the creature that had killed her threw back his head and howled—a high, piercing cry that bounced from the black clouds and echoed across the bloody field. Blue flame flickered around the outline of the Rider's body and the length of his sword. Tristan saw the skin of Aileen's back shrivel and fall away, and then the flesh, until only white bone remained.

The howl of the Bloodrider grew to an awesome pitch, until finally, the gruesome horseman gave a casual flick of his sword, throwing the lifeless hulk to the ground.

Tristan's nerves froze, and the knowledge came, in a flood of painful knowledge that his foolishness in taking the Rider's feint had led to Aileen's death. Unconsciously, he retched.

A wave of hatred rushed over him, and he forgot his despair in the single-minded desire to slay the murderous Rider. Avalon sprang forward, and the silver sword reached for its victim, but a group of Bloodriders charged in to block his path.

He stabbed one, watching in satisfaction as the creature's mouth gasped silently for a moment before falling to earth. The others pressed

him back, but his weapon clashed and clanged against a succession of
enemy blades. He swung wildly, striking the head off another Rider, but
the attacks still forced him back.

The Bloodrider who had killed Aileen sprang away like a flickering
shadow, and the prince lost sight of him. He found other opponents, and
fought them mechanically. He caught a glimpse of Gavin, with perhaps
half his company remaining, fighting a desperate battle against the surrounding horde of northmen. The town militia fought bravely but was
trapped against the town wall.

The clouds boiled and twisted overhead, and thunder rumbled across
the battlefield like a funeral dirge. It did not seem possible for such a
black and threatening sky to yield no rain, but the air remained dry.

Tristan joined Brigit, as the sister and her proud gelding struck
down one after another of the raiders who charged, on foot, toward
the knights. As Brigit's flashing long sword lifted the head of one raider
from the man's shoulders, another of the northmen swung a monstrous
battle-axe.

The gelding twisted from the blow, protecting its mistress, but the
vicious axe sliced into the horse's unprotected loins. The horse screamed
its death cry as its entrails spilled onto the ground, then collapsed into
the gory mess.

Brigit managed to unbuckle her belt as the horse fell. The sister
knight sprang free, then crashed to the ground, stunned. A dozen raiders, bloody weapons upraised, sprang toward her.

And then the air exploded in sound and fire. The springing northmen
were outlined in flame against darkness, and then they fell, black and
dead. A hundred others were knocked senseless by the force of the blast.

Again the explosion ripped through the air, and this time Tristan
discerned its source. White lightning erupted from the heaving clouds,
horribly burning another group of northmen before him. The force of
aroused nature crackled again, leaving a third circle of blackened corpses
in its wake.

Instinctively, Tristan looked toward the castle, high above. Silhouetted against the dark sky atop the parapet of the high tower was an even
darker shape. From the figure, a black robe whipped sideways from the
force of the wind, and a long ribbon of black hair waved like a pennant.

The prince smiled as he discerned Robyn, holding the Staff of the White Well over her head, and gesturing toward the battlefield.

The black clouds spit another deadly bolt, and panic began to spread through the ranks of northmen as the fighters turned to watch the crackling attacks. Soon the northmen saw the pattern and fled in panic from the path.

And so the lightning crashed, upon the shore, and the moor, and the castle road. It splintered great chunks of the ground, blistering turf, and slaying any northmen foolish enough not to flee.

In minutes, the road to Caer Corwell lay open.

xxxxxxxxxxx

A thousand wolves sat, immobile, in a great circle, staring intently at the duel for mastery of the Pack.

Erian snarled in triumph as he felt the moorhound's neck between his jaws. The spikes of the iron collar bent and snapped against the crushing power of the wolf's bite. Finally, the collar itself snapped and fell to the ground . . .

. . . baring the soft, thin torque of silver.

A flash of light and fire burst outward from the torque, singeing the inside of Erian's mouth. With a startled cry, he sprang backward. Rage fogged his vision. His tongue felt as if it had been seared by flame.

Canthus lunged at his foe, unaffected by the blazing wounds around his neck. The great werewolf was still shaking his head in pain, choking as if trying to spit out a sliver of bone. This time the moorhound's teeth found flesh. The power of the goddess surged through those teeth as they tore off an ear and punctured a red, glowing eye.

The wolf cringed backward, yelping, but Canthus turned without mercy and bit the monster in the shoulder, driving it to the ground. Then his widespread jaws flicked forward and he buried his teeth in the soft flesh of the werewolf's neck.

Canthus felt his teeth tear skin and flesh, and he tasted salty blood pumping through his mouth. He heard the rush of air as his murderous bite finally cut the great beast's windpipe.

The wolf sagged, finally collapsing completely, but the great hound held the even greater body aloft by the neck.

Canthus looked around, wondering what would happen next.

BESIEGED

19

Laric stared up at the tiny figure, poised on the brink of the tower so far away. Strong and arrogant, he throbbed with the vitality of the sister knight whose life he had extinguished.

Yet now that knight was forgotten, a mere morsel in comparison to the fresh strength now emanating from the woman on the parapet. His hot, liquid sockets fixed their gaze upon the black robe and flowing black hair. Hunger surged within him, forcing the memory of his recent repast from his mind.

That one, he vowed, cracking his blackening lips into a wide smile, he would have. Could he but slake his thirst with her blood, Laric knew his own strength might grow to match that of the Beast itself.

✗ ✗ ✗ ✗ ✗ ✗ ✗ ✗ ✗

Kazgoroth, too, looked at the tiny figure on the distant tower, and the body of Thelgaar Ironhand twitched with mindless rage. Only with great concentration and effort did the Beast prevent its real body from emerging. Hatred inflamed the Beast's mind, and gave it determination for vengeance.

This human would die in Kazgoroth's own clutches.

Still, the Beast's inherent caution warned it against a rash attack. The human must be a druid, for she had great command over the forces of the goddess. Kazgoroth knew even Genna Moonsinger, Great Druid of the isle, could not match such a display of magic.

This new druid required caution.

Thelgaar Ironhand left the rest of the battle to his underlings, and disappeared into his tent to plan.

xxxxxxxxxxx

Looking down from the gatehouse, Tristan saw the raiders plunder Corwell Town. The army lay like a great blight upon the pastoral view he had known all his life.

The rearguard had almost reached longbow range. The Lord Mayor stood in the middle of the fray, surrounded by the loyal men of his militia. His brown horse, apparently, had fallen.

As the archers unleashed their first volley, the thrust of a northman's sword cut the mayor, and he fell to the road. Tristan saw the rotund little man struggle to his knees, but then the raiders surrounded him and his body disappeared. Several seconds later, arrows from the castle walls began to fall into the raiders. They turned and fled, leaving the militia to enter the castle unhindered.

Sickened, Tristan watched the last Ffolk enter the castle, and heard the great oaken gates thud solidly shut. Suddenly seized by the need to see Robyn, Tristan turned from the battlefield and hurried into the castle.

Outside of her door he hesitated, and then knocked softly at the heavy oaken boards. For seconds he heard nothing, and then came the faint invitation to enter.

Slowly he pushed the door open. For a moment he could not see Robyn—only a huge mound of a bed, opposite the narrow window.

Robyn's pillow and heavy quilts swelled around her, seemingly smothering the bed. The maiden in the middle of it all looked very, very small.

Her black hair, lying in a shiny black cloud across the great pillow, accentuated the exceptional pallor of her skin. Her green eyes seemed to have sunk deep within her head, and dark circles marred her cheeks.

But she smiled at him, and that lit up the room. Tristan rushed to the bed and knelt, wrapping his arms around her. For a long moment the two friends who had been through so much held each other.

Then, the prince lifted his head and brushed back a thick tress of Robyn's black hair. He leaned forward to kiss her, and she pulled him to her lips eagerly. After long moments during which the world stopped, they broke apart.

They each saw that the other was short of breath, and they laughed together.

Robyn's face turned somber. "I thought I'd never see you again," she whispered.

"If not for your magic, you wouldn't have—nor would anyone else." Tristan saw the Staff of the White Well beside her bed and silently thanked the goddess for it.

The prince touched the circles of weariness under the new druid's eyes. "Are you hurt?"

"No. I'm just very exhausted. That was not my power that called the lightning down. It came from the staff, through me, but it seemed to drain me as well. " She looked sadly at the ashwood rod. "I fear that its might has been expended. Still, it served very well!"

"You have given us the chance to persevere!" exclaimed Tristan, trying to cheer her. "We can remain within the castle for months, and even if we don't drive them off, the coming of winter shall!"

She smiled sadly, easily penetrating his bravado. "I fear for their attack. They are still very mighty. " For a brief moment, her composure slipped, and she looked like a small, frightened child. "Tristan, hold me!"

He gathered her in his arms, and pressed her to him. For a minute, she shivered uncontrollably, but then, slowly, she calmed. She turned her face toward his ear.

"I love you," she whispered, squeezing him.

All of Tristan's concerns vanished in his joy at her words. He held her close, and imagined peaceful days in the future, when they would be together always. The moment suddenly vanished as an insistent tapping came at the door. Robyn sighed, but she relaxed her hold as the prince stood.

Tristan opened the door to reveal Friar Nolan, who nodded politely at him and then looked curiously at Robyn. The cleric's wide eyes were soft with concern, though lines of weariness had carved themselves into his face. His hands were chapped and raw, but a clean robe covered any other signs of battle.

"Pardon the intrusion," said the cleric, as he entered. "I hope you are not too tired?"

"What do you want?" demanded Robyn.

"I can help protect you," the cleric said simply. "You realize, of course, that you have made of yourself a very visible target."

"This had not occurred to me," replied Robyn.

"But, of course, you have. I am sure you are well aware that our enemy is not—how shall I say?—not entirely natural?"

"I am aware of that, yes."

"I feel certain that the driving force behind this evil will seek you out. I will stay here and help you drive it off."

"But if Robyn remains here, in her room . . . " began the prince.

Nolan cleared his throat pointedly, and nodded at the window. Tristan walked over to it and looked out. As he had known, it was fifty feet up that wall of the keep which looked out over the courtyard within Caer Corwell's walls.

"I fear for you, my child," said the cleric. "We both know that there is something dark and unnatural about this enemy. I am not altogether certain that a high window is enough of a safeguard.

"If you'll allow me. " The stout cleric crossed to the window. He muttered some mysterious phrases as he passed his hands along the frame.

"I will stay here with you," Nolan announced, returning from the window to sit in a soft chair. Robyn seemed ready to object, but when she looked at the cleric's face, she said nothing. If anything, thought the prince, she looked slightly relieved.

Tristan rose to leave, squeezing Robyn's hand in a private gesture of farewell.

Leaving Robyn's room, the prince suddenly became acutely aware of the great weariness that had crept into his body. Still, he had one last, unpleasant task to perform before retiring. He had already postponed it for too long. He would have to talk to his father, the king.

He walked ponderously to his father's study, knocked once on the door, and entered. The great fire blazed on the hearth, and his father still lay upon the long couch. He looked up, expressionlessly, as the prince entered.

"I'm glad you could finally find the time to report," said the king.

"I had to see Robyn." The prince was determined not to let his father bully him.

"Indeed. From what I hear, you owe her your life."

"I know that! Everyone in that town owes her their life!"

"If you had evacuated the place, like I ordered—"

"Dammit, Father, I tried! We lost one company—all of Dynnatt's men—and the goddess knows how many more before the northmen cut us off!"

His father closed his eyes, as if struggling to regain his patience. Tristan seethed, but he kept his mouth shut.

"So what have you accomplished since returning to the castle?"

"Not one thing! I saw that the last of the column from the town had reached safety, then I went to Robyn. I will see to the defenses at first light."

"My son! Listen to me!" His father spoke with a strange urgency. "Your presence on the walls and towers is very important! You must be seen, and you must be in command!"

"I will do this," Tristan responded, trying unsuccessfully to suppress his irritation. "Now, I'm going to sleep."

He left the study, slowly climbing the stairs to the family living quarters. He walked silently down the corridor toward his room, stopping outside of Robyn's door and leaning his ear toward the portal.

Hearing nothing, he walked on. The opening of his own door brought awareness of an overwhelming tiredness. It was all he could do to think of leaving his door open a crack, and to place the Sword of Cymrych Hugh upon a chair near his bed.

In another minute, he slept.

XXXXXXXXXX

The serpent, tiny and black, slithered along the ground, keeping always to shadow. All around it, the rolling moor sparkled with the fires of the army of northmen, but the small reptilian thing avoided all contact with the raiders.

Soon it slipped through the picket line, leaving the lighted region behind. Here, with none to see, Kazgoroth grew and stood, stretching its flesh into a new form, uniquely suited to this purpose. The Beast sprouted great, leathery wings from its shoulders, and reached forth long, muscular arms, tipped with a multitude of taloned fingers.

The wide mouth gaped, displaying row upon row of wickedly curved teeth and a long, forked tongue. A flat nose, like a pig's snout, separated two tiny but intensely glowing eyes of fiery crimson. The head was rounded and smooth, though the entire body—except for the wings—was protected by a layer of tiny scales.

The Beast flew toward Caer Corwell. The castle stood out from the pitch darkness of the night like an island of light. A hundred or more torches lined the parapet upon the wooden palisade ringing the fortress, and outlined the squat block of the keep itself. High above the army of the northmen, the castle remained a symbol of the Ffolk's resistance.

Kazgoroth glided soundlessly through the air, descending toward the broad courtyard. The black body blended perfectly with the night, and none of the sentries suspected its presence.

Circling about the keep, the Beast remained a hundred feet in the air. The grotesque nostrils quivered delicately, soon finding what they sought. Now the Beast dived, veering toward the keep and centering its dive toward a narrow window, high in the smooth stone wall.

The druid, Kazgoroth sensed, slept in the room beyond this window. Soon, reflected the Beast with a drooling leer, she would sleep much more deeply. The supple fingers, with their cruel claws, clenched and flexed in eagerness. Tucking its wings at the last moment, the Beast narrowed its body and dived into the window.

Instantly the night exploded in crackling fire, sending sparks of raw pain shooting through the monster. Kazgoroth bounced from the protected window, crashing heavily to the courtyard. Shouts of alarm rang from the guards in the courtyard, but no one saw the black shape near the keep.

A barrier! Rage flared through Kazgoroth as it understood its own carelessness. Shaking its scaly head to clear it, the creature lumbered to its feet and flapped its wings powerfully.

Kazgoroth leaped into the air again, soaring quickly to the height of the druid's room. This time the Beast hovered outside for a moment, and saw the magical barrier faintly crisscrossing the window. Sneering at its limited scope, he dived against the granite wall of the keep.

An explosion of rock and dust tumbled into the room, with the monster in its midst. Kazgoroth shook itself, rising to its feet in the center of the room, and looked around. The druid, starkly beautiful in her terror, sat up in the bed.

The toothy jaws gaped in a reptilian smile, and the venomous tail flickered toward the maiden's unarmored breast. From somewhere, she pulled a plain staff across herself, and the Beast cursed the earthen power of the wood.

A force of cold power smashed into the Beast from the side, sending it lurching into, and almost through, the window. With a lightning grab of its muscular arms, Kazgoroth caught itself by the window frame, and heaved itself across the room, into the squat form of the man it now saw there. The two large bodies crashed into the floor, and the Beast felt the man's bones snap and splinter.

But the man blazed with a strength that was new to the Beast, after its long centuries of battle with the goddess. The man's harsh magic was powerful, even if it could not master the hot, fiery might of the Darkwell.

Kazgoroth's claws snaked into the cleric's face, leaving long and bloody gashes. But somehow the man raised a potent silver circlet and pressed it toward the Beast's drooling visage. His cold magic surged through the circlet, forcing Kazgoroth back. The man lay where the monster had pushed him, one leg bent unnaturally to the side. Lines of horror and pain stretched his face into a garish mask.

Kazgoroth spun to attack the druid. Robyn had now left her bed and stood, staff held protectively before her, against the wall. She leaned against it, shivering. But her face betrayed no hint of frailty.

The Beast focused the energy of his eyes, compelling her to stare into those orbs of fire and death, but she resisted with impossible strength. Death magic flashed from the monster, but the protective shield of the staff dispersed it harmlessly throughout the room.

The broken man lying upon the floor groaned, a piteous wail of pain, and the druid looked at him with obvious concern. For a split second she forgot her opponent, and in that time Kazgoroth crossed the room and snatched the staff from her hands. It blazed against his grip with the white fire of the goddess. The Beast felt the wood draw strength from its body, but it ignored the pain and slammed the potent rod to the floor.

Now the woman recoiled backward, eyes widening as her talisman was torn from her. She shrank along the wall, but with a casual push the Beast knocked her into a corner. She lay stunned, moaning slightly in fear, as the venomous tail again lashed toward her.

XXXXXXXXXX

Tristan awoke, slowly, as always. He shook his head and sat up in bed, wondering why he no longer slept. Vaguely, he recalled some sense of purpose when he went to bed, as if there was something he was supposed to remember.

He suddenly heard a groan from the hallway, and his body tensed with energy as he suddenly recalled the threat to Robyn.

Suddenly he felt the Sword of Cymrych Hugh calling to him from its position on the chair. The sword, always bright against a dark night, now glowed with an intensity that shone brilliantly through the leather scabbard. Tristan saw, or imagined he saw, the sword vibrating with excitement, calling him to battle with a voice that tugged inaudibly at his will.

Instantly he sprang from the bed. The sword seemed to leap from the scabbard into his hand. He burst into the hall, and the sword tugged him toward Robyn's bedchamber. Only with great difficulty did he retain his grip on the smooth hilt.

Together, Tristan and the Sword of Cymrych Hugh crashed through the door of Robyn's room. The blazing white light from the weapon threw the entire room into a stark contrast of light and shadow. As the door fell inward, the prince saw the broken form of Friar Nolan, and he saw Robyn's staff glowing on the floor amid the rubble blasted away from a gaping hole in the wall.

Then, in the far corner, he saw the hideous body of the Beast crouching over a shapeless form on the floor. Tristan saw the barbed tip of the monster's tail lashing toward the motionless Robyn.

In a blur of movement the sword pulled him across the room and sliced unerringly downward, through the scaly surface and bony frame of the serpentine tail. The Beast howled in pain and stumbled backward, clutching at the stump of its mangled tail. Robyn shrieked instinctively as the dismembered tip dropped onto the floor, twitching reflexively. Overcome with shock, she collapsed in the corner.

The prince turned to face the snarling monster, and for the first time saw the grotesque features of the Beast. But even as he watched, the monster's great rage seemed to cause its face and body to bend and shift, changing shape before Tristan's astonished eyes.

He thrust with the gleaming sword, and saw that the monster recoiled in fear. The blade, on the other hand, compelled the prince to attack the creature mercilessly, driving it ever backward.

Finally, with a parting snarl, the Beast leaped through the hole in the wall and soared into the night. Though the sword nearly pulled the prince through the same aperture in an attempt to pursue, Tristan could not see the black shape for more than a second after it had escaped into the darkness.

He sprang to Robyn's side and lifted her head from the floor as Keren carried a torch through the broken door. With relief, he saw that the maiden breathed, though all of the color had left her skin.

"Help me carry her to the bed," he asked, as the bard knelt beside him. Together, they made the druid as comfortable as possible, then turned toward the unconscious cleric. Streaks of blood ran from the deep claw marks across the cleric's face, but at least the attack had missed his eyes. His left leg jutted sideways at an odd angle, and the prince knew that the bone was broken.

The bard splashed a little water upon the cleric's brow, and his eyes flickered open. Wincing in pain, the wounded cleric reached downward and adjusted the bone of the broken leg, muttering a mysterious prayer to his gods. Then, to the astonishment of Tristan and Keren, he stood and walked solidly to Robyn's bed. Her long black eyelashes fluttered upward as his strong palm rested upon her forehead.

"There, my child," he said softly. "Your strength prevailed when it was most crucial. Now sleep."

Robyn stared at the cleric, and the prince, and the bard, and shrunk more deeply into her quilt. The prince laid the Staff of the White Well beside her, and then selected a chair. Keren did the same, while Nolan took his original seat, reflexively caressing his small silver circlet—the sign of his gods.

For the rest of the night, Robyn slept while the three men stayed restlessly awake and guarded her. They held sword, circlet, and harp, ready to drive back the darkness again.

But it did not return that night.

× × × × × × × × × ×

Canthus turned curiously, watching the thousands of wolfish eyes return his stare from every point of vantage within a mile. The wolves made no move to attack, however, so the moorhound ignored them.

His task done, the dog had little remembrance of it. The fight had been hard, but the enemy was slain, and the wound in his shoulder had already begun to heal. His thoughts returned to his people, and his home. He grew lonely for the men, and the woman, who were his.

He sniffed the air, ignoring the scent of the ravaged farm, and of the gathering crows and other scavengers. He sought the scent of his home. For long minutes he studied the horizon.

Finally, served by some mysterious animal instinct that pointed him in the right direction, he walked slowly toward the south. The journey, he felt, would be a long one, and his shoulder had not healed entirely, so the hound would travel slowly, only breaking into his patient lope when he felt stronger.

A thousand wolves watched their new leader walk from the desolation of the farm. The animals dropped the meat and bones they had been gnawing, and moved from the surrounding hills. As one column, they fell in behind Canthus.

× × × × × × × × × ×

For a tenday, the army of the northmen bustled about in the town, and across the moor below the castle. Much to Tristan's surprise, they did not burn Corwell Town as they had the eastern cantrevs. Apparently the raiders preferred instead to usurp the buildings of the town as quarters during the siege.

At night, the enemy's campfires spread across the moors in all directions, for the town was large enough to shelter only a small fraction of the army. During the day, the defenders could see tall frameworks take shape, out of range of bowfire from the castle walls, and they knew that the attackers were building huge siege engines.

The Ffolk, meanwhile, prepared Caer Corwell as best they could for defense. Huge pots of oil were gathered in the gatehouse, and on the walls. Arrows by the hundred were made and collected for the six or seven score archers in the garrison. Food was rationed at a rate that would allow for many months of siege.

Tristan spent much time with Robyn. Her strength slowly returned, but she stayed in bed most of the time. They had moved her to a safer room, near the center of the keep, and she was never unattended. The prince, Friar Nolan, the bard, and Daryth alternately stayed with her, so that one or two of them was always present. No additional attack materialized, however.

Several days passed before the prince had a chance to be alone with her, but one evening he arrived to keep her company as Keren, who had been there, was ready to retire for the night. When the door closed behind the bard, Tristan knelt beside Robyn's bed and took her hand.

"I've been thinking about you," she admitted, with a frankness that had nothing of the coy in it. "You stayed away too long!"

"I know. I'm sorry. There's a lot to do in the castle, but everything seems unimportant compared to being with you."

She pulled him to her, and he felt the cares of the castle fall from him.

They remained awake throughout the night, talking or simply sitting beside each other. Near dawn, the prince finally fell asleep in his chair, and Robyn cradled his head and wondered what he dreamed that made him shiver in his sleep. She was too content to waste a moment in sleep.

At times when Tristan could not be with Robyn, he stood upon the palisade, or climbed the gatehouse or high tower, to observe the northmen. Each day he looked out, expecting to see an attack, but time passed and still the raiders labored upon the moor.

The prince saw them build a series of gargantuan catapults, rising like ungainly insects from broad, wooden carts. Daryth joined him, upon the palisade, as he counted a dozen of the great war machines.

"We'll stop them, you know," said the Calishite with easy confidence. He laughed, quietly, and said reflectively, "You know, I never thought I'd be one to fight for any kind of cause—a grand purpose that I would champion. I'm too proud to think that, after all this trouble to find a cause, my cause might fail!" Daryth smiled at Tristan's worried expression.

Another time he discovered Keren reclining against the parapet of the high tower, gently strumming his harp. Sable perched on the stone rampart, higher than anything within his field of vision, and preened his inky feathers.

The bard looked quite pleased with himself as he set the harp aside and greeted the prince. He saw Tristan nod at the instrument, and understood his question.

"Yes, indeed, the song is coming along quite well," the bard said, grinning. "I hope you'll be able to hear it very soon."

Life began to feel almost normal within the castle, crowded though it was with the citizens of the town and nearby cantrevs. Food was plentiful, if not terribly varied, and the position on the little knoll seemed very secure. But always, the besieged had the knowledge that, beyond their palisade, an implacable foe awaited—an enemy that would not hesitate to slay or enslave them all.

And then, eight days after the fall of Corwell Town, the army of the northmen surged forward again. Great engines of war trundled across the moors, leaving traces of black smoke in the clear morning air. From the smoke emerged a monstrous column, and the prince recognized the Firbolgs of Myrloch. The creatures marched in a long file, and Tristan could see the massive log they carried as a ram.

Tristan stood with Daryth and Pawldo on the ramparts of the gatehouse, overlooking Castle Road. The two men stood against the stone rampart, while Pawldo scrambled onto a box to look over the wall.

"What's that?" cried the halfling, squinting into the distance at the giants' ram.

"It's a knocker for the door," said Daryth. "I think they want to come in."

XXXXXXXXXX

Kamerynn lay in the stinking mud. Waves of pain assaulted him, again and again, until he no longer noticed them. The pain had faded into the background as simply another fact of life.

Suddenly Kamerynn heard a rustling of leaves, and froze, straining to hear the approach of a possible enemy. Then he felt a warm wetness upon his face, and his back, and the rustling increased to a steady patter.

Rain.

At first the water was only warm, driving the deepseated chill from the unicorn's bones and bringing his shiver under control. The balmy liquid washed over the huge, soiled body, driving the acid sludge from the Darkwell off what remained of Kamerynn's snowy coat.

Then the water cleansed the wounds of the unicorn, soothing like a fine salve, mending shattered bones. The goddess wept for the suffering of her child, but her tears healed and restored and replenished.

Eventually, the great unicorn managed to stand and shake himself, sending a clear spray of water through the air. His eyes remained shut, damaged such that even the tears of the goddess could not restore them.

The rain spattered upon what was left of the Darkwell, washing more oily sludge through the wreckage of the Firbolgs' dam. The water cleansed the ground, and healed it, nearly everywhere it fell. Slowly, Kamerynn lurched away.

Only in the center of the Darkwell, where still lingered a potent mixture of pollution and earthen enchantment, did the dark power resist the balm of the Mother. Here the water swirled and bubbled very darkly indeed.

BOOK
FIVE

BOOK
FIVE

A CONTEST OF MIGHT

20

XCompelled by a mysterious sense of urgency, Canthus broke into the patient lope that he could maintain for many days. The great moorhound felt a need to return to his home, without understanding why.

Behind, the wolves of the Pack matched their leader's pace. No longer did the wolves strike at animals protected by fence or barn, nor did they molest the humans they saw in passing. Canthus, in his natural caution, led them around settlements, and maintained too steady of a pace for the leisurely plundering of isolated farms.

But though the great dog's strength and endurance were mighty, his distance from home was long.

It would be many days before he again saw Caer Corwell.

×××××××××××

Kazgoroth advanced in the lead of the raiders' army, personally directing the placement of two of the great catapults. The great wooden wheels sucked turf from the moor as the huge war machines lumbered forward. Two hundred northmen pushed each to the bottom of the steep slope. The wooden palisade of Caer Corwell loomed a hundred feet above.

Creaking noisily, the vehicles lodged in position. Great, smoking cauldrons of smoldering pitch, hauled in carts drawn by several dozen raiders, followed the catapults. Black and acrid smoke swirled around the raiders, but the stench bothered Kazgoroth not in the least.

All around the Iron King, the legions of the northmen advanced upon Caer Corwell. The structure was well fortified, yet never did Kazgoroth's confidence in the outcome of the battle falter.

To the left, Groth and his company of Firbolgs carried a heavy ram up the exposed length of the castle road. Each of the creatures wore a hood and cloak of heavy leather, protecting it against attacks from above. The ram—a massive trunk of oak, capped with a fist of iron—carried within it the power of the Darkwell, and the Beast knew that the mortal gates of Caer Corwell could not stand against it long.

Against the slopes of the castle's knoll hurtled the thousands of northmen. Armed with ropes, spikes, ladders, and firepots, the raiders began to scramble up the steep and rocky sides and attempted to breach the wooden palisade at the top.

Only the Bloodriders did not participate in the attack, for their steeds became liabilities upon the steep slopes, or within the narrow confines of the steep road. When the gates fell, however, or the wall was breached, the Riders would have their opportunity.

Smiling inwardly, Kazgoroth knew that the Bloodriders would not fail.

A shower of arrows suddenly descended upon the crews of the catapults, sending several northmen screaming to the ground. Others swiftly replaced them, and the machines continued their fiery assault. Already, several of the pitch-soaked missiles had struck the palisade, forcing the defenders to scramble.

But Thelgaar's brows knitted in concern, as the Beast cloaked in his body considered the one unknown quantity facing it during this battle.

Where was the young druid?

XXXXXXXXXX

"Now!"

Tristan's order echoed through the courtyard, and the archers of the Ffolk sent hundreds of missiles sailing into the ranks of the attackers on the slopes below the palisade.

"Now the oil!"

Fifty men of the castle guard, including Daryth, Pawldo, and the prince himself, had occupied the gatehouse platform. Now, several men, insulated with heavy gauntlets, hoisted a bubbling cauldron of oil to the edge of the stone parapet and poured it over the side.

There was a moment's hush as everyone waited to see the effect. Then a young trooper at the wall cried hysterically, "It's not stopping them! They're still coming!"

Tristan looked over in disbelief. Indeed, the scalding oil simply splashed off the Firbolgs' hoods, spattering to the road and swiftly cooling upon the gray paving stone.

The hulking Firbolgs shoved their battering ram against the stout oaken gates. Splinters flew, and the barrier sagged inward from the force of the blow.

"They won't hold much longer!" observed Tristan quietly.

"How can we stop them?" asked Daryth, shouting over the din of the pounding. "We can't let them through the gatehouse—they'll have the run of the castle!"

"Come on!" called Tristan, drawing the Sword of Cymrych Hugh and yanking open the trapdoor leading down into the gatehouse.

"Might as well die downstairs as up," muttered Pawldo, darting into the winding stairwell after the prince.

Daryth leaped after them. A half dozen men-at-arms followed the trio down the stairs.

Tristan burst through the door leading into the lower gatehouse just in time to see the great wooden portals crash inward. One broke free and fell to the ground, while the other hung loosely from a single hinge. Immediately, the press of ponderously cheering Firbolgs tumbled through the breach.

With the main gates smashed, the gatehouse gave the Firbolgs two routes into the castle. If they could also crash through the portcullis with their ram, they could charge directly into the courtyard. If they could overcome Tristan and his companions, the monsters could climb through the trapdoor onto the roof of the gatehouse, and from there reach all of the defenders on top of the wooden palisade.

Tristan hurled himself and his sword at the nearest Firbolg, spilling the creature's guts onto the stone floor. Before his first victim had fallen, the prince struck another, and then a third. In seconds, the bellows of the wounded Firbolgs reverberated through the hollow stone structure. The rest of the monsters dropped the ram, pulling their crude stone daggers or heavy wooden clubs from beneath their leather cloaks.

The prince was vaguely aware of Daryth at his side, and he saw a silvery flash dart suddenly from between them, low to the ground. He knew the valiant halfling stood with them.

"Look out!" The cry from Daryth alerted Tristan to a blow from a Firbolg to his left, and he barely ducked the murderous cut of a heavy blade. Before the Firbolg recovered, however, the Sword of Cymrych Hugh visited his heart, hissing eagerly, and the creature fell heavily to the flagstones, which were quickly dyed red by the blood from his death wound.

More Firbolgs crowded into the gatehouse, as the flagstones grew slick with blood. As Tristan lunged toward one giant, his boots slipped and he fell, knocking the wind from his lungs. The giant kicked him in the ribs with a hobnailed boot, and he curled involuntarily from the pain, waiting for a final blow from above.

Through the red haze of his vision, the prince saw Daryth leap, driving his blade deep into the Firbolg that had kicked him.

"Come here!" Pawldo grabbed the prince's arm and pulled with surprising strength for one of his size. Another fighter helped, and they yanked him from the thick of the melee and got him to his feet. Ducking a pair of huge clubs, Daryth sprang away from the Firbolgs and landed by his companions, checking to see that Tristan was all right.

"I'm fine. Thanks," gasped the prince.

Without waiting to acknowledge him, Daryth again leaped into the fray as a Firbolg came close. The slender Calishite gave the mountain of a creature a swift cut to the neck.

For a few seconds, Tristan rested and regained his breath, looking at the progress of the battle within the tight confines of the gatehouse. Several dozen Firbolgs still raged against the few humans. Fortunately for the humans, the close quarters and their own lack of imagination played against the Firbolgs. A half dozen or so of their numbers lay on the flagstones, dead, and near those bodies lay at least three men-at-arms, skulls crushed.

Once more, Tristan pushed forward into the fight, selecting a stupidly grinning Firbolg as his next target. The monster's foul breath nearly made the prince gag. Ignoring the prince's first blow, the perspiration-covered Firbolg drove his heavy club downward, but with a clear anticipation of the blow, Tristan stepped quickly to the side, and then disemboweled the creature with a slashing cut of his sword.

Bellowing in pain, the monster slumped to the ground, trying in vain to hold its intestines. In moments, the Firbolg died, and the gore on the flagstones grew thicker and more slippery than ever.

The stench of blood and death filled the gatehouse, and weariness began to drag at defenders and attackers alike. Tristan looked quickly around, and saw that only himself, Daryth, Pawldo, and a single man-at-arms stood between the Firbolgs and the door giving access to the castle.

Breathing deeply, the prince realized that the Firbolgs, too, had stepped back from the pace of battle for a brief rest. As sweat poured down his forehead, the prince angrily wiped it from his eyes. He knew he could not allow the Firbolgs time to rest and regroup, or they would certainly pick up their ram and smash the portcullis.

"We must attack," gasped the prince, raising the Sword of Cymrych Hugh, though the effort shot burning pain through his arm.

"Hi-eeee!" With a screech, Pawldo bounded forward, striking deeply into the calf of a startled Firbolg. Before his companions could build on his initiative, however, the flat of a Firbolg cutlass crashed heavily into the halfling's little body, sending him flying into the stone wall. Then Pawldo dropped senseless to the floor.

"All right, you stinking bastard," growled Daryth, in a low voice than somehow carried clearly through the din of battle. The Calishite advanced in a low crouch, and the Firbolg that had struck Pawldo recoiled instinctively from the sight of coming death.

Daryth sprang forward, and Tristan stepped quickly beside him. As the prince fended off a series of attacks against the Calishite's back, Daryth forced the offending Firbolg backward.

With an inarticulate gurgle of terror, the monster stepped into the ram that still lay in the middle of the gatehouse and tumbled over backward to the floor with a mighty crash. As his face twisted into a mask of hatred, Daryth drove forward and sank his shortsword to the hilt in the Firbolg's belly.

Darting back with lightning speed, Daryth avoided a blizzard of blows aimed in vain by the other Firbolgs. Tristan took advantage of the enemy's singlehanded pursuit of the Calishite. The Sword of Cymrych Hugh seemed to relish each hissing touch of Firbolg flesh, and the prince carved several deep wounds before he, too, fell back against the wall.

But this ebb and flow of combat could not continue for more than a few minutes more, Tristan realized. Even as he looked for a solution, a wicked swing cut the head from the one remaining man-at-arms standing with them. Now Daryth and Tristan stood alone before the wide wooden door leading to the upper level of the gatehouse.

"When the Firbolgs came to Corwell . . ."

The strong voice, lifted in song, emerged from the hall behind them. Like magic, the prince felt renewed strength flow through his sword arm. The song, accompanied by aggressive yet melodic harp chords, seemed to have the same effect upon Daryth. The Calishite wiped the sweat from his eyes, and the weariness distorting his face gave way to a look of deadly determination.

And then Keren stood between them.

The bard quickly slung his harp behind his back and brandished his silver long sword. Even without his instrument, however, the bard sang out a lusty song of battle, turning between verses to wink at the prince and say, "A few minutes, my prince. That's all the longer we have to hold!"

"The ram!" cried Daryth, pointing with his bloodstained blade.

Tristan realized then that, with an unusual show of intelligence, some Firbolgs had been keeping them busy while others had cleared and hoisted the heavy ram for a final assault.

"Let's go!" the prince called, and immediately the three men dived between the slower giants and threw themselves into action.

Tristan struck quickly at a Firbolg holding one end of the ram. Daryth whirled past him, spinning and dodging as he struck the other confused giants. Keren, too, pressed in, striking more slowly, but coolly keeping the enemy from the backs of his two companions.

The entire squirming mass of Firbolgs slipped and cursed as the ram once again tumbled to the floor. From somewhere, however, a Firbolg's club spun sideways and crashed heavily, into Keren's ribs. The bard stumbled back to the door, his face ashen with pain.

Trying to protect their companion, Tristan and Daryth fell back again as the Firbolgs once more forced them to the wall. As before, the press of heavy bodies actually restricted the actions of those engaged in the fight, and several more of the monsters added their blood to the crimson surface of the floor, victims of their own side.

"We . . . can't hold out . . . for long," gasped Daryth, twisting frantically to avoid a swinging cutlass. The heavy iron blade struck sparks from the stone wall and cut a deep gouge, barely missing the Calishite's head.

"We have to try," grunted Tristan, too busy fending off attacks to look at his friend.

A rattling clang sounded through the gatehouse, and the prince recognized the sound with a numbing shock.

Someone had reached the crank and winch, and was now raising the only barrier between the Firbolgs and the courtyard of Caer Corwell.

"The portcullis! It'll let them into the courtyard!" shouted the prince. "Get to the stairs! Fall back!"

"Run, you overgrown bags of blubber!"

The harsh voice, ringing through the gatehouse, sent a thrill of hope through the prince. He saw that the portcullis had been raised only about four feet from the ground before being stopped. Instead of letting the giants out of the gatehouse, it let Finellen and her dwarves in.

"Now, get back to Myrloch, where you belong!"

The prince could not see why, but the Firbolgs began to bellow and yell, both fear and frustration in their voices as they milled about in the gatehouse like a herd of sheep that has scented the hungry wolf. One cried out in pain, another dropped to the ground, slain.

Tristan and Daryth gasped as they leaned against the door, momentarily forgotten by the Firbolgs. An occasional dwarven curse sounded from the courtyard, confirming Tristan's guess as to their rescuers.

"I told you," said Keren, struggling to his feet. "A few minutes!"

"And not a second too soon," admitted the prince, relieved to see the bard apparently recovered.

"Now run, you stinking cowards!" taunted Finellen, punctuating her cry with a vicious thrust into the groin of a retreating Firbolg. The monsters fell back more quickly than ever, slipping and scrambling across the gory floor.

"Charge!" cried the dwarven warrior, her beard bristling aggressively. Immediately, she and her company sprang forward, their steely spearheads advancing as a glittering and impenetrable wall of death.

"Go!" cried Daryth, sagging against the wall in relief.

Tristan grinned weakly at the Calishite, as they were ignored by the Firbolgs. Together they watched the rout as panic spread among the hulking creatures and they turned, en masse, and fled the gatehouse. Two dozen dead or badly wounded Firbolgs lay sprawled and bleeding about the small structure, while a smaller number fled down the castle road.

The fight for the gatehouse was won.

XXXXXXXXXXX

Clouds of black smoke spiraled skyward from the flaming walls of the palisade, obscuring the Beast's view of the castle. The monster recalled the ease with which the Firbolgs had broken into the gatehouse. Kazgoroth wondered how the battle following the break-in had fared. Were the Firbolgs in the courtyard yet?

Angrily, the Beast compared this swift success to the plodding progress of the raiders against the palisade.

The steep and rocky slopes leading to the wall had proved too sheer in many places for men on foot to climb. In other places, a few hundred northmen had managed to reach the top and hurl themselves against the wooden walls, which, the Beast noted in anger, still stood.

Now, Kazgoroth could see the walls smoldering and smoking in many places, but nowhere did a truly massive conflagration blaze.

And what of the female druid? She had not yet used her power during this part of the battle. Surely she would be there, with the defenders, during these darkest hours in Caer Corwell's history. The Beast hoped that she would strike soon, revealing her location. Once this was done, she would belong to the Beast.

Frustrated, Kazgoroth could barely restrain the urge to use the unbridled power of the Darkwell. A blast of savage magic could blow away an entire section of the palisade, giving the raiders easy access to the heart of the castle.

Cursing, the Beast knew that such a display would have a disastrous effect upon his own troops. The superstitious northmen might very well flee the battlefield in confusion and panic. They would realize that something powerfully magical was in the body of Thelgaar Ironhand.

Then the Beast saw the Firbolgs, lumbering heavily, emerge from the black and swirling smoke. A dozen of the creatures raced down the castle road in sheer panic. Kazgoroth could only deduce that the rest of the monstrous company lay dead in the gatehouse or the castle proper.

And finally the Beast's careful control snapped.

Involuntary shudders of rage flexed Kazgoroth's body, warping and shifting his shape. Though few northmen were near enough to see this, those that did drew back in fear and astonishment.

First, the Beast grew several feet taller, while retaining basically a human shape. With a force of will, Kazgoroth brought its size back toward the earth, but could not prevent an outbreak of scales across its exposed arms and face. Snakelike, a forked tongue emerged from the grotesque face and the eyes grew red hot in anger and frustration.

With an inarticulate scream, Kazgoroth released his anger in a blast of explosive magic. The fleeing Firbolgs, led in their panic by Groth, disappeared in a thundering explosion as a great chunk of the castle road blew up. Chunks of paving stone, clods of dirt, and small pieces of Firbolg flew upward through the air, arcing out to land hundreds of yards away from the road.

The thundering eruption brought the fighting to a momentary halt as the warriors on both sides gaped in shock. Two hundred feet of the castle road had vanished, replaced by a crater twenty or thirty feet deep. Not a single Firbolg lived, nor could the body of any of the creatures be located. Fortunately for the morale of Kazgoroth's army, few witnessed the Beast's loss of control or realized the source of the explosion. But even as the battle raged, rumors of the king's mysterious nature continued to spread throughout the army of raiders.

Tremendous willpower allowed Kazgoroth to regain control of its human body, and once again the form of Thelgaar Ironhand strode forward among the ranks of northmen.

"Send fire, and more fire!" he roared, and the raiders hastened to obey their king. Trailing streaks of black smoke, another barrage of missiles sped toward the high wooden walls. With satisfaction, the Beast watched many of them strike the timbers, igniting a half dozen new fires.

Perhaps yet, thought the Beast, Caer Corwell would burn.

×××××××××××

Acrid smoke burned her eyes, and the din of battle became a constant, dissonant theme in her ears as Robyn did what she could to help contain the fires. Now the missiles from the enemy catapults struck with alarming accuracy, and it seemed that fires erupted faster than the Ffolk could quench them.

Robyn's long black hair, confined into a long braid, twirled around her head as she ran from one crisis to another. Despair threatened to overwhelm her, but she drove the emotion back.

In a momentary lull, she looked around and saw Gavin nearby, straining to operate a pump designed to be run by six men. He nodded and gave her a slight smile. She nodded back as she wiped a sweatsoaked strand of hair from her face, heartened by the strength of her friend. Stumbling wearily, she stepped to his side and strained with him to raise and lower the heavy lever. All around, the fighters of the Eastern Cantrevs followed Gavin's occasional shouted commands.

But the fires threatened to strip the palisade from the castle and expose the inhabitants to the attackers.

"You fight well, my lass," grunted the smith through clenched teeth as he strained at the pump.

"I have little choice," responded Robyn.

"As do we all," said Gavin, smiling. "You! Pick up those buckets and move!" he bellowed at a group of firefighters who had paused to catch their breath. Several more men joined the smith at the pump, and Robyn went back to the palisade to direct the water onto the fires.

A spattering ball of pitch struck the top of the palisade, soaking one of the defenders in blazing flame.

The man staggered backward, and Robyn quickly chanted the words to a simple spell—one she had learned from her mother's book. Cool water appeared, in the air above him, splashing across the man's body and clothes, extinguishing the flames and hissing into steam.

But her store of magic had to be conserved, and again she picked up a heavy bucket and poured its contents over a smoldering section of the palisade. She had tied a thong to her staff and slung it across her back. Now it lay there, and she could feel the energy of its power through her sweatsoaked blouse. Still, she dared not use the staff yet—its power, too, was limited.

The springs below Caer Corwell were deep, and many pumps had been placed throughout the castle to reach the water in the event of attack, but the fires were spreading now. Already, great sections of the palisade had begun to crackle and roar as they were consumed by hungry flames. The druid looked around her in horror.

Suddenly the strains of a peaceful ballad caressed her ears, overcoming the surrounding cacophony. Like a ray of sunshine through storm, the music of the bard's harp penetrated the air of the courtyard, and the defenders took heart.

Keren walked calmly through the ranks of the desperate Ffolk, strumming his instrument and softly singing a tale of tragic love. His cape was battle-stained, and he favored his right leg slightly, but war seemed to be the farthest thing from his mind. Robyn instinctively looked up to see the black falcon, circling above the defenders.

With a wry smile, Robyn imagined her appearance. Soot and dirt coated her skin. Her hands were chapped and sore.

"Have you seen Tristan?" she asked Keren.

"He led the defense of the gatehouse!" exclaimed the bard, and then added soberly, "Pawldo was hurt, but I don't think it's serious."

"And the fight?"

"The gatehouse is secured," replied the bard. "The Firbolgs have fled, and now the great threat lies to the walls themselves. How do they stand?"

Robyn's despair rose to the surface and her voice cracked. "We cannot contain the fires much longer, I fear."

As if in taunting mockery of her words, a great section of the wall suddenly collapsed in a cloud of smoke and sparks.

Immediately, northmen appeared in the gap, crossing the ruins of the wall and charging into the courtyard.

"To arms!" Gavin's bellowed command thundered through the courtyard, and the warriors of his company dropped buckets and pumps, reaching instead for sword and shield. Keren slung his harp over his shoulder in favor of his sword and joined the line, anchoring the far flank. But Robyn knew that a hundred or more northmen would enter the courtyard before Gavin's company could organize.

Again, she called upon the knowledge gained from her mother's book, chanting an arcane command and drawing the power of the goddess from the earth. With a sharp, chopping gesture, she waved at the northmen scrambling across the wreckage of the fallen wall.

Immediately, the ground below their feet split and twisted, as an eruption of plants burst upward. Bushes, vines, creepers, and thorns crawled forth, snakelike, grasping the legs and waists of the raiders. Caught by the druid's spell, the attackers hacked and slashed frantically at the writhing plants.

But the stalks and branches would not slow the attack for long. However, the plants gave Gavin and the Ffolk of the Eastern Cantrevs time to form a long line, three ranks deep, in preparation for a savage charge. The northmen who did not fall instantly began to retreat. Breathing heavily from the exertion and excitement, Robyn shouted in triumph as she saw the attacking force broken. Gavin and his company now patrolled the entire length of the breach.

"We did it!" Robyn cried, running up to the smith and seizing him excitedly. "They ran away! We stopped them!"

Gently, Gavin removed her arms from his neck, nodding his head toward the moor a hundred feet below. "But" cautioned the smith, "the enemy is not quite finished."

XXXXXXXXXX

Laric's skull-face split into a ghastly caricature of a grin as the dozens of prisoners were prodded toward the Bloodriders. For a moment, the captain's thoughts turned toward the druid who was somewhere up there, in the castle. The lust within him twisted his features even more horribly. Even the gaunt black stallion underneath him sensed his anticipation, prancing and snorting nervously.

On the field that had once been the site of the Festival of the Spring Equinox, Laric let his gaze linger upon the steep slope, almost a sheer cliff, that stood between him and the quarry he so desired. The palisade atop the slope had burned to ashes, and now a line of Ffolk stood along the crest of the knoll, weapons ready.

The prisoners—mostly elder Ffolk who had not fled before the advancing enemy—were pushed toward the Bloodriders, who set upon them with complete mercilessness. Few of the prisoners even had time to scream, or turn in horror, and none escaped the quick and killing blows. Rich, red blood welled forth, to be trapped by the eager cupped hands of the Bloodriders.

Each of the Riders spread a leather pouch below a bleeding body, quickly gathering a deep, crimson pool. Laric could barely control the trembling in his skeletal hands as his pouch drained the life from a frail old woman. He turned slowly to his gaunt black mount, kneeling at the steed's flank.

Carefully, Laric held the pouch open and lifted the stallion's foreleg. He dipped the black hoof into the warm blood, relishing the aroma that wafted upward when the two met. As the hoof emerged, it pulsed with a glowing vibrancy. Slowly, deliberately, he anointed each of the stallion's hooves, while each of the other Riders of his company did the same to their mounts.

As each hoof, thus enchanted, struck the ground, a sharp crack of noise broke upon the field. Should the hoof happen to strike a stone or the tip of a sunken boulder among the soft loam of the field, then the crack was amplified tenfold, and a shower of sparks burst across the grass.

Prancing eagerly now, the horses of the Bloodriders awaited their masters. Leaving the drained corpses sprawled about the commons, Laric's creatures leaped into their saddles, turning the snorting heads toward Caer Corwell. Laric drew his sword and held the black, tarnished blade in the air before him. Its tip indicated the breach in the palisade, high atop the looming cliff. The cracking and sparking of the enchanted hooves shot across the battlefield like the bursting of lightning, drowning out all other sounds.

Quickly the great horses broke into a trot. The clattering noise of their hoofbeats rose to an unbelievable din.

As the Riders picked up speed, Laric saw the world slow around him. Men turned to watch the Riders, and they moved as if suspended in molasses. Balls of pitch, launched by the catapults, seemed almost to freeze in the air, inching forward finally like puffballs balancing on a light breeze. The dark enchantment speeded the Bloodriders far faster than mortals, and the rest of the world slowed to a crawl.

And now the Bloodriders began to gallop, charging straight for the sheer wall. Laric, in the lead, pulled his stallion into a mighty leap. The creature's hooves now left a blazing trail of fire every time they struck the ground, and this fire extended onto the slope. Quickly, impossibly, the horses of the Bloodriders thundered onto the sheer slope leading up to Caer Corwell. To watchers, they were a blur of shadow and fire, leaving a land black and tortured in their wake. To the Riders, the rest of the world was a mosaic of stunned observers and slowly tumbling fireballs.

××××××××××

Newt buzzed lazily among the groves of aspens along the shore of crystalline Myrloch. The summer day warmed him and made him sleepy, yet he felt propelled by a strange uncertainty.

Flitting like a hummingbird through the trees, Newt blinked into invisibility for a second, before reappearing and again disappearing. In his agitation, he continued to pop in and out of sight, unconsciously hurrying through the forest, ever southward.

Finally, the summery air grew rank with the stench of decay and death. Flies and gnats buzzed heavily in the still, humid air. Newt realized that he had flown to the Fens of the Fallon.

The knowledge brought a sudden memory of his adventure with the maiden and her companions. He giggled happily as he recalled the Firbolgs thrashing about in the grip of Newt's illusionary magic.

Still blinking, he decided to have a look at the scene of his adventure—the stronghold of the Firbolgs. Buzzing low, under the drooping branches of willows, hovering above the brackish water, he suddenly noticed a trail.

He could not see, nor smell, nor otherwise identify how he followed the spoor, laid down tendays earlier in brackish water and clutching pools of mud.

Racing quickly, Newt vanished entirely from the sight of anyone who might have been nearby. He took notice of nothing but the spoor before him, winding through the fens until he finally entered the sunnier realms of forest.

In his darting speed, Newt traveled many miles in an hour, never flagging in his determination. And finally, near the end of the day, he came upon the source of the long trail.

A FORTRESS FALLEN

㉑

Pawldo recovered consciousness as Tristan and Daryth carried him to the barracks, where the wounded were cared for as best as possible. Here they encountered Friar Nolan.

"How goes the fight?" asked the cleric, pulling a woolen blanket over the face of a blankly staring fighter. He stood and looked at the prince, and Tristan could barely hold back an expression of shock.

The formerly stout cleric had grown much thinner, and the skin seemed to sag upon his body. His face had an unhealthy pallor, with black circles under the eyes. He looked as if he had not slept for tendays.

"We've stopped them for the time being," answered Tristan as he lay the halfling upon a relatively clean patch of straw.

"Let me up, I tell you!" shouted Pawldo, twisting away from the prince. "I'm going back out there and—"

"You're staying right here!" stated the cleric, silencing the feisty half-ling. A garish streak of blood ran down the side of Pawldo's head, and he could not conceal the deep pain that shot through him when he moved. Meekly, Pawldo relaxed into the bed of straw and closed his eyes.

As Tristan and Daryth returned to the courtyard, a shower of sparks tumbled over the palisade beyond the stables, threatening to ignite the straw. Daryth joined a group of Ffolk rushing to extinguish the flames. Tristan, seeing the fire quickly under control, ran to look for Robyn.

He saw her, standing beside Gavin, on the far side of the courtyard. The two were peering down the slope of the knoll, toward the commons. The prince, starting toward them, noticed that the line of Ffolk at the wall seemed suddenly thrown backward as if in shock.

And then he saw the Bloodriders strike the courtyard.

XXXXXXXXXXX

"What's happening?" cried Robyn, as the Bloodriders became a blur of movement. She heard the horrifying lightning and thunder of the hooves, and saw the fire-blackened path behind them, but the horsemen themselves moved too fast for her mortal eyes.

Only Gavin seemed capable of reacting as the black horses climbed the knoll. The giant smith stepped before Robyn and lifted his huge hammer.

The woman saw a blur of red eyes, black skin, and grinning teeth, and then the horsemen were upon them. Robyn felt something massive— perhaps a horse's shoulder—slam against her, and she fell to the ground.

Dimly, she saw Gavin's hammer whirl and strike a Rider from his saddle with enough force to shatter his body into pieces. She saw a slashing blade cut a chunk of red from the smith's shoulder as Gavin stepped backward, straddling Robyn's body with his giant legs.

Sparks and chips of rock stung her exposed skin. But the smith stood firm, dividing the onrush of horsemen so that none of the crushing steeds could step on the druid.

Blood splashed onto her, and she saw weapons pass over her in a blur. The blades left deep red slashes all over Gavin's body. His neck, chest, arms, and head all spurted blood, but somehow Gavin still stood, like some inexorable force of nature.

Then the horsemen were past, galloping unhindered into the courtyard, leaving the battered remnants of the company moaning and bleeding on the parapet. Gavin slumped to his knees as Robyn squirmed from beneath him and sat up. The smith's eyes glazed as he looked dumbly at his lifeblood, running freely into the ground. Then he slowly toppled backward to lie, motionless, among the many other bodies.

XXXXXXXXXX

The body of Thelgaar Ironhand seemed like an inefficient vehicle for climbing the steep slope, but the Beast forced itself to retain the bothersome shape. Now, with the fall of the fortress so near at hand, it could not afford to distract the northmen from their task.

Grasping chunks of sod or outcrops of rock with its hands, Kazgoroth moved upward at the head of a thousand northmen. The breach in the palisade, formerly held by a company of Ffolk, was empty once more.

For the charge of the Bloodriders had passed here. Not a single defender along that line still stood to meet the advancing raiders. The charge had cut like a scythe through the Ffolk, and now the men of the Iron King reached the crest of the knoll and rushed through the opening.

XXXXXXXXXX

"In the name of the goddess . . ." Robyn whispered.

When she saw Gavin, dust-covered and bleeding, she sobbed uncontrollably. Kneeling beside the man who had died to protect her, she gently closed his sightless eyes. For the first time since they had seen his village in flames, she thought that he looked peaceful. He had joined his family in death.

She stood and carefully took the staff from behind her back, holding it close before her. Its smooth surface, so warm against her hands, calmed and strengthened her. She felt very old, but as if that age had weathered and toughened her.

"Thank the goddess you're all right," said the bard, as he ran to her.

"The smith saved my life," she said simply, and then turned away.

She saw the Bloodriders sweep through the courtyard of the castle, her home. Now they moved at a more normal speed, killing anyone who stood in their path until they were galloping through a courtyard empty except for themselves and their dead victims.

"Are you all right?" From somewhere, Tristan appeared next to the druid, touching her shoulder with concern. She looked at him, and the sight of his tired, careworn face made her nearly burst into tears again.

"I'm fine," she replied, gulping. She knew that she could not yet let go.

"Come on, let's get away from here!" Willingly, she grabbed the prince's arm and ran. They raced through the choking, swirling smoke until they reached the stables. Here, as he had hoped, Tristan found that the sister knights had begun to mount their white horses.

Brigit opened the stable doors to let them slip in, and they turned and watched the Bloodriders wreak havoc in the courtyard.

Heartsick, Tristan counted eleven white horses, and eleven silvery knights. How these valiant warriors had suffered in his service! Yet now they mounted again, prepared as always to charge a foe that outnumbered them five to one.

"Wait," cried Robyn, as a man-at-arms prepared to throw open the stable doors. "Give me time to get out there near the doors to the keep!"

"Tristan, I need you to come with me," she said, and he could not refuse.

Robyn turned again toward the eleven knights. "When the doors open, charge across the courtyard once, and then return this way. You must lead the Bloodriders past me!

"And please—" Robyn's voice was low, her tone grave, "all of you must pass before they reach me—you must be certain!"

Brigit looked slightly puzzled, but nodded.

Robyn and Tristan slipped through the stable doors and sprinted toward the keep, under cover of the acrid smoke. Soon they reached a position near the great oaken doors.

Suddenly the stable doors burst open, and the Sisters of Synnoria charged into the embattled courtyard.

The silver plate mail of the sisters gleamed in the afternoon sun, and the colorful pennants, proud as ever, trailed from the silvery lances. Those lances now leveled at the circling mass of the Bloodriders, as the two groups of riders came together with brutal impact.

The Bloodriders swerved from the path of the advancing knights. But before the black horses could swing around the knights and trap them, the Sisters of Synnoria, swung about and raced back toward the stables.

Howling their victory cry, the Bloodriders pursued the fleeing knights. The white horses were swift, however, and the sisters outdistanced nearly all the Bloodriders in their short spurt across the courtyard.

All but one.

The captain of the Bloodriders hurled his black stallion forward with lightning speed, and the powerful horse carried him to the very heels of the sisters.

The knights, trailed closely by Laric, galloped past Robyn as she stepped from the doorway onto the paving stones of the courtyard. Her oaken staff pounded sharply on the ground, once and then again. She uttered words of arcane power, a call upon the benevolence of the goddess.

And the goddess heard.

The goddess split the ground asunder, along the line Robyn had marked with the staff. The goddess called upon the wells of heat lying deep within her bowels—vast pools of liquid rock glowing with white-hot fire. And the goddess gave this power to Robyn.

A wall of fire exploded from the ground, stretching across the path of the charging Bloodriders. Paving stones flew upward as the fires of the Earthmother reached toward the sky, creating a barrier of intense heat.

The Bloodriders struck the wall of white fire. Their horses turned instantly skeletal, mutilated and black as they fell to the ground. The goddess's fire took hold of the body of each Bloodrider and scoured the force of the Darkwell from his bones. Only ashes emerged from the fire.

XXXXXXXXXX

Like a gray-brown wave, the wolves of the Pack followed their leader across the moors, hills, and forests of Gwynneth. Canthus took them quickly from the highlands, through the sparse settlements of the northern cantrevs, closer and closer to his home and his master.

For more than a tenday, the mass of animals maintained its steady course, resting only for a few hours in the darkest hours of the night. Before dawn they were off again, always rolling forward with that steady lope.

Finally, Canthus sensed the nearness of his home, for he passed through fields where Tristan and Daryth had taken him during the training. Ahead lay his castle and his beloved master.

The great black column towering into the sky marked the location of Caer Corwell. The hound loped steadily on, his long tongue hanging limply from his jaws. His shaggy flanks were tangled and matted with burrs, and his ragged breathing panted from his huge chest.

Now his nostrils picked up scents of home—scents ominously mingled with the more powerful aromas of threat and danger. He could smell the salty waters of the firth, and the musty dankness of the stables, but these odors were far overshadowed by the smells of fire, death, and decay.

Like a brown legion, the followers of Canthus raced to Caer Corwell. But even as they ran, warriors died, and the castle burned.

xxxxxxxxxxx

In a brief second, Laric saw the towering wall of fire, and he sensed that the long line of debris—bones of horses and ashes of Riders—represented all that remained of his company. He felt no sadness at the loss of his companions, for he was no longer capable of such an emotion—only anger.

The black stallion veered from the sisters, for the odds no longer favored Laric here. He noticed, dimly, that Thelgaar Ironhand now led a large band of raiders through the breach in the lines created by the Bloodriders—the battle was far from over.

And always his decayed nostrils searched the smoking, swirling air of the courtyard for the scent of her whom he sought. The druid, he knew, must be responsible for the destruction of his company. That only made his longing for her deeper.

Suddenly, a delicious scent floated past his nostrils, and the smoke parted enough for the Bloodrider to see his quarry. She lay motionless against the stone walls of the keep. Before her stood that arrogant human, the one with the mighty sword. The human would be a powerful enemy, Laric knew, but his lust for the druid compelled him to attack.

His skeletal jaws clenched into a smile as the black steed sprang forward, the hard hooves clattering against the paving stones. With hot pleasure, Laric saw that the prince did not yet notice him coming. His attention seemed focused across the courtyard toward the advancing ranks of northmen . . .

Toward Thelgaar Ironhand.

×× ×× ×× ×× ×× ×× ×× ×× ××

Kazgoroth paused among the corpses of the Ffolk left by the charge of the Bloodriders. The human lungs of Thelgaar Ironhand gasped for air, but no matter, the Beast felt no energy drain from the long climb.

The Beast watched the Sisters of Synnoria charge from the stables, and it watched the Bloodriders pursue them back across the courtyard.

And then the flames blossomed from the courtyard, and Kazgoroth bellowed inarticulately at the destruction of his own creatures. The white flames soared high and burned the Beast's eyes with the power of the goddess. Roaring in a rage, Kazgoroth was forced to avert its eyes until the goddess's power receded.

The Beast saw, finally, the ruins of the Bloodriders, and again its body twisted from the consuming rage. The power of the Darkwell surged uncontrollably, exploding in flames from Thelgaar's distorted mouth and flexing his brawny arms into serpentine tentacles.

But the cool intelligence at the center of the monster's being brought it quickly under control. Quickly the tentacles withdrew into human arms, and the white-bearded face melted back into the likeness of Thelgaar. Some northmen rubbed their eyes, attributing the alarming sight to the swirling smoke, the confusing din of battle. Others spoke silent prayers to their foreign gods.

×× ×× ×× ×× ×× ×× ×× ×× ××

Tristan gasped as the white flames devoured the Bloodriders. He dimly heard a clattering beside him, and turned to see Robyn's staff fall carelessly to the ground. The druid sagged backward against the wall of the keep, and slowly slumped.

The prince leaped to her side and caught her unconscious body before she hit the ground. Robyn's face was frighteningly pale, but she still breathed. Obviously, the effort to cast the awesome spell of destruction had drained and exhausted her.

For a moment, Tristan let the battle surge forward without him. Anguishing, he carried his beloved Robyn into the shelter of the alcove before the doors of the keep, laying her carefully upon his outspread cloak. Then he took her staff and placed it across her chest, hoping that the talisman might offer some enchanted aid to her recovery.

The prince noticed that the oaken shaft seemed to have cooled somewhat—it felt like a normal piece of smooth oak, no longer throbbing with that strange and deep sense of vitality he had noticed before.

And then Tristan forgot all about Robyn, as the Sword of Cymrych Hugh compelled him to stare across the courtyard. He saw the advancing form of the enemy king—a huge, white-bearded northman leading the charge of his countrymen with berserker intensity.

But the prince, aided by the power of Cymrych Hugh, saw much more than this. He saw the king as it truly was—not human, nor even animal, but the spawn of some force deeper and far more malignant than any living organism.

He recognized the king as the demon that had attacked Robyn in her room, only to be driven off by the combined efforts of the druid, the cleric, and the prince.

And he knew that the Beast recognized him.

Robyn moaned slightly, and stirred upon the steps of the keep. The prince half-turned toward her, and saw her eyes flutter open. He wanted to go to her, but the sword would not let him.

Resolutely, the Prince of Corwell turned his back upon Robyn and advanced to do battle with Kazgoroth.

XXXXXXXXXX

The final rise north of Corwell passed below the loping paws of the Pack, and finally Canthus saw his destination. The castle before him stood high upon its familiar knoll, but its appearance was much changed.

Black smoke and orange flame roared skyward from many places along the wooden palisade. All about the base of the knoll pressed the army of northmen, as catapults bombarded the fortress from all sides, and raiders scrambled up the steep slopes of the hill to attack every breach in the palisade.

With a growl, Canthus leaped to the defense of his master's home.

This loyal hound, however, was accompanied by a thousand drooling, aroused, and fiercely hungry wolves. The Pack set upon the army of the northmen. A hundred raiders died without knowing what killed them, for the Pack approached from the rear of the battle. Slowly, as the screams of the dying and the snarls of the killers spread across the field, the raiders turned from the castle to behold canine doom inexorably loping toward them.

The wolves approached from the north, where the attack had been weakest. On the opposite side of the castle, the Bloodriders had already breached the palisade, and fighting raged in the courtyard. But here, the palisade still stood, and the stone bulk of the keep rose directly beyond. Here, too, much of the slope leading to the castle consisted of sheer cliffs of weatherworn rock, unclimbable by even the most determined of attackers.

The raiders now turned to save themselves, ignoring the castle. In a flash, the wolves were among them, and each northman who confronted a wolf with his weapon found two more creatures setting upon him from flank and rear.

The blows of sword and axe killed many a wolf, but the Pack rolled forward with single-minded determination, always following the form of the great moorhound that inspired them.

As the carnage continued, the blood-letting drove the wolves to the height of frenzy. More and more, the raiders simply fled, and quickly a wave of panic spread. Within a few minutes, the enemy had been cleared from the northern side of Caer Corwell.

xxxxxxxxx

A great carnivore leaped at Grunnarch, but he split the creature's skull with a crushing blow from his axe. He turned in time to see Raag Hammerstaad, fighting nearby, move too slowly to avoid the rush of another of the beasts.

The wolf sank ivory fangs through Raag's beard and into the flesh of his throat, tearing out the windpipe and jugular. The Isles of Norheim lost their king in that instant, but Grunnarch was more concerned with the loss of an entire army.

All around him, the raiders had begun to turn their backs and flee these unnatural attackers. Another of the snarling canines threw itself at the Red King, and once again his battle-axe saved his life.

But Grunnarch had little spirit for this fight. A bolder warrior than he it would be hard to find, should the enemy be a man, with flesh and blood and weapons and armor. But too often during this raid, the enemy had been rain, or insects, or crags of mountains. And now these wolves.

It seemed as though the land itself fought against the northmen, and this thought gave the Red King profound misgivings.

He looked about him, seeing more and more of his men fleeing from the Pack. In a moment, he saw that he would be surrounded by the rampaging horde.

With little regret, Grunnarch turned his back to the wolves and joined the flight. His attention focused not on the army of Thelgaar at the castle, or even the status of the fortress itself.

Instead, Grunnarch fled toward his longship on the beach of the firth. Foremost in his mind was home.

×××××××××××

The prince steadily moved across the courtyard toward the approaching mass of the northmen. He ignored the vast numbers of the enemy, focusing his attention solely upon the Beast. The remaining fighters of the Ffolk, remnants of the companies that had fought in the castle's defense, now emerged from behind barricades, and streamed from within the buildings.

A hundred fighters of Gavin's company, grimly determined to avenge the death of their captain, fell in behind Tristan. A score of dwarves, anchored by the staunch Finellen, emerged from the gatehouse and marched to his right. The Sisters of Synnoria emerged from the stables, lances leveled, to the left of the prince.

Those men-at-arms surviving from the castle's garrison and from other companies also swarmed into the courtyard. Soon the number of Ffolk behind the Prince of Corwell nearly matched that of raiders standing with Thelgaar Ironhand.

For the first time, the Iron King drew his sword from behind his back. The mighty steel blade, nearly five feet long, extended menacingly. His great hands, heavy with muscle, clasped the hilt, so that the heavy weapon floated like a thin wand in the air.

The Sword of Cymrych Hugh, feathery in Tristan's hand, pulled him forward. But the prince needed no encouragement to fight the creature before him. He understood that this creature was the source of all of the evil that had befallen Gwynneth during the long and fatal summer.

The raiders and the Ffolk paused, instinctively, one hundred yards apart. Thelgaar Ironhand strode forward, and Tristan Kendrick, Prince of Corwell, met him with steel.

Tristan eyed the towering figure before him, watching the long blade intensely.

Suddenly, the Iron King's long sword slashed toward Tristan's knees, and he parried the attack at the cost of a numbing blow to his hands. His own sword cut toward the northman's shoulder, but the king's parry was as fast as his own had been. Again and again, the two weapons clashed and clanged in the otherwise eerily silent courtyard.

The weight of the Beast's weapon, backed by the power of the Darkwell surging through its body, crashed against the Sword of Cymrych Hugh with many times the might of a normal blow, and Tristan had to back away from the Iron King's steady attack.

The numbness in his hands turned to pain, and Tristan found himself dreading the next blow. As each one fell, it seemed impossible that his blade was not knocked from his hands.

They fought near the edge of the slope, and Tristan spun away from that deadly sword seconds before the Beast cornered him against the drop. He nearly stumbled among the wreckage of the palisade, dodging a downward blow that slashed completely through a heavy timber.

✗ ✗ ✗ ✗ ✗ ✗ ✗ ✗ ✗ ✗

"Look!"

The cry came from an unknown warrior among the Ffolk, but it called the attention of the gathered multitudes to the moor below them.

A thousand or more northmen streamed away from the castle knoll, and behind them rushed the thousands of wolves. Panic had spread through the entire army, except for those upon the knoll with the Iron King. Now these looked nervously past the hulking form of their leader to the massive retreat being enacted below them.

And they saw the visage of their leader and king begin to change into something not imagined even in their deepest nightmares.

XXXXXXXXXXX

The Beast watched its army flee, and it felt the momentum of disaster building. The Firbolgs and Bloodriders were dead, and its army now ran away. Rage welled within the demonic breast, and the Beast exploded into its true form before the terror-stricken eyes of the northmen and the Ffolk. Its tail grew longer than the timbers of the palisade and with an angry lash a dozen northmen were toppled from the knoll. It grew in height until it towered above the humans, its head higher than the walls of the courtyard. It stood upon two mightily muscled, heavily scaled rear legs.

Wicked barbs tipped the clutching forelegs, and these thrust forward to try and pull the heart from the breast of the Prince of Corwell. But the Sword of Cymrych Hugh met those claws with the eternal power of the goddess.

The flesh of the Beast could not withstand the weapon's enchantment. Screaming in pain, Kazgoroth reared away from the Prince of Corwell and his potent sword.

Momentary astonishment rooted the prince to the flagstones, as the transformation of the Beast sent shivers of horror through the fighters of the Ffolk and the enemy alike. And the attackers stood immobile, for the briefest of moments.

All of them, that is, except one.

XXXXXXXXXXX

Engrossed by the clash of prince and king, the people in the courtyard did not notice the shadow of Laric as he stealthily maneuvered away from the press of bodies, trying to choose his moment precisely. Dimly, Laric noticed Kazgoroth's transformation as the Beast assumed its true form, but the Bloodrider's attention focused far more diligently upon the unconscious maiden.

As the others in the courtyard stood transfixed, Laric spurred his snorting mount toward the druid. Its hooves cracked and sparked against the paving stones. Laric drew up before her as she blinked and opened her eyes. Her mouth opened in a gasp of terror, but by then the Bloodrider's clawlike hand had grasped her shoulder.

Cruel spurs of bone punctured Robyn's skin, and the creature lifted her across the haunches of the stallion, noting with pleasure that she had lost consciousness at the horror of his touch.

But she still lived, and this was important. Laric would kill her, certainly, but in order to feast upon her essence as he did so, the killing must be very carefully arranged. For now, he would be content to place distance between himself and this scene of chaos.

The others in the courtyard, still riveted by the tableau before them, now heard the thundering of hooves across the courtyard. Those who turned saw the flash of a black horse and its red-cloaked Rider ducking under the half-raised portcullis. Any who looked quickly enough saw the motionless body of the maiden draped across the stallion.

And then Laric was through the gatehouse, racing like the wind down the castle road and across the open moors. Sparks flashed and smoke billowed where the black hooves struck the ground, and the surface of the earth lay black and ruined where the Bloodrider passed.

XXXXXXXXXXX

Kamerynn turned his broad head toward the buzzing that approached from behind, almost as if he still had eyes. He heard a voice, squealing in excitement. A series of questions assailed the unicorn, far too rapidly for him to understand. He felt certain, however, that the strange visitor was not an enemy.

Newt blinked in agitation and despair as he looked at the once-mighty unicorn. Kamerynn had grown gaunt in the recent tendays. His broad ribs stood out clearly against the ragged, scratched pelt that had been his gorgeous coat. But mostly Newt noticed the unicorn's scarred and pale eyes, and sensed the creature's blindness.

Like all creatures of Myrloch Vale, Newt was aware of the unicorn as the benign son of the Earthmother and protector of the Vale. Now, seeing the creature thus crippled, the little dragon was gripped by a sense of danger and despair. He desperately wanted to help the unicorn. But how?

Newt buzzed along with Kamerynn, thinking and talking. The unicorn obviously did not understand his speech, for the faerie dragon had asked many questions without getting an answer. Instead, he just kept plodding along the forest trail. How he found his way—albeit a very slow one—Newt couldn't guess.

A small brook splashed across their path, and the unicorn slowed cautiously. Newt buzzed over the stream. Hardly thinking, he imagined a bridge across the stream—a casual gesture of his illusionary magic. The bridge popped into view. It was a solid stone structure, much too large for the stream, but Newt liked it anyway. He turned his back upon the illusion, gleefully deciding to leave it there and hope something attempted to cross it before the magic wore off in a few hours.

Then Newt stopped, forgetting to buzz his wings in his astonishment. He saw, as he plopped lightly to the ground, the unicorn's sightless eyes tracing the outline of his illusionary bridge.

The unicorn could see illusions!

Newt's mind, normally rather undirected, leaped rapidly from this piece of knowledge to a simple deduction, and then to a plan. He knew how to help the unicorn!

Clapping his hands gleefully, and blinking again in his excitement, Newt cast an illusion before the unicorn—an illusion that precisely matched the reality of the path stretching before them. Kamerynn sprang forward in joy, tearing off at such a gallop that Newt had to buzz himself forward at top speed to catch up. Just as the unicorn reached the end of the spell's range, Newt let go with another tidbit of magic, and another, and another.

Finally, the faerie dragon settled onto the unicorn's head, then crawled forward to perch on the broad horn. Thus, with the dragon casting his spells, and the unicorn leaping over the ground magically duplicated before him, the pair raced through the byways of Myrloch Vale.

MIST-WREATHED MOOR

22

A trailing plume of black hair caught Tristan's eye, and he whirled in time to see the Bloodrider's stallion clatter across the courtyard. For a second, his mind did not grasp the full impact of the scene—then he saw the pale face and limp body draped across the horse's withers.

"Robyn!" The name caught in his throat. Without thinking, he leaped toward the stables to get Avalon.

But already the Rider had streaked through the gatehouse and raced down castle road. With a feeling of revulsion, Tristan looked at the shining long sword in his hand and knew that the weapon would not let him leave as long as the Beast remained here.

Tristan tried to throw the weapon to the ground. He must rescue Robyn! But the hilt of the sword remained, as if glued securely in his palm. Despite the strongest efforts of his will, he could not drop the sword.

"Damn you," he snarled, turning toward the Beast that had recoiled toward the edge of the courtyard. Even as Tristan had watched the racing Rider, so now he saw that the monster also eyed the Bloodrider and his captive. The Beast's eyes flamed, and its face twisted into a grotesque mask.

He lifted the Sword of Cymrych Hugh and advanced toward the towering creature.

The northmen fell away from the Beast in droves, turning to roll or

XXXXXXXXXXXXXXXXXXXXXXXXXXXX **334** XXXXXXXXXXXXXXXXXXXXXXXXXXXX tumble down the slopes of the knoll in their eagerness to escape.

With a shattering howl of frustration, the great scaled head turned from the Prince of Corwell to follow the blackened trail across the moor left by Laric's stallion. Before the prince could attack, the monster slipped over the crest and sprang like a huge cat down the steep slope. In moments, it too disappeared across the rolling expanse of the moors.

The monster followed the Bloodrider's trail.

XXXXXXXXXX

Canthus's jaws coursed with the red blood of the northmen, and his shaggy coat bore cuts and nicks from a dozen wounds. But the press of the Pack had been too much for the northmen, and the last vestiges of the raiding army now fled the snarling attackers.

They abandoned their siege of Caer Corwell, running through the streets of the town toward the familiar security of the longships, still safely beached a mile away.

The pace of the wolves' attack gradually lightened, as weariness and wounds took their tolls. The field around them ran red with the blood of slain northmen.

But now, as the wolves paused, the bloodlust slowly passed from their eyes. Suspiciously, and curiously, they looked around. The Pack ignored the last few fleeing raiders as they realized, as a group, that they had entered a human settlement.

Slinking and growling nervously, the wolves left the town, hurrying to reach the moors. A dozen wolves raced to the south, followed by a score, and then a few more in a small band. Several score loped to the east, and others ran to the north. The Pack dispersed to the points of the compass.

The call of the goddess no longer bound them together. Instead, they heard the voice of the Mother telling them of dens, and forest glens, and smooth clear pools of crystalline water.

The wolves thought of deer and rabbits, and their bellies stirred with their natural hunger. None stopped to eat of the meat that their merciless attack had left behind. Instead, no longer the Pack, the wolves returned to the wilds.

XXXXXXXXXXX

The huge, malign shape moved with an easy grace across the moors, racing down the black, smoldering trail left by the Bloodrider and his captive.

Upon Caer Corwell's knoll, Tristan and the rest of the defenders watched the monster run, and slowly felt the heat of combat fade.

The prince's eyes stung with tears. He looked about the castle—the home of his family for generations—and saw the death and debris wrought by the Beast and its minions. And he looked across the rolling moor, to the disappearing shape of the Beast, and then to the mass of northmen retreating beyond Corwell Town.

The sword's possession of Tristan diminished, as the Beast moved farther and farther away. Finally, the prince turned and looked for his friends among the crowd of silent, stunned watchers.

"Daryth! You must take command of the force," he called to the Calishite, who stood nearby. Daryth's dark skin was streaked with black grime, but his face shone with determination. Smiling, he nodded.

"Brigit! Finellen!" Tristan turned to the two females who had been such staunch allies during the fight. "Can you aid Daryth and the Ffolk in chasing the northmen back to their ships?"

"It'll be a pleasure!" growled the bearded captain of the dwarves, fingering her bloodstained axe.

"Of course," added Brigit, quietly.

"Fighters of the Ffolk!" called Tristan, addressing the growing congregation of his people in the ruined courtyard. "The invaders of our land have fled! It only remains to drive them back to their ships and away from here! . . . with such memories that they shall never want to return!"

"Death to the northmen!"

"Drive them into the sea!"

The cries swelled to a crescendo as the people of Corwell realized that the battle was nearly won. All that remained was the final harvest of retribution.

Keren stood among the crowd, watching the prince with renewed respect in his eyes. Tristan turned to the bard and met his gaze.

"Will you come with me?" He did not need to explain his mission.

"Our horses are being saddled even as we speak," answered the bard. "We'll have her back or die!" Even the mellifluous bard, gifted speaker though he was, did not radiate conviction.

"I'm going, too!"

The pronouncement, in a high-pitched but very determined voice, came from Pawldo. Tristan turned and saw the halfling, his forehead and one eye masked by a white bandage.

"Thank you, old friend," answered the prince, kneeling beside the halfling. "But you must stay here and recover your strength. Your wounds—"

"My prince," said Pawldo, with a rare pleading tone in his voice, "it's the Lady Robyn . . ."

"Of course." Tristan stood, clenching his teeth to hold back his own sudden rush of tears.

"You'll have to find somebody else to chase the northmen," said Daryth. "I'm coming with you, too."

"But . . . " Tristan began to object, but gratitude toward his friends flowed warmly through his body.

"Very well. The four of us shall ride as soon as we can." In desperation, he looked about the castle for someone else who might be able to command the situation.

As if in response, the stable doors burst open, and several men-at-arms emerged, leading a large chestnut mare. Seeing the rider, Tristan had to blink in amazement. At the same time, a ragged, lusty cheer arose from the throats of the Ffolk in the courtyard.

King Bryon Kendrick rode his warhorse once more.

Running forward, the prince saw with surprise that his father had been lashed into the saddle. His shattered legs had been tied to the stirrups, and his left arm was hung in a sling. Yet his strong right arm waved vigorously, and in his hand he hoisted a heavy broadsword.

"Ffolk of Corwell! Follow me to battle! Rid our kingdom of this invading scourge!" The king's words roused his people anew.

King Kendrick looked down at the prince, standing beside his horse. "Good luck, my son. I know you will find her."

Gripping his sword under his injured arm, he reached out with his good hand and clasped Tristan's shoulder. Then his silver-black beard jutted forward aggressively. "To arms, my Ffolk. We will drive them into the sea!"

As the fighters in the courtyard milled about, organizing for the pursuit, the prince and his three companions ran to the stables and mounted. Already, stableboys had three white horses of the sister knights saddled, and they were busily stuffing provisions into saddlebags.

Tristan retrieved Robyn's staff from the doorway to the keep. "She might be wanting this," he told the others as he mounted Avalon.

Suddenly, a delighted and familiar barking broke through the courtyard, and Tristan turned to see a moorhound bound through the gateway toward him.

"Canthus!" Tristan jumped to the ground as the great moorhound ploughed excitedly into him, knocking him to the flagstones. Canthus's jaws were stained with dried blood and his body marked by many wounds, but his behavior was that of a gleeful puppy welcoming his master home from a long absence.

"Good dog," sighed Tristan, scratching the hound's wooly neck. Canthus wagged his tail wildly.

"Quite a hound!" Daryth, kneeling beside them and hugging the dog's neck, choked back tears. "I could never bring myself to believe that he was dead!"

Canthus turned and licked the Calishite's face. Then he broke free and his head swiveled around the courtyard and castle, cocked to the side, as if looking for someone else. Knowing the dog could understand, Tristan spoke to Canthus.

"She's not here," he said tightly, again mounting the white stallion. "Let's go get her back!"

×××××××××××

The fiery, magic-driven hooves of the black horse carried Laric and his prisoner for many miles before the enchantment wore away. Even then, the powerful steed raced forward with impressive speed. Moving at a steady canter, the mount and his two riders moved farther and farther from Caer Corwell.

Laric knew that there would be pursuit. In fact, he suspected that both the druid's friends and his own former master would be vengefully inflamed. Neither of these pursuers would be a match for him, though, thought the ghoulish Rider.

The pale moon rose into the evening sky. Two more nights, guessed Laric, and the moon would be full. That did not seem like an impossibly long time.

Robyn moaned and stirred. Pleased, the Rider looked down at his prisoner, roughly pulling her shoulder back so that he could see her face. The maiden's skin had a ghostly pallor, and her left arm was streaked with dried blood from the wounds inflicted when Laric grabbed her. She winced in pain, holding her eyes tightly closed.

Though the flesh and skin had rotted away from most of his face, crimson lips still outlined Laric's mouth, and he spoke with a swollen, festering tongue.

"You are mine, now, druid." His skeletal claws stroked her long black tresses, almost tenderly. He ran a cracked fingernail, extending from a bony and grotesque finger, along Robyn's cheek, chuckling as she winced and shuddered.

Feeling her muscles tense, he was ready when she suddenly squirmed, trying to break free from his grasp. Mercilessly, Laric the Bloodrider tightened his grip upon her hair and forced her harshly down upon the withers of the horse.

"Very nice," he chortled, lisping thickly. He squeezed his claws together on the back of her neck, feeling warm blood break from her skin and flow across his fingers. Robyn lay very still.

"Do not try to leave me, my dear," he continued. A thick, gurgling laugh bubbled in his rotted chest. "We shall be together now, forever."

He pulled Robyn's hands behind her and bound them tightly with a leather thong, hoisting her to a sitting position in front of him on the steed.

"Ride with me, my . . . love." He chuckled, his breath hissing against her ear.

Laughing again, Laric spurred the gaunt horse. The moon, nearly full, had risen higher now. White mist had begun to condense in the evening air, and the outline of the moon and its tears became hazy and indistinct.

For two days, Laric knew, he must keep her alive, avoiding the dogged pursuit. Two more nights, before the moon rose full and powerful into the sky.

Then, under the baneful eye of that moon, her power would become his. Her life would end, as his truly began. And after he had drunk of her power, he would need flee from nothing in the world again.

On, into the mist that slowly turned to a cool rainfall, rode the Blood-rider and his helpless captive.

✕ ✕ ✕ ✕ ✕ ✕ ✕ ✕ ✕ ✕

Genna Moonsinger turned her round and wrinkled face toward the sky. The lines of age deepened into a frown of anxiety. The moon was visible only as a white outline against the fog.

The Great Druid stood poised for several minutes, listening. Once, she jerked slightly, in agitation. A watcher who could have moved close to her would have seen pools of salty moisture collect at the corners of her eyes.

"I understand," she whispered finally.

In seconds Genna assumed one of her favorite forms—that of the tiny swallow. The speed and agility of the little body always caused her a thrill of excitement, but now pleasure was subordinate to the urgency of her mission.

Darting into the sky, she raced above the moors and forests. She had much to do, and very little time.

Chirping, the bird flitted among the glades of Myrloch Vale, seeking one that she knew would be near, but she could find no trace of her quarry. Her worry grew as she realized that she would soon be forced to abandon this mission, in favor of another, yet more urgent, task.

Still, she felt that she must allow herself more time. Racing as fast as the tiny wings could propel her, the druid frantically sniffed and hunted through the ways of Myrloch Vale. The hours passed, and still she searched.

Finally, she admitted defeat. The little bird darted upward and began winging south and west. But then, as she flew, the faint spoor of the trail she had sought wafted to her senses on a gentle breeze. The source of the spoor was near!

Chirping in excitement, Genna swooped low to the ground. Just a few minutes, she told herself—minutes that might make the difference between life and death.

Soon Genna found him she sought, and she spoke urgently for a few moments. Then she took to the air again, determined now to find the Prince of Corwell.

XXXXXXXXXX

The great clawed feet pounded the turf with a relentless cadence as Kazgoroth pursued the traitorous minion. The monster dropped to all fours, loping somewhat awkwardly because of its small forelegs.

The long, forked tongue snaked from between bristling rows of teeth, tasting the air. Very faintly, the Beast detected the spoor of the druid, salivating at the stimulus. But within its dark brain, Kazgoroth had begun to worry.

For many months now it had been away from the Darkwell, thriving upon the spreading of evil. But now the forces of evil had suffered a dire reverse, and the power of Kazgoroth was beginning to wane.

The Beast slowed to a trot, and then to a plodding walk. The trail of the Bloodrider beckoned, mocking the Beast's weakness.

Snarling, the great head lifted high, its gaze fixed with murderous intensity. Once again the powerful rear legs propelled the huge body at a steady lope, this time striding erect.

The forked tongue slipped forward again, tasting the air. No longer did it seek the sweet scent of the druid, nor the fetid spoor of Laric the usurper. Instead it sought its primary source of nourishment—the power that had brought the Beast into the world.

Kazgoroth had no choice but to return to the Darkwell.

XXXXXXXXXX

"Everyone stay close," said Tristan, as the mist closed thickly about them.

"Can you see Canthus?" asked Daryth, nearly invisible only ten feet away.

"Barely," answered the prince.

Darkness had fallen, and with it had come a mist that threatened to cloak every feature of the terrain from the pursuers.

Avalon and the other horses foamed and lathered from the exertion of the long ride. Canthus loped steadily before them, unfailing in his strength and endurance.

Now, as darkness concealed the blackened trail of Laric's stallion, the hound kept on the track of the spoor, and no torches were necessary.

For several more hours they pushed forward, talking low to maintain contact with each other. Finally, after they had lost Canthus for the eighth or ninth time, Tristan wearily acknowledged the inevitable.

"We had better break for some rest. We'll never catch him by wearing ourselves out."

The others agreed, so they dismounted and stretched on the ground to savor a few hours of sleep before dawn. Keren whistled softly, and Sable glided from the mist to settle onto a tall boulder beside the bard. Unable to sleep, Tristan ate some dried beef and drank wine, but even this could not relax him. After what seemed an eternity, he noticed that the heavy mist had begun to glow. Dawn was near.

"Let's go," he called. Stiff and sore, they climbed onto their white horses once again.

The trail left by Laric's stallion stood out like a line of ink across a page, and they started at a canter to warm their bodies and jolt their sleep-drugged senses into alertness. For an hour they rode in silence, and gradually the murky fog turned bright. It did not disperse, however, and they traveled across a featureless moor that vanished from sight a hundred feet away.

Only the black trail stood out from the pale green grass and the perpetual whiteness of the mist. They followed in single file, Canthus leading, with Tristan behind, then Keren, and Pawldo and Daryth bringing up the rear on a large gelding.

Always beside the trail of the Bloodrider ran the huge prints left by Kazgoroth the Beast in its constant lope of pursuit. The heavy rear feet sank deeply into the soft loam and left a clear, claw-studded outline.

Early in the morning they reached a parting, where Kazgoroth turned east, while Laric and his captive had continued north.

Tristan looked at the fork, for a moment uncertain. The others stopped silently and watched as his face suddenly twisted into a grimace of indecision.

To follow the Beast—the deadliest creature to walk the Moonshaes—and slay it?

Or to hasten to the rescue of the woman he loved, if she was still alive?

He thought of the sword at his side, sensing that if he grasped its hilt he would be compelled to follow Kazgoroth. Yet, could he responsibly do otherwise?

The Sword of Cymrych Hugh had been forged centuries ago, for the purpose of slaying that very Beast. If he did not follow its trail, the monster would soon vanish into the vastness of Myrloch Vale, and the Ffolk would have to suffer its evil once again.

Should Robyn be abandoned to her fate?

"I must go after her. The Beast will have to wait," he finally said, dropping his eyes to avoid meeting their gazes. He was sickened at his own words, and felt he had betrayed his companions, his Ffolk, and the Sword of Cymrych Hugh.

The chirping of a swallow, diving close overhead, distracted him. As the bird settled to the ground, its shape shifted quickly in the curling mist. Tristan started to reach for his sword, thinking the Beast had come among them, but suddenly an old woman stood before them. Her eyes sparkled, and she smiled wisely at the prince. Slowly, her expression turned sorrowful.

"You know what you must do, Prince of Corwell. If you do not seek the Beast now, and destroy it before it can rekindle its power, you will never have another chance." Her voice was cool and forceful, much like a younger woman's.

"I know you, druid," said the prince, remembering. "You spoke to me that night at the Spring Festival! But how can you command me, when Robyn—a druid!—may still be alive?"

"She lives," said the druid, and his heart leaped involuntarily, "and she is not forsaken."

"But—"

"She is a favored daughter, smiled upon by the goddess! Can it be that you do not know this?" Her voice now rose indignantly. "We shall do everything in our power to save her."

"I cannot—" Tristan prickled at the rebuke, about to argue. Something within the druid's eyes made him hold his tongue.

"You are a worthy prince of the Ffolk," said the druid, more kindly. "One day soon you will be king, if you can succeed in your final task. Now go, and do what you must!"

Miserably, Tristan knew that she was right—the Beast must be slain, and it was his duty to accomplish that. He turned away slowly, and then he remembered the staff.

"Wait!" he cried, untying the wooden rod from its position behind his saddle. The druid smiled and stepped closer as he held it out to her. "It's hers. I hope you can give it to her."

"I will try," she promised, and her smile soothed Tristan's torment.

With a whirl of her woolen cloak, she disappeared. This time, a little bat darted through the mist, its tiny wings straining in desperation. For all her brave talk, Genna Moonsinger knew she had precious little time.

✕ ✕ ✕ ✕ ✕ ✕ ✕ ✕ ✕

Robyn grew more alert through the long, fog-bound day, but her body still seemed gripped by a paralyzing weakness. She could raise her head and look around, but she could not turn to see behind her. She had lost all feeling in her hands, for the numbing leather thong cut cruelly into her wrists.

A smell of death and foulness seemed to surround her, rising from the bodies of the horse and Rider. Every so often, Laric would lean close and say something unintelligible to her, and then his rank, polluted breath would make her head spin with nausea.

Even more revolting than his breath were his cold and skeletal fingers. Occasionally, he would encircle Robyn's waist with those hands, or run a long, leisurely caress down her back or across her shoulders.

Each time he did this, Robyn shuddered in revulsion. She wished for death to release her from this nightmare but death did not come, and the nightmare stayed the same.

All during the long day, the fog hung thick and low across the moor, as if the goddess could not bear to open the curtain upon the play enacted there. Yet the fog would provide no protection for the actors.

The long day of riding ended with dusk, when a patch of light rose against the clouds to the east, and Robyn knew that the moon was full. Laric reined in the black horse and dismounted. Roughly, he pulled his prisoner to the ground and pushed her across the grass. For a moment, Robyn allowed herself to hope that they had stopped for rest.

Something in the Bloodrider's fiery eyes told her otherwise.

Laric pulled her off the horse onto a broad, flat stone, cuffing her shoulder so that she fell, stunned, upon the rock.

Then the mist parted very briefly, and the rays of the full moon spilled unfiltered into the clearing. Robyn saw Laric draw his stained, blackened sword. Even through the tarnish the weapon seemed to burn with a deep corruption, which hurt her eyes as she looked upon the blade.

The Bloodrider turned to her, weapon upraised, his face distorted in a horrible leer. She tugged frantically on the bonds restraining her wrists, but she was held too securely.

Sensing his purpose, she could do nothing to save herself. She resolved that the creature would not know of her terror, and she lifted her proud face toward Laric in an expression of disdain.

As he reached for her, a deathly chuckle bubbling from his chest, she spat in his face.

XXXXXXXXXX

Newt's tiny claws gripped the horn of the unicorn, holding on for dear life as Kamerynn raced through the tangled ways of the forest. Always the little dragon maintained the flow of illusory magic, reproducing the world so that the blind creature could once again proudly inhabit his domain.

Newt had not understood the message that the Great Druid brought to Kamerynn, but her words filled the unicorn with fanatical energy. Shivering, the faerie dragon struggled to retain his perch and still work his magic.

Never before had Newt performed such sustained illusion, and the effort now brought a throbbing ache to his little scaled head. Normally, some errant butterfly, or toothsome frog, would have long since diverted Newt's attention. Instead, he rode diligently and attentively, ignoring the pain in his head in order to bring sight to the blinded unicorn.

For a long night, and an even longer day, the pair raced over the mist-wreathed moor. The encloaking mist surrounded and assailed them, and even Newt found his bearings difficult to maintain. Finally night—the night of the full moon—fell again, and at last fatigue forced the unicorn to slow his resolute pace.

Around them, the fog seemed to press heavily. The mist felt very cool, and exuded a sense of danger.

THE SONG OF KEREN

23

The bat darted through the mist purposefully, soaring above the blackened track that marred and tore the ground. Night fell with frightening suddenness, surrounding her with tendrils of fog. Menacing shadows moved the boundaries of her vision.

The Bloodrider had ridden impossibly fast—she could not understand how or why. The full moon, rising above the fog, did little to penetrate the mist, or to remind the druid of the benign presence of the goddess. Genna Moonsinger, Great Druid though she was, felt frightened and alone on this night of foreboding.

From somewhere in the mists before her, a shrill female voice, laden with terror, screamed through the night.

×××××××××

Tristan and his companions rode steadily along the path of the Beast. As darkness fell, they were forced to dismount, since the trail left by Kazgoroth was much less obvious than that left by the Bloodrider.

Still, Canthus had no difficulty following the spoor. The moorhound loped ahead, disappearing into the mist, and then stopped and waited for the men and horses to catch up. When they did, the dog bounded forward again, quickly swallowed by the fog.

A deep and hollow sense of loneliness gripped Tristan.

"Did I make the right choice?" he asked the bard, miserably. Yet he already knew the answer: It was not the right choice for the heart.

"She'll be all right," said Keren, in a quietly comforting tone. "The druid spoke the truth—she carries the divine blessing of the goddess."

"But I turned from her trail!" The prince heard his own voice take on a wail of grief.

"But you are doing the right thing, all the same."

Little comforted, the prince rode in silence. Darkness soon surrounded them, and the mist grew even thicker, if that were possible. Faintly, they could make out the patch of light where the full moon—a moon of dire omen, Tristan felt certain—rose into the late summer sky.

"Should we stop and sleep for a bit?" the prince asked his companions, though he did not feel tired.

"I don't think I can sleep," declared Daryth, peering forward to keep Canthus in sight.

"Me either," added Pawldo.

Keren remained silent, but his eyes, like the Calishite's, stared resolutely ahead. Silently, they continued forward through the cold and oppressive night.

XXXXXXXXXXX

The Bloodrider laughed harshly at Robyn's futile gesture of defiance, and suddenly his eyes grew white hot with bloodlust. The image changed so quickly, and so frightfully, that she could not suppress a shriek of terror.

A skeletal hand grasped her ankle. She kicked at Laric's frail-looking chest, but her foot was deflected by an invisible force as from a stone wall. Twisting, she tried to escape, but her hands were bound tight, and he held her fast.

Now Laric held her flat on her back, against the stone, with one clawlike hand pressing hard against her chest. She could barely breathe, she could not move, she was helpless. With the other hand the ghoulish creature lifted his sword high. The sinister weapon rested directly above her neck.

Brown spittle leaked from Laric's cracked lips, as he drooled in anticipation of his feast. He began to lower the blade.

Suddenly brilliant flashes of light exploded through the mist. Laric's black stallion screamed and reared in panic, flailing the air with his deadly hooves.

The explosions of light sent barbs of color arcing in the sky, lighting the scene first in red, then blue, then green.

A white shape galloped from the mist, snorting in anger, and her heart filled with hope.

"Kamerynn!" she called, immediately recognizing the mighty creature. "Look out!"

The black stallion lunged forward, breaking his tether, and driving his forehooves into the unicorn's flank. Kamerynn turned clumsily, striking with his horn but missing the stallion by a wide margin. Suddenly, next to the fighting steeds, Robyn saw the little figure of the faerie dragon, Newt, blinking in and out of sight in agitation.

A shadowy image appeared next to the stallion, mimicking the black horse in appearance and movement.

Now Kamerynn struck more surely, the ivory horn cutting a deep gash in the steed's flank.

Laric turned toward the fight, momentarily forgetting the maiden stretched on the rock. He crept toward the unicorn, raising his long sword.

"Kamerynn! Newt! Look out!" shouted Robyn, as the Bloodrider hurled himself into the fray. But her warning came too late, and the flickering blade caught the dragon unawares. With a tiny, highpitched scream of pain, Newt dropped to the earth.

Immediately, the colored lights and the illusionary vision of the black horse vanished. Kamerynn was blind once again. The unicorn stepped backward, as if confused, and the stallion charged him savagely. Laric, too, advanced toward Kamerynn, readying the fatal blow.

"Stop, spawn of the Beast!" The voice rang harshly through the clearing, and Robyn turned to see a plump old woman scurry from the mist. There was nothing pleasant or kind about her voice, however.

"Now, see if you can stand against the power of the goddess!"

Genna Moonsinger held her finger before her, pointing at the breast of the Bloodrider. She called upon the power of the goddess, asking for the use of her most baneful spell. A crackling beam of light sizzled from her finger, into and through the body of the Bloodrider, only to disappear into the night beyond.

Laric's hollow, liquid laugh was frightful in its supreme arrogance. "You seek to slay me, druid—but you cannot slay that which is already dead!"

With a snarl, he leaped forward, but Genna stepped back quickly and uttered another casting, raising the power of the goddess's own body into a tool of the druid.

The ground below Laric's feet shifted and roiled, and the Rider tripped. Rolling across the heaving turf, he leaped to his feet and snarled at the shape of a creature, vaguely humanlike but composed of the elemental materials of the earth itself, that rose from the ground. It rose with a ripping sound, smelling strongly of moist dirt, and lashed out with an earthen fist, trying to crush the ghoulish figure.

With incredible agility, Laric jumped aside and managed to hack a great chunk of dirt from the earth elemental. Genna, concentrating, commanded her creature to attack. Another clublike fist sprouted from a different spot on the creature's trunk, and this one smashed into Laric's chest.

The Bloodrider sailed backward, crashing into Robyn's stone and slumping to the ground. But in a second, Laric sprang to his feet again. He charged the elemental and marked a dazzling series of slashes with his sword. Each blow struck off a piece of the creature, until shortly it collapsed into motionless, mundane rubble.

Still snarling, Laric turned his deathshead gaze upon Genna Moonsinger. Slowly the Rider advanced, extending a gruesome claw as Genna stumbled backward. Suddenly, the druid tripped upon a hummock of grass and fell.

Robyn gasped, and at the same moment felt the grip of tiny claws upon her leg.

She looked down to see Newt scamper up and perch beside her. He remained visible for several seconds.

"You poor thing," she whispered. One of his butterflylike wings had been severed, and he moved tortuously because of a long gash in his neck.

"Why do you not help them?" queried the dragon, tilting his head toward the fight. Genna had rolled away from the Rider, but could not get to her feet before Laric closed in again.

"My hands," replied Robyn, turning her back to reveal her bound wrists. Newt looked positively enlightened and in an instant had set upon the thongs, chewing energetically.

Across the clearing, Kamerynn grunted painfully as the black stallion once again crashed into his unprotected flank. Newt paused in his task and squinted solemnly at the fight, sudden tears welling in his eyes. "I can't do it!" he sobbed. "My magic is broken!"

"Hurry and untie me," urged Robyn. "And there's still hope."

Again the unicorn cried out in pain, and then Laric's howl of triumph rose above all. He leaped toward the Great Druid, dropping his sword in his eagerness to sink his claws into her flesh. As he grabbed her, however, he found himself holding a coiling viper. The snake's wedged head darted forward to bury long fangs in the rotted flesh of Laric's arm.

"Bah," cried the Rider, disdainfully throwing the serpent to the ground. He swept up his sword, aiming a killing blow. Suddenly, the confident chanting of Robyn's voice carried toward him.

And then the Bloodrider cried in pain and dropped the weapon, which glowed red, then white, before turning liquid and running into the ground. With Newt clapping in glee, Robyn rose from the stone and faced the Bloodrider, meeting his hate-filled gaze with her own look of pride and determination.

For an instant, the little faerie dragon disappeared. Then he popped back into sight, shouting, "I've got it back! My magic's fixed!"

Immediately the clearing shimmered as blue and orange light streaked through the mist. The image of the black stallion appeared, confidently mirroring the steed as it leaped at the hapless unicorn.

But now Kamerynn perceived the image and dodged the stallion's murderous assault. As the stallion stumbled past, the unicorn reared high, his heavy forehooves landing with crushing force upon the stallion's forehead. The horse dropped instantly to the ground, dead.

With a gurgle of choking hysteria the Bloodrider lunged toward Robyn. The young druid tried to break away across the wide stone, but the ghoulish creature met her with horrifying speed. His eyes seething like the guts of a volcano, Laric's clawlike hands reached for Robyn's throat.

And then Laric's death scream split the night, deafening Robyn with its shrill intensity. The Bloodrider soared into the air above Robyn as the unicorn's horn emerged from his chest, clean and white as bone.

The wasted, rotted body tossed like a rag doll upon the impaling horn as the unicorn bucked and reared. Finally Kamerynn threw his head back and kicked his forelegs toward the full moon. His whinny of triumph resounded through the night as the body of the Bloodrider sailed into the mist to fall, broken and forever useless, among the rocks.

Robyn stood, frozen, for several seconds. She saw Genna limping toward her, and the two women collapsed into each other's arms for a minute, breathing heavily. A slender form hesitantly crawled up Robyn's leg, and she hoisted Newt to cradle him in her arms.

"My, my," clucked Genna, inspecting the wounds upon the little dragon. She murmured a low prayer, stroking the soft scales. Robyn's eyes widened as she saw the gash along Newt's neck heal and a stubby bud appear over the scar of the lost wing.

"Now, now, my little hero," whispered Genna as Newt wriggled in delight up to Robyn's shoulder. "You must treat that wing gently—it will take some time to grow back.

"But until then, you've someone to carry you," said the druid, sadly turning to Kamerynn. She scratched the unicorn's broad forehead and stroked the ruined eyes. "Just a little longer, my child, and then you can rest."

Genna's manner became businesslike.

"Come come, child! You must ride now, while there is still time!" She took Robyn by the arm. "I almost forgot! Your prince gave this to me, for you. " She took the staff from across her back and offered it to Robyn.

Robyn took the shaft of wood reverently, though it seemed as if the fire of the goddess's power had been extinguished from it. Suddenly, Genna snatched it from her.

"Of course! You don't know about *charging* it! And tonight, of all nights, you can find out." Genna held the staff toward the full moon, chanting a rolling phrase. The words entered Robyn's mind and would stay there, forever. And once again the staff hummed with power.

"Every month, my dear, during the full moon, you can bless it with the might of the goddess. One time, each month, it will bring forth her power at your command. Use it wisely, for it is the blood of our Mother herself!"

Quickly the druid told Robyn about Tristan and the others, their pursuit of the Beast. "Go to him! Ride like the wind, girl!"

"But ride what?" questioned Robyn, not daring to guess what Genna meant.

In answer, Kamerynn trotted to her side and knelt upon the soft loam. Reverently, feeling a sense of deep awe, Robyn climbed onto the unicorn's broad back. Scampering like a squirrel, Newt leaped to Kamerynn's shoulders, then his head, and soon perched like a figurehead upon the great horn.

Before Robyn could say farewell to the Great Druid, Kamerynn sprang forward. In seconds, they vanished into the mist, but the paleness of the light was augmented by the many colors Newt added to the illusionary fog.

XXXXXXXXXX

The Beast reached the Darkwell and paused in shock. The wide, polluted pool it remembered had been reduced to a small pool of scum in the center of a brown wasteland. Kazgoroth's eyes took in the shattered dam, and its brain thought vaguely of the failure of the Firbolgs.

For a moment, the Beast regretted the sudden disaster he had wrought upon those same Firbolgs. If they lived now, their punishment would be far worse than mere death.

A bubble broke from the black sludge in the middle of the pond, and the Beast crawled through the mud to wallow there. The power was not great, but could still be felt. The goddess had not yet been able to reclaim her Moonwell.

Slithering deep into the muck, until its entire body lay buried, Kazgoroth began to feed once again on the power of the Darkwell.

XXXXXXXXXX

In the harsh days of pursuit, always, it seemed, through the cloaking, chilling fog, Canthus never strayed from the trail of the Beast. It led through a low pass entering Myrloch Vale, and from there, due east. It was Keren who realized that the monster's destination was none other than the Fens of the Fallon.

"My prince," asked the bard, "do you recall a hidden sense of menace there? A presence that could be felt even more acutely than the threat of the Firbolgs?"

"Perhaps you're right," responded Tristan.

A thundering of hooves called their attention to the rear, as Daryth and Pawldo caught up with them. The pair, both upon the sturdy gelding, had been riding well behind Tristan and Keren as a precaution against ambush.

"The fens!" cried the Calishite. "Do you recognize them?"

They stopped, briefly, upon a low rise, overlooking the expanse of black ponds, thorny thickets, and soggy marshland. Somewhere in the distance, they sensed, lay their destination. Restlessly, Tristan looked back along their path. The monster was near, and he knew that he would soon face a climactic showdown, yet these thoughts were far from the forefront of his mind. One question forced all other thoughts from him.

Where was Robyn?

×××××××××××

"I'll try green now! Aren't you getting tired of red and blue all the time? I know *I* am—I think green will be a nice change of—"

"I'm afraid I'm too tired to pay much attention," apologized Robyn, opening her eyes at the sound of Newt's voice. The gentle pacing of the unicorn had lulled her to sleep.

"Just for a little while?" pleaded Newt. "Can't you watch?" The little dragon still perched upon the unicorn's ivory horn, peering forward into the night. Involuntarily, his mouth opened in a wide yawn, but he quickly snapped his tiny jaws shut.

"Now look what you made me do!" he pouted, turning his back toward Robyn in a huff. She sighed, but let the smooth rocking of her mount settle her back toward sleep. The unicorn moved more gracefully than any horse—Robyn felt as if she rode in a comfortable boat along

XXXXXXXXXXXXXXXXXXXXX DARKWALKER ON MOONSHAE XXXXXXXXXXXXXXXXXXXX

a smooth-flowing river. Suddenly she jerked awake, seeing an ocean of
darkness before them.

"Newt! Wake up!"

The fairie dragon lifted his head, but by then Kamerynn had
reached the limit of the last illusion. The unicorn stopped sharply.
Robyn fell forward, clutching the broad neck and holding on, but
Newt lost his hold and sailed into the darkness, landing with an
outraged squeal.

"Hey!" squeaked the tiny voice, indignantly. "What's the big idea?
That's no way to treat somebody who's been helping you out all day!
Why, you big lummox!" The dragon pranced up to the unicorn, glaring
at him.

Robyn laughed and slipped to the ground. "I think we could all use
a little sleep. Why don't we rest here until morning?"

The dragon curled up quickly, and even the unicorn seemed to sense
the purpose of her words, for he knelt and rested his travel-weary muscles. Robyn, leaning against the broad flank, easily fell into a refreshing
slumber.

The following days passed quickly, a blur of pursuit as the valiant
unicorn sped over the moor.

Somehow the unicorn knew the path to follow, and he led them unerringly toward the Fens of the Fallon. Robyn, too, recognized the dank
reaches and sensed the nearness of her destination.

"Do you think we'll find him soon?" asked Newt, peering forward.

"Find who?" asked Robyn. She had not talked to the faerie dragon
about their destination.

"Your prince, naturally! Why, who in the world else would I be talking about? You really haven't gotten much smarter, you know."

"Yes," said Robyn, laughing, "I think we'll find him soon."

"Are you going to be his queen? He's a king or something, I know, and,
well, I think it would be just delightful if you two humans did what you
do, you know, as a king and queen. You really should, you know!"

Robyn laughed again, and was surprised to feel her face growing
red.

The unicorn stepped into a murky pool, wading through water that
reached nearly to his belly.

XXXXXXXXXXXXXXXXXXXXXXXXX 355 XXXXXXXXXXXXXXXXXXXXXXXX

Robyn's heart pounded with anticipation, and she eagerly examined the fens before her. Kamerynn sprang onto a patch of dry ground, and crossed a sunlit clearing.

There she found her prince.

x x x x x x x x x x

"I guess we should move on," mumbled Tristan. Giving a last look over his shoulder, he remounted Avalon and turned to regard the festering marsh.

"Wait!" said Daryth, holding up his hand.

Branches rustled and parted a hundred feet away. At first, the prince thought that a large white horse struggled from the woods, but then he recognized the unicorn and its rider, even through the sudden tears that threatened to blind him.

"Hi, guys! Boy, are we glad to see you! Hey, wait for us!" Newt chattered at them from the unicorn's horn, as Kamerynn lurched out of the muck and trotted up the low rise toward them.

Tristan jumped to the ground and ran to the unicorn as Robyn slid from her mount, falling right into his arms.

"I can't believe . . . " she started to say, but her own tears choked her.

The prince said nothing, just held on for dear life. He even refused to relinquish his hold on his Robyn when Keren and Daryth tried to give her warm, happy hugs.

Finally Robyn freed herself enough to turn and smile at Newt, and then she kissed the prince again. The faerie dragon clapped happily, exclaiming, "I love a happy ending!"

Finally, Pawldo, holding the reins of the three horses, said, "Let's get a move on. You two will have plenty of time for *that* when this is over!"

Tristan sighed and held Robyn for one more second before relaxing his arms. As the other men went back to the horses, he looked straight into her eyes.

"I had no idea how much I loved you," he whispered, awe in his voice.

Reluctantly, he climbed to Avalon's back. Choosing their path carefully, they entered the fens following the great moorhound. Canthus had no difficulty finding the trail even here, where it commonly entered a foul-smelling pool only to emerge from the opposite side.

They left the white horses and the unicorn in a bright meadow that somehow sprouted wildflowers in the midst of the fens' decay.

Pawldo and Daryth now led the way, after Canthus, with Keren in the middle and Robyn and Tristan to the rear. As they forced their way into the thicket, following a narrow and tangled trail, Robyn heard a whimpering noise behind her. She turned to see Newt, left behind, perched upon Kamerynn's horn, plaintively calling to her.

Suddenly, the little faerie dragon leaped to the ground and scampered after her, only to pause fretfully and dart back to the unicorn. Finally, he made up his mind and bounded into the forest, whimpering until he caught up with Robyn. She hoisted his shuddering little body to her shoulder.

And then the Darkwell lay before them.

"Can you feel it?" Robyn whispered, giving a shiver. She pointed at the center of the sludge-lined pond. "There!"

"Yes," nodded Keren, removing his harp from its shoulder sling. "Shall I call to the creature? I suspect that the longer it stays down there, the more powerful it becomes!"

"Wait," cautioned Tristan.

"I'll get around to the other side of the pond," volunteered Daryth.

"Good. We should all spread out," suggested the prince.

"You, with the Sword of Cymrych Hugh, must get close," said the bard. "The rest of us should try to distract it so that you can strike a free blow."

Robyn looked at Tristan, her face pale, but she nodded with the rest of them.

They readied the attack. Daryth circled around the pond, concealing himself in the bushes on the far side. Keren strung his bow and leaned his weapon against a tree. Pawldo scrambled into the high branches of a tree, and placed several arrows within easy reach.

Tristan and Robyn stood together as their companions deployed for the confrontation. He felt a curious sense of detachment now that the most important thing had been accomplished—his reunion with Robyn. Hesitantly, he turned toward her.

"I was thinking . . . " whispered Tristan. He looked nervously at Robyn, then away again. "That is, I would like to be king of this land, someday. I know this now. And, if I should be fortunate enough to win the crown, well . . ."

"Let's talk later," she said, but the answer to his unspoken question shone in her eyes.

She seemed to be full of peace, and the prince envied her calm.

"Good luck," Robyn whispered, kissing him again. Then she took her staff and walked to her position.

Tristan drew the Sword of Cymrych Hugh, and the weapon seemed to hum with anticipation. He slogged forward, each footstep sinking to the knees. He nodded at Keren.

The bard struck a jarring chord from his harp. It was not music—it sounded more as if he were trying to tune a badly warped instrument. Again, and once more, the harsh notes jangled through the heavy air.

The mud in the center of the pond started to shift and bubble as if a great upheaval had occurred within it. Gradually, the center of the mass began to rise, and then mud flowed from a mountainous form that slowly became visible. Black, fetid muck flowed quickly off the huge, scaly body.

Tristan stopped short, as the monster rose above him. "You have grown," he whispered, unconsciously. Indeed, the Beast towered nearly twice as large as it had been in the castle. Stunned at the awesome size of the Beast, the prince stared in awe and was unable to move.

The thick shoulders and the two forelegs broke free of the mire as the creature grew. It blinked slowly, showing mud-stained but fiery red eyes, and looked around for the source of the discord that had disturbed it.

Keren was the first to react. As the monster climbed from the sludge, the bard dropped the harp into the mud at his feet, swept up his bow, and drew the weapon with the nock of an arrow pressed tightly against his cheek.

Kazgoroth loomed above Tristan, the mudspattered jaws spread wide. The whitened flesh inside the Beast's mouth cut a garishly bright streak across the blackened, muddy body. Above the mouth, two red eyes glinted with cunning and determination. The eyes focused on the prince.

Keren loosed his arrow, and the missile thunked into the Beast's left eye, puncturing the orb in a shower of gore. The monster bellowed—a deep rumbling cry that shook the roots of the tallest trees. Then the baleful gaze of its lone remaining eye fixed upon the bard.

Even as Keren whipped another arrow onto the string and began to draw the weapon, Kazgoroth's jaws opened wide. A crackling beam of hot magic exploded from the monster's mouth, striking Keren in the chest and flowing around him until the bard's rigid body was outlined in a blazing light.

A loud explosion rocked the pond, and the bard was gone. All that remained was his harp, lying in the mud where he had dropped it.

"No!" screamed Robyn, staring in disbelief and horror.

The prince felt a cold stab of fear, for the Beast was mightier than he had imagined. But he also felt the burning heat of his own fury, and he turned back toward the towering shape.

"I'll kill you," he said evenly, stepping forward through the clutching mire. Each footstep slurped loudly as he pulled his boots free, and the progress seemed agonizingly slow.

Canthus raced through the mud to bite at one of the monster's feet. Kazgoroth ignored the savage hound, and turned to find another two-legged opponent.

Pawldo reacted quickly. Balancing on a high limb, he let an arrow fly. The tiny missile struck the monster's other eye with enough force to puncture it. Kazgoroth, now blinded and shrieking with rage, turned vehemently toward the source of the new attack. A black shadow dropped from above as the falcon Sable tore at the monster's face. With a sweep of its mighty claw, the Beast sent the bird spiraling to the ground, trailing a cloud of feathers.

Kazgoroth lunged forward, one clawed foot splashing into the mire beside the prince. Tristan swung with all his strength, and the enchanted blade hissed through Kazgoroth's flesh, but the Beast was not distracted from its next target.

Kazgoroth seized the branches of Pawldo's tree with its foreclaws. The powerful shoulders clenched, and the trunk broke free from the ground. Pawldo twisted and struggled, trapped in the high branches, but could not break free. Clutching and gasping, he vanished below the surface of the pond.

Tristan felt a growing sense of despair.

He lurched toward the monster, slipping and falling in the mud. Desperately, he tried to sink the potent blade into the monster's body, but he could not scramble quickly enough.

Newt, perched upon Robyn's shoulder, was chanting one magical casting after another. An illusionary ball of fire exploded around the monster, and then a plague of flying scorpions appeared to attack it. The illusions seemed quite real to Tristan, but Kazgoroth paid no attention to them.

Tristan struggled toward the Beast. The sword continued to tug him forward, and he could feel the desire to destroy evil flow through the silvery blade. He turned briefly, and saw Robyn gesture him away as she raised the staff and chanted a spell.

A moment, and then another, passed, and still nothing happened. Kazgoroth turned toward the druid, the wide nostrils twitching in the still air.

Suddenly, the ground and water of the Darkwell crackled, as towering sheets of flame leaped from the earth to curl around the monster's body.

Kazgoroth screamed in pain and stumbled, batting wildly at the flames, but the fire surged all around it. Suddenly the Beast shuddered, as if in deep concentration, ignoring the searing flames that scarred and scorched its scales.

Quickly, a black fog bubbled from the center of the Darkwell, extinguishing the flames and spreading across the ground. In seconds, the fire had vanished.

Robyn stared weakly, not believing the ease with which her magic had been countered. The monster lunged in her direction, as Tristan struggled to put himself between them. The mud pulled at his feet, tripping him in his haste. Splashing to his hands and knees, he watched helplessly as the creature approached the woman he loved.

Wrenching to his feet again, his vision clouding in fear, again he slogged toward the Beast, and again he fell.

Kazgoroth was looming over Robyn. Then, the prince saw a flash in the bushes across the pond, and Daryth ran forward, his silver scimitar extended. Tristan stared in amazement as the nimble Calishite leaped across the monster's scaly tail onto its rough, plated back.

As if he were climbing a field of boulders, the Calishite leaped from one horny scale to the next, climbing all the way to the monster's neck in a single, fluid charge. There, he raised his arm, and then buried his sword to the hilt at the base of Kazgoroth's brain.

With a bellow of sheer rage the Beast reared backward, and Daryth flew through the air to land, senseless, at the shore of the pond. Canthus again lunged forward, but the dog could do nothing to slow the Beast but nip at its giant trunk.

Tristan finally made contact, stumbling into the form of the monster, hacking wildly with the Sword of Cymrych Hugh. A great gash was torn in its leg, but the wound did not seem to impair it seriously, and Kazgoroth lurched away. Suddenly, the great tail lashed around to smash Tristan's back and send him sprawling to the ground.

Gasping for life, Tristan spun around and tried to leap to his feet, but the prolonged exertion had completely drained him. Panting, he knelt in the mud and looked up at the monster.

Black blood ran from the wound in its neck, but Kazgoroth still threatened. The Beast stopped moving for a second, as its forked tongue and scaly nostrils twitched in the humid air. Slowly, the great head swiveled around to fix upon Robyn, transfixed by the tableau.

"Tristan, my beloved."

The prince heard the voice in his ears, through the haze of his abject despair. He shook his head, clearing it slightly, and heard Robyn continue speaking, very quietly.

"Be careful, my prince, and think! Control!"

The message finally penetrated to the deepest fount of his emotion, and a warm feeling of calm spread over him. He breathed slowly, and deeply, and felt strength flow once again into his tired muscles.

Standing up, he stepped carefully through the mud toward Robyn, his sword tingling with prospect. At last he turned to look up at the monster, for Kazgoroth had begun to move again.

A clawed foot kicked Canthus out of the Beast's path, and the loyal dog crashed into a tree trunk before sliding to the ground. The forked tongue of Kazgoroth snaked forward with appetite, as it seemed to sense the druid before it.

But between the monster and the woman stood the Prince of Corwell.

As the Beast stepped toward him, Tristan crouched low. The bulging gut, smooth and white like a snake's belly, swung over him.

And Tristan struck.

The Sword of Cymrych Hugh parted the white skin easily, and hissed with gratification as it sank into the warm bowels of the Beast. The blade grew hot as the power of the goddess flooded through the weapon, wracking the corrupted body. Tristan stepped quickly back, but not before the sloshing contents of the monster's insides spilled over the prince's own body.

Gagging and choking, Tristan felt himself surrounded by filth and poison. His skin burned as caustic acids poured over him, and polluted gases filled his lungs. He was aware of the monster stumbling and bellowing.

Then everything stopped.

××××××××××××

Robyn gasped in shock as she saw Tristan fall beneath the flailing body of the Beast. The sinuous tail, the great jaws, and the powerful legs all thrashed mindlessly in the center of the Darkwell.

Kazgoroth's body settled into the mire, and the Beast's struggles finally ceased. The great, gaping wound in its belly continued to pour the creature's essence into the sludge at the bottom of the Darkwell.

As the monster's lifeblood mixed with the stuff of the Darkwell, a strange metamorphosis began.

A small spot of light burned through the surface of the sludge. The light began to swirl, and the spot grew until a burst of white flame shot upward from the spot where Kazgoroth had collapsed. The flame was cool and clean—Robyn knew instinctively that this was the power of the goddess manifested upon the world.

The white flame burst higher, and the brightness spread across the filth and mire in the pond. Somehow, Robyn knew, the blood of the Beast had given the goddess the power to cleanse the pollution from the Darkwell, purifying it once again into the Moonwell of old.

As the flames spread, they left behind a small pool of crystalline water, surrounded by a smooth and grassy bank. A finger of fire reached for the motionless body of Daryth, wrapping him in white, and then withdrawing. As it left, the Calishite sat up and looked around, scratching his head curiously.

The white light burned away the tree that had dragged Pawldo into the pond, and as the glow subsided, Robyn saw the halfling, standing knee deep in clear water, and looking around in amazement.

And in the center of the pool, the Beast's body had vanished entirely. The silvery surface broke apart and Tristan stood, sputtering, waist deep in the pond. With a cry of elation, he ran toward the shore, meeting Robyn as she splashed toward him. Laughing and crying at the same time, they hugged each other and fell headlong into the water.

Canthus bounded around the shore, barking, while Newt rode the moorhound's broad back and chattered insults at the spot where the Beast had disappeared.

A last tendril of white fire flickered from the pond, seeking and swirling about the spot where Keren had stood. The flame probed and twisted, as if searching, but all it could find was the harp, lying now on green grass.

The white fire settled into the strings and frame of the harp, and for a moment the clearing resounded with unspeakably beautiful music. Then the flames surged to a brightness that seemed to equal the sun's, and blinked out, leaving the companions staring at each other in amazement.

The harp was gone.

✕ ✕ ✕ ✕ ✕ ✕ ✕ ✕ ✕

The travelers rode wearily toward Corwell, trailing an empty horse—a forlorn reminder that their mission had been not without cost. But they rode, at last, without urgency.

Behind, the wilderness of Myrloch Vale harbored a tiny sentry, perched upon the horn of a gallant and proud unicorn. The watcher, a small dragon, wept unashamedly at the departure of his friends. Then, the unicorn turned into the woods and the little dragon once again showed him the path.

Daryth and Pawldo in the lead followed Canthus as the moorhound raced through the countryside.

Tristan rode slowly beside Robyn, holding the hand of his lady.

×××××××××××

The goddess smiled, and her smile was the warmth of the late summer sun. Her breath was the smooth caress of the wind that cleansed the countryside. She saw the fleet of northmen sail from the shores of Corwell, and she ignored them for she had no need for vengeance.

She wept for the deaths of her people, and for the destruction that had been wrought upon her lands. But she knew that the Ffolk were strong, and would soon restore their homes and fields, and their heritage would be renewed.

And she thought of the bard, whose songs had so soothed her. The wind spread throughout the lands of the Moonshaes, carrying the enchanted memories of the great Keren's harp. And wherever there were bards, a new song was learned—a song of evils, and heroes, and lovers, and death. It was a song of rare beauty, a song that would be sung for many centuries.

It was a song by the greatest bard of them all. And though Keren no longer lived, his legacy of song rode the wind across the Moonshaes, and all the bards of the land shared in its sweet refrain.

×××××××××××

The trees at the edge of the Moonwell parted shortly after sunset, and a hooded figure advanced cautiously to the muddy shore. Slowly it probed the pond with a long staff, hesitantly stepping into the water.

Trahern of Oakvale had suffered much, this summer, because of the enchantment of the Beast. The blessings of the goddess had been stripped from him, and he no longer had the protection of his master. But now he had nothing else to turn to, and so he sought any tiny fragment of his master to hold and cherish.

The staff clicked against something hard, and the corrupted druid pulled a black chunk from the bowels of the pond. Gratified, he clasped the skull-sized object—black, like a lump of coal—to his breast.

Cackling and gibbering, Trahern turned from the pond and lurched into the forest. He was completely mad. The nearness of the goddess he had formerly served had driven the last vestiges of sanity from his shattered mind. Clutching his dark possession, the old man stumbled into the forest.

And with him he carried the heart of Kazgoroth.

The Elven Nations Trilogy is back in print in all-new editions!

FIRSTBORN
Volume One

Paul B. Thompson & Tonya C. Cook

In moments, the fate of two leaders is decided. Sithas, firstborn
son of the elf monarch Sithel, is destined to inherit the crown and
kingdom from his father. His twin brother Kith-Kanan, born just
a few heartbeats later, must make his own destiny. Together—and
apart—the princes will see their world torn asunder for the sake of
power, freedom, and love.

New edition in October 2004

THE KINSLAYER WAR
Volume Two

Douglas Niles

Timeless and elegant, the elven realm seems unchanging. But when
the dynamic human nation of Ergoth presses on the frontiers of the
Silvanesti realm, the elves must awaken—and unite—to turn back
the tide of human conquest. Prince Kith- Kanan, returned from
exile, holds the key to victory.

New edition in November 2004

THE QUALINESTI
Volume Three

Paul B. Thompson & Tonya C. Cook

Wars done, the weary nations of Krynn turn to rebuilding their
exhausted lands. In the mountains, a city devoted to peace, Pax
Tharkas, is carved from living stone by elf and dwarf hands. In
the new nation of Qualinesti, corruption seeks to undermine this
new beginning. A new generation of elves and humans must band
together if the noble experiment of Kith-Kanan is to be preserved.

New edition in December 2004

Strife and warfare tear at the land of Ansalon

FLIGHT OF THE FALLEN
The Linsha Trilogy, Volume Two

Mary H. Herbert

As the Plains of Dust are torn asunder by invading barbarian forces, Rose Knight Linsha Majere is torn between two vows— her pledge to the Knighthood, and her pledge to guard the eggs of the dragon overlord Iyesta. To keep her honor, Linsha will have to make the ultimate sacrifice.

CITY OF THE LOST
The Linsha Trilogy, Volume One

Available Now!

LORD OF THE ROSE
Rise of Solamnia, Volume One

Douglas Niles

In the wake of the War of Souls, the realms of Solamnia are wracked by strife and internecine warfare, and dire external threats lurk on its borders. A young lord, marked by courage and fateful flaws, emerges from the hinterlands. His vow: he will unite the fractious reaches of the ancient knighthood— or die in the attempt.

November 2004

Follow Mina from the War of Souls into the chaos of post–war Krynn.

AMBER AND ASHES
The Dark Disciple, Volume I

Margaret Weis

With Paladine and Takhisis gone, the lesser gods vie for primacy over Krynn. Recruited to a new faith by a god of evil, Mina leads a religion of the dead, and kender and a holy monk are all that stand in the way of the dark stain spreading across Ansalon.

First in a new series from *New York Times* best-selling author Margaret Weis.

August 2004

The War of Souls is at an end, but the tales of Krynn continue...

THE SEARCH FOR POWER:
DRAGONS FROM THE WAR OF SOULS

Edited by Margaret Weis

After the War of Souls, dragons are much harder to find, but they should still be avoided. They come in all hues and sizes and can be just as charming and mischievous as they are evil and deadly. The best-known DRAGONLANCE® authors spin tales of these greatest of beasts, in all their variety and splendor.

PRISONER OF HAVEN
The Age of Mortals

Nancy Varian Berberick

Usha and Dezra Majere find that a visit to the city of Haven might make them permanent residents. The two must fight both the forces of the evil dragon overlord and one another in their attempts to free the city—and themselves.

WIZARDS' CONCLAVE
The Age of Mortals

Douglas Niles

The gods have returned to Krynn, but their power is far from secure. Dalamar the Dark, together with the Red Mistress, Jenna of Palanthas, must gather the forces of traditional magic for a momentous battle that will determine the future of sorcery in the world.

THE LAKE OF DEATH
The Age of Mortals

Jean Rabe

Dhamon, a former Dark Knight cursed to roam in dragon form, prays that something left behind in the submerged city of Qualinost has the magical power to make him human again. But gaining such a relic could come at a terrible price: his honor, or the lives of his companions.

October 2004

Long before the War of the Lance, other heroes made their mark upon Ansalon.

Revisit these classic tales, including the *New York Times* best-seller *The Legend of Huma*, in these brand new editions!

THE LEGEND OF HUMA
Heroes, Volume One
Richard A. Knaak

STORMBLADE
Heroes, Volume Two
Nancy Varian Berberick

WEASEL'S LUCK
Heroes, Volume Three
Michael Williams

KAZ THE MINOTAUR
Heroes, Volume Four
Richard A. Knaak

THE GATES OF THORBARDIN
Heroes, Volume Five
Dan Parkinson

GALEN BENIGHTED
Heroes, Volume Six
Michael Williams
November 2004

The Elven Nations Trilogy is back in print in all-new editions!

FIRSTBORN
Volume One

Paul B. Thompson & Tonya C. Cook

In moments, the fate of two leaders is decided. Sithas, firstborn
son of the elf monarch Sithel, is destined to inherit the crown and
kingdom from his father. His twin brother Kith-Kanan, born just
a few heartbeats later, must make his own destiny. Together—and
apart—the princes will see their world torn asunder for the sake of
power, freedom, and love.

New edition in October 2004

THE KINSLAYER WAR
Volume Two

Douglas Niles

Timeless and elegant, the elven realm seems unchanging. But when
the dynamic human nation of Ergoth presses on the frontiers of the
Silvanesti realm, the elves must awaken—and unite—to turn back
the tide of human conquest. Prince Kith-Kanan, returned from
exile, holds the key to victory.

New edition in November 2004

THE QUALINESTI
Volume Three

Paul B. Thompson & Tonya C. Cook

Wars done, the weary nations of Krynn turn to rebuilding their
exhausted lands. In the mountains, a city devoted to peace, Pax
Tharkas, is carved from living stone by elf and dwarf hands. In
the new nation of Qualinesti, corruption seeks to undermine this
new beginning. A new generation of elves and humans must band
together if the noble experiment of Kith-Kanan is to be preserved.

New edition in December 2004

The Minotaur Wars

Richard A. Knaak

A new trilogy featuring the minotaur race that
continues the story from the *New York Times*
best-selling War of Souls trilogy!

Now available in paperback!
NIGHT OF BLOOD
Volume One

As the War of Souls spreads, a terrible, bloody
coup led by the ambitious General Hotak and
his wife, the High Priestess Nephera, over-
takes the minotaur empire. With legions of
soldiers and the unearthly magic of the Fore-
runners at his command, the new emperor
turns his sights towards Ansalon. But not all
his enemies lie dead...

New in hardcover!
TIDES OF BLOOD
Volume Two

Making a bold pact with the ogres, and with
the assurances of the mysterious warrior-
woman Mina sweetly ringing in his ears, the
minotaur emperor Hotak decides to invade
Ansalon. But betrayal comes from the least
expected quarters, and an escaped slave
called Faros, the last of the blood of the lawful
emperor, stirs up a fresh, vengeance-driven
rebellion.